# When the Storm Ends

## Rebecca L. Marsh

Visit the author's website: rebeccalmarsh.com

Cover design by Trim Ventures

www.TrimVentures.com

ISBN:978-1-949498-01-1

James 1:17
"Every good gift and every perfect gift is from above, and cometh down from the Father of lights, with whom is no variableness, neither shadow of turning."

For my family and all the others who helped me find the courage to begin this journey.

Samantha,

May your days be filled with rainbows.

# Chapter 1

Beth sprang up in bed gasping for air as her heart galloped in her chest. Images swirled through her mind—running, hiding in a cabinet . . . being found and dragged out by her hair. Sometimes it was hard to tell which parts were just dream, and which parts were memories from her childhood.

She glanced at her husband lying next to her. His chest was still rising and falling rhythmically with sleep. Beth breathed a sigh of relief that she hadn't awakened him this time. She knew her nightmare driven screams woke him at least once already during that night. It had been a particularly bad night, but she didn't want Nolan to know just how bad.

Quietly, Beth eased out of bed, took a quick shower, and padded down the hallway toward the kitchen. She glanced at the rose petals still scattered on the carpet. They should make her smile, but instead, she glared at them. Standing still for a moment, she tried to recapture the joy she'd felt the night before when she and Nolan came home from their anniversary date and she saw them there, but she couldn't. The awful feeling she woke up with was wrapped around her like a shroud, and she couldn't seem to shake it loose.

Looking away from the petals, she shuffled to the back door, where her dog, Lulu was begging to be let out. She mindlessly patted the dog's shaggy head and opened the door.

Pushing her dark hair back behind her ears, Beth scooped coffee into the maker, and waited for it to brew. Then, carrying her cup into the living room, she flipped on the TV and turned to a local news channel. She stood behind the couch and focused her blue-green eyes on the flickering screen.

"A few weeks ago we were shocked to learn that James Clifton, CEO and major shareholder of Bentwood Industries, was murdered in his home," the blonde anchorwoman spoke in a grim tone that didn't match the smile on her makeup encrusted face.

A picture of James Clifton flashed in the corner of the screen. Beth glanced at it and felt a chill rush up her spine. He looked like any other businessman with blonde hair combed neatly, and a confident smile, but there was something disturbingly familiar about that man's face, the eyes maybe. Beth couldn't put a finger on it, but it nagged at her.

"Even more shocking, James was killed by his daughter, Erin Clifton, who pulled the trigger of her father's gun as her mother and sister watched in horror. Yesterday it was decided that Erin will be tried in juvenile court after an emotional plea from her mother, Victoria Clifton."

Beth relaxed a little as relief washed over her.

The anchorwoman continued, "We were able to catch up with Victoria outside the courthouse and this is what she had to say."

The picture changed to Victoria Clifton's flawless face. "James was a great man and a wonderful father. I'm heartbroken by his death." Tears streamed down Victoria's face. "Erin was a good kid, but a couple years ago she started to change. I only wish we had realized how serious those changes were. Maybe we could have gotten her the help she needed in time to prevent this tragedy. I still want to get her help, though, and perhaps if she is tried in juvenile court she will have that chance." Victoria looked right into the camera's lens, a pained look on her face. "It's the best I can do for her now that —"

Beth snapped the television off just as Nolan walked into the room, a curious look on his face. She followed him into the kitchen and waited as he poured a cup of coffee.

"Last night was wonderful. You really outdid yourself this year," Beth said, pasting on the smile that was required for this conversation.

"Only the best for my wife of seven years," Nolan said, smiling back. His brown hair was still messy, and the eyes that nearly matched his hair were not yet fully alert.

"I don't know how you can possibly top it next year."

"I'll just have to find a way." Then his expression sobered as he looked her in the eye. "I wish all the screaming that went on in our bed last night was a result of my romantic prowess."

Beth looked down into her coffee cup, as disjointed images from her dream the night before raced through her head—being chased by someone without a face. Of course, she knew who it was, it could only be one person—and yet, there was a strange quality about this dream. It felt almost as if the man chasing her might not be who it should be, but instead someone she didn't know, as if she'd been dropped into someone else's nightmare.

"We might as well talk about it," Nolan said when Beth stayed silent. "You were having another nightmare." Nolan paused, waiting for Beth to answer. When she said nothing, he continued, "That's the third time this week. You can't keep ignoring this and hoping it will go away."

Beth looked up at him, a little stab of anger flaring. "What do you want me to do about it? I can't control my dreams."

"I think you should talk to someone about it ... a professional."

"In case you've forgotten, I am a professional."

"Okay," he spoke in a pinched tone. "Physician, heal thyself. What do you think is causing this?"

Beth gave him a defeated shake of her head. "I don't know."

"Think about it for a minute. Maybe there's something going on that's making the memories surface

3

again. What about the kids you're working with? Are any of them from abusive homes?"

"No." Then she thought about it. "Well, none that I'm sure about."

"What do you mean?"

"I'm helping Lisa on a court case." Lisa, a lawyer, and a friend, worked on many juvenile cases and occasionally needed a child psychologist's help.

"Do you think the kid is abused?"

"I don't know. She won't talk to me. It's just … something in her eyes, like they're pleading for help even when she insists she doesn't want any."

"Maybe she's the cause of all the dreams."

"Maybe." Beth glanced at the clock on the stove. "We better get moving. We're supposed to be at Dad's house for brunch in half an hour."

Beth and Nolan rushed up to the front door of a yellow two-story house with black trim and a row of purple pansies growing beside the front sidewalk. Behind the house was a small wooded area and beyond that, you could see the Blue Ridge Mountains, still capped in white. Every time Beth looked at this house, she thought about the first day she'd come here to live. The pansies were blue and yellow that year, and she was filled with a mix of fear and hope, which seemed to fit perfectly with the colors.

Beth knocked quickly, then let herself in with Nolan right behind her.

"There you two are," said Beth's stepmother, Grace, hurrying over to embrace them. Taller than Beth, Grace leaned down for the hug, her wavy, blonde hair that was streaked with just a little gray brushing Beth's shoulder. "We were beginning to wonder about you."

4

"I know," Beth said, "we overslept a bit."

"That's okay," Grace said with a sly smile that made her hazel eyes twinkle. "How was the anniversary date?"

Smiling a little Beth responded, "Wonderful! Nolan picked a great place for dinner. He was very romantic as usual. So, where's Dad?"

"He's outside cleaning the table and chairs so we can eat on the patio. He should be about done and brunch is almost ready. Why don't you go on out there, Nolan, and see how he's doing?"

"Sounds good. And the food smells great," Nolan said walking toward the back door.

"Come on in here with me." Grace put her arm around Beth as they walked into the galley style kitchen that was covered in floral print wallpaper. "Ronnie and Ashley called yesterday. That baby should be here any day now."

This, Beth knew, was not just information, but Grace's idea of a subtle nudge. After all, Beth's seventh anniversary had just passed. Her little brother Ronnie had been married only two. Not to mention the fact that Beth was thirty three. The clock was ticking and everyone knew it. "I'm sure you're getting excited."

Grace smiled enthusiastically and said with less subtlety, "And I hope we'll get some more grandchildren soon."

When Beth looked away, saying nothing, Grace sighed and changed the subject. "I heard from your little sister this week."

"How is Sarah?"

"Good. She likes her new job in the big city. She's made friends there. Roberta, next door, has a nephew in New York, so I'm thinking I might try playing matchmaker," Grace said piling pancakes and sausage onto a platter.

"That can be a dangerous job," Beth responded as she and Grace carried the food out the back door to the patio where her father and husband sat waiting.

The early spring breeze wafted, fluttering the green leaves of the trees that towered over the backyard. Beth took a deep breath, sucking in the cool morning air; it was one of her favorite things about living in western North Carolina.

As they ate, the conversation jumped from sports to the weather and then to the latest family news. Beth listened but said very little. Thoughts of her nightmare kept floating into her head. The words *I gonna get you* echoed in her brain, making her appetite go south.

Her thoughts drifted to her patient, the one with the pleading eyes. She'd tried every way she knew to convince the girl to talk to her. In normal circumstances, patience was the best course of action. Give the patient space and time to get comfortable with her until she was ready to open up. Time was running out, though, and the interview room at the juvenile detention center offered little space and no comfort. But she had to do something because the girl's haunted, gray eyes never left her mind.

Then a crazy idea bloomed in Beth's mind. But, no, she couldn't. To do such a thing went against the ethical standards of her practice ... Still, what if it could work?

# Chapter 2

Beth spent Monday morning talking to her young patients about their troubles. Her mind, however, kept wandering back to her crazy idea. *Could something that was wrong be right? If it helped someone, did that make it right?*

When three o'clock came, Beth hurried from her office and drove twenty miles to the juvenile detention center.

Pulling into the parking lot, Beth spotted her friend right away. Lisa was just stepping out of her car, her tailored suit showing off a tall, slender build. She pulled her briefcase out of the car with one hand and with the other, checked to make sure that none of her blonde hair had escaped the twist at the back of her head.

"You ready to get this girl talking?" Lisa asked as Beth walked over.

"I hope so." Beth looked at Lisa tentatively and thought about her idea. Of course, she couldn't do it, but the idea refused to leave her head. What if something unorthodox could help?

"I hope so too. I'm working on getting a continuance on her trial date, but even if that happens, her time is almost up."

Beth nodded. "I'll do my best."

Beth was already seated at the metal table in a small meeting room when her patient was led in by a guard, a man with clean-cut brown hair and a bit of a baby face. He glared at Erin as he pushed her into the chair on the other side of the table, then marched back out the door.

The room was cold and stark with cinderblock walls and a gray tile floor that may have once been white. Erin's sandy blonde hair was a little messy and her gray eyes stared at Beth with a look that was both sullen and defiant.

"Hello, Erin," Beth said. "Are you ready to talk?"

"What's there to talk about? Everyone knows what I did." Erin's words held an edge of bravado, but her eyes were filled with misery.

"That's true. But I don't want to talk about *what* you did. I want to talk about *why* you did it."

"What does it matter? I shot my father with a gun that I took from his gun cabinet. I stole the key, I took the gun, and I shot him. Now he's dead." The shakiness in her voice contradicted the indifference that Erin tried to convey.

"It does matter. If you tell me *why* you killed him, the judge might decide it was justifiable homicide."

"Why would he take my word over my mother's? She's the victim, right? And she's a face everyone knows and loves. She heads up charity luncheons and all that."

Beth nodded, looking Erin straight in the eyes. "That may be, Erin, but just because she's a public figure and people love her, does not mean she's a good mother, or that she has your best interests at heart."

Erin leaned forward on the table with her head down, her sandy-colored hair falling around her face. Beth reached over and gently placed her hand on Erin's shoulder. "Talk to me. I want to help you."

Erin lifted her head, revealing a tear on her cheek. "It doesn't matter what they do with me. It can't be worse than where I've been."

"But it could be better," Beth pleaded. Looking into Erin's eyes, she saw a brokenness that was so familiar that, for a moment, Beth felt as if she was twelve years old again. The next words out of Beth's mouth seemed to come without thought, almost against her will. "Erin, maybe it's time for me to tell you a little about myself."

Rebecca L. Marsh

# Chapter 3

My mother's name was Annabella Edgewick, and she was nineteen when I was born. She never spoke of my father except to say that he'd left her and that he didn't want either of us. I didn't even know his name. That didn't stop me from longing to have a father in my life, though sometimes I felt angry at this man I didn't know just as my mother did.

For the first few years of my life, my mother and I lived with my grandparents and my mother's twin sister, Amelia, whom we called Amy. I was happy there.

When I was four years old, my mother met a man named Jeff and began spending a lot of time with him.

Jeff brought me small gifts or candy when he came to take my mother out. He even played with me sometimes, and he seemed like the father I longed for.

A few months later, my mother and Jeff got married, and the three of us moved into a little yellow house in a small neighborhood. The houses were spaced far apart, and a small wooded area separated us from another neighborhood. We fixed up the house, and I had my own room for the first time.

About three months after we moved in, Jeff called before dinner one night and told Mama that he'd be late. Mama fixed us dinner, gave me a bath, and a little while later, put me to bed.

Later that night I awoke to the sound of Jeff shouting at my mother. I couldn't hear all the words, but his voice was loud and angry, and he seemed to think that someone had been at the house while he was gone.

Soon I heard my mother crying along with crashing sounds. I pressed my hands over my ears and curled into a ball.

After a brief silence, I heard Jeff ask, "Where is she?"

"Where is who?" Mama responded, fear resonating in her voice. "What are you talking about?"

"Your little brat, bitch! Where is she?"

"In bed. She's been asleep for hours."

"We'll see if she's sleeping. I'm sure that noisy little monster is still awake. I bet she knows who you had over here, probably listened while you were fucking him."

"There wasn't anyone over here. Beth has been asleep since eight-thirty. Please don't wake her."

Jeff didn't respond, but I heard his loud, clumsy footsteps stomping down the hall toward my room.

As time went on, I learned to close my eyes and pretend I was asleep when Jeff came to my room drunk. But that night, when I was only five years old, I didn't know enough to try that. He stormed in and found me lying on my back with my eyes wide open.

He grabbed me by the front of my nightgown and pulled me up close to his face. I tried to turn away from his pungent breath, but he shook me until I looked at him. A whimper escaped my lips, but fear and shock kept me from crying.

"Who was it?" he screamed at me. I stared at him, wide-eyed, as a warm trickle ran down my leg. "Answer me, brat! Who was in my house?"

"Leave her alone, Jeff," Mama pleaded running into my room, her eye swollen and nightgown ripped. "She can't tell you anything because there's nothing to tell. No one was here!" Tears streamed down her face. "I'll be a better wife, Jeff, but don't hurt Beth! Please!"

"You're a liar!" Jeff knocked Mama to the floor with the back of his arm, never looking away from me. "I'll give you one more chance. Who was here?"

"No one was here." The words squeaked out of me.

By the time the last word left my mouth, his hand was already slashing across my face. "Tell me the truth you little heathen!" He shook me hard. I cried and begged him to stop, but every word I said made him angrier. I could hear Mama crying and pleading with him, but she didn't get up.

I tried a couple more times to tell him that no one was there, but he hit me each time and demanded a different answer. Eventually, I stopped talking. After I was silent for a few minutes, he dropped me onto the bed and stomped out of my room. I heard his heavy footsteps go back into his and Mama's room, and the door slammed.

For a moment the only sound I heard was my own muffled cries. After a few minutes, Mama picked herself up. She carefully changed my pajamas and my sheets with a quiet efficiency that made me feel like she had done all this before. Afterward, she crawled into my little bed with me. "I'm sorry," she said stroking my dark hair, "I can't stop him." For the first time in my life, I felt no comfort from her presence.

I awoke late the next morning to the smell of bacon and eggs cooking. I sat up, feeling the pain of my bruises with every movement. Mama was gone, and everything seemed quiet that morning as if nothing had happened, but my bruises told me it hadn't been a dream. I sat in my bed a while, wishing I could turn my room into a fortress to keep me safe. I did not relish the idea of leaving it, but the smell of food had my stomach growling.

I eased my door open and tiptoed down the hallway to the kitchen, and stopped just before entering. Jeff was in the kitchen with Mama. She was kissing him! A vase of roses sat on the counter and Jeff was cooking. Still, in her ripped nightgown and with her eye black, Mama acted as though the night before had never happened.

I stood there staring for a few minutes before they noticed me.

"There you are, sleepy head," Mama said. "Jeff's cooking us breakfast this morning. Isn't that nice? And look on the table, Beth. He got you a present." She spoke with a smile on her face and an eye that was almost swollen shut.

I didn't know how to respond. I wanted to scream.

I was about to speak up when I saw the fear in my mother's eyes.

Not sure what to do or say, I stood there a moment longer studying them. "Aren't you going to open the gift I got you, Beth?" Jeff smiled at me as though I might have forgotten what he'd done.

I glanced at the wrapped box on the table, then back at my mother's eyes. I slowly made my way over to the table and unwrapped the box. Inside was a fluffy brown teddy bear. Had I been given the gift a couple days earlier, I would have loved him dearly. But knowing from whom he had come, I thought he was the ugliest teddy bear in the world. I wanted to rip off his head and throw him in the garbage. I knew I couldn't.

"What do you think," Jeff asked, "It's cute, right?"

I didn't answer. "Beth, don't be rude," said Mama. "Tell Jeff *thank you* for the gift."

As I sucked on my swollen lip, I was afraid, but more than that, I was angry. I didn't want to speak to him at all. When I looked at my mother again, her eyes begged me to say the words Jeff wanted to hear. I squeaked out a quick "Thank you" and sat down at the table, dropping the bear on the floor.

Jeff put the food on the table, and we ate as though nothing was wrong. Mama and Jeff smiled at each other, touching their hands together like lovesick teenagers. I ate in silence wishing I could wake up from the nightmare my life had become.

I had to stay home from kindergarten for a week until the bruises were lighter. The next week Mama used make-up to cover the yellow spots that remained and told me that I was not to touch my face or talk to the teacher about what had happened. If I did, terrible things could happen. I wasn't sure what could happen that would be more horrible than what already had, but I didn't want to find out.

A few weeks passed without incident, and I allowed myself to believe that night had been a one-time thing. Maybe Jeff really was sorry. Maybe he hadn't meant to hurt us.

Then, on a rainy night in early December, he came home drunk again. Mama told me that I should pretend to be sleeping when Jeff came to my room. I listened while he beat her. Then, with my heart pounding, I closed my eyes when he opened my door. Her idea worked. He didn't hurt me that night, but I was forced to listen as he beat my mother again.

Rebecca L. Marsh

# Chapter 4

At Christmas time Jeff came home with a big tree that filled almost half of our living room. As we decorated the tree we drank hot chocolate and roasted marshmallows in the fireplace. We seemed like a happy family, especially when Jeff lifted me to put the star on top, just like any other kid would do.

On Christmas morning I woke up very excited, but afraid to wake Jeff, I tiptoed down the hall to wait in the living room. I found it filled with more gifts than I'd ever seen. And to my surprise, Mama and Jeff were already waiting for me.

We spent most of the morning opening gifts. My favorite was a brand new bike with pink and white with streamers on the handlebars and a little basket attached to the front.

When all the presents were opened, Mama brought another out from the coat closet and handed it to Jeff.

"This one is special," she told him, "I wanted it to be opened last. Merry Christmas, darling." She gave him the gift, kissing his cheek.

"Well, I wonder what this could be," Jeff teased, tearing off the paper. Once he got the box opened, he gave Mama a puzzled look and held up a tiny shirt. "I don't think this will fit me, Bella."

"No, but it will fit our baby in about seven months."

"Are you serious? You're pregnant?"

"Yes. Are you happy?"

Jeff's face lit up, and he threw his arms around Mama. "Of course I am! We're going to have a baby. That's great. Isn't that great, Beth?" He turned to me. "You're going to be a big sister."

I nodded my head, but I couldn't imagine how this might impact my life. Perhaps it would be a good thing. I hoped so.

For a couple months things were quiet around our house. Jeff taught me to ride my bike and spent Most of the day on the weekends outside watching me ride. I even found myself trying to show off and impress him.

In the evenings we all sat together and discussed names for the baby. We debated many girl's names, but Jeff refused to discuss boy's names. "If it's a boy," he said, "his name will be Jeffrey Jackson Jones, Jr."

One Sunday Mama and I went shopping for baby things and came home to find Jeff drunk.

"Where have you been, Bitch?" He screamed at Mama when we walked in the house. His words were slurred and his breath was pungent.

"You know where I was, Jeff," Mama answered hesitantly, "Beth and I were out shopping for baby stuff."

"Yeah, I'll bet you were. Spending all my money. Do you think I'm made of it?"

"No, Jeff. We didn't spend that much. But we have to buy some things; a crib and clothes for the baby."

"You don't buy anything without my approval!" Jeff backhanded Mama, knocking her to the floor.

Mama scooted back against the wall, protecting her slightly protruding belly with both hands. "Jeff, please," she gasped, "our baby."

Jeff stopped short of hitting her again, standing over her as if he was trying to decide how important this baby was to him. I saw a good opportunity to slip away, but my attempt didn't go unnoticed.

"Are you trying to run away from me?" Jeff hissed, grabbing the back of my shirt and pulling me close to him.

"Children don't run away unless they've done something wrong. What did you do, Beth?"

"I didn't do anything. I promise." I shook my head vigorously.

Jeff slapped me across the face. "Don't lie! What did you do?" He narrowed his eyes at me and shook his forefinger in my tear-streaked face. "I couldn't find my wallet this morning. You took it, didn't you? You're a lying little thief!"

"No. I didn't take it. I wouldn't."

"I know you did," he slurred, throwing me on the floor. "You lie just like your mother!" Jeff kicked me hard in my side, and I yelled out in pain, but my cries didn't stop him. He kicked again. I curled into a ball, trying to protect myself. His foot still made contact with my chest, and I heard a crack and felt a sharp pain. My mother was crouched against the wall crying. After a couple more kicks, Jeff left me on the floor. My body hurt so much I didn't think I could move.

Mama came to me when Jeff was gone. She stooped down, speaking to me in a soft voice. "Beth, come on, sweetie. We have to get you to your room before he comes back." She eased her arm behind my back and helped me sit up. I wanted to scream out in pain, but fear kept me quiet. I managed to get up with my mother's help and hobble to my room. She helped me ease onto my bed and lie down. Her eyes were filled with pain. "You'll be okay now. Just stay in here and you'll be okay."

"Why does he hurt us, Mama?" I asked. Mama shook her head, pulled the blanket over me, and left my room.

Mama decided to send me to Aunt Amy's apartment that summer during the last months of her pregnancy. Amy took me places I had never been. We went to the zoo where I looked at each animal in awe, and a museum with beautiful paintings. What I loved most was the swimming pool at her apartment complex, where I'd splash around for hours. She taught me to swim, and by summer's end, I was playing in the deep end and having the time of my life.

Then on July 30th, Jeff called with news. The baby was here.

Hanging up the phone, Amy turned to me. "You're a big sister, Beth. Aren't you excited? You have a little brother."

I was worried, angry, sick to my stomach. I wasn't excited. I didn't really want a brother, and I didn't want to go home.

Amy drove me to the hospital that afternoon. First, we went to see Mama in her room. She smiled weakly and hugged me. "Did you have a fun summer with your aunt?"

"Yes," I replied. "Thanks for letting me go. Was everything okay at home while I was gone?"

Mama nodded. "Have you seen your brother yet?"

"Not yet. We're going there next."

"He's a beautiful baby. We named him Jeffrey Jackson after Jeff, but we're calling him Jack. Go see him, Beth. Go meet your brother."

Amy walked me to the nursery and we peered through a window at a room full of babies. Some were crying while others were sleeping. Some were bald while others had heads crowned with hair. Amy pointed to a baby in the front, near the window. "There he is, Beth. There's your little brother. Isn't he cute?"

I looked at him. He had chubby cheeks and was mostly bald, but other than that, he looked just like Jeff. I felt repulsed and thought of all the times Jeff had been drunk and had hurt me and my mother. Would this tiny person who looked like him also be like him?

Without thinking, I said what was going through my mind. "He looks just like the devil."

As soon as the words left my mouth, I knew I shouldn't have said them. Amy grabbed my arm and swung me around to face her. Anger flared in her eyes, and for the first time in my life, I was afraid of her. I closed my eyes, bracing myself for a slap, but it didn't come. When I opened my eyes, Amy was kneeling in front of me. She still looked angry, and her words stung. "Beth, I'm ashamed to hear you say that! He's your brother. You may not realize this now, but he's just as much a part of you as he is a part of your mother or Jeff. He's *your* brother and he's going to need his big sister to help him. He's only a baby. He'll need you to take care of him."

I looked at her in shock, my eyes wide and unblinking. Her expression softened and she cupped my face in her hands. "Just take care of little Jack. And don't ever say that again. You wouldn't want anyone else to hear it."

Rebecca L. Marsh

# Chapter 5

August second, Jack came home from the hospital. Jeff drove Mama and Jack home in his car. I rode with my grandparents and Aunt Amy. I sat slumped in the back of my grandfather's Buick. I didn't want to go home.

As we drove up to the house, Amy reached over and rubbed my arm. There was sympathy in her eyes. "This is it, Beth. You're home."

"I liked staying with you," I said in a sullen tone. "I hope I can do it again sometime."

Before Amy could reply, my grandfather cut in as he turned off the car. "Okay! Let's go see that grandson of mine." He jumped out of the car with more energy than I ever knew he had and hurried over to Jeff's car, opening the door for Mama.

Next thing I knew, everyone was huddled around Mama and Jack. They took picture after picture of his wrinkled little face and cooed at him in unintelligible words. They chattered about how cute he was and who they thought he looked like. All I could see in that tiny red face was Jeff.

A few hours later, Amy and my grandparents went home and it was just the four of us. That night, when Jack began crying, I slipped away to my room. No one noticed I was gone and no one came to tell me goodnight.

Several weeks went by in a similar fashion. Mama paid attention to me at times, but most of the time she was busy with the baby. When she asked me to help with the baby, I did everything she asked just to be noticed for a while, but I felt no love for Jack.

One Saturday when Jack was about two months old, Jeff went to Charlotte for a football game with some of his friends. Mama, Jack, and I spent the day at home.

It was clear when Jeff staggered from his friend's car that he was drunk. Mama raced to pick up the bassinet, then grabbed my arm and frantically pulled me down the hall to my room. "Stay in here, Beth. Keep the lights off, and try to keep the baby quiet." She placed the bassinet on the floor near my bed and left the room, closing the door behind her. For a few minutes, all was quiet and dark. I climbed onto my bed and cuddled a doll.

Then the front door slammed.

First Jeff asked Mama where his dinner was, and I could hear her taking a plate out of the oven. After a few minutes of silence, I heard a loud crash. "What is this? It's horrible! Are you trying to poison me, bitch?"

There was shouting and loud banging. Jack seemed to be sleeping through all the noise. I curled myself up into a ball and folded my pillow over my ears.

I lay like that for about ten minutes before Jack began to whimper. I flipped around on the bed and looked down into the bassinet. Just enough moon-light glowed through the window to see his little scrunched up face.

"Be quiet Jack. We don't want him to come in here," I whispered, hoping that he would understand, but he only cried louder. I didn't want to pick him up or be close to him, but my fear of Jeff was stronger. I slipped out of bed and reached into the bassinet. Sliding one hand under Jack's head, I lifted and held him. He stopped crying immediately, and, even in the darkness, I could see the trust in his eyes.

I wanted to put Jack back in the bassinet, but I was afraid he might cry again if I did. So I carefully laid him down next to me on my bed. He was quiet despite all the noise in the next room. He went back to sleep, and I fell asleep beside him.

The next morning, Jeff told me that Mama was sick and she'd be staying in bed all day. I was put in charge of

Jack. My heart ached thinking of how bad my mother was hurt if she could not even care for the baby. But I did what Jeff demanded of me and didn't ask any questions. I'd seen how Mama heated the bottles and I knew how to change him. I tried not to let myself like Jack, yet I was beginning to feel close to him. Maybe Amy was right; Jack needed me, and maybe I needed him.

Rebecca L. Marsh

# Chapter 6

As Beth finished talking, Erin slowly met her eyes. Erin's expression had changed a little. She was looking directly into Beth's eyes rather than avoiding them. Beth thought they might be forming a connection and she felt hopeful.

"Erin," Beth began. "Would you like to talk now? Is there anything you want to say?"

Erin looked at the table. "There're always people like that."

"People like what, Erin?"

Erin looked up, and there was a touch of anger in her eyes. "People like your aunt."

"I don't think I know what you mean." As Beth finished speaking, the door opened and a tall guard with a mustache stepped in wearing a stern expression. Their time was up. It didn't matter if Erin didn't answer the question. Beth was pretty sure she knew the meaning of Erin's statement. That moment at the hospital was when Beth had first realized that Amy knew the truth about what was going on in her home. Erin was likely referring to people who knew about abuse, but did nothing.

Erin got up and walked toward the guard. She looked at Beth again before leaving the room. Her expression was back to a mask of indifference. "It doesn't matter anyway," she muttered.

Beth walked out into the hallway. Lisa was waiting on a bench and stood up as Beth came out. "You were in there a while this time. Did she say anything?"

"No, nothing helpful, but she was different this time. Maybe I'm on the right track."

"I hope so."

"I'll come back and see her again in a couple days. There's still time before her trial, so I'll try everything I can to get through to her."

"I know you will. Now, putting that aside, you and Nolan are still planning to meet us for dinner tonight, right?"

"Definitely! So long as I can drag Nolan away from his sketches."

Beth drove home with Erin on her mind. She wished that she had been more successful, but, despite no discernable progress, her anxiety level was down.

Arriving home, she pulled her Acura sedan into the garage and hurried inside. "I'm home," she called. "Nolan, are you here?"

"Back here."

Beth hung up her blazer, and with their dog, Lulu hot on her heels walked down the hall to a small room that Nolan called "his study." The room was a medium shade of green but most of the wall space was covered with drawings.

Nolan made his living as an elementary school art teacher, but he hoped to someday devote himself to his own art. For the time being, however, he had his drawing room and his students, including a few "rising stars" as he called them.

Beth walked up behind the chair and wrapped her arms around his chest. In front of him was a sketch of an elderly couple sitting on a park bench holding hands. The couple gazed at each other with such affection in their eyes that Beth found herself almost moved to tears. "That's beautiful, darling,"

"That's going to be us someday, old and wrinkled but still madly in love."

"Absolutely," Beth agreed.

"Of course we'll have a bunch of grandchildren to spoil by then," Nolan said hopefully.

Beth looked down and sighed. Having children was always coming up, but she wasn't ready to talk about it. "We're supposed to meet Lisa and Keith for dinner in less than an hour."

Nolan nodded with sad resignation, making Beth feel guilty—and she supposed she should.

"Tell me about your day. Did you have any breakthroughs?" Nolan asked rallying cheerfully.

"Not exactly, but I think I might be on the right track."

"That's great, honey. So, dinner tonight with the Larson's. Do I have to dress up?"

"No, we're not going anywhere fancy. But you will have to wear pants. I don't think anyone at the restaurant would appreciate your Mickey Mouse boxers the way I do."

Nolan swiveled his chair around to face Beth and pulled her down onto his lap. "If we hurry maybe you can enjoy Mickey before I get dressed."

"I think that can be arranged." Beth leaned down and met his lips. His kiss was soft and sweet and reminded Beth of the first time.

At six-thirty Beth and Nolan pulled up to Angelina's, a small Italian restaurant. Beth spotted Lisa's silver BMW a few spaces over. "I guess they beat us here. They probably already went in to get a table."

Nolan leaned over and brushed his lips against Beth's. "Nothing wrong with being the last to arrive. I sure enjoyed getting ready."

Beth smiled. "I can't argue with that, but you'll have to control yourself for a while."

"Do my best." Nolan stepped out of the car, walked around to open Beth's door, and gallantly leaned over offering his arm. She smiled and took his hand.

They walked inside arm in arm. Beth inhaled deeply and smelled rich tomato sauce and freshly baked garlic bread. It was pure heaven.

"There they are." Nolan pointed to a table near the front window where Lisa was waving them over.

Beth and Nolan scooted into the booth sitting opposite Lisa and Keith. "Did you catch that game last night?" Keith asked Nolan, slapping him on the shoulder.

"Yeah, I saw it. Not much of a game though. Chicago won by a landslide."

Nolan and Keith continued talking about sports while Beth and Lisa ignored them and started their own conversation. A few minutes later the waitress came to take their order.

"I know what I want," Lisa started, "I'll have—"

"She'll have the eggplant parmesan and, let me guess, a Caesar salad." Nolan grinned.

Lisa gave Nolan a half-hearted expression of annoyance and then looked at the waitress. "What he said."

"You are nothing if not predictable, Lisa," Nolan laughed.

"I'm a vegetarian. That narrows it down a little."

"Alright, Nolan, stop tormenting my wife. She can't help it if she's predictable. At least I always know what to expect," Keith said. The rest of them gave their orders and the waitress left.

They continued talking and a few minutes later their food arrived. "Beth," Lisa began, noticing how close Beth and Nolan were sitting, "you never did tell me how the anniversary was. You two have a good time?"

"We sure did." Beth smiled. "Candlelight dinner at this fancy place near the top of a mountain, with a spectacular view. And when we got home I found out why Nolan had whisked me away without letting me freshen up. He had the CD player set up with romantic music, candles waiting next to the bed, and a dozen roses on my dresser. He even scattered petals down the hallway floor."

"Wow! Nolan, that's so sweet," Lisa looked at Keith and hit him with the back of her hand. "Why can't you be more like that? I can't even remember the last time you were that romantic."

"Give a guy a break," Keith held a hand in front of his face. "I took care of Josh and Anna last Saturday, so you could spend the day shopping. I didn't even complain when Anna threw up on my favorite shirt."

"That doesn't count. They're your kids too. I have them every Sunday so you can watch whatever sporting event is on at your brother's house."

"He's got the big screen."

Lisa rolled her eyes. "You see what I'm working with here?"

"Come on!" Keith raised his hands in a defensive gesture. "It's harder to be romantic when you have kids. Our entire house is covered with toys. The last time I tried to be romantic I missed one of Josh's G.I. Joe men on the living room floor. When I took Lisa in there to dance she stepped on it and cut her foot. We ended up spending the rest of that night in the emergency room waiting to get it stitched."

"That's true," Lisa agreed. "Kids do make romance more challenging. But they're so worth it. I can't believe you two haven't had one yet."

"Oh, not you too!" Beth said. She was trying to think of a way to change the subject when her phone rang. "Saved by the bell." She flipped the phone open. "It's Grace," she said to Nolan and then answered the call. "Calm down, Grace, I can't understand you . . . She is? Okay, we'll be right there." Beth closed her phone and looked at Nolan. "We need to get to the hospital. Ashley is having the baby."

"We don't have to go right away, do we? It takes hours, right?" Nolan asked.

"Apparently it's already been hours. Ashley went into labor early this morning but she and Ronnie didn't tell anyone right away. They didn't want anxious grandparents-to-be hovering over them the whole time."

"I sure can understand that," Keith said. "When Josh was born, both sets of parents were so annoying that we almost had to have them kicked out of the hospital. When Anna came along we got smart and didn't call anyone until after she was born . . . Oh sorry, don't let me hold you up. Go see the baby."

Nolan scrunched up his nose in disgust as he and Beth walked through the whooshing automatic doors of the hospital. Beth hadn't been inside this place since Joey Reed, one of her first patients, had gotten hostile and took a bite out of her arm. That was when she learned that Professor Yakomora was right about keeping a professional distance from patients, even if they were kids.

Beth pushed the elevator button for the 4th floor, maternity ward. When they stepped off the elevator, Grace rushed up with Ron trailing behind.

"It's going to be any minute now." Grace embraced Beth. "I still can't believe they didn't call us sooner."

"Give them a break, hon, they just wanted a little privacy. When Sarah was born, you didn't call your parents until after the fact," Ron said.

"That's only because Sarah didn't give me time to call them. She was almost born in the car. If I had been in labor all day long, I would've called them. I might have even called your parents."

"Now I know you're lying." Ron smiled.

The four of them walked to the nearby waiting area and sat in green and blue vinyl covered chairs. The waiting area had blue carpet in contrast to the white and green tile that covered the hallway floor. A few tables were arranged with outdated magazines and a small TV was mounted in a corner and played the news on low volume.

"Did you call Sarah?" Beth asked.

"Right after I talked to you," Grace answered. "She won't be able to come until the weekend. She can't take any time off work yet since she's still new."

"What about Ashley's family? Are they coming?"

"Her parents are on their way. Since they live in Florida, Ashley did call them this morning, but there's a bad storm there and all the flights have been delayed. Her sister from Texas isn't coming. She's raising two kids alone, so it's hard for her to make a trip like that."

A few minutes later Ronnie walked into the waiting grinning. "It's a boy!" he announced. "The doctor says you can come in and see Ashley and the baby now as long as you don't cause too much commotion."

They all jumped up and followed Ronnie to a small room. Ashley was sitting up in bed holding her newborn son. The baby was squirming in his mother's arms and looking up at the fluorescent lights through squinted eyes.

Grace rushed over first and looked the baby over. "Oh, he's just perfect, Ashley."

"Here, grandma, hold your grandson."

Grace carefully lifted the infant from his mother's arms. Holding him close, she cooed and swayed side to side.

"He really is beautiful," Beth said. "Does he have a name yet?"

Ashley and Ronnie looked at each other and smiled. "He does," Ashley said, "Hunter. Hunter Allen Collier."

"I love that! You gave him Ronnie's middle name." Beth looked over where Grace had been holding the baby and saw that Nolan now held little Hunter. He looked down at the child, talking to him softly. Beth found herself staring spellbound at her husband. She wondered if she would ever again feel that comfortable holding such a fragile life in her hands.

Rebecca L. Marsh

# Chapter 7

It was late when Beth and Nolan got home from the hospital. They went to bed without talking. Beth felt as though there was a weight on her chest. Nolan had driven them home looking so sad. He loved her, Beth knew that, but how long would he wait for the child he wanted?

When she and Nolan first got engaged, they had talked often about the family they wanted to have, but after they were married and Nolan initiated serious conversations about having children, Beth began to feel terrified at the very idea. She was still unable to overcome the fear. She hadn't even been able to hold her nephew. What was wrong with her that she couldn't even do that?

Well after one o'clock, Beth fell into a fitful sleep and dreamed vividly. She heard the muffled cry of a baby. She knew immediately it was Jack, and he needed her. She ran down the hall to her room. Jack wasn't there. Her heart racing, she ran to Jack's room. The crying was louder, but she still didn't see Jack. The little oak crib was empty, but the mobile was still spinning its colorful clowns and rainbows around in a circle while the music box played a lullaby. The clowns seemed to be staring at her.

Where was Jack? Panicked, Beth ran from the baby's room toward the room her mother shared with Jeff. Jack's crying got louder and Beth ran with all her might, but the door seemed to get farther away.

"No! I have to help Jack!" Beth screamed, waking Nolan from a sound sleep.

"You were having a nightmare," He told her. "You were screaming something about helping Jack. Do you want to tell me about it?"

Beth glanced at the clock. The glowing red numbers read three-thirty. Nolan sat up waiting for her answer. She sighed and switched on her bedside lamp. "Jack was crying, but I couldn't get to him. I was sure Jeff was hurting him, but I couldn't save him."

Nolan nodded. "Maybe seeing the baby tonight got you thinking about him … at least subconsciously."

"I guess so," Beth responded. She didn't want to talk about it. She wanted to cover the wound and forget. "Listen, I'm okay. Really, I am. Let's just go back to sleep. It's late and we both have to work tomorrow."

"Are you sure? We can talk if you want. I'm here for you."

"I know you are." Beth felt guilty by the love in his voice. "But I'm okay. I'm ready to get some more sleep."

"Alright. If that's what you want." Nolan wiped a tear from Beth's cheek. She reached for his hand and gripped it in hers. She hadn't even realized the tear was there. All of a sudden more were coming and she couldn't hold them back.

Nolan put his arms around her and held her close until she stopped crying and fell back to sleep.

On Wednesday afternoon Beth's last patient of the day canceled, so she used the extra hour to go to the juvenile detention center. She hadn't been able to stop thinking about Erin, or Jack for that matter, for the past two days.

She drove to the detention center, calling Lisa on the way. As Erin's lawyer, Lisa had to approve Beth's visits. "I'm glad you're going to see her again. I was there this morning, and she asked for you."

"That's a good sign. Maybe I'll get something from her today."

"I hope so. I can't do much to defend her until she tells her side of the story … Her mother was on TV again today. It never ceases to amaze me how she talks like a mother that wants to get her kid help and simultaneously makes that child look like evil incarnate."

"Yeah, that's some kind of gift Victoria has. I'll do my best with Erin. But I think her mother makes her feel helpless ... Or maybe there's something else holding her back."

"Good luck. I'll call the center and let them know you're coming."

When Beth arrived at the front office, a guard escorted her to the same room as her previous visit. She sat in one of the rickety metal chairs and waited.

After about five minutes a stocky guard entered, pushed Erin into a chair, then stomped back out the door.

"Are you okay, Erin? That guard was a little rough," Beth said.

"Most of them are with me. I scare them."

"Why would they be scared of you? That one was at least twice your size."

"Most of the guards here are married men with kids. When they see me, they worry about what *their* kids could be capable of doing."

"That's quite an assessment. You're a smart kid, Erin." Beth studied Erin as she sat silently with her hands in her lap. "The way the guards treat you ... Does it ever make you angry?"

"Maybe a little, but I can understand why they feel the way they do."

Beth nodded. This was one together kid for the most part. She didn't get upset easily, so why did she kill her father?

"I really want to hear your side of the story, Erin."

Erin was quiet for a moment. She looked down at the table. Then looking up at Beth, she used her sleeve to wipe moist eyes. "Would you tell me more? About you, I mean. I'd like to hear the rest. Did things ever get better for you?"

Beth knew she shouldn't continue telling her story, but maybe it really would help Erin open up. She nodded. "If that's what you want, I can do the talking today." Beth thought for a moment and then began. "I was about ten when something changed in my life. I'll never forget that day."

# Chapter 8

The day started quietly. Jeff was out with his friends and Mama was helping Jack and I make cookies. We were having a good time. Jack was only four and just wanted to help by licking the last bit of cookie dough out of the bowl. I relished every moment with Mama when Jeff was not there.

Late that afternoon Jeff swerved into the driveway. Mama peeked out the window, shaking her head. "I can't believe Ricky and Charlie let him drive home like that. One of these days he's going to get himself killed."

Mama's words brought a smile to my face. I knew that I shouldn't want someone to die, but I did. The fantasy danced in my head, but my smile vanished when Mama turned around and looked at me. "Take Jack to your room, Beth."

I grabbed Jack by the hand and rushed to my room, pulling him behind me. I locked the door and ran to the window. Jack and I had gotten good at avoiding the inevitable drunken rages. If Jeff could not find us, he was happy to focus his attention on mama. I didn't love that idea either, but protecting Jack was most important. Every time it was my hope that Jeff would pass out before he even noticed we were missing.

I opened the window, which was on the backside of the house, and motioned Jack over. I held my hands together for Jack to boost himself up and through the window, dropping easily to the ground just below. Then I stepped up onto a small chair by the window and wriggled through. I held Jack up so he could pull the window most of the way shut from the outside. We were free, but we couldn't stay too close.

"Let's go see Mr. Kim," I said. Jack nodded and we took off into the woods. Mr. Kim was an elderly Asian man who lived in the house on the other side of the woods. Mama and Jeff didn't know him, but Jack and I had gotten to know him well and frequently used his house as a refuge. He was always in his yard gardening, and often let us help. He was kind, and I enjoyed learning from him.

Jack and I raced through the woods hand in hand. We dodged the occasional briar patch as we moved through the trees and rhododendrons. When we reached Mr. Kim's yard we saw him kneeling in the grass pulling weeds. We stopped running and I took stock of our appearance. Mr. Kim didn't know why we came to his house so much and I wanted to keep it that way. I brushed some leaves and dirt off both of us and straightened our clothes. Then I cleaned a cookie dough smudge off Jack's face with my thumb.

We waited a minute to catch our breath before meandering over to Mr. Kim. "Hi, Mr. Kim," I said brightly. "We came to visit. Can we help you?"

"Hey, Misser Kim. We made cookies and I got to ..." Jack stopped short and gaped at the man who turned around to look at us. His hair was short and dark like Mr. Kim's, but it was not Mr. Kim. This man was taller and stouter with a salt and pepper goatee.

"Who are you?" I demanded. "Where is Mr. Kim?"

The man looked at us with amusement. "My name is Ron. I own this house. Mr. Kim was renting it from me, but he had to leave because his son got sick and needed him. Now, may I ask, who are you?"

I looked him over, trying to decide if I should talk to him. He was, after all, a stranger. However, Mr. Kim had been a stranger once as well. He looked nice enough, and I decided that if he knew Mr. Kim he was probably okay. "I'm Beth and this is my little brother Jack. Is Mr. Kim coming back soon?"

"Actually, he's not coming back. His son will need him for a long time, so he's decided to move to Charlotte, where his son lives."

"Who's going to live here?"

"I am. My wife and I were planning to move to this area. I grew up in this house.

"Where are you moving here from?"

Jack had lost interest in the conversation and skipped off into the yard.

"Virginia. That's where I went to school and I've been living there ever since. But I've wanted to come back, and I finally talked my wife into it. We were looking for another house to buy, but since Mr. Kim had to leave, we're moving in here."

I nodded. I was worried that Jack and I had lost our best hideout. I didn't know where else to go.

"I guess you were friends with Mr. Kim. I'm sorry he had to leave so suddenly and didn't get a chance to tell you. Your little brother might enjoy playing with my son, though. I'd guess they're close to the same age."

I smiled. Maybe this man would be as nice as Mr. Kim. "You have a son? Jack will love that."

"I have two children, actually, but my little girl is only two. Their names are Ronnie and Sarah."

"I can't wait to meet them. I guess I didn't tell you that Jack and I live in the house on the other side of the woods. We used to come by and help Mr. Kim with his gardening."

"Great! I could use some help. I promised Grace, my wife, that I would have the whole place in perfect shape by next weekend for her and the kids to move in." Ron stopped and looked at me. "I guess when she gets settled in we should pop over to meet your parents. What's your last name, Beth? I want to know what to call your parents when I meet them."

I froze. Mr. Kim had never asked to meet our parents. I didn't want them to know where we went when we ran away. "Beth?" Ron gave me a curious look. "Is something wrong?"

"Oh, no, nothing's wrong," I spat out panic racing through my body. "It's just that my parents don't really like company. They never knew Mr. Kim."

"Okay." Ron furrowed his brow. "Well, I don't want to disturb them. Just thought I should be friendly. They do know you're here, don't they?"

"Yes. Of course, they do," I said in a slower and more controlled tone.

"My name is Ron Collier. You can tell them to come and see me if they want to know who you were over here talking to. So, tell me, Beth, what's your last name? I like to know my neighbors."

"It's Edgewick."

"Edgewick," he repeated looking thoughtful. Then he looked up at me.

"Hey, that's neat," I said. "Your eyes are the same color as mine. My mother says they're unique. I got them from my father."

He looked closer. "Well, look at that. You're right. Our eyes are the same color." Ron paused for a moment watching the sky turn pink. "I have to get inside now and do some painting, so I'll have to say goodbye. I hope I see you again Beth and Jack Edgewick."

"Oh, he's not an Edgewick. His last name is Jones. He's my half-brother."

At that moment recognition flashed on Ron's face. "You wouldn't happen to know an Annabella Edgewick, would you?"

I smiled. "I know her. She's my mother. But her name is Jones now. How do you know her?'

"I met her one summer when I was home from school. We were friends."

I smiled back at Ron as I grabbed Jack's hand and ran off into the woods.

I didn't see Ron again until the day his family moved in. Jeff had lost his temper after watching his favorite football team lose a big game. Jack and I were in the kitchen when trouble was obviously brewing. I grabbed Jack and pulled us down behind the cabinets before Jeff looked in our direction. Since he didn't see us, he stormed off down the hall and began yelling at Mama.

When he was gone I took Jack and tried to get out of the house, but I knew there wasn't enough time when I heard Jeff and Mama coming out of their room. I hurried Jack over to the couch and pointed for him to go behind it. I moved in next to him and hoped we wouldn't be found.

We huddled behind the couch while Jeff beat Mama. I tried to protect Jack by covering his ears, but he still knew what was going on. There was no hiding from the violence in our home.

Jeff passed out about thirty minutes later and we were able to leave our hiding spot. We ran over to Mama, who was lying on the floor looking like a battered rag doll. Jack laid his head down on her chest and sobbed. I looked down at her with sorrow. I didn't understand how she could allow herself to keep living this way.

"I'll be okay," she whispered, "Just get out of the house before he wakes up."

I crouched down next to her. "Let's get you to bed first. He'll be out for a while," I said, "Move out of the way, Jack, so I can help her up."

Jack kissed her cheek and moved aside. I helped her get up and limp to her room.

"I know you don't understand," she said when I looked at her with pity. "You wonder why I don't just leave him, but it's not that simple."

I nodded in resignation, "I know. You've told me before."

"But you don't believe me."

"There has to be a better way," I said before leaving the room.

When I got back down the hall, I found Jack standing over Jeff. "What are you doing?" I pulled him away.

"Why is Daddy so mean?"

I shook my head. "I don't know, Jack."

"Do you think he loves us at all?"

"He says he does. And he's pretty nice when he isn't drinking."

"Then why doesn't he just stop drinking?"

"I don't know. Maybe he doesn't love us enough."

Jack's lip poked out and began to quiver. I pulled him close and gently turned his face up to look into my eyes. "*I* love you, Jack. And I'll always be here for you. Now let's get out of here before he wakes up. We can go see Mr. Ron."

When Jack and I got to the other side of the woods, we stopped running and sat for a few minutes just inside the tree line. Once we caught our breath I dusted us both off, and we walked into Ron's backyard. He wasn't there, and I wasn't sure if I should approach the house or just leave.

When we heard voices coming from the front, I held Jack's hand and led him cautiously around the house. Ron was walking toward the front door holding a large box.

"There he is." I pulled Jack along.

"Hi, Mr. Ron," Jack and I said as we ran up to him.

"Well look who's here! Come on inside with me and you can meet Grace and the kids." Ron stopped and paused for a minute. "Or I could have them come out here if you're not allowed to come in or if you aren't comfortable with that."

"That's okay," I replied, "We can come in. If you knew Mr. Kim, then you're not a stranger."

Ron smiled. "Alright then, come on in."

Jack and I waited by the front door while he went to find his family. He came back with a woman and two young children. The woman was tall with wavy blonde hair and warm hazel eyes. "This is Grace, my wife," Ron said, "and these are my children, Ronnie." He pointed to a little boy about Jack's age who looked just like Ron except for sharing his mother's hazel eyes. "And Sarah." He pointed to the little girl in Grace's arms, a tiny carbon copy of her mother. "And these two nice kids are Beth and Jack," Ron told his family.

"It's very nice to meet you," I said politely.

Grace smiled. "It's very nice to meet you as well."

"I see you're moving in today. Can we help you?"

"Oh, I don't think so," Grace began, "We're just unpacking boxes and getting things put away."

"I could watch the kids for you if that would help." Grace looked at me closely and seemed very unsure. "I've been helping take care of Jack since he was a baby. I know what to do. I can even change diapers," I assured her.

Grace nodded and handed Sarah to me. "I guess that would be okay since we'll be right here. But let me know if there're any problems or if Sarah needs me."

"Of course," I answered.

Jack and Ronnie ran off, becoming fast friends. I played with Sarah. The house felt calm even with the boys playing. It felt safe.

About an hour later, when I went looking for some toys for Sarah, I overheard Ron and Grace talking in the next room.

"You need to find out the truth about this, Ron. From what you've told me the timing seems about right and you can't deny what you see when you look at her," Grace said.

"I know. I see it. But what do you suggest I do? Charge over there and demand to know?" Ron said.

"You could always ask Beth. She might know something."

There was a brief pause. *Ask me about what?*

"Alright, I'll ask her about it." I heard Ron's footsteps coming toward the door and rushed back to the living room.

When Ron walked out, I was sitting with Sarah in my lap while the boys chased each other around the room. Grace came out behind him, and Sarah wiggled free from my lap and ran to her mother.

"Can I talk to you outside for a minute, Beth? Grace will keep an eye on Jack."

He seemed very serious. "Did I do something wrong?" I twisted my hands in my lap.

"No, no. I just want to ask you about something if that's okay."

I stood up and nodded, dragging my feet as I went toward the door. Ron put his arm around me to guide me out and I jumped at the contact.

"I'm sorry," Ron said, "did I startle you?"

I could never tell him that physical contact in my home usually only happened in a negative way. "I'm okay. You just surprised me."

We got outside and I faced him. He bent down close and looked me in the eye with a serious expression. "Beth," he began, "I noticed that your last name is your mother's maiden name. And you said that Jack was your half-brother. Is that right?"

I nodded.

"Do you see your father on weekends or something like that?"

I shook my head.

"Do you ever see your father?"

I shook my head again, staring at my feet.

"I know this might be none of my business, but do you know who your father is?"

"No," I said, "My mother won't talk about him."

"But you told me you have his eyes." Ron stroked his goatee.

"Yes," I said becoming squirmy and uncomfortable with the questions. "But that's all I know."

"Okay." He gave a slow, unsatisfied nod. "You can go back with the kids now."

I slept very little that night, Ron's questions nagging at me. I wondered why he was so interested in me and who my father was. And, I realized, his questions made *me* want to know who my father was. I knew my mother hated him because he had left her alone and pregnant. She had never forgiven him, and I wasn't sure I should forgive him either. Still, I wondered who he was, why he'd left, and if it was because of me.

I decided to ask Mama about him. I was getting older, maybe she would tell me about him now.

On my way to the kitchen the next morning, I heard voices. I knew Mama wasn't talking to Jeff because he always got up early and went fishing with his buddies on Sunday. That made Sunday my favorite day.

When I stepped to the end of the hallway, I was shocked to hear Ron's voice.

"Who do you think you are coming to my home and making ridiculous accusations?" My mother spoke in a low but angry tone.

"They're not ridiculous. I've seen her, Bella. She has my eyes. She looks just like me. Do you want to keep denying, or should we get to the truth? If you don't want to talk, I could always get a court order for DNA and find out myself," Ron spoke forcefully. "But I'd rather not put Beth through that."

There was a pause, and even from the hallway, I could feel the tension. Then my mother spoke again in a quiet, relenting tone. "Okay, the truth is this: she's your daughter, but that gives you no right to her. You left, as I recall, and I'm the one who's been raising her." Mama sobbed. "I was so scared. I was only nineteen and I didn't know what to do. You weren't there for me."

"I would have been if you'd told me, Bella. Why didn't you tell me?"

"I didn't tell you because you didn't love me. You were leaving. If you'd loved me, you would have stayed."

Ron's voice lowered as he began again, "I was leaving to go back to college." He paused for a moment. "I was young too. I don't know if I can say I loved you, but I cared for you. I wanted to stay in touch with you, but you refused." I heard footsteps pacing around the kitchen. "You should have told me. I would've tried to be there for you and I would have done my best to be there for Beth."

I stood motionless in the hallway. Ron was my father? He was the man my mother hated, the one who left us? But Ron was so nice. I didn't want to hate him.

"It's too late," Mama said, "There's nothing you can do to help us now."

"She's my daughter. Either you agree to give me time with her or we can take this to court. It's up to you."

There was a brief pause before Mama answered. "Only Beth. I won't have my son spending time at your house anymore. And Beth is to spend time only with you."

"That's ridiculous! She lives here with your husband and son. She should get to know my family as well."

"No!" Mama shouted, "I'll let you take me to court before I will agree to her spending time with the woman you left me for."

"I didn't leave you for her! I met Grace two years after we split."

"I don't care." I heard a fist slam into the counter. "I won't have it, Ron."

Ron spoke again in a pinched tone. "Alright, Bella, she doesn't have to spend time with Grace, but I will insist that she has the chance to get to know her little brother and sister."

"They're not her brother and sister!"

"They are as much her siblings as Jack is. I won't negotiate this one. Either you agree, or we take it to court."

After a pause, Ron growled, "I can afford a very good lawyer, I assure you."

Mama relented and they decided that I would spend one day with Ron every weekend. I waited until Ron left before going into the kitchen, then stood there waiting for my mother to notice me. When she did, tears were streaming down my face.

"Beth, what's wrong, sweetie?" Mama asked as if nothing had happened.

"I heard you, Mama," I hissed, emotion surging through me. "Why didn't you tell me who my father was before?"

"You know why, Beth. He left us. He's a sorry excuse for a man."

"No-! He's not!" I shouted, "He's nice. And he's a good father to his kids, a lot better than Jeff. I could have had a good father! I thought he didn't want me. But he didn't even know about me. It's not fair what you did!"

Bewildered, my mother stared at me. Perhaps she expected me to always be her ally. She turned away, and almost whispered, as if to herself, "He hurt me and I wanted to hurt him back."

"You hurt me too," I spat back at her.

Rebecca L. Marsh

# Chapter 9

The first day I spent with my father was a warm, sunny Saturday in late May. He took me to a nearby park along with Ronnie and Sarah. Ronnie immediately dashed off to play, but I sat on a bench with Ron near the sandbox where Sarah played. For a while, neither of us spoke. Now that I knew he was my father, I had no idea what to say. I still liked him as Ron, but I didn't know how to forgive him as my father.

After several minutes, he spoke, "I'm really glad we're spending time together, Beth. I hate that I've missed so much of your life."

A moment passed in silence as I mustered the courage to ask the question that was on my mind. "Would you have stayed?" I began tentatively. "If you had known about me, I mean."

He stroked his goatee before answering. "I can't answer that with a simple yes or no. I wasn't leaving your mother, Beth, I was returning to college for my last year."

Ron looked me in the face. "Even if I had known about you, I would have returned to school, yes. I needed to finish and get my degree so I could get a good job. Had I had known about you, a decent income would've been even more important. But I would have done what I could to care for you and your mother, and I would have been there to see you born. I would have provided for you financially and spent time with you as much as possible."

Ron paused, stroking his goatee again. "I can't change the past, Beth, but now that I do know about you, I'm here for you, *anytime you need me*."

Emotion rose through my body, and a tear ran down my cheek. I scooted closer to him and reached for his hand. "I'm glad I met you, Ron."

He squeezed my hand and kissed the top of my head. "I'm glad I met you too, Beth. But now that we know I'm your father, I'd like you to call me Dad... if you're comfortable with that."

I nodded, "Okay, Dad." I felt strange but good saying that word. And for a brief moment in time, my heart was content.

After that day, I continued to spend time with my father and siblings every weekend. Dad was kind and gentle, and I enjoyed the time we shared. The only drawback was leaving Jack alone with Mama and Jeff. I taught him to stay quiet and out of the way, and I made sure he remembered the best hiding places. But I knew there might come a day when that would not be good enough.

In the summertime, Jack and I stayed with Aunt Amy during school vacation. I knew Jack would be safe at her apartment, so I didn't need to worry when I was gone.

One of the best times I can remember as a child was the summer when I was eleven. Mama gave Dad permission to keep me for a week, so he could take Ronnie and me on a camping trip in the woods.

Dad taught us how to pitch the tent and build a campfire. We hiked through the woods, and Dad showed us how to catch fish. Ronnie and I had a great time playing in the stream and crossing on the rocks.

But the best part for me was after Ronnie went to bed. As Dad and I talked, he listened to me and showed interest in my thoughts. The more we talked, the closer I felt to him. I wished that I could tell him the truth about the hell I lived in, but same fear always stopped me. Jack safety.

# Chapter 10

Beth stopped talking when the guard walked in, wondering what he'd heard. She looked at her watch. "I thought we had an hour."

"Sorry to interrupt a little early, but Ms. Larson is here and wants to see you right away.

"Okay," Beth replied, glancing across the table. Erin was looking right at her with a soft expression. "I'll come back and talk to you in a day or two, Erin." The girl quietly nodded, and Beth got up to leave.

As Beth reached the door, Erin whispered in a wistful tone, as though thinking aloud. "I wish I'd had a dad like that." Beth longed to push the guard out of the room and sit down again to ask Erin just what kind of dad she'd had. But their time was up for today, and the guard was waiting impatiently.

As she walked out into the dingy hallway, Lisa strode over. "I just came from the courthouse, and I have good news. The judge has agreed to postpone the trial for a couple of weeks. I managed to convince him that Erin was too traumatized to tell her side of the story. He was skeptical, but I showed him your report, and he reluctantly agreed to give us more time." Lisa stopped and turned away in thought. "Now our big problem is not just getting Erin to talk, but finding proof of anything she tells us."

Beth patted Lisa's arm. "I'm sure you'll work your magic somehow, Lisa. I have faith in you."

"I hope your faith is not misplaced." Lisa paused for a moment, rubbing her cheek in a motion of discontent. "Say your prayers. We're going to need all the help we can get."

Lisa turned toward Beth. "Listen, Keith and I have a babysitter for Saturday night, so we can go catch a movie. You and Nolan want to join us?"

"Can't this time. Sarah's coming into town this weekend to see the baby."

"That's nice. I know you haven't seen her in a while. Tell her that Keith and I say hello."

"I'll tell her. I can't wait to ask her about the blind date Grace arranged."

"A set-up, huh? Could be a dangerous game Grace is playing. Make sure you call me with all the dirt on Monday."

"Don't worry, I will. You never know, though, sometimes set-ups turn out good. As I recall you set me up, and that one is still working out."

"That was a little different considering the circumstances."

"True. But you never know. Maybe he will be Sarah's Mr. Right."

Lisa raised her eyebrows. "We'll see." Then she glanced at her watch. "I gotta go. I promised Keith I would be home for dinner with the kids tonight, and I still have to meet with one more client. I'll see you next week."

Beth woke up Saturday refreshed and at ease. Four nights without nightmares and the darkness had all but faded away.

She and Nolan arrived at her father's house right on time. Sarah opened the door, beamed at them, and embraced Beth first, then Nolan. "It's so good to see you guys. Come on in. Mom is fixing breakfast, and it smells great."

Beth looked her little sister over and couldn't help but think of the first time she'd met Grace. Sarah looked just like her, but their personalities were so different. Grace had always been devoted to caring for her family, and Sarah was a career girl. She had studied advertising and now worked at an agency in New York City.

"Are Ronnie and Ashley here yet with the baby?" Beth asked.

"Not yet, but they should get here soon. I hear little Hunter is quite a cutie. I can't wait to see him for myself, though, since Mom says he looks like Ashley, and Dad says Hunter looks like him."

Beth raised her eyebrows trying to fit those descriptions with the infant she'd seen at the hospital several nights before. "Opinions do vary. I thought he looked like Ronnie only with Ashley's nose and Grace's chin."

Sarah shook her head and rolled her eyes.

"I don't think you can tell what a baby is going to look like when they're newborn," Nolan spoke up. "To me, he just looked like a baby. He is cute, though," Nolan added in a suggestive tone as he kissed Beth on the cheek. "I think I'll go find Ron now and see what he's up to. You girls have fun catching up."

Nolan headed for the living room while Beth and Sarah went into the kitchen where Grace was cooking pancakes and bacon, wearing an apron that read "Grandma's Kitchen." Grace turned and grinned. "Both my girls at once, and my grandbaby coming over, too."

Beth gestured toward the apron. "I see you didn't waste any time getting into the spirit of being a grandmother."

"You like it? Ronnie and Ashley gave it to me when Hunter came home from the hospital. Maybe I'll soon have more grandchildren to play with." Grace looked at Sarah slyly.

"And how *did* the blind date with Roberta's nephew go?" Beth asked.

Sarah wrinkled her nose. "You mean Steven? He was clumsy. He kept knocking things over. By the time he got me home, I had tea on my shirt and marinara sauce all over my favorite skirt. It's not going to work out. I don't make enough money yet to cover what he's going to cost me in damages."

Grace looked at her daughter, disappointed. "Oh, give him another chance, Sarah. Maybe he was just nervous."

"She could be right," Beth said, "I dated a guy like him in college. He stopped spilling things on me after the third date."

"What made you keep going out with him that long?" Sarah asked.

"I wasn't going to. But one day, after the first date, my car broke down. I called all my friends, but no one answered. His number was still in my purse, so out of desperation, I called him. Not only did he pick me up, but he paid to have my car towed after I realized I didn't have enough money. That day made me look beyond his awkwardness and see what a nice person he was."

"Okay, okay. I'll give Steven another chance. But if he doesn't start talking about something other than scientific facts that I don't understand, he's gone."

"That's my girl." Grace kissed Sarah on the cheek just as the doorbell chimed. "There's my baby!" Grace exclaimed, dashing out of the kitchen.

Beth and Sarah looked at each other and smiled. They walked into the living room where Grace was already on the couch next to Ashley and Hunter. Grace stroked Hunter's bald head and spoke to him in a soft voice. Ron, Nolan, and Ronnie sat off to the side of the room discussing the noise Ronnie's car was making.

"Hey, Sis," Ronnie said to Sarah. He got up from his seat and walked over to embrace his younger sister. "Come have a look at our little man."

Sarah moved to the couch and looked over her mother's shoulder to see the baby. "He's beautiful. Can I hold him?"

"Of course you can." Ashley handed Hunter to Sarah, and she moved to a rocking chair and sat down.

A short while later they were all seated around the table, eating and talking. Hunter was passed from person to person, so his mother had a chance to eat. About half-way through the meal, Nolan tried handing the baby to Beth. She turned and looked at her husband, panic suddenly flashing in her eyes.

"My pancakes are getting cold. You hold the little guy for a few minutes." Nolan, acting innocent, placed the child in her arms before she could stop him.

Panic gripped her like a noose around her neck. *Why did she feel this way?* He was only a baby, and he was her nephew. She couldn't avoid holding him forever. And why did she want to? She urged herself to calm down. *You can handle this, you've done it before.* Perhaps that was the problem. Holding Hunter felt too much like having Jack in her arms.

A few seconds ticked by that felt like an eternity. *I tried,* Beth thought, *I really tried. But I just can't do it.* She turned to her father, on her other side, and thrust the infant into his arms. She jumped up from the table. Seeing her father's surprised face she mumbled, "I have to go to the bathroom."

Beth hurried down the hall and into the bathroom. She sat down on the toilet lid and buried her face in her hands. She wondered what her family must think of her. Could they see the panic she felt?

She went to the sink. Then, looking into the mirror, she straightened herself up. She looked directly into her own blue-green eyes. She should go back out there. Her family would at least try to understand... But how could they when *she* didn't even understand her feelings?

When Beth opened the bathroom door, her father stood in the hallway looking concerned.

"Can we talk?" he asked putting his arm around her, a gesture she'd learned to find comfort in. She nodded and walked with him to his small office, and they sat down facing each other.

"So tell me," Ron began, "what's going on with you?"

Beth took a deep breath and began. "I don't know how to explain. I hope Ronnie and Ashley aren't taking it personally, though."

"They don't know what to think. None of us do. So tell me as best you can." Ron stroked his goatee, now more salt than pepper.

"The baby is adorable and part of me wants to hold him and enjoy him just like everyone else. But at the same time, the thought of having him in my arms and being responsible for his care, even for a moment, scares the hell out of me. When Nolan put him in my arms I was so panicked that I couldn't catch my breath." Beth paused for a moment looking at the beige carpet. Then she looked up at Ron again. "The night Hunter was born I had a terrible nightmare about Jack."

Ron nodded. "You think this fear you have is related to Jack somehow? That's not so hard to understand."

"But it is. I was never afraid to take care of Jack. I loved him."

"Yes, but you were often responsible for keeping him safe in a very unstable home. I can see how being reminded of him, and those years would make you fearful." Ron smiled faintly. "I know you're the one with the psychology degree, but maybe you should tell me about the dream."

When Beth finished telling her father about the dream, Ron asked, "How did the dream make you feel?"

Beth thought for a moment. "The same way I felt when I held Hunter... a suffocating panic."

Ron sighed. "I wish I was a therapist, so I could help you more. Maybe you should see someone."

Beth sighed. "That's what Nolan thinks. But I want to try and work it out on my own. I think I can find the answer myself. In the meantime, I hope the family won't shun me for not holding the baby. I'm also hoping that Nolan won't leave me and go in search of a better wife."

"Sweetheart," Ron began encircling his arms around his daughter and hugging her tight. "This family will always support you and help you through whatever you're going through." Ron released Beth from the hug and lifted her chin with his hand as if she were still a little girl. "And don't worry about Nolan. He's loved you for a long time. I don't think anything could ever change that."

Ron gently wiped away the tear running down Beth's cheek with his thumb.

Beth stood up. "I love you, Dad. Thanks for talking it out with me."

"I love you too. I'm here for you anytime."

Beth nodded. "I know. That's what makes you such a great father."

Sunday night, after a busy weekend with family, Beth and Nolan said good-bye to Sarah and returned home to prepare for the coming week. Nolan was quiet on the way home and went straight to his study to work on his sketches. Beth sat at the small desk in their bedroom and pulled out the patient files she had brought home. Lulu nuzzled her leg, and she patted the dog's head. Then she separated the file Donald Whitman's name printed at the top in bold letters and pulled the papers out.

Donald was a new patient whom she would be seeing first thing Monday morning. His parents had called her sounding very distraught, claiming their son was having an identity crisis. Beth had very little information on the boy, but she could gather clues about him from the basic information, and from what his parents had offered. She looked at the address typed on the first page. *He lives in Crescent Hills, so I know his parents have money.* His parents had also told her that "Donald was behaving like a hoodlum and dressing like a street kid." So now all Beth had to do was find out why a suburban boy with yuppie parents was insisting on dressing and acting like an inner-city gangster. She suspected it wasn't an identity crisis.

After writing the questions that she wanted to ask Donald, Beth put the file away and got ready for bed. Nolan came to bed a short time later. After a short period of silence, Nolan rolled onto his side, facing her, and said, "I'm sorry about Saturday. You weren't ready to hold the baby. I won't pressure you like that again."

Beth looked through the darkness, her eyes still adjusting, and tried to make out the features of her husband's face. She wished she could see how his eyes looked, the emotions in them. Though Nolan's words comforted her, His melancholy manner overwhelmed her with guilt.

# Chapter 11

Donald Whitman was dragged into Beth's office by his parents right on time Monday morning. His father indicated a chair, and Donald dropped into it, attitude and resentment evident in his jerky movements. His parents sat on the leather sofa and faced Beth.

Mr. Whitman gestured toward Donald with one hand. "You see what we are dealing with here? This is every day now; every minute. He used to be different. He was courteous and respectful. He had straight A's and he was a member of the chess club."

"Yes, I know," Beth said. "I spoke to some of his teachers. They all told me that he changed quite suddenly. We need to try and determine why." She looked at Donald when she said the last part and was rewarded with an angry stare.

"Clearly he's having an identity crisis," Mrs. Whitman said. "You must help him, Dr. Christopher."

Beth nodded. "I'll need to spend a little time talking to Donald alone."

"But what's that going to do? We're his parents. We are the ones who can help you understand who he is, or was so that you can fix him."

Beth wanted to put her head in her hands. How did this woman expect Beth to *fix* her son? Was she supposed to hypnotize him and tell him how he should be behaving? Instead, she just smiled and said, "I need to talk to Donald alone. That's how this works."

Donald's parents left grudgingly, and Beth spent some time talking to Donald. At the end of her session, she still didn't know what had caused his transformation, but she did know that she was going to need some help understanding some of the more colorful phrases he liked using.

At one o' clock, Beth hurried to her car and drove to a little diner called Nick's about three miles away where she was meeting Lisa for lunch.

When Beth arrived, Lisa was waiting for her at an outside table on the sidewalk. Beth sat down across from her.

"I already ordered for us," Lisa said. Since they were busy women, whoever arrived first ordered for both. Sometimes they didn't get exactly what they wanted, but they had been friends long enough to guess correctly most days.

"I hope you ordered me something greasy. I'm in the mood to indulge," Beth said.

"Cheeseburger and fries," Lisa responded. "Garden salad for me. I haven't been able to indulge since Josh was born. The last time I ate fries, I gained three pounds."

Beth scrutinized her tall, slender friend. "I doubt anyone noticed. The only time I've ever seen you look different *was* when you were pregnant. And you lost the weight in less than a month both times."

"Yeah, because I worked out every day."

Beth pulled a file out of her briefcase and laid it on the table. "I'm going to see Erin tomorrow. I've scheduled my whole morning for her."

"That's good. I should warn you, though . . ." Lisa paused, looking uncertain about how to finish her thought.

"What is it, Lisa?"

She took a deep breath and pushed a strand of hair from her face. "Erin's going to look a little beat up when you see her."

Beth looked Lisa in the eye, more upset and angry than she should have been. And she knew deep inside this case was far more personal to her than any in the past. "What happened?"

"She got into a scuffle with another girl. I'm not sure how it started, but the other girl was a lot bigger than Erin."

Beth struggled to shake off the rage. This wasn't an uncommon occurrence. In juvenile detention centers, fights were expected. "How bad is it?"

"She has a black eye, some bruises and abrasions and one broken rib. She's been patched up, but I just wanted you to know."

Beth nodded, trying to calm herself. "I was wondering...has anyone talked to her sister?"

"No. Victoria won't allow it. She says Kayla has been through enough."

"She might know something helpful."

"I've thought of that, but I would have to get an order from the judge to over-ride Victoria's wishes. And the judge isn't going to issue that order unless I know what I'm looking for and have good reason to believe Kayla can help. Right now I have nothing."

Beth looked down at the papers in front of her, more frustrated than ever if that was possible. Somehow, she had to get through to Erin.

Beth looked up again when she felt Lisa's hand on her arm. "We'll figure it out."

Just then the waitress arrived with the food. Lisa opened her packet of dressing and poured it over her salad while Beth picked up a french fry and doused it in ketchup. Maybe the greasy food would improve her mood.

When she talked to Erin, Beth intended to share a memory that she had kept out of her mind for years. But perhaps this part of her story would make Erin see that sometimes what you thought was impossible isn't.

Rebecca L. Marsh

 *Chapter 12*

It was a sunny day, but the ground was still wet from the previous three days of rain. Jack, now six years old, sat at the table while I stood at the kitchen counter making lunch for us. Mama was at the grocery store, so I was taking care of Jack.

"Maybe we can go outside for a while after lunch," Jack said.

"I don't know. It's still pretty muddy."

"But I want to go out while the worms are still squirming around on the sidewalk," Jack protested. "Then I can catch some before they all dry up and die."

I shook my head, *what is it with boys and creepy crawly critters?* "Why do you want to catch worms?" I placed a slice of bologna on a slice of bread. "What are you going to do with them?"

"Nothing. I just want to watch them. And maybe cut one in half to see if it turns into two worms."

I walked out of the kitchen with two plates and set one down in front of Jack. "That's gross," I said, joining him at the table. "And it's mean."

He rolled his eyes at me. "But they're going to die anyway if they stay on the sidewalk." Jack stopped for a moment and took a bite of his food. "Why do they do that?"

"Do what?"

"Stay on the sidewalk until they die. Why don't they go back into the dirt? Don't they know they'll die?"

"I don't know, Jack. Maybe they're just dumb."

Jack looked up at me, his eyes wide with excitement. "My teacher says that worms are asexual. That means they can make babies all by themselves. They don't need another worm to do it with. And they're all boys *and* girls at the same time. Isn't that cool!"

I didn't share his fascination with worms, but to make Jack happy, I agreed with him. Then he looked at me curiously. "Do you think that's why they're so dumb?"

"What do you mean?"

"Well, since they have girl parts and boy parts, maybe there isn't enough room left for brains."

Jeff was home that day, as well as sober, and laughed out loud from the living room, where he was watching the end of a baseball game. Jack and I laughed too.

We finished our lunch just as the baseball game was ending. I cleaned our dishes, and we both hurried into the living room just in time to watch Jack's favorite show, *Scooby Doo*. I flipped the channel, same as I did every Saturday after lunch, but this time Jeff grabbed my arm— hard. I cried out in pain.

"What do you think you're doing?" He yelled at me, holding a firm grip.

"It's time for Jack's show." I fought back tears as pain shot up my arm. "I was just changing the channel for him."

Jeff tightened his grip and pulled me, stumbling, closer to his face. "This is *my* house and *my* TV," he hissed at me, his breath hot on my face. "You don't touch it without my permission! Is that clear?"

Tears streamed down my cheeks. "Yes, Jeff. It's clear," I forced the words out as Jack looked on, horrified.

Jeff loosened his grip, and the look on his face changed from rage to shock, as if he had just realized what he was doing. He released me and jerked his hand away in one quick motion. Jumping up, he moved to another chair and put Jack in his lap. He tousled Jack's hair and began talking about *Scooby Doo* as if nothing had happened.

I eased away to my room. I lay down on the bed and cried until I fell asleep. Jeff wasn't even drunk this time.

Pain sliced through my arm as soon as I awoke the next morning. I pushed the sleeve up on my nightgown and rubbed my forearm. I could see blue-black bruises where Jeff's fingers had dug into me. Despair overwhelmed me, but I pushed the bad feeling away, remembering that today was Sunday and my day with Dad.

I showered and dressed before I went out to the kitchen for breakfast. Jack was already done eating. He and Mama were snuggled on the couch together in pajamas watching cartoons. Mama smiled at me as I passed her and went into the kitchen.

I reached for a box of cereal but stopped when I noticed a small box on the counter. Underneath was a note addressed to me. I picked it up and read it.

*Beth, I love you.*
*From, Jeff.*

Inside the box was a silver chain with a small moon-shaped pendant, his apology. He thought that made up for what he'd done as if the gift could erase the hurt.

I hated his gifts even more than the abuse. I snapped the lid closed and threw the box into the trashcan. I would lie and say I'd put it away in my jewelry box. At some point, I would have to make up an excuse for not wearing it. What I really wanted to do was rip the chain in half and throw it in Jeff's face. I knew I couldn't.

I ate my cereal and started back to my room when Mama asked about Jeff's gift.

"I put it away," I told her, but she insisted on seeing it. I should wear it today, she told me. That way Jeff could see it on me when I got home from Dad's house tonight. I dug the box out of the trash and fastened it around my neck. The chain felt like fire on my neck, but I smiled and showed it to Mama as if I was proud of it. I had already decided to rip it off and throw it away in the woods on my way to Dad's

67

house. I would say it had fallen off and gotten lost. Only I would know different.

Dad took Ronnie, Sarah, and me hiking on the parkway. It was a slow walk since Sarah was only four, but her pace made talking to Dad easier. I liked talking to him about most anything, but the one and only topic I never brought up was my home life. Fortunately, I didn't have to lie since he rarely asked me questions. He was usually content to let me lead the conversation.

I also had fun playing with Sarah and talking to Ronnie, who was so much like Jack... No, he was what I imagined Jack might be like if he lived without fear. I hoped that someday Jack would have what Ronnie had—I hoped we both would.

About halfway through our hike, we stopped and sat on a log to take a break. Dad opened a small cooler he'd been carrying and took out drinks and snacks. I munched on trail mix as I watched Sarah, who never sat still for more than a couple minutes, inspect the leaves and sticks covering the ground. She picked something up and ran excitedly over to Dad. "Look, look, Daddy. I found a rock." She held out her hand to him.

While I knew this was nothing too exciting for Dad, he still gave a broad smile, acting as if this little gray rock was a great find. "Wow, Sarah! That's great. It's really a pretty one." Sarah smiled with pride and walked off to see what else she could find.

"I'm getting hot, Dad," Ronnie said. "Can I take my jacket off now?"

"Sure. Just tie it around your waist, because I'm not carrying it for you."

Ronnie peeled off his green jacket, and I realized that I was getting hot too. Without thinking, I rolled up the sleeves of my sweatshirt and nibbled more trail mix. When I felt Dad's hand on my arm, I glanced at him sheepishly.

"What happened to your arm, Beth?" His tone was serious and his face filled with concern.

How could I have been so stupid, I wondered? For two years I'd been careful, never letting Dad see the marks Jeff's beatings left.

I worked my mind trying to find an excuse for the marks. I could think of nothing specific to explain them. "I guess I'm just clumsy," I said. "I bumped it a few times the other day."

I could tell by the look on his face that he didn't believe me. "Beth, I know what these marks are. The question is who put them here?"

"I ... I ..." My mind whirled as I tried to find words. But I couldn't think of an explanation. "He didn't mean to. It was just an accident." The words flew out of my mouth, my haste and emotion speaking their own story.

Dad knelt down in front of me, taking both of my hands in his. "Who did this, sweetheart? You don't have to be afraid to tell me."

I shook my head, and a tear streaked down my cheek. "He really didn't mean it," I pleaded and then I lied. "He won't do it again." A voice inside my head screamed at me to tell him the truth. I ignored it.

Dad brushed the tear from my face and asked again in an even but demanding tone, "Who?"

I looked at the worn sneakers on my feet. There was no way out of this. I had to tell him that Jeff had bruised my arm. I raised my head a little without meeting his eyes. If I looked into his eyes, I would spill it all. I couldn't do that. For Jack, I had to keep the secret.

"It was Jeff." I made no more excuses for him but volunteered no more information.

"You're right about one thing." Dad lifted my chin up with his hand so that my eyes met his. "He won't do it again. I'll take care of it."

His words were meant to comfort me, but instead, they filled me with fear. *What did he intend to do?* My breath came in quick, sharp bursts as I considered the possibilities.

"Ronnie! Sarah! Come on, kids, we're walking back to the car now," Dad called.

"But, Dad, you said we could walk the whole trail this time," Ronnie whined.

"I know I did. And I'm sorry, but something has come up that I need to take care of," Dad told him. Then, before Ronnie could start another protest, Dad looked at him with a seriousness that no kid could fight. "This is important, Ronnie. Don't make me tell you again."

Ronnie's eyes widened, and I could see that Dad didn't often take this tone with him. He nodded his small head and started back down the trail without another word. I followed behind everyone else, dragging my feet, my stomach churning with dread.

Dad dropped Ronnie and Sarah off with Grace and returned to the car where I was waiting. Usually, I walked home, but this time Dad insisted on driving me.

I breathed a small sigh of relief when we drove up in front of my house. Jeff's car was not there. So at least it was possible a confrontation might be avoided.

When we got to the front door, Dad asked me to get Mama while he waited. I did as he said and returned a few minutes later with my mother.

"Why don't you come in, Ron. You don't have to lurk in the doorway," Mama said as if he was always welcome and should know it, which we all knew was not the case. Dad accepted her invitation, and we went into the kitchen. "Beth says you want to see me. What's this about?"

My father motioned me over to him. He gently took my arm and pulled up my sleeve, exposing the blue-black marks. "This is what it's about, Bella," he said calmly, but with a dark and angry tone. "Can you tell me why you're allowing your husband to manhandle our daughter?"

Mama's eyes registered shock, which perhaps Dad thought meant she really was surprised about the bruises. But even though Mama hadn't actually seen *these* marks before, I knew she was only shocked by the confrontation.

"Well, I've … I mean …" Mama fumbled for words, just as I had. She opened her mouth again and then closed it shaking her head. "Ron, I haven't seen these marks before. But Jeff would never hurt her. Certainly not on purpose." I watched my mother, wondering how she could lie so convincingly.

For a few moments, there was silence. I could feel Dad's anger. Mama kept an expression of innocence. "What did Beth tell you happened? Did she say he did this on purpose? That he meant to hurt her?"

Dad answered honestly. "No. She insisted that it was an accident."

Mama's face betrayed her briefly, showing her satisfaction. She shrugged. "You see? It was just an accident. Beth told you herself."

Dad nodded. "Yes, she did. But I don't believe her. I can see through her, and I can see through you too, Bella."

Mama stared at him, looking aghast. She wasn't fumbling for words now or making excuses. She was stunned. In the seven years since the abuse began, no one had ever questioned her.

"I don't care how you choose to live, Bella. But I do care about how it affects Beth. I won't let her live this way any longer," he paused to let his words sink in. "She's coming home with me. She's going to live with me now."

My jaw dropped as I heard my father's words.

Mama's expression turned dark. "How dare you assume to know what our life is like! How dare you think you can walk in here and take my child away! I gave birth to her… alone. And I've been taking care of her. Just because she has your DNA doesn't mean you have any right to her! Jeff has been more of a father to her than you have. You weren't even here for the first ten years of her life!"

"How could I be?" Dad slammed his fist down on the counter. "You didn't tell me she existed! You stole those years from me. There's nothing in my life I regret more than missing that time with her. And I may never forgive you for that. But she *is* my daughter and I'm going to make sure she's safe. I don't believe she's safe here." Dad looked at me with pain in his eyes. I stared back at him bewildered. "I'm just sorry that for two years I didn't realize what was going on here. I feel like I failed you, Beth." He turned his gaze back to Mama. "But I'm going to fix it. She's coming to live with me."

I saw Jack watching us from the hallway, his eyes filled with fear and hurt.

"I won't go," I said with a forceful tone.

"Beth," Dad began, looking confused and upset. "You don't have to live this way. I promise I'll keep you safe. Please … come with me." He looked at me with a deep penetrating expression. Then his look softened as he spoke to me again. "I would never hurt you. You know that, don't you?"

I nodded and struggled to keep back the tears threatening to flow. A part of me wanted more than anything to go with him. He loved me. He wanted to protect me. I couldn't imagine anything more wonderful than that. "I know that. But I won't go with you. I live here."

I looked at Jack, holding his eyes for a second, then back at Dad. I could see he intended on convincing me to go with him. I took his hand, leading him outside to the front porch. I closed the door behind us, and we sat down on the steps.

"Beth, I want to help you, take care of you."

"I know," I responded. "But I don't need you to. I told you he didn't mean to hurt me."

Dad put his hands on my shoulders and turned me to face him. "And I told your mother that I don't believe you." He looked down for a moment and then straight into my eyes. "I'm going to take care of this. And I'm going to take care of you ... one way or another."

Still meeting his eyes, I spoke with total honesty. "I won't go, Dad. If you make me, then I'll run away and come back here. And I'll keep running away day after day. I will always come back here."

Dad looked confused. He'd seen through me. And though he had no idea how bad the abuse was, he knew there was more going on than Mama or I were willing to say. Then I said what I felt would clear up his confusion without letting him know just what Jeff really put us through.

"I love you, Dad. I'm so glad we found each other. And I want to keep spending time with you. Mama says that Jeff has been more of a father to me than you have, but that isn't true. You're the father I used to dream about. But I can't live with you. I won't leave Jack."

He must have heard the conviction in my voice. He stared at me for a second, then put his hands over his face. Then he raised them both in a gesture of surrender. "Okay. If you feel that strongly about this, I'll let it alone... for now." Holding my chin in his hand and looking deep into my eyes he continued, "You say he didn't mean to hurt you. I find that hard to believe, but I can't prove that I'm right. So I'll have to take your word for it. But if he ever hurts you again... in any way ... call me. I promise you it will be the last time he hurts anyone."

Rebecca L. Marsh

# Chapter 13

About two weeks after I had talked with Dad, I found myself spending an evening at home with my mother and Jack. Jeff had gone out with his buddies.

We played Monopoly, then I went to my room to do a little homework while Mama took a phone call and Jack watched TV.

Around ten o' clock I heard Jeff's car pull up out front. Less than five seconds later Jack ran into my room. We had already stuffed his bed with pillows to make it look like he was sleeping there.

I'd also learned to only use a small lamp on the nights Jeff went out. That way I could turn it off before Jeff saw it through my window.

I switched off the lamp. Then Jack hid under my bed and I hurried under the covers and prepared to be asleep.

As I got into bed, the front door slammed, and an object shattered on the floor. I squeezed my eyes shut, my breath shortening as I prepared for what I was about to hear.

Jeff's voice boomed out in a slurred shout. I couldn't even tell what he was saying. *This is bad. He's really drunk this time.* He was probably yelling ridiculous accusations at Mama. That's what he usually did. Once he had even torn the house apart looking for Reverend Holiday, the minister from our church, because he was convinced Mama was having an affair with him.

I heard Mama cry out, followed by a thud. Next came a jumble my mother's cries and Jeff's shouting. I reached down to grab Jack's up-stretched hand and held onto him tightly as I sobbed into my pillow.

All at once, the sounds stopped except Mama's crying. Then she yelled, "No, Jeff! Please! The children are sleeping. Leave them alone!"

Mama knew Jeff wouldn't listen. Her outcry was a warning, her way of saying, "he's coming!"

I dropped Jack's hand and he slipped it back under the bed. I kept my eyes closed, but not too tightly. I willed myself to slow my breathing as if I was really asleep.

I heard Jeff stomping down the hall and cursing when he stumbled into the wall. Then the doorknob started to move. He was so drunk that he had trouble turning it, but he finally succeeded. For a few seconds, I felt him staring at me. Then all hell broke loose.

My eyes flew open when I heard Jack's high pitched scream. I wasn't sure how Jeff knew Jack was there: maybe his foot had been sticking out, or maybe he had moved. When I looked, Jeff was dragging Jack out from under the bed by one arm.

I screamed and hit Jeff's arm, trying to make him let go of Jack. He knocked me back and laughed at my attempt.

Mama started yelling again. "Please, Jeff! Don't hurt them. It's me you're angry with!" She didn't come running. He was probably unstoppable by any of us, but she didn't even try. Only Jack and I fought back.

I continued to hit Jeff and, in a desperate attempt to free Jack from his grip, I bit Jeff's arm. He screamed but retained his hold. He swung with his left arm, slapped me hard across the face, and dragged me off the bed by my hair. When he let go, I fell to the floor with a hard thud. Before I had a chance to catch my breath, Jeff pulled me back up by my arm. Holding each of us by one arm, he dragged Jack and me out of the bedroom. Jack's head banged against the doorframe as we went through.

Halfway down the hall, Jeff stumbled and slammed me into the wall. I hit my forehead—hard—on a picture frame. The glass shattered and fell to the floor. A sharp pain stabbed through my head, and blood trickled down my face.

An odd thought went through my head about school. I wouldn't be able to cover this injury up. I would probably have to miss at least a week. And I couldn't let Dad see it. I'd have to make up an excuse to cancel my visit with him this weekend.

By the time we reached the living room, I felt like my head was on fire. I knew Jeff was just getting started. He slammed me on the floor and turned his attention to Jack. Slightly dazed, I saw Jeff pinning Jack up against the wall. He screamed in Jack's face. "What do you think you're doing sleeping in your sister's room? You sick little fuck!"

"Daddy, please! I didn't do anything," Jack cried.

Mama crouched in the corner with a horrified expression on her face. Tears ran down her cheeks, as she continued to beg for mercy she knew Jeff would never give. Her eyes were swollen from crying, but that was the only evidence you could see of her beating. She had bruises, I knew, in places that could not be seen. Jeff made mistakes with Jack and me this time, much as he had that first time he'd beaten Mama and me, but usually, he was careful to leave marks only in places that could be covered.

I jumped up and kicked the back of Jeff's leg, knocking him off balance. "Leave him alone! He's just a little boy!"

"You're right," Jeff spat back at me. "You put him up to it, didn't you? What were you making him do, you little whore? Was he touching you? Did you like it?" Jeff knocked me to the floor and began kicking me. I curled into a ball as a sharp pain in my chest took my breath away.

The police didn't knock when they showed up with their sirens blaring. They kicked the door down and swarmed into the house. One officer grabbed Jeff and, slammed him into the wall, slapping handcuffs on him, while another screamed in his ear about what a big man he was hurting kids.

Paramedics rushed in and tended to Jack, Mama, and me. They gently lifted me onto a stretcher.

As they rolled me to the front door, I looked at the mess. Objects were strewn about. On the floor near the door, a broken porcelain angel laid on the floor. I remembered Jack giving it to Mama the previous mother's day. Beside it, the phone receiver was off the hook, beeping nonstop.

A man with a kind face sat next to me in the ambulance. I looked at him fearfully, wondering what would happen to me now.

"It's going to be okay," the man said in a gentle voice, "We'll take good care of you."

"What about my mother and my brother?"

"You'll see them soon. We're taking you to Adam's General. The doctors will check you over and take care of your injuries. Your mom and little brother will be going there too."

I nodded and closed my eyes. I felt safe with this man. His voice was quiet and soothing as he reassured me, and his hands were gentle as he tended to the cut on my head.

When I opened my eyes a few minutes later, the ambulance was already coming to a stop outside the hospital. The paramedics wheeled me out of the ambulance and into the hospital.

A doctor stood over me and looked at me with sad eyes. "I'm Doctor Rifkin. What's your name?"

"Beth."

"I think we can fix you up just fine, Beth. We'll need to stitch that cut on your head. Can you tell if anything else is hurt badly? Is there anything that feels worse than a bruise?"

"It hurts when I breathe."

"That's probably a fractured rib. We'll do an x-ray to see for sure." He paused for a moment and looked me straight in the eyes. "Beth, has this ever happened before?"

I opened my mouth to lie. I was so used to doing it, but I saw in his eyes the possibility of a different future. I didn't want to lie anymore. All I could do was cry. Pain seared through my chest as I sobbed. The doctor spoke quiet words of comfort, trying to calm me, but even as he did, tears streamed down his cheeks.

After the doctors fixed me up, I was taken to a small area closed off with a curtain. I still hadn't seen Mama or Jack, but no one was around to ask and I was tired. I closed my eyes and went to sleep.

When I woke up a little while later, a woman was sitting near my bed. I blinked my eyes a few times to clear the sleep, and then looked her over. She was a small black woman who looked to be around twenty-five. She was dressed in nice slacks and a tailored jacket.

"Who are you?" I asked sleepily.

She looked up, smiling warmly. "My name is Martha Edmonton. I work for social services."

"Why are you here?"

"It's my job to find out as much as I can about what happened to you and your brother tonight, and make sure you're safe. I'm here to help you. But you have to be honest with me. Do you think you can do that?"

I nodded and rubbed my eyes. I would tell her what she wanted to know. I didn't have the energy to lie anymore. I had no idea what would happen if I told her the truth, but I knew what would happen if I lied again. The pain in my head and chest constantly reminded me.

Martha took a pad of paper and a pen out of her briefcase. She looked me directly in the eyes and began asking questions.

"The first thing I need to know is if your injuries the result of an accident."

Gathering my courage, I returned her gaze and answered, "No."

Martha paused for a moment looking surprised as if she'd expected me to lie. "Did your mother hurt you in any way?"

"No."

"Did your father hurt you in any way?"

"He's my step-father. And, yes, he did."

Martha nodded. "Your doctor told me that your x-rays showed evidence that you've had broken ribs in the past. Has he ever hurt you before tonight?"

I nodded, barely able to speak.

"I know this may be difficult, but I have to ask you to describe, in detail, what happened tonight."

I took a deep breath. I wanted her help, but I had not expected to relive every horrible part of that night. I swiped at the tears rolling down my cheek and then told Martha everything, from Jeff coming home drunk to the police arriving.

Martha listened in silence, keeping her warm eyes on mine. Something about her that told me she understood where I had been. Somehow her presence made me feel safe.

When I finished telling her everything, I thought about Jack.

"Is my brother okay? Have you seen him?"

"Yes, he's fine. I haven't talked to him yet. You're the oldest and I wanted to hear it from you first. But I talked with the doctor and he says you will all be fine once you heal."

I felt better knowing he was all right, but I knew he must be scared. "When can I see him?"

"I'm going to go talk to him when we're done here. After that, you will both be released to child services. You'll spend whatever is left of tonight there. You may be there for a day or two while I find you a foster home."

"We're not going to live with our mother anymore?" I felt strange thinking about that. I didn't want to go back there and yet I would miss her.

"Not right now. Whether or not she regains custody will be determined later. I'm going to look into the possibility of you and Jack staying with another family member."

"What about Jeff? What's going to happen to him?"

"I don't know," Martha said. "That's for a judge to decide."

Rebecca L. Marsh

# Chapter 14

Wednesday morning Beth sat in her office filing her notes on the patient who had just left, but Erin's image floated around in the back of her mind. When she'd left the detention center on Monday Erin had looked terribly vulnerable. Her eye was black, and she could barely sit up straight because of the broken rib. Beth had hoped the unfortunate turn of events would push Erin to talk, but her determination to stay silent remained intact. The one thing that gave Beth hope in her unusual tactics was that Erin was definitely interested in hearing the next part of the story.

The phone rang just as Beth was reaching for it. She picked it up and heard Lisa's voice on the other end.

"I have something new to tell you about Erin," Lisa sounded hopeful.

"Don't hold me in suspense!"

"I spent time yesterday and this morning calling the schools Erin has attended. I talked to as many of her teachers as I could. At first, I didn't think my calls would amount to anything. All of her elementary teachers raved about what a fantastic student had been. They said she was happy, enthusiastic, and very bright. Their only complaint was that, while Victoria was always willing to make donations and sponsor events, she and James were never available to help in the classroom and were often too busy to attend school programs."

"Okay, so what did you find that was interesting?" Beth fiddled with an oddly shaped paperweight one of her patients had given her last Christmas.

"It didn't get interesting until I spoke with her seventh-grade teacher, Mrs. Abernathy. She said that at the beginning of the term, Erin was a model student. She did all her homework, participated in class, and was popular with the other students." Lisa paused a moment. "Then something changed after Erin's birthday in November. Apparently the day after her birthday, Erin came to class in a foul mood. And she continued to have problems for a while. Mrs. Abernathy wasn't able to talk to me on the phone for very long, so I scheduled a meeting with her today during her lunch break. I was hoping you would join me. You're the psychologist. You might be the best one to talk to her."

"I definitely want to talk to her. What time is her lunch break?"

"Twelve o' clock. I'll pick you up, and it will take us about fifteen minutes to get there from your office. We want to get there a few minutes early, so we have time to check in at the school office. So why don't I just pick you up at eleven thirty?"

"Sounds good. I'll have Juanita reschedule a couple of appointments."

Beth and Lisa arrived at Stonewood Academy and proceeded to the office where they were given visitor's passes and directions to Mrs. Abernathy's classroom.

The bell rang just as they arrived, and young students came pouring out. Beth and Lisa waited until the last student left the room and then went in. Mrs. Abernathy was sitting at her large wooden desk with a bagged lunch. She was middle-aged with brown hair pulled back in a bun and stylish glasses.

She looked up as Lisa approached, with Beth a step behind, and extended her hand. "I'm Lisa Larson." She shook the teacher's hand. "We spoke on the phone this morning." Lisa gestured to Beth. "This is Beth Christopher. She's a child psychologist who's been working with Erin."

Mrs. Abernathy nodded. "Pull up a chair and we'll talk. I hope you don't mind if I eat. It's the only chance I'll get."

"Of course not. We appreciate your taking the time to see us on such short notice," Lisa responded.

Beth and Lisa looked around the room for chairs. It was an amazing classroom; unlike any Beth had ever spent time in as a kid. The walls were covered in wood paneling and two blackboards hung behind the teacher's desk. The large pupils' desks were in perfect shape. Not one of the desks or chairs had anything etched on it, nor was there any chewing gum stuck to anything.

On the back wall was a long table with six computers set up and chairs facing them. Beth and Lisa walked to the back to retrieve chairs.

They sat down facing Mrs. Abernathy, who was just digging into a ham and cheese sandwich. Lisa began the conversation. "Mrs. Abernathy, you were telling me on the phone that Erin changed right after her birthday when she was in your class. That was her thirteenth birthday, right?"

"That's right. It was in early November. The day of her birthday, Erin was happy just like always. I remember the whole class singing "Happy Birthday" to her. But the next day she was a different kid."

"How was she different?" Beth asked.

"At first she was just quiet and sullen. She looked tired and I thought maybe she hadn't slept well. During our science lesson, I called on her. She had her head down on the desk and I wanted to see if she was paying attention." Pausing, Mrs. Abernathy took another bite of her sandwich. "Erin said she didn't know the answer and I pressed her. I reminded her that the question was covered in the homework I had assigned the previous day. She got angry, which was very unlike her. She started to yell over and over, 'I don't know! I don't know!' Then she started crying. I was taken aback. I'd never seen Erin behave that way. It's not as though she always knew the answers, but she'd never gotten upset before."

"What did you do about her outburst?" Beth leaned closer to the teacher's desk.

"I called her up to the front and quietly asked her to go see the school counselor."

Beth nodded. "Can we talk to the counselor?"

"Sure." Mrs. Abernathy dabbed her mouth with a paper napkin.

"Was Erin's behavior strange on any other occasions?" Beth asked.

"Well, she only showed anger with me one other time, but from that first day on, she showed less interest in her studies and her friends. Her grades dropped from mostly A's to mostly C's and didn't start to improve until the end of the year. She quit cheerleading and stopped attending dances and other school functions she had enjoyed."

Beth nodded as she scribbled notes. "Tell me about the other time she got angry. When was that?"

Mrs. Abernathy thought a moment while biting into an apple. "It was about two weeks after the first incident. Erin came into class and was very quiet again. And again she seemed tired. I didn't call on her that time, but I approached her just before lunch break and asked about her mood. I told her I was concerned. She said she didn't want to talk about it. I told her that if she didn't want to talk to me then she could go have another talk with the counselor. That's when she got angry. 'I don't need a shrink!' she yelled at me, 'I'm not crazy and there's nothing wrong with me!' I told her she could either see the counselor or the principal. She went to the counselor."

"And that was the last time she behaved that way?"

"It was the last time she got angry with me. There were a few other times when she seemed tired or moody and didn't participate in class."

"Okay. Just one more question. Did Erin ever say anything to you about her father that was negative or cause for concern?"

"The only discontent she ever expressed was that her parents were always busy and didn't have time to do things with her or Kayla. But...she didn't have to tell anyone that. James and Victoria were obviously more interested in making the society page than in spending time with their children."

Beth nodded and smiled at the teacher. "I think that's about it unless Lisa has any other questions."

"No," Lisa said, "I think that covers it. Thank you for your help, Mrs. Abernathy."

"You're welcome. I hope it does help. And if you want to talk to the counselor, his office is just down the hall on the left."

Beth and Lisa did talk to him even though they knew anything Erin had said to him would be confidential. However, he was able to tell them that Erin had simply sat in his office and refused to talk, just as she was refusing now.

The next day, sitting in her office with young Lindsay Arnold, Beth found herself struggling to pay attention to her patient talking. She blinked a few times and shook her head a little to bring back her focus. Lindsay was relaying her feelings about her father. He had left Lindsay and her mother a year ago. At first, he'd sent Lindsay letters and cards in the mail, but in the last few months, Lindsay hadn't heard from him.

"I really love him. And I thought he loved me too. But if that's true, why doesn't he call or write? I haven't seen him in ten months. I didn't even hear from him on my birthday. He's never forgotten my birthday before. Do you think he stopped loving me?"

Beth was fighting to keep her attention in the room, but her mind kept wandering back to Erin. *Help Lindsay now*, she told herself, trying to focus. She looked at the twelve-year-old girl in front of her. Lindsay was a very pretty girl. She had golden blonde hair that fell around her face in loose curls, pale skin, as perfect as porcelain and big blue eyes that were, at the moment, filled with sadness.

"Lindsay, I can't answer that question. Have you tried contacting him yourself?" Beth wanted to tell Lindsay that no parent could ever stop loving their child, but she knew that wasn't always true. And offering false hope was not her job.

"Yes, I sent him a letter and asked him why I don't ever hear from him anymore. I haven't heard anything back though."

"When did you send the letter?"

Lindsay pushed her hair from her face and wiped her nose with a tissue. "Two months ago."

"How do you feel about him not responding? Does it make you angry?"

"A little, I guess, but mostly sad. My mom keeps telling me he'll call soon or I'll get a letter. But sometimes when she doesn't know I'm there, she says bad things about him. I don't think she really believes he'll call."

"Does it upset you that she isn't totally honest with you?"

Lindsay paused a moment and thought out her answer. "Well sometimes I feel like she's lying to me, and it hurts me to hear the things she says about him. I wish we could all be a family again. Last week I saw the movie *The Parent Trap* on TV and it made me cry, 'cause I know that happy endings like that don't usually happen when parents split up." Lindsay looked up at Beth, her big blue eyes filled with tears, "I don't think my father is ever coming back."

Beth offered Lindsay another tissue. "I don't know what will happen with your father, Lindsay, but I think when your mother tells you that he'll call, she wants to take away your pain. She loves you and she wants you to be happy, so she tells you what she thinks you want to hear." Beth stopped and looked at the wall clock. "It looks like our time is up. We'll talk more in a couple weeks. In the meantime, I think you should talk to your mom. Tell her what you've heard and how you feel about it."

Lindsay nodded and left the room. Beth sat at her desk and prepared her files on Erin, with whom she was going to spend the rest of the afternoon. She'd listened to a girl suffering because her father had left her, and locked behind bars was a girl who had killed her father. What had she suffered?

Rebecca L. Marsh

# Chapter 15

Jack and I spent three days at child services before Martha moved us to our new foster home. She packed us, and two suitcases full of items brought from our old home, into a small white car and drove several miles. We drove through a neighborhood of beautiful houses with manicured lawns and stopped in front of a gray house with black shutters. The bushes along the front of the house were cut perfectly rectangular, and on the porch was a large pot that I imagined would hold flowers during the summer. A man, a woman, and a little girl who looked to be about four years old stood in front of the house.

Martha turned and looked at Jack and me in the backseat. "It's time to meet your foster parents." She smiled reassuringly. "Don't be afraid. I met with them yesterday and they're very nice people."

As I wandered up the walk holding Jack's hand, I felt a little queasy, but I wasn't sure why. It couldn't be worse, could it? Martha shook hands with the couple and introduced us. "I'd like you to meet Beth and Jack," she gestured toward us. "Kids, this is Matthew and Karen Zimmerman. And this," she pointed to the little girl, "is their daughter Tamera."

Tamera moved behind her mother's legs, trying to hide, but her bright red hair was difficult to conceal.

I smiled and shook hands with the Zimmermans. Karen smiled back bending down to Jack who looked terrified. "How about we go in and show you around. I think you'll like your new rooms."

Jack nodded and we all went into the house, which was pretty, bright, and clean. Mama had always kept the house clean, but I knew there was more to a home than what the eyes could see.

We walked through the family room and kitchen toward the bedrooms in the back. It was a big house, and even though they had another child, Jack and I would have our own rooms.

Karen took us into Jack's room first. It was a large room, filled with new toys, but Jack noticed right away that his Lego set and favorite stuffed dog from home were in the room. He ran to the dog and hugged it tightly. He then ran around the room checking out the other toys. Like any six-year-old, he noticed the bed last. It was a brand new twin size bed with a comforter covered in cowboys on horses swinging lassos. The wallpaper border around the top of the walls matched the bedspread.

Jack bounced a little on the bed, then looked up at Karen. "This room is so cool. But how did you get my dog and my Legos?"

"I'm glad you like the room." Karen beamed. "We asked Martha to bring a few things over to help you feel more at home. She could tell how much you love that dog."

I looked over and saw Matthew standing in the doorway with little Tamera at his feet. He grinned at Jack's joy while his small daughter hugged his leg. *Maybe this would be a good home*, I thought. On the other hand, even Jeff could be really nice at times. I looked at their smiling faces, and I wanted to believe this home would be different.

From the doorway, Matthew smiled my way and waved me over. "Come on. Let's go see your room, Beth."

The warmth of his smile was infectious, and I couldn't help but smile back. I followed him out of Jack's room and walked to a room two doors down the hall. On the way, we passed Tamera's room, painted pink and yellow with shelves full of toys and books.

My room took my breath away. Blue and purple flowers bordered the pale lavender walls. Centered on the far wall was a beautiful, full-sized white canopy bed with lavender coverings in just a slightly bolder shade. On the opposite wall, stood a large matching dresser with a mirror on top. Blue and purple pillows flanked the seat of the bay window.

Looking closer, I saw a painful reminder of the past. Sandwiched in between two new stuffed animals sat the brown teddy bear Jeff had given me after the first beating.

I stood motionless staring at the bear in shock. Then I remembered the rest of the room these nice people had given me and how happy Jack was. *It doesn't matter. Just pretend it isn't here.* I closed my eyes a minute and imagined the room without the dreadful bear. I thought of Matthew and Karen's smiling faces. Then I opened my eyes and turned to the entire group, now gathered in the doorway. I told them that I loved the room, and thanked them for making Jack and me feel so welcome.

"You're not just welcome," Karen replied. "You're wanted."

For a while, we were happy with the Zimmermans. The only part I didn't like was not seeing Dad. I wondered if he missed me and if he really loved me as much as he said he did. I couldn't be sure, but I assumed he was the one that called the police the night they came. He was the only one I could think of who cared about Jeff hurting me. But if that was true, why didn't he come for me?

Within a few weeks, Karen started noticing that Jack was sneaking into my room most nights, sleeping there with me, then going back to his room early in the morning.

"Matthew and I are concerned about this behavior," she took a deep breath. "Not only are we dismayed by this behavior because the two of you, especially you, Beth, are too old to be sleeping in the same room when one of you is a girl and one a boy, but we're worried about the kind of message it may send to our daughter."

Jack and I sat silently on the couch. How could I explain to her about the terror we had experienced? Karen knew a little about what we had come from, and that wasn't enough to make her understand. So how could anything I said help?

She waited a few minutes looking at our mystified expressions but neither of us responded.

"I want it to stop. You will both sleep in your own rooms and in your own beds." With that, she walked away.

The next day Matthew took Jack and me aside when he came home from work. I wasn't surprised—I'd heard him talking to Karen the night before. He'd tried to convince her that Jack coming to me at night wasn't such a bad thing, but when she asked him how he'd feel about it if Tamera began to join in, he admitted she had a point, and agreed to talk to us himself. I couldn't even argue with her point. I knew Jack sleeping in my room wasn't normal. But for years I was the only one who tried to protect him. We were in a safe place now, but the fear didn't just disappear instantly.

"I know Karen already talked to you about the ... night time problems. I want you both to know that we understand why you're doing it. The thing is, we have to think about what it says to Tamera. But I want you both to know that if you get scared at night and need someone, you can come to us."

"Jack's used to coming to me at night," I said. "He does it without thinking."

Matthew nodded. "That's what I figured. But, Jack," he turned his attention just to Jack, "please try to come to us instead of Beth. And, you know, if that nightlight we got you isn't bright enough, we can get another one. Just let us know what will help you feel safer at night. We want to help you."

"The nightlight's okay. I just get so scared sometimes," Jack said.

Matthew knelt down in front of Jack and put a hand on his shoulder. "I imagine you do, but remember we're here for you. Karen didn't mean to be so harsh. She's just concerned for Tamera. She's a mother, and mother's worry about everything."

Jack leaned forward and wrapped his small arms around Matthew. Then he leaned back and said, "I'm glad they brought us here. I like having you for a dad."

"And I like having both of you for my kids," Matthew responded with tears in his eyes.

Things went fairly well for about a week. Jack started going to Matthew and Karen at night, which made Karen happy. But, even though I knew we were in a safe place, not having Jack around at night affected me more than I'd imagined. Nightmares began to plague my sleep. They were vivid and violent causing me to scream out in my sleep. Matthew and Karen tried to comfort me, but my screaming woke up everyone in the house, and it was very upsetting for little Tamera. So Matthew stayed with me while Karen tried to calm Tamera down.

As the dreams continued, I could see how the hard nights were stressful for everyone and I wondered how long we could all go on that way.

A couple weeks later, Jack and I went on our first visit with Mama since we had been taken away from her. I tossed and turned the night before, and when I did sleep, the nightmares came.

I knew Jeff wouldn't be there. He wasn't allowed to see us.

Still, I wasn't sure I wanted to see Mama. I did miss her, but life with her had always been turbulent. With the Zimmerman's I was, for the first time since age five, enjoying some calm. They weren't perfect parents, but they never hurt us. The choice, however, was not mine. The court was allowing Mama to have supervised visits with us, so there was nothing I could do.

Martha came to pick us up mid-morning and took us to a nearby park for the visit. We were not supposed to go back to our old home for the visits because social services had decided it would be too traumatic for us considering our history there. That was fine with me. I didn't care if I ever saw my mother's house again.

Mama was waiting for us when we got to the park. Jack jumped out of the car and ran to hug her. I eased out and walked to her. It felt like my shoes were full of lead. She held out her arms, and I let her hug me, but I gave very little back. If she noticed my reluctance, however, she didn't say anything.

Mama sat down on a bench and motioned for us to sit with her. Her face was bright, and she seemed more alive than she had in a long time.

"So how have you two been?" Mama sat between Jack and me, holding each one of us by one hand. Martha sat on another bench across the walking path from us and listened without interrupting.

Jack told Mama all about the Zimmermans, from the size of the house to his cowboy room. Despite the smile Mama kept plastered on her face, I could see the disappointment she felt at Jack's joy.

Jack talked non-stop, but I stayed quiet. When the visit was nearly over, Mama looked at me. "So, Beth, what about you? How are you doing? You've hardly said a word today."

"I'm fine," I said in a disinterested tone. "And the bruises are almost all healed."

Her face tightened, but she forced the smile to stay in place. "That's good, honey," she said in a pinched tone.

Martha stood up and walked over to us. "Alright kids, it's time to go. I'm just going to walk over there a bit, and you can have some privacy to say goodbye. Two minutes and I'll be back."

As she walked away, Mama bent down and pulled us both close. "I know this has been hard for you two, but I don't want you to worry. Grandpa got a real good lawyer for Jeff and pretty soon I think we'll all be a family again."

I felt ill. I swallowed hard and fought nausea. "I thought Jeff was going to stay in jail."

"If that does happen, then I'll get you back and when Jeff does get out, then we can be a family again. We'll get there someday, I promise."

Mama kissed us both on the head when she saw Martha coming back. "Okay, you two. Be good and I'll see you again soon. I love you."

"Love you too," Jack sang back to her. I said nothing.

In the car, I felt frozen. My mind raced around the idea that we could end up back with Jeff. Since we had been taken away I'd wondered what would become of us. I'd imagined several different scenarios, but living with Jeff again wasn't one of them. I simply wouldn't allow my mind to go there. Would Martha really let that happen? Did she have the power to stop it?

"Beth?" Martha's voice snapped me out of my thoughts and I realized I had chewed my thumbnail down to a nub. I jerked my hand away from my mouth and looked up at her.

"Yes?"

"We're here, sweetie. You can get out of the car now." Martha smiled back at me. "I'll be back for your visit next week."

I nodded, opening the door to the car. "Okay."

I went to my room without saying a word to Karen or Matthew. I didn't want to talk. My head hurt and my stomach was rolling. I went to my bed and sat down on the lavender spread. I looked around the room, and for a moment I was comforted. I was in a good place now, with good people.

Then I looked over at the window seat, and the brown bear seemed to be smirking at me. I had hated that bear since the first time I saw it, but now in place of its cuddly brown face, I saw Jeff's face. I could hear Jeff's voice taunting me. As I stared at the bear my rage grew stronger and stronger. Suddenly the anger became uncontrollable. I jumped off my bed, and flew toward the bear, throwing pillows off the bed as I went. I grabbed the bear and began to tear its limbs off. Stuffing fibers spewed out, as I was tore at its face, plucking its eyes off, and ripping off its head.

When the bear was completely destroyed, I stood still, looking at it with satisfaction. I had wanted to do that since the first moment I'd laid eyes on that dreadful thing seven years earlier.

What I hadn't realized is that while I was tearing apart the bear I had also been screaming at it. And while my fit of anger had been directed at the bear, by the time I was finished, several other things in my room were destroyed and the bear's filling fibers were all over the room.

The screaming brought Karen to my room to check on me and when I turned around, I saw her standing in the doorway. She looked horrified, staring at me with her mouth agape. Tamera held onto Karen's right leg was, her eyes wide with terror. Karen and I seemed to stand for an eternity staring at one another.

Finally, she broke the silence. "What did you do?" She spoke at first in a soft and bewildered voice but then it raised causing Tamera to cry. "My God, Beth, what did you do? Have you gone mad?"

I opened my mouth to explain. Then I knew she could never understand. "I'm sorry."

Karen reached down and lifted Tamera into her arms. The child put her head on her mother's shoulder and stopped crying. "You're sorry? That's all you have to say? I don't even know how to respond to that." She shook her head and looked down at the face of her daughter. Her eyes were filled with sorrow when she looked at me again. "I can't do this. I just can't do it. I wanted to, but I don't have what it takes."

She turned and walked away from my room.

I wasn't sure what she meant by that, but I knew it wasn't good. I didn't know what else to do when she left, so I started to pick up the mess as well as I could. When I had done all I could to make it better I laid on my bed, curled my legs up to my chest and wept. Eventually, I fell asleep.

When I woke up I could hear Matthew and Karen talking in the living room. Then I heard Martha's voice. I eased off my bed and opened the door to my room just a crack so I could hear them better.

"I understand that, Martha, and I'm really sorry. We've tried. Honestly, we have. But this is the last straw. We can't go on like this. We have to think about Tamera," Karen said.

"I understand," Martha said. "You'll have to give us some time to find a new placement."

"Of course," Matthew spoke up, "We want you to find a good place for her."

"I would like to talk to Beth about it today though if that's okay. This won't be easy for either of them. But she's old enough to know that something is going on. I think it will be better if she knows the truth."

"Go ahead and talk to her. She's in her room," Matthew said.

There was a short pause and I heard Martha starting toward my room. I closed the door again and hurried back to my bed. A minute later Martha knocked.

"Come in," I called to her.

"Hi, Beth." She sat on the bed next to me and put her arm around my shoulders. "I wish I had better news for you, sweetie. It seems you really upset Karen. She feels unable to deal with you." Martha looked down at her lap as she continued. "That means I'll have to place you in another foster home."

"What about Jack? Is he coming too?" I asked.

"Actually, that's what I have to talk to you about. Normally we like to keep siblings together, but we're very short on foster families right now and I'm not sure I'll be able to find anyone who will take two kids." Martha turned toward me. "Beth, the Zimmermans want to keep Jack, and I think that might be best. If I can find someone to take both of you, then I will. We'll work this all out as soon as we can."

I nodded, struggling to control the tears that threatened to come.

"It'll be okay, Beth. I'll find a good place for you," she said. "Now, would you like to tell me what happened here today?" She gestured around the room that was still somewhat disheveled.

I took a deep breath. "I was upset because Mama said something about her and Jeff getting us back. Then I came home and I saw that bear... I just couldn't stop myself."

"Why did the bear upset you, Beth?"

"Jeff gave it to me when I was five, the day after he beat me for the first time. I've wanted to tear it apart ever since I first saw it. And today, after what Mama said about Jeff, I just felt so angry and scared. Then I saw that bear." Starting to cry, I looked at Martha with her kind eyes. "I just couldn't stop."

Martha pulled me close to her and let me cry on her shoulder. "I'm so sorry. I brought that bear here. I guess that makes this at least partly my fault. I'll talk to Matthew and Karen about it, explain to them. But I don't know if it will change things."

I nodded. I was pretty sure it wouldn't change things, but at least Karen would know the reason and I was grateful to Martha for trying. "It's not your fault," I told her. "You didn't know. But, Martha, could it happen?" I asked. "Could Jeff really get us back?"

She stroked a hand down my hair. "Beth I'm so sorry for what you're going through, and I wish I could tell you that you have nothing to worry about ever again. But I can't. I promise to always try my very best to look out for you. And I will always be around if you need to call me. But I can't say with absolute certainty that you will never be put back with your mom and Jeff. However, to ease your mind a little, I will say, considering the circumstances, it's very unlikely."

I nodded and was quiet for a moment. "What about Mama? Could she get us back? I mean if it was just her?"

"Maybe. She didn't ever abuse the two of you herself, so as long as she does the right things and shows herself to be capable, it is possible."

My stomach felt sick again at the thought. "But what if she got us back and then got back with Jeff. You know, when he gets out of jail. Could that happen?"

Hearing the panic in my voice, Martha held me close stroking her hand down my hair again. "I can't tell you how much I wish I could fix it all for you, sweetie. I wish I could fix it for all the kids I work with. But I can only do what the law allows and requires. And sometimes that doesn't work out so well."

She pulled away from me and looked me in the face. "I don't know for sure what's to come in your life. The only thing I can promise is that I will try my very best to keep you and Jack safe." She furrowed her brow and shook her head. "I want you to do something for me. Try to just live now, Beth. Don't spend all your time worrying about what might happen down the road. Doing that, you could waste your whole childhood. And the way I see it, you've lost enough of that already. I'll keep a watch on you two no matter what happens. And you both can come to me anytime you need me, okay?"

I nodded and reached my arms around her as I began to sob again. I didn't know what was to come, but I did know one thing. This woman really cared about me and I loved her for it.

Rebecca L. Marsh

# Chapter 16

Beth tried her best to focus on her patients on Friday, but she couldn't shake the bad feeling from her nightmare the previous night. She was running down the hall of her mother's house in a long cotton nightgown. She felt the old, worn carpet under her bare feet as they slapped across the floor. She looked for a hiding place when she got to the living room, but the only one she could think of was the space behind the couch. She squeezed herself into the space and then realized that Jack was not with her. Panic gripped her until she saw that he *was* already there, crouched low with his head down against his knees. Beth slid in next to him and reached her arms around him, but he remained still and he felt cold. Her heart pounded wildly as fear rose up through her. Was he dead?

She wasn't sure how she could help Jack because she had to stay quiet or Jeff would find them. She shook him and whispered his name, but he didn't move.

Then, in an instant, everything changed. It was not her mother's house behind the couch but in a dark bedroom closet. As the person in her arms lifted its head, she saw that it was not Jack, but a girl with long hair. Beth was confused by the darkness, and could not see clearly until the door opened and light spilled in.

It was Erin sitting with her. She looked at Beth with desperation and pleaded, "Help me." Beth looked up and saw a large male figure looming in the doorway, but she could not make out a face. Before Beth could react, Erin was ripped from her grip. A howling scream rang in Beth's ears, though she wasn't sure if it had come from herself or from Erin.

She'd awakened with that scream echoing through her mind, and she must have screamed out loud because

Nolan had awakened as well. He jumped up and pulled her close. Then he gently rubbed her back and mumbled soothing words into her ear while she trembled in his arms.

Now here she was, wanting to help all the kids who needed her. Erin, however, was the only one whose time was running out, and Beth couldn't get the urgency out of her mind. So why wouldn't Erin help herself? She kept saying she didn't care what happened to her, but Beth saw fear in the girl's eyes. She did care, but whatever her father might have done to her, he was dead now. Something else was holding her back.

At three o' clock Beth pushed her dark thoughts away to answer the phone. "Elizabeth Christopher." She put the receiver to her ear.

"I love the way you answer the phone at work. You sound so sexy."

"If that's all it takes to turn you on, then you really are too easy," Beth giggled as she responded to her husband's voice.

"Would you rather I played hard-to-get?"

"Not really. It's nice that I don't have to work too hard for your attention." Beth pushed back in her chair and swung her feet up on the desk.

"No worries. We both know I live to be your love slave."

Beth laughed despite the uneasiness she had felt all day. "So did you call just to bolster my confidence or was there another reason?"

"Actually, I was calling to remind you to stop at the store on your way home and pick up what I need to make my famous potato salad for the picnic this weekend."

"You mean you want me to buy the pre-packaged stuff so you can put it in a different bowl and pass it off as your own?"

"I do add some of my own seasonings, but, yes, that's what I mean."

"Don't worry. Your secret's safe with me. I may even pick up some of my famous brownies at the bakery while I'm there."

"Umm ... now if you bring a couple of those to bed with you tonight, I'd really be turned on."

"We might be able to arrange that, but you know the rules. I only bring chocolate to bed for my massage therapist."

"You get those brownies, and I can promise you that your massage therapist will be ready and waiting. I'll even speak with the French accent if you want."

"I wouldn't turn it down. See you in a couple hours." She hung up the phone and realized she was smiling. Nolan always had a way of lifting her spirits.

Beth and Nolan arrived at Lisa and Keith's house around noon on Saturday. They were both feeling good, and two brownies were missing from the dozen she had bought.

As they got out of their car, five-year-old Josh came running up to them, going straight to Nolan. "You're here! You're here!" Josh cried out. "My dad's setting up in the backyard and he says we can all play basketball later."

"Sounds good, buddy!" Nolan said. "I can't wait to see Anna make a basket."

"Not everyone is going to play." Josh rolled his eyes. "Just us guys." Josh looked over at Beth. "Well, you can play, Beth, but Anna can't. She's just a baby, and Mom has to watch her. She's into eating stuff off the ground these days." He made a face of disgust. "Babies are soooo gross!"

"If I remember correctly," Beth began, "you were into eating dog food at her age. And one time you ate a worm."

"Yuck! No way!" Josh said. "Are you making that up?"

"No. As it turns out, all babies are gross. And you were no exception." Beth tousled the boy's blonde hair as they reached the house where Lisa stood on the porch.

"What shall I do with these?" Beth held up the food she was carrying.

"Oh, it's the famous potato salad and the famous brownies. Aren't we lucky today?" Lisa said. "You can take them out back with the rest of the food. And you know, you really could leave it all in the store packages. You're not fooling anyone by putting it into your own containers."

Nolan put on his most innocent face. "I don't know what you're talking about. I slaved over this potato salad for hours last night."

"Of course you did." Lisa raised her eyebrows. "And that's why two of the brownies are missing."

"Do you women have to talk about everything? I mean, is nothing sacred?"

"Sorry, my friend. Talking about our husbands is what we do best."

They walked to the backyard where Keith was chasing Anna around the picnic table while she laughed. Beth set the food on the table. Anna stopped running to look up at her and then at Nolan. Her round little face was bright with a smile and her big blue eyes sparkled. "No-nan … Beh-beh." She held her arms up to them. Nolan reached down and picked the child up. She wrapped her little arms around his neck and placed a sloppy wet kiss on his cheek. Beth felt a surge of emotion as she watched the affectionate greeting. Nolan would make a great dad, and she had once longed to share a family with him. What was holding her back— making it next to impossible for her to even hold a small child? What had changed?

She had held Josh when he was a baby, and she had even held Anna when she was first born. True, she had been feeling unsure about whether or not she wanted to have kids of her own for a while now, but only since the dreams returned had she felt such paralyzing fear about holding a child.

Beth shook away her bad feelings. She was going to enjoy this day. She watched her husband play with the kids while Keith manned the grill, then they all ate together. Nolan gave Lisa a hard time about eating a veggie burger. Then they all got to hear Josh's rendition of *The Pledge of Allegiance* which he learned in school.

After that, it was time for the basketball game. Keith had put up a hoop over their garage so everyone trekked into the front yard so the "guys" could play ball and the "girls" could watch. Lisa and Beth sat in lawn chairs to watch while little Anna explored the yard. Nolan and Josh paired up to play against Keith.

"I'm still gonna win," Keith boasted looking at his son. "You should have stuck with me, kiddo. I've always been a better player."

Nolan tousled Josh's hair. "That's what he thinks. We're gonna whip his butt!"

"Yeah! We're gonna whip your butt!" Josh jumped up and down.

"Get him, Josh!" Lisa piped up from her chair. Keith looked over at her and raised his eyebrows in question. "Sorry, honey. I have to support our son."

"No love for me, I guess." Keith pretended to be hurt.

Anna stopped what she was doing, looked at her father and said, "I wuv you, Da-Da."

"Oh, come here, sweet girl." Keith bent down to hug Anna when she toddled over to him. "At least somebody's on my side. Now I'm gonna win just for you." Keith tapped a finger to Anna's little nose and she toddled back to her mother saying, "Da-Da win."

The guys began their game and Beth took a deep breath of fresh air as she looked around the yard. She had always liked this house. It reminded her of the house in the movie "Father of the Bride" with its big front porch, beautiful green grass, and white picket fence. And the flower garden was in full bloom and looked wonderful, although Beth didn't know how Lisa found the time to care for it. She was sure Lisa must have a hired gardener and just didn't want anyone to know—either way, it was beautiful, and Beth was enjoying it. Feeling nice and relaxed, she clinked her wineglass to Lisa's and settled in to watch and chat.

# Chapter 17

Beth and Nolan left the picnic after ten on Saturday. What a lovely day with good food and great company in a beautiful setting. Now Beth was comfortably tipsy in the passenger seat while her sober husband drove home.

Just as they stepped out of the car, Beth's cell phone rang. She jumped at the sudden trill, then holding one hand to her racing heart, retrieved her phone from her purse. "Hello." She said.

"Beth," came a very upset female voice.

"Katie, what is it? What's wrong?" Katie was the daughter of Beth's second foster parents, and to Beth, she was another sister.

"I went to see dad today. Beth, he's getting worse—" Katie sobbed. "I'm losing him so fast. I knew this was coming, but it's so fast."

"Slow down, Katie. Tell me what happened."

"He always has to think for a moment before he knows who I am. And sometimes he thinks I'm someone else, and I have to help him remember. Today he didn't know me at all." Katie's voice broke as she began to cry.

"Maybe it was just a bad day for him." Beth wanted to console Katie, even though she didn't want to believe that John could be fading away from them so quickly. He'd been diagnosed with Alzheimer's less than two years ago, and within that first year, Katie had to move him to a nursing home in Wilmington, where she lived. "I'm sure he'll remember you tomorrow. It always comes back to him."

"I'm not so sure this time. If you had seen him … he was so lost. And it wasn't just that he didn't remember me." Katie began sobbing again. "He was afraid of me, Beth, and so confused. He got so violently upset that they had to sedate him. It was awful seeing him like that. I'm so afraid of losing him completely." Katie stopped for a minute to collect herself. "Oh, Beth, he could be nothing more than a vegetable soon, and I'll be all alone. I feel alone already."

"You're not going to be alone, Katie. I'm here for you."

"That's true. I'm so glad I have you."

"I'm glad too," Beth said. "Listen, Katie, it's late. I'll call Juanita in the morning and ask her to cancel all my Monday appointments. Then I'll pack some things and come to see you and John. I'll be there tomorrow afternoon."

"Thank you, Beth. It'll be good to see you."

The next morning, after making a few calls, Beth threw clothes and toiletries into a suitcase and began her drive to Wilmington. Nolan had offered to come along, but Beth insisted that he stay behind this time. There was no need for both of them to take a day off from work. Besides, she and Katie needed time together, just the two of them.

Five hours later, Beth pulled up in front of Katie's apartment complex. Katie raced out the front door before Beth was out of her car. Beth pulled her suitcase from the back seat and walked over to Katie, who pulled her into a hug with the suitcase still in her hand.

Katie stood back, still holding Beth's shoulders. "It sure is good to see you, little sister."

"It's good to see you, too." Beth hadn't seen Katie in several months, but her older foster sister never seemed to change much. She was a beautiful combination of her parents, tall like her father with her mother's slightly larger stature, along with curly auburn hair contrasting with John's sparkling green eyes.

Beth followed Katie into the apartment and set her suitcase down. "Are you hungry?" Katie asked. "I thought we could go out and have an early dinner before we see Dad."

"That sounds good." Beth's stomach rumbled in anticipation. "I am getting hungry. I didn't take time to stop for lunch, and I forgot to pack something."

"Good. I'd love to catch up with you a bit before things get serious."

"Yeah, that would be nice. You know any good places to eat around here?"

"Certainly. You know I make a point of cooking as little as possible. That's one talent I didn't get from Mom."

"She was one great cook." Beth rubbed her belly at the thought.

"Yes, she was. And, if you're in the mood for it, I know a little place down the road that has food almost as good as Mom's."

"I'm definitely in the mood for it. I'm also in the mood to let someone else do the driving."

"No problem, little sister." Katie put an arm around Beth's shoulders. "I'm happy to drive."

They left Katie's apartment and drove a few blocks to a little diner.

"This is the place?" Beth asked as she skeptically eyed the place.

"It doesn't look like much, I know, but the food is fantastic."

"Okay, I'll take your word for it." When Beth saw the shabby exterior, she wondered what grade they'd received on their last health code check.

As they were seated at a window booth, she noticed that the inside was clean and well kept. She also noticed that the place was busy despite the fact that it was late for lunch and early for dinner.

From the many tempting choices on the menu, Beth finally decided to try the fried chicken. She hoped for chicken as good as the chicken Katie's mother, Ellen Sue, had fried the first night she stayed with them.

"So," Beth began after they had placed their orders. "How's work?"

"Okay. Things are a little tense right now, though, since I had to fire someone."

"You had to fire someone? Anyone I've met?" Beth looked at Katie with interest.

"You remember Aaron?"

"You mean the Aaron you were dating?"

"That's the one. But I'm afraid my having to fire him got in the way of our relationship. I haven't seen him in a couple weeks." Katie shrugged.

Beth wondered if Katie was really that cool about it or if she was covering hurt feelings. "What happened?"

"You mean why did I fire him?" Katie paused a moment. "He was trying to use our relationship for special treatment. You know, more time off, showing up late and thinking that he wouldn't be reprimanded. And, honestly, his work was getting shoddy." Katie let out a long breath. "I miss him. But I love my job too much to jeopardize it for a man. Soooo … now I'm thinking I may have to join one of those internet dating sites to find a good man."

Beth was surprised. "I've never known you to have a hard time meeting men."

"Meeting them, no. Finding one I can really connect with who doesn't try to abuse the relationship, now that's another story." Katie tipped her head and shrugged her shoulders. "And let's face it; I'm not getting any younger. That big four-oh hit last year, and you know what they say about women over forty."

"You mean about how they have a better chance of getting struck by lightning than they do of getting married?"

"That's it." Katie rolled her eyes.

"Come on, Katie." Beth waved the whole idea away. "Love after forty can still happen. Besides, not all women are as beautiful, smart, and funny as you."

"Thank you, sis. But it's not the end of the world for me if I never get married. At least I have a job I love," Katie said, referring to her job at the North Carolina Aquarium in Fort Fisher. "The only thing is, I feel like I'm letting my parents down by not having any kids. I mean being their only child and all. Well, only natural child that is."

"I don't think they would feel let down. They would be thrilled that you're happy and doing something you love."

"Yeah, I know. Maybe it's just something I'm feeling now because Mom's gone and Dad's slipping away from me. Sometimes I think it would be easier if I had a husband to lean on. And if I had kids I'd feel like the family is going on." Katie stopped as the waitress arrived with their food.

"Is there anything else I can get for you?" The waitress asked as she set the plates on the table.

"No. It all looks good," Katie answered.

"It *does* look good." Beth inhaled the scent of the food. "Katie, if you want to have a family, you shouldn't lose hope in that, but if you don't want it, then you shouldn't worry about your family going on. You should do what makes you happy." Beth bit into the chicken. She closed her eyes, savoring the taste. "Oh, this is so good."

"Yeah. Not as good as Mom's, but close." Katie patted her mouth with her napkin. "And as far as the family thing goes… the real answer is, I don't know. I've thought a lot about it, but I'm not really sure what I want. I might even consider having a baby by myself. Maybe I need to visit you and spend time with that new baby. See what it feels like."

"A baby by yourself? Would you really want to do that?" Beth was a little shocked by this idea, and she hoped her sister would think through all the possible consequences.

Katie shrugged. "I don't know. Maybe."

"You know you're welcome anytime you want to come. Grace and Dad would love to see you. And I'm sure you'd do better with Hunter than I have so far."

Katie looked up at Beth, her eyebrows lifted. "Not dealing well with the baby? I thought you would be a natural."

"I don't know what's wrong with me. I haven't even been able to hold him without panicking."

Concerned, Katie kept her eyes on Beth. "I remember the terrible dreams you had that first Christmas when I came home from school—when we first met. That night you woke up screaming ... you looked so terrified." Katie looked down, pushing her food around the plate with her fork. "I felt so bad for you. I couldn't even imagine what it felt like to have parents who hurt you. And I was so glad you ended up in our family. I knew Mom and Dad would help you." Katie looked up again, searching Beth's eyes. "Is it like that now? Is it that bad?"

Beth shook her head. "Not that bad. But bad enough that Nolan wants to send me to therapy."

"Maybe you should listen to him."

"I'm thinking about it, but I want to try to work it out on my own first."

Katie nodded. "I understand—just don't wait too long."

After finishing their meal, Katie drove Beth across town to the nursing home where John now lived. Beth had never seen the home because every time she'd visited, Katie had brought John to the apartment. This time was different. From what Katie had told her, Beth knew John was far too upset and confused to be taken anywhere.

When they pulled into the parking lot, Beth was struck by the beauty of the place. The building was immaculate, with a fountain in the front, and well-maintained gardens surrounding the building. Beth was not surprised that John was in such a nice place. In fact, she was sure Katie had taken great pains to ensure that her father received the best care possible. It seemed ironic to feel such sadness and angst in this picturesque setting.

"This place is really something," Beth said.

"Only the best for Dad," Katie responded. "It is pretty, though, and the gardens out back are even more beautiful. They have chairs and benches out there so the residents can enjoy it. Dad and I used to have a picnic lunch out there every weekend when the weather was good." Katie's eyebrows drew together in sadness. "But in the past couple months … well, it's been so hard just to get him to remember me."

Beth wrapped an arm around Katie's shoulders, comforting her as they walked toward the building. They checked in at the front desk, then took the elevator to the second floor. When they reached the door marked 209, Beth turned to Katie. "Maybe it would be best if only one of us went in at a time. Two might be too much for him."

"That's a good idea," Katie agreed. "I've already seen him today, so why don't you go in first."

"Okay." Beth took a deep breath, and then knocked on the door. When John replied, she pushed the door open and walked inside.

John stood in front of the window looking out at the gardens below. He wore an old pair of tan pants and a checkered button-up shirt. The white hair atop his head had thinned since Beth had last seen him.

When the door closed, he turned and looked at her, his face breaking into a wide grin. At first, Beth thought it was because he recognized her.

"Ellen Sue!" John's face beamed joyfully as he wrapped his arms around Beth. "Darling, I thought you would never come."

Hating to leave the warm hug and shatter her foster father's happiness, Beth forced herself to pull away. She took John by the shoulders and looked into his eyes. "No, John. I'm not Ellen Sue. She died twenty years ago." Before Beth could say any more, John's smile faded and he looked broken and lost. Beth searched out his eyes. "I'm Beth, John. Do you remember me?"

"Beth?"

"That's right. I'm Beth."

When John's face changed, Beth knew that something had clicked. He knew who she was now. "My poor Beth. I'm so sorry. I'm so sorry." A tear slipped down his cheek.

Beth took his hand in hers. "It's okay, John. I know you did what you thought was best. Everything turned out okay, remember?"

John nodded as the memory returned, then he reached out to hug her. "My Beth."

As she pulled away, Beth felt John's legs begin to wobble. "Let's get you to bed." She guided him there. Then as she tucked him in, she thought maybe she should take advantage of John's moment of clarity. "Katie's here, John. She's right outside the door. Would you like to see her, too?"

John smiled again, and his face was almost as bright as when he thought she was his dead wife. "My Beth and my Katie? Yes, of course, I want to see you both."

Beth went to the door and called Katie in, telling her that John was remembering. Katie smiled and rushed into the room. They sat on either side of John, each holding a hand.

John smiled at both of them then closed his eyes and slept. They expected that when he woke up he would have forgotten both of them.

Beth glanced at Katie, and then, looking back at the man who had been just as much a father to her as her own, she thought about the first time she'd met him. She would tell Erin about it the next time they met.

# Chapter 18

Two weeks after my teddy bear episode, Martha called to say she had found a new foster home for me. Though grateful for her efforts, I woke up feeling sad the next morning. Her talk with Karen and Matthew had given them more understanding, but I could sense that they still felt unable to deal with my issues. And I knew they were especially worried about the effect those issues were having on Tamera. So in a few short hours, Martha would take me to my new foster home.

In the meantime, I had to pack and say goodbye to Jack, something I didn't even want to think about. I knew Jack was safe with the Zimmerman's. That gave me some peace.

I got out of bed and dressed, then grabbed my suitcase and started to pack my clothes. I was almost finished when someone knocked on my door. I didn't feel like talking to anyone, but I knew I couldn't avoid it. Taking a deep breath, I called out, "Come in."

Karen walked in with a hesitant expression. She gestured toward the suitcase. "Do you want help packing?"

"No. I'm almost done."

She sat down on the bed that was no longer mine and waited quietly while I closed my suitcase and set it on the floor. Then, patting the bed next to her, she said, "Come sit down for a minute. I want to talk to you."

I sat down, letting out a sigh.

"I'm not really sure how to say what I want to say. I just want you to know that I'm sorry we couldn't help you. I wish I knew how, but maybe we're just not the right people." She stopped and turned toward me. "I know this must be hurting you. It isn't easy for us, either. Matthew and I really care about you. Most of all, I want you to know that anytime you want to see Jack, you're welcome to."

Hot tears stung my eyes as I looked up and met her gaze. She wiped a tear from my cheek and then wrapped her arms tightly around me.

After letting me go, Karen walked to the door again. Once there, she paused and looked back at me. "We'll take good care of your brother. I promise you that."

After I finished packing, I went to Jack's room and knocked before going in. He was sitting on the floor, still wearing his pajamas and clutching his stuffed dog. I walked over and sat down next to him.

"I won't say goodbye." He said sternly, refusing to look at me.

"You don't have to because I'm gonna' come see you all the time."

"Only once a week—that's what Martha said."

"Well, Karen just told me I can come anytime I want to." I reached over and lifted his chin, insisting he look at me. "And even if she hadn't, I wouldn't let her, or anyone else, stop me. I'll always be looking out for you, Jack. You know that."

He pulled away from me and looked down at the floor, squeezing his dog. "It's still not the same. You won't be here at night if I have a bad dream."

"That's true, but you have Matthew and Karen. You've been going to them the last couple weeks anyway."

"Yeah, but I knew you were here." He looked up at me again. "You make me feel safe."

I scooted closer to him and wrapped my arm around his shoulders. "I wouldn't have let them split us up if I didn't know you were safe." He didn't answer and I thought for a minute about what to say. "You know, Jack, with me leaving, you're going to be the oldest around here. You know what that means don't you?"

Confused, he looked at me and shook his head.

"That means you're the big brother. You're the one who has to look out for Tamera, just like I've looked out for you. And I want you to be the best big brother you can be."

"How do I do that?"

"Well, you have good parents here, so that helps. But you can still do a lot for little Tammy. You know, teach her things. Help her out when she gets stuck sitting at the table with food she doesn't like. And when she gets older and goes to school, you'll have to watch out for her there too. She'll need you, Jack."

Jack nodded his head. "Just like I've always needed you."

I took a deep breath and ruffled his hair. "Yeah, just like you've always needed me."

Late that morning Martha arrived, and, with a heavy heart, I got into her car, and left Jack behind. Martha was quiet. She didn't try to cheer me up or make light of the situation. When we pulled out of the driveway, I turned around in my seat and waved to Jack until I couldn't see him anymore.

When I lived with my mother and Jeff, I had endured much trauma, both physical and emotional, but I had never experienced heart ache like I did that day.

I turned to face forward and rubbed my hand on my chest as it began to heave with anguish. Martha pulled to the side of the road and handed me a tissue. "We'll just wait here until you're ready." She got out of the car and opened the door next to me. Scooting in beside me, she reached her arm around me and held me close until my cries became quiet sobs.

"There now. Let's get you cleaned up." She dried my tears with a tissue.

As my sobs began to calm, I put my hand on hers. "Thank you."

She patted my hand. "You don't need to thank me, sweetie."

After I was settled and calm again, Martha returned to the driver's seat and drove for a few minutes to a modest ranch-style house. Black trim outlined the white house, with a small front porch where two white rocking chairs sat. Two enormous oak trees dominated the front yard, and, hanging from a branch in one of them was a swing with a wooden seat.

Martha carried my suitcase to the front door. We rang the bell and a moment later a plump woman of about five-foot-three opened the door with a warm smile. She had welcoming brown eyes and curly auburn hair that was tied back with a red ribbon.

"You must be Beth," she said, her smile beaming. "I'm Ellen Sue McMillan. I'm so glad to meet you. Come on in and meet my husband."

Martha and I walked into the house and the first thing I noticed was the delectable smell. As I took a deep breath, Ellen Sue's smile brightened. "That's the pie I'm making for us to have after dinner tonight. I hope you like apple."

"I do. My grandmother used to make apple pie for Christmas, but I haven't had any in a while."

"You'll get plenty of it around here," said a man as he walked up behind Ellen Sue and put his hands on her shoulders. "This one is always in the kitchen. Best cook I ever met," he said in a matter of fact tone. "Of course, that's why I married her."

Ellen Sue giggled and patted the hand on one of her shoulders. "Beth, dear, this old rascal is my husband, John."

John reached around his wife and offered his hand for me to shake. A tall man, more than six feet, his salt and pepper hair was starting to thin on top. His green eyes sparkled when he smiled, and I could tell by his mischievous grin that he enjoyed life.

"Beth, would you like to see your room now?" Ellen Sue asked.

"Okay." I nodded.

"It's right this way," Ellen Sue motioned toward the hallway that branched off the living room. The house was nowhere near as big as the Zimmerman's, and the short hallway had only four doors. Ellen Sue opened the first one on the left. "Here's the bathroom," she said, and then opened the next door revealing a small room decorated with a flowered wallpaper border. On the far wall stood a double bed covered with a lacy off-white quilt. Next to it was a nightstand that matched the bed's head and footboard. On the wall across from the bed was a matching dresser. Both the dresser and nightstand were adorned with lace doilies.

"This was the guest room, but we can fix it up different if you want," Ellen Sue said.

I shook my head. "No. It's fine the way it is."

"Why don't I show you the rest of the house and then you can settle in."

Martha sat my suitcase on the floor, and then we all went back into the hall. John opened the door straight across from my room and said, "This is our room." I glanced inside and saw that their room was not too much larger than mine and was decorated with blue and white striped wallpaper and a blue bed cover.

John opened the next door to a room covered in posters and pictures. A colorful spread covered the twin bed in the corner, and, on the wall above, hung a triangular flag with the name of the local high school printed on it.

"This is our Katie's room," John said. "I imagine Martha told you that she's away at school now."

"Yes, she did tell me. Will I get to meet Katie soon?"

"She won't be coming home for Thanksgiving because she's going to a friend's house. She'll be home for the Christmas break next month, so you'll get to meet her then," Ellen Sue replied.

I nodded. "I'll look forward to meeting her. It'll be different. I've always been the oldest."

"I hope you won't mind being the little sister here," John said. "Katie will be thrilled. She always wanted us to have another child. I think you'll like her."

"I'm sure I will. And I don't mind being the little sister at all. It might be nice for a change."

After John and Ellen Sue showed me around the house, I returned to my room while they finished the necessary paperwork with Martha. I unpacked my suitcase, then lay on the bed a while. I couldn't say why, but I felt at ease. Of course, a part of me was filled with worry over leaving Jack behind, but even so, I felt calm in my new room and with John and Ellen Sue. They possessed a kindness that showed from the start.

A while later, Martha knocked on my door and said goodbye to me. I hadn't slept well the night before, so once Martha was gone, I lay down on the bed again and fell asleep for a little while.

I woke up to a wonderful smell and went out to see what it was. John was in the living room watching a football game on TV. He didn't see me walk by as I went into the kitchen.

"What smells so good?" I asked.

Ellen Sue turned around, smiling at me. "That's the fried chicken I'm making for dinner." She dusted her hands off on a pale green apron. "Do you like fried chicken, Beth?"

"The only kind I've ever had was from KFC. I liked that."

"I hope you'll like mine at least as much. And I've got green beans, mashed potatoes and biscuits to go with it."

"And apple pie." I smiled back at her.

"Of course. That's the best part." She patted her stomach. "And my waistline is proof of how much I like dessert."

A short while later we all sat around the kitchen table eating Ellen Sue's wonderful meal. It was the most amazing food I'd ever eaten. But the true joy was being with them.

"That was the best food ever, Ellen Sue," I said. "I don't think I've ever eaten that much."

She looked at me, her eyes twinkling, and patted my cheek. "Thank you, dear. That's the best compliment I've gotten in a while. I'm so glad you enjoyed it."

John leaned back in his chair and with a serious look, he said, "Now that's not really fair. I compliment your cooking all the time."

"Oh, yeah?" Ellen Sue put her hands on her rounded hips. "And that's why you stay so skinny."

"I can't help it if I have good metabolism." John tried to sound wounded. "You're gonna blame me for having good genes?"

Ellen Sue raised her eyebrows at him. "Alright now, John, if you're going to be argumentative, you can just go on back to your football game and leave us girls alone."

"Is that right?"

"It most certainly is."

I watched them, amused as they pretended to argue. Much as they tried, neither one of them could keep a straight face.

Later that night, while I was getting ready for bed, a knock came on my door. "Come in," I called out. Ellen Sue stepped into the room.

"Getting all settled in?" She asked.

I nodded.

"Good. It's going to be nice having you here, Beth. It's been so quiet since Katie went off to school. I'll be happy to hear something other than John snoring in front of the TV."

I smiled at her remembering the way they had been together during dinner.

"Can we talk for a minute?" She walked over to my bed and motioned for me to sit with her.

"Sure." I joined her on the bed.

"Martha told us a little about your past. It's been pretty rough, hasn't it?"

I squirmed, feeling uncomfortable about being confronted with the events of my past. "At times," I whispered.

"You can talk to me about it if you want to."

I nodded again keeping my head down.

"You know," Ellen Sue went on, "when I was a girl and I had a bad day I would tell my mother all about it thinking that she could tell me how to make it better. But every time, no matter what my trouble was, she always answered me by saying 'Ellen Sue, into every life some rain must fall.'

"One day when she said that I got angry with her. 'You say that all the time, but what kind of answer is that?' I demanded. She looked me square in the eye and said, 'The reason I always say that is because I want you to remember that everyone has difficulty in life sometimes, but it's only when the storm ends that you can see a rainbow.'"

Ellen Sue put her hand under my chin, lifting my face to look at her. Her brown eyes, full of compassion, looked straight into mine. "Beth, I know you've had more than your fair share of the rain. I hope you can find that rainbow here with John and me." With that, she kissed me on the cheek and left my room.

I sat there on the bed for a while thinking about what she'd said. It had been a long time since I'd believed my life could be good. I wondered if these people really would stick by me when the going got tough.

I had a few good days with John and Ellen Sue before my demons haunted my dreams again. Very early one Sunday morning, I woke up screaming after a terrifying dream. In mere seconds Ellen Sue was at my side with John just behind her. He stood just inside my door, looking concerned, while Ellen Sue rushed over and sat next to me. She gathered me up into her arms and held me until I stopped crying. Then John walked over and handed her a tissue, which she used to wipe the tears from my face.

"There now, dear." She pushed damp hair back from my face. "What's wrong?"

I opened my mouth and, with trembling lips, told her I'd had a very bad dream.

She hugged me again. "Can you tell us about it? Sometimes it helps to talk about it."

John sat on the other side of my bed, and they both looked at me with concern.

"It…it was about my step-father." My voice quivered.

"What happened? What was he doing?" Ellen Sue asked.

I opened my mouth again to speak, but the words got stuck in my throat. I had dreamt about Jeff beating my mother to death while Jack and I listened from inside a closet. Then Jack had vanished and I was left alone.

Tears streamed down my face and I shook my head as I remembered the terrible images. Ellen Sue pulled me close and held me while John stroked my hair soothingly.

"That's okay, honey. You don't have to tell us if it's too hard," Ellen Sue said. "John, dear, why don't you go on back to bed? I'll stay here until she's settled."

John leaned over, kissed my head, and then left the room.

Ellen Sue held me until I stopped crying again. Then she tucked me back into bed and sat next to me until I fell asleep.

Rebecca L. Marsh

# Chapter 19

As I got off the school bus the Friday before the Christmas, I felt overwhelming joy. I hadn't smiled so much since my camping trip with Dad. In the past school had been a refuge, a safe place away from the worries of home. I had never been able to enjoy holiday breaks, but this year was going to be different.

The air was cold, but I was so warm inside that I barely noticed. As I walked home from the bus stop, snowflakes began to fall. I put my arms out and turned circles tilting my face up and letting the flakes hit my cheeks. I felt free in a way I never had before.

When I got home, I rushed inside to tell Ellen Sue that it was snowing. "I saw that," she said. "And I have another surprise for you. Katie is home a few days early."

"Really? Katie's here already?"

"Yes. And she can't wait to meet you. I told her I would let her know the minute you got home."

I smiled and glanced around. "Where is she?"

"She's in her room getting unpacked." Ellen Sue reached an arm around me and guided me toward the hall. "C'mon, I'll introduce you."

We walked to Katie's room and knocked on the door, but she didn't answer. Ellen Sue shook her head and raised her eyebrows. "Just like old times." She opened the door without knocking again.

Inside the small room, a tall young woman was unpacking a suitcase and dancing with earphones on her head. She didn't see or hear us, so Ellen Sue yelled at her, but she didn't hear that either. Ellen Sue looked at me, rolled her eyes, and then tapped her daughter on the shoulder. Katie yelped and jumped a few feet back, falling backward onto the bed.

Pulling the earphones off her head, she looked up at Ellen Sue with exasperation. "Mom! You scared me half to death. I keep telling you not to do that."

"And I keep telling you not to turn the music up so loud."

"I like it loud, and that's why I wore the earphones."

"I appreciate that courtesy, dear, but if you're going to have it so loud, you should be prepared for a tap on the shoulder. It's the only way I can get your attention. And I have someone I want you to meet."

Katie leaned forward and looked around her mother to see me standing in the doorway. I smiled bashfully, and she smiled back.

"You must be Beth." She got up from the bed and walked over to me. "It's really good to meet you."

Katie was tall like her father, so she had to stoop down a bit when she embraced me.

"It's really good to meet you, too," I said as she released me, and stepped back.

We looked at each other for a minute. Katie's green eyes sparkled like her father's always did, showing joy that came from within. "This is going to be a great Christmas. I always wanted a little sister."

Katie reached out and took my hand. "C'mon, the first thing we need to do is make Christmas cookies."

Katie walked me into the kitchen with Ellen Sue close behind. "I suppose you want me to make the cookie dough for you?"

"Well, of course." Katie drew her eyebrows together. "You know I can't cook, and we don't want to poison anyone."

Ellen Sue tried to look annoyed as she went to work, but I could see the smile in her eyes. I sensed that she would do just about anything for her daughter.

Once the dough was made, Katie wiped down a countertop and sprinkled it with flour. She placed the dough on top and rolled it out flat. Then we cut out snowmen and reindeer, Christmas trees and stars. Katie had a boisterous personality, and she was fun and easy to be with. I had a wonderful time with her.

When John got home and found us covered in flour, he insisted on getting a picture. After our photo op, Katie and I put the cookies in the cookie jar and cleaned up our mess while Ellen Sue cooked. Then we sat down and had dinner together. Everyone happily chattered about the cookies and everything else they'd done that day. I looked around the table at this family I was with, and a warm feeling glowed inside me. I had never expected to live this way.

I realized I was smiling, and that I had been smiling most of the afternoon. Almost in wonderment, I raised my hand to the corner of my mouth to confirm the smile was real and not an illusion. I remembered what Martha had said to me about living in the moment. And I knew she was right. A day of simple happiness felt so good.

The rest of that week was a flurry of activity. John and Ellen Sue had waited on Katie for all the Christmas activities, including getting a tree. One night the four of us went to a tree lot and picked out a beauty. John set it up on the stand and we all helped decorate. When we were done, it was a medley of different ornaments, a shiny silver garland, and multi-colored lights.

John handed a lovely ceramic angel to Katie. "Time for the final touch."

Katie looked at the angel and walked toward the tree, but then turned to me. "I'm not the youngest anymore. This should be your job now, Beth." She put the angel in my hands.

"Are you sure you don't want to do it?"

She nodded, smiling. "I want you to do it."

I looked at John and Ellen Sue and they were smiling too. I reached up and, standing on my tiptoes, placed the angel on top of the tree. Stepping back, I looked up at her and felt like she was looking at me; a guardian angel.

A couple of days later, Katie took me ice skating. The next day I went with Ellen Sue and Katie to finish our Christmas shopping. I didn't have much money, but Ellen Sue gave me some to buy a gift for Jack, and Katie helped me pick something out. Then Ellen Sue handed me more money. "Take this and go buy something for your mother."

I shook my head and tried to refuse the money, but she insisted. "She's made some bad choices that hurt you. I know that. But she's still your mother."

I reluctantly accepted the money, and then asked if I could be alone for a while to look around. I decided on a small figurine. The price was half of what Ellen Sue had given me, so I decided to use the rest to buy her and John a gift. After shopping a bit longer I found something that grabbed me. I paid for the items and then found Ellen Sue and Katie in the clothing department.

After we finished, we talked and laughed at lunch until our sides nearly split.

On December 23rd I had my weekly visit with Jack, and this time Mama would be there as well. It was too cold for the park, so we met at a nearby McDonald's. Martha picked me up first and then drove to the Zimmerman's house.

Jack was so excited, he jumped into the car and hugged me, then sat back on the seat holding a bag.

"Whatcha got there?" I asked him.

"Some presents. One's for you, and the other one is for Mama. I can't wait to see her. I want to tell her about our Christmas tree. It's huge! You should see it. Do you have one at your house?"

"Yeah, we got one."

"Is it big?"

I shook my head and smiled at his happy face. "No, it's not that big, but it's really pretty, and I got to put the angel on top."

"That's cool. Ours has a star that lights up with lots of colors. Does your angel light up?"

Jack bounced in his seat as he talked, and I smiled at him. I really missed seeing him every day. He was the one and only person I had ever loved this much.

"No," I answered him. "The angel doesn't light up."

"Too bad. I like the lights." Then he changed the subject. "I'm doing what you said, Beth."

"What do you mean?"

"I'm helping Tammy like you said I should. I'm teaching her to tie her shoes."

"That's great, Jack." We pulled up to McDonald's. "I knew you would be a great big brother. And now I get to be the little sister."

"Really?" Jack said in disbelief. I suppose it was hard for him to think of me as anyone's *little* sister.

"Yeah. The McMillan's have a daughter named Katie who's in college, but she's home now for the holiday. She's really nice."

Jack's smile brightened and he put his small hand on top of mine. "Now you have someone to take care of you."

"I guess I do," I said almost to myself as we got out of the car and walked inside with Martha.

Mama hadn't arrived yet, so Martha took us into the playland. I was a little big for the equipment, but I wanted to spend as much time with Jack as possible, so I squeezed through the tunnels as best I could.

Mama arrived about thirty minutes late saying she'd had car trouble. When she joined us at the table, Martha excused herself and sat at a nearby table where she could still see us.

Jack had thrown himself into Mama's lap the moment she sat down and he stayed right there chattering away about the big Christmas tree.

Jack said something about the gifts he brought and Mama said she had some for us too. She looked at me. "What about you, Beth. I see you have a bag there. Is it a present for your brother?"

I looked down at the bag. "Yes, and one for you too, Mama."

Mama smiled, and I could see she was surprised. "That's nice of you, Beth. But I want you kids to open your gifts first."

She handed a wrapped gift to each of us. Jack opened his first, and his face lit up. "Wow! My own ant farm!" he said.

I said nothing. That was going to be Matthew and Karen's problem.

Jack jumped up and hugged Mama hard around the neck. Then they looked at me. "Okay, Beth, it's your turn," Mama said.

I looked down at the small gift in my hand and began to tear the paper away. Inside was a small box covered in blue velvet. I ran my fingers across it, then lifted the top. In the box was a silver locket in the shape of an oval with flowers etched on the front. "It's really pretty."

"Open it."

"Okay." I popped it open. In one side was a picture of her and in the other a picture of Jack. I was relieved because I feared that a picture of Jeff would be inside.

I looked up at Mama who was smiling at me. "Thanks, Mama. This is really nice."

Next Jack and I exchanged gifts. I let Jack open his first and he loved the toy dinosaur. His gift to me was a bath set with scented soaps and lotions.

"Thanks, Jack. This is really nice."

"I think that stuff is stupid, but Karen said girls your age like that smelly junk."

"She's right, we do."

"Good. And thanks for the dinosaur. It's really cool."

"Glad you like it. Katie helped me pick it out."

"Your big sister?"

"Yeah."

"She's *not* your sister!" Mama snapped.

Jack and I snapped our heads up in surprise. She hadn't yelled, and she was trying to keep her voice even, but her face was red with anger.

I wasn't sure how to respond because I wanted to make it all better so Jack wouldn't be hurt. I stammered. "W-well I know she's not my real sister. Just a foster sister."

"She's not your sister at all. She's just someone you live with. You can't think of them as family, Beth. This is your family."

I wanted to yell at her and tell her that our family was not the family I wanted. Tell her that John and Ellen Sue and Katie were a better family and that I would rather stay with them than live with her again if given the choice. But I looked at Jack's stunned face, and couldn't ruin this day for him. I said nothing.

Mama took that as agreement on my part and continued as though if nothing had happened.

Jack quickly recovered and handed Mama her gift—refrigerator magnets and a folded piece of paper.

Mama opened up the paper, and then looked at Jack, her eyes smiling. She turned the paper to face us. It was a drawing of flowers and on the bottom, it read, "I lov you." Mama pulled him close to her and hugged him. "I love you too, sweet boy."

When Jack pulled away I handed Mama my gift. She pulled the paper off, opened the brown box inside, and pulled out the small teddy bear figurine. Her jaw clenched, but she smiled when she looked at me and tried to pretend she wasn't hurt. The figurine was exactly like one that Jeff had once broken when he'd thrown it at Mama's head. It ended up smashing against the wall when she ducked. "And I love you too, Beth." She hugged me as she had Jack, and guilt washed over me.

On Christmas Eve, I spent the morning and afternoon with John and Ellen Sue while Katie visited with a friend from high school. Ellen Sue had last minute items to pick up for Christmas dinner, so we ran errands all morning, and then John took us to Arby's for lunch.

All afternoon Ellen Sue rushed around the house doing chores.

"Can I help you?" John asked her at one point.

She gave him a questioning look. "We both know you're useless around the house. Now, you just take yourself into the living room and take a nap in front of the TV."

John smiled. "That's what I was hoping you would say."

"Then why did you even ask, you old fool?"

"I had to be polite and seem helpful, didn't I?" John put his arm around me and said, "Come on, Beth, I think there's a game on. Want to watch it with me?"

"I don't really know much about football," I said hesitantly.

"Great! I'll teach you."

"And that might even keep him awake for a few minutes," Ellen Sue snickered.

John and I headed off to watch the game while Ellen Sue continued with her work. For about thirty minutes John taught me about football, but the lesson was finished when he fell asleep in his recliner, just as Ellen Sue had predicted.

When he began to snore, I went to the kitchen to see what Ellen Sue was doing. I found her standing in front of a large bowl stirring ingredients.

"Can I help?"

"Well finally," she responded. "Some real help is offered. The old man's asleep, is he?"

"Yes. And he's snoring."

"That sounds about right." She laughed. "Well, dear, if you want to help, why don't you come and take over stirring this while I get the dough for the crust ready."

"Sure." I walked over to her. "What kind of pie are you making?"

She looked at me raising her eyebrows. "*We* are making a pumpkin pie."

I helped Ellen Sue cook and clean until Katie came home and pulled me away.

"Come with me, Beth." She dragged me toward her room. "Let me give you a makeover before church."

As soon as we got into her room, Katie turned on her stereo, at a reasonable volume, and sat me down in her desk chair. "We'll do makeup first and then your hair." Katie opened a makeup kit, ran her fingers over the various lipsticks and eyeliners, and finally showed me her selection.

"You have the most amazing eyes, Beth. I think some eyeliner and mascara will really bring them out."

I sat quietly as she applied the makeup to my face. "So, do you have a boyfriend?"

I felt my cheeks grow hot. "No."

"Are there any boys that you like?"

I looked away from her as I answered. "There's one boy at school that I think is cute. But he's never even noticed me."

"That's hard to believe. You're such a pretty girl." She applied powder to my face. "If he sees you tonight, he'll notice you. I can promise you that."

I smiled bashfully. "Do you have a boyfriend?"

As she smiled back at me, I could tell she enjoyed this girl bonding.

"There was someone last semester, but he was a little too needy. I'm not seeing anyone right now." She looked at me slyly. "But there is someone that I've been flirting with. I think he's going to ask me out when we get back to school."

Katie finished my makeup with a little blush and then got out a brush, a comb, and a selection of hair ties and clips. She ran her fingers through my hair and then started brushing.

"So what's the boy's name?" she asked.

I looked at her, confused.

"The one you like, Beth. What's his name?"

"Oh, his name is Richie," I said. "What about the guy that you're flirting with? What's his name?"

"Mike. And he's really cute, and nice, too." She slipped her hand under my bangs and pulled them back. "You should grow your bangs out. You have a nice forehead and with the bangs gone, your eyes will show up even better."

I looked into the mirror, and I had to agree, but I had never even considered it before. My life had always been so full of turmoil that I really didn't worry about my looks. Maybe now my life would be calm enough to think about the things that most girls my age were concerned with.

"I'll think about it," I said. "It does look pretty good."

"For today, we'll have to do something else with it." She stooped down in front of me and played with different ideas. "I think it looks best down, so I'll use clips on the sides and then curl your bangs a little."

Katie finished my hair as we continued to talk and laugh. When she finished, I was surprised by the girl who looked back at me from the mirror.

"Wow! You're really good at this."

"I only used the makeup and fixed your hair to bring out what's already there. You're a real beauty, you know."

I looked down, not used to such compliments. Katie lifted my chin, looking earnestly into my eyes. "That's why the boys don't notice you. You're trying so hard to not be seen. Keep your chin up and look confident. That's what boys really notice." She let her hand drop, but kept her eyes locked on mine. "And after they notice the confidence, they'll notice your eyes."

Moments later, we were all in John's old blue station wagon, heading to church.

As we entered, I was stunned by the crowd and by how beautiful the place was. I had already been to this church with John and Ellen Sue, but never had it looked so spectacular or felt so filled with magic.

We walked down the center aisle and found a seat on the right side. As we sat down and took our coats off, I looked around in awe. The lights were dimmed down as much as they could be without being off, and candlelight surrounded the altar. An advent wreath hung from the ceiling with all the candles lit. To one side of the altar, a brass quartet played regal Christmas hymns.

The choir took their places, and joined in singing the hymns, their voices sounding like angels. Then the pastor came out and took his seat until the hymn was finished. He spoke eloquently about the first Christmas and the meaning for each of us. I listened with interest.

Some would say it was only church, but that night was the first time I felt God's presence.

Christmas morning I woke up with a joyful heart. I slipped on my bathrobe and went out to see if anyone else was up. When I got to the end of the hall I heard noise in the kitchen and found Katie making coffee and pouring a bowl of cereal.

She smiled at me. "I guess I should make it two bowls."

"Okay," I said. "I'm surprised you're up. You usually sleep later."

She glanced at me again, her green eyes twinkling, as she poured the cereal. "It's Christmas. I always get up early on Christmas. She poured milk into both bowls. Then we sat down and ate Rice Krispies.

"Mom and Dad will be up as soon as they smell the coffee. That's why I always make some on Christmas morning." Katie put her spoon down and placed her hand on mine. "I just wanted to tell you, Beth, that I've really enjoyed having you around and getting to know you. You're the little sister I've always wanted." She looked at me sincerely. "I kinda hate that I have to go back to school next month."

I met her gaze. "Me too. I like having a big sister." I looked down, unsure if I should be ashamed of my feelings. My mother would think I should, but I didn't care. Without looking up I said, "I wish this was my real family."

Katie didn't answer right away, and for a few moments we sat there hearing only the coffee maker brewing, and our Rice Krispies crackling. I wondered if I had said the wrong thing. I looked up as I felt Katie's eyes on me. Her expression was warm. "I know you may not be able to stay here for the rest of your childhood. And there's nothing we can do about that. But no matter what happens, you are a real part of this family as far as I'm concerned. I'll always be your big sister … as long as you want me anyway. I'm only a phone call away if you need me." She smiled again. "Or if you just want to talk about boys." We both laughed just as Ellen Sue walked into the kitchen with John a couple steps behind.

"Apparently we missed the joke, dear, but at least the coffee is already made." Ellen Sue took two mugs out of the cabinet.

"Sounds good," John replied with an eye-twinkling smile. "Coffee and presents."

In the living room, Katie and I sat on the floor in front of the Christmas tree while John and Ellen Sue sat in their recliners sipping coffee and watching us.

"Okay, Beth, this is how we always do it," Katie began. "First I open all my gifts, then Mom and Dad open their gifts from me, then they open their gifts from each other. But this year we'll do it just a little different." She gave me a meaningful look. "Since you are the new member of the family, you get the first one and then you and I will take turns. After that, we'll each take our gifts to Mom and Dad. Then they can open their gifts from each other."

I looked around me at the gifts and back at Katie. "I don't know where to start."

"Start with my gift to you."

I stopped stunned for a moment. "You got me a gift? But I don't have one for you."

"Beth." Katie placed a hand on my shoulder. "Don't worry about that." But she saw the distressed look on my face so she leaned forward and whispered in my ear. "I told you I always wanted a little sister. So your being here is a gift."

Blushing from the compliment, I smiled and took her gift. I ripped the paper off and pulled out a small pink box. Inside was a complete make-up kit with a little mirror built into the lid.

"This way when I leave you can do your own makeovers," Katie said.

I got up on my knees and reached over to hug her. "Thank you. Now it's your turn to open one."

Katie picked up gifts, giving each a little shake. After testing a few, she selected one. She looked up, her face as bright as a five-year-old's. She ripped the paper off the gift. Inside was a new CD, and Katie got very excited. She jumped up, ran to Ellen Sue, and hugged her. "Thanks, Mom. I love it." Then she hugged John. "Thanks, Daddy."

When the only gifts left were for John and Ellen Sue, I insisted Katie give them her gifts first. Afterward, I took my one gift over and stopped between their chairs. "I just have one gift for both of you, so I don't know who to give it to."

"Not a problem." John got up from his chair. "We can both sit on the couch and open it together." Ellen Sue moved to the couch along with John.

"It isn't much." I handed them the gift. "But I hope you like it."

John held the gift while Ellen Sue removed the paper, and pulled out a small, framed picture of a rainbow spread over a green hilly landscape. She stared at the picture for a few moments and looked at me with damp eyes. She reached out her arms to me and I hurried into them.

"Beth, this is a beautiful gift." Then seeing John's confused expression, Ellen Sue said, "I'll explain it to you later, dear."

"I'm glad you like it." I smiled, feeling pleased with myself.

"It's wonderful and thoughtful. If this is what I got, I can only imagine what you found for your mother."

My face flushed as I remembered the gift I had given my mother. For the first time, I felt bad because the gift I had given her was hurtful and vindictive. As much as I loved Mama, I couldn't seem to stop reminding her of the past.

# Chapter 20

Two days after Christmas Martha called. I thought she was calling to wish me happy holidays and ask about my Christmas until I noticed the tightness in her voice.

"What's wrong, Martha?"

"I don't even know how to tell you this."

I took a deep breath to prepare myself for Martha's news. I couldn't imagine what could be so bad that she didn't want to tell me. I prayed that nothing was wrong with Jack.

"There's no way to sugar-coat it, so I'll just have to say it like it is," Martha went on. "I'm at the courthouse today, Beth. Jeff's trial has come to an end."

"Well, what is it, Martha? What happened?"

"It's not good. They let him go with community service and time served."

I was stunned that I couldn't reply for a few seconds. "W-what does that mean, Martha? Could he get us back?" My heart pounded like a drum in my chest. I had been free of Jeff for several months now, and I couldn't bear the thought of going back to that life. I couldn't let that happen. I would run away with Jack if I had to.

I gasped for breath as my mind raced with escape plans. When Martha's voice broke through, I realized she'd been trying to answer me, and I hadn't been able to hear her over the noise in my head.

"Beth! Can you hear me?" she shouted into the phone.

"Yes. Sorry. I hear you." I willed myself to calm down and listen.

"The state isn't going to give you or Jack back to him. Don't you worry about that. We're already working to terminate his parental rights to Jack. And your mother knows she won't get you two back if she has any contact with him—so we'll be watching her."

Relief flowed through me, and I was able to breathe again. Still, I worried. Jeff wasn't the type to let anyone else tell him what he could or could not do. "What if he comes after us? What if he finds us, Martha?"

"Sweetie, he's not going to come after you. He has no idea where either of you is living, and neither does your mother," Martha reassured me. "Don't worry about him, Beth. He's not going to get anywhere near you."

I thanked Martha and assured her that I wouldn't worry about Jeff. But how could I not? He was on the loose and probably very angry that he'd been caught. He would want someone to take it out on and might find a way to get to us.

Suddenly, I was frightened for my mother. She may have gotten us into the whole mess, but she was still my mother and I loved her. Jeff would have no trouble finding her, and no matter how badly he beat her, she would never turn him in. That thought made me angry with her again. Why did she let him hurt her, and Jack and me for so long?

I placed a hand on my stomach, now churning with all my conflicting emotions, and leaned against the kitchen counter.

Ellen Sue came in with a bright smile that faded when she saw me. "Beth, sweetie, what's wrong?"

I told her about Martha's call, and how worried I was that Jeff was going to hurt Mama. She held me close and let me cry on her shoulder.

That night I went to bed troubled, my stomach rolling with the anxiety I was feeling, and I was plagued by a nightmare about Jeff.

I was back in my mother's house, alone in my room. I heard Jeff beating Mama; her screams and breaking glass. I found Jack in his room and took him back to my window so we could escape, but the window had been nailed shut. Our escape route was cut off.

When the sounds stopped, I knew that Jeff was coming for us. I pushed Jack into the closet, and squeezed in next to him, as we heard Jeff stumbling down the hall. "I ... gonna ... get ... youuuu!" he slurred loudly, as he crashed into the walls.

Jeff searched for us, and when the closet door opened, I pushed Jack behind me to protect him. In a split second, Jeff pushed the clothes out of the way, and his breath ran hot against my face.

His hand closed around my throat. "Please!" I choked out, but Jeff's steely eyes stared into my eyes without mercy. He lifted me by the throat and flung me out of the closet onto the floor. I closed my eyes expecting a blow, but when it didn't come I opened them and saw Jeff going after Jack.

"No! Not Jack!"

The next thing I knew I awoke with Ellen Sue's worried face looming over me, her brow furrowed with concern. "It's okay, dear. You had a bad dream, but you're okay. I'm here for you."

Her eyes were compassionate, and I found myself crying in her arms. She held me close and whispered soothing words in my ear.

"Is she gonna be okay, Mom?" I heard Katie's voice and turned to see her standing in the doorway.

"She'll be alright. She just needs a little time to recover. Why don't you bring us a box of tissues?"

Katie returned a few minutes later with the tissues and looked at me with heartfelt sympathy. "Can I help?"

"You just go on back to bed, sweetie. I'll take care of her," Ellen Sue said.

Katie leaned down and hugged me before going back to her room.

"Do you want to talk about it?" Ellen Sue asked.

I shrugged my shoulders. Part of me wanted to talk, but another part of me didn't know how to tell anyone what went on in my head. That would be almost the same as telling them about the things that had gone on in my mother's house. Even though life here was so different, it was hard for me to talk to anyone about it.

New Year's came and went and before I knew it Katie had returned to school. My nightmares continued to plague me at least once or twice a week. making me tired. My teacher called John and Ellen Sue to a conference because I had fallen asleep in class a number of times. When they got home, they sat me down for a talk.

"Am I in trouble?" I asked before they could say anything.

"No. Of course, you're not in trouble, dear." Ellen Sue reached out to take my hand.

"It's not a matter of doing something wrong, Beth," John began. "It's just that we're concerned about you and so is your teacher."

"But I'm okay," I protested. "I've just been tired."

"You've been tired because the nightmares are making it hard for you to get a good night's sleep," John said. "And when you're having bad dreams this often it's because you're anxious about something. We need to find a way to help you work through that."

"Like what?"

They looked at each other and then Ellen Sue spoke up. "Your teacher thinks you should talk to a counselor."

"You mean a shrink?"

"Not exactly," John said. "We're talking about a psychologist. Someone you can talk through this with, and who can help you understand what's causing the nightmares." John placed a hand on my shoulder. "Don't be scared about seeing the psychologist, Beth. Let him help you."

I nodded, but I still wasn't sure I liked the idea of talking to a stranger about my past.

Nevertheless, after John and Ellen Sue consulted Martha, I found myself talking to Dr. Ruskin. He had a nice office with plush carpet and walls paneled in dark wood. In front of the window, he had a large mahogany desk with a leather swivel desk chair. Across from the desk were two chairs and on the wall to the left was a couch and a cushy chair along with a coffee table.

The office was warm and welcoming, and so was Dr. Ruskin. I was still apprehensive about telling him my dreams, my worries, and my past. So for a while, he let me talk about school, my friends, and other things that interested me.

Before the end of my second session, I found myself telling him about the dreams, and a week later I was telling him my concerns about Jeff and how I worried about Jack because we lived apart now and if he needed me, I wouldn't even know.

Dr. Ruskin talked me through my fears, and over time, the dreams came less frequently, and, within a year, all but stopped.

The following October when Martha called me with news, I felt ready to deal with it.

"What is it, Martha?" I asked.

"It's about your mother." A wave of fear rushed through me. *Had something happened to my mother?* I felt pain in my chest and at the same time a faint amount of surprise that I was even this upset about someone who had hurt me so much.

I tried to speak, but only managed to sputter a few words. "W-what about my mother?"

"Now don't panic. She's not hurt."

My brow furrowed as I tried to process that. *If she wasn't hurt, then what was this about?*

"The thing is," Martha began. "She's been seeing Jeff again. We think it's been going on for a while now, but she's been sneaky."

"How did you find out then?"

"We got an anonymous call telling us we should pay her a visit and see what kind of company she's keeping."

"Who would make a call like that?" I was confused. All those years that Jeff was beating us no one ever spoke up, so why now?

"We don't really know. Maybe a neighbor who saw him going into the house and knew he wasn't supposed to be there."

"I wish the neighbors had cared so much eight years ago."

Martha sighed. "I wish they had too, sweetie. But this time they did and we have to act."

"What does that mean though, Martha?"

"For now you and Jack will still go on your visits. And I think it's best not to tell Jack what's coming, but we're starting the process of stripping your mother's parental rights."

"Does that mean we won't see her anymore?" The weird thing was that a part of me felt sad about not seeing Mama again, but another part hoped it was true.

"Once the process is complete…yes. She will no longer visit with you, and she will never have custody of you and Jack back again."

"Well … I'll miss her. Or at least part of me will. But this is good news, right? I mean I won't have to worry about Jeff anymore."

"That's true. And that's very good, but you won't see your mom at all once it's done."

"I know. I think it's mostly for the best though."

"There's one more thing, Beth. After your mother's rights are taken, you and Jack will be available for adoption."

"You mean we could get a new mom and dad?" I wasn't sure how I felt about that idea.

146

"Yes. But you should know that the Zimmermans have already expressed interest in adopting Jack."

I stood speechless for a few moments. Even though Jack and I were in different homes now, I hadn't thought about the possibility of being adopted by different people.

"Beth, are you still there?"

"Uh … um … yeah, I'm here." I stopped for a minute and thought about what to say next. "Martha, if the Zimmermans adopt Jack … what happens to me?"

"That's hard to say. For now, you'll stay with the McMillan's. You'll be up for adoption, but I should tell you, teenagers aren't adopted as often as younger kids. It could happen, but I don't want you to get your hopes up too much." Martha's voice was heavy. Any other social worker might have tried to sugarcoat the situation, but Martha always told me the whole truth.

I asked the question weighing the heaviest on my heart. "Will I still get to see Jack after he's adopted?"

Her sigh prepared me for bad news. "I can't answer that with certainty because that would be up to the Zimmermans. And if you are adopted, then your new parents would have a say as well."

That wasn't the answer I wanted to hear, but at least it wasn't an absolute. So far the Zimmermans had expressed no discontent with me seeing Jack. But I wondered if that would change once they were his parents.

A few months later, after my mother's parental rights had been stripped, Jack and I visited her for the last time. On the day of the visit, when Martha picked me up, my feelings surprised me. When I had first heard that they were taking Mama's rights away, I had been relieved. My anxiety about living with her and Jeff had washed away, but knowing I might never see her again, I felt sad and somewhat empty. I wasn't just losing the threat, I was losing her.

When we arrived at the Zimmerman's house to pick up Jack, he was already crying. He clung to Karen, his head pressed into her belly. She encouraged him to get in the car, trying to peel back his arms, but he only held on tighter.

"I don't want to," he cried. "You can't make me say goodbye to her!"

I got out of the car and went to Jack. I put my hand on his back and bent down close to his ear.

"I know this is hard, Jack. It's hard for me too," I said in a soothing tone. "But it won't make a difference if you go today or not. You still won't get to see her anymore." Jack whimpered, but he at least looked at me. "This is your last chance to see her. If you choose not to go, you might wish you had … And I know she wants to see you."

Still sobbing, Jack released his grip on Karen and dropped his arms to his sides. His red and tear-streaked face made my heart ache.

I felt Karen's hand on my shoulder and looked up at her. She nodded slightly and mouthed the words, "Thank you." She bent down to Jack. "You go, sweet boy. Beth is right. You need to do this. You need to see her this last time." Karen hugged Jack, then walked over to Matthew and Tamera. Jack watched her walk away and then looked at me. I took his hand and led him to the car.

Martha drove us to a park where Mama was already waiting. Jack jumped out of the car as soon as it was parked and ran into Mama's waiting arms. I hurried after him and surprised myself by running into her embrace as well. Now that I knew I would never see her again, I was oddly drawn to her.

She smiled down at me. "This is the best gift you've ever given me, Beth."

"I do love you, Mama." I looked into her eyes. "But I don't understand why you would be with him again. Don't *you* love us?"

She was silent for a few long seconds as she stared into my eyes. All I saw in hers was pain and misery. "I do love you." Jack was still holding onto Mama, and his body shook as he sobbed. She looked down at him and lifted his face to look at her. "Both of you, but Jeff is still my husband. I won't shut him out . . . I can't."

I shook my head, wishing I could understand. Weren't mothers supposed to love their kids more than anything? "How can you still love him after all he's done?"

Mama was still looking me in the eye, but now I saw more than pain. Now there was something else there, but I couldn't say exactly what. "Maybe," she said. "You'll never understand." There was a conviction in her voice that didn't seem to fit and I wondered just what she meant. Before I could think about it, she put her arm around me and led the two of us to a cart where a man was selling balloons and cotton candy.

"I know this is hard for all of us, but let's try to enjoy this last time together." Mama looked at Jack and then me. "No more sad faces. Now, let's get some cotton candy and balloons."

Jack and I picked out balloons. We ate blue cotton candy until we were almost sick, and all three of us played on the playground. One thing I could say for Mama is that she was very good at lightening the mood. She'd had a lot of practice.

Our visit was longer than in the past since it was going to be the las, but it did have to end. I knew the time had come when I saw Martha standing under a tree near the playground. She nodded her head, letting me know that it was time to say goodbye.

My stomach knotted as I pointed my mother's gaze in Martha's direction. I didn't know how to say goodbye.

Mama looked at me, and I could tell she was fighting to keep control. She grabbed Jack and me in a fierce hug that almost knocked the wind out of me. That's when she lost control and I could hear her crying and feel her body shaking.

"Just do one thing for me," she said.

Jack and I nodded with tear-streaked faces.

"Whatever happens just remember that I'm your mother. And don't forget that I do love you. Please tell me you won't forget." Her voice strained with emotion.

"We won't forget, Mama," I said.

"Promise," Jack added.

She nodded and held us close again. "Okay, you two go now and be good. I love you. I'll always love you."

"Love you too," Jack and I both said not wanting to leave her. But as Martha approached, Mama broke free from us and turned away. Martha took us by the hand and led us away while Mama stood sobbing, unable to look at us.

# Chapter 21

When Beth stopped talking, Erin was studying her. Beth wished she could go on telling Erin her story. She felt the girl was on the verge of opening up. Unfortunately, the guard had already knocked on the window to let her know their time was up. This meant they had only a precious few minutes before he would come in and insist their session end.

She placed one of her hands over one of Erin's and looked into her eyes. "I'll be back on Thursday and we'll talk some more."

"Will you tell me what happened?" Erin was still looking Beth in the eye. "After you saw your mom for the last time?"

Beth assured Erin she would and then asked one direct question. The five words Erin responded with tore at Beth's heart, but at the same time gave her hope. They told her that this crazy approach might not be so crazy after all. Perhaps it was working. Those five words, if they were honest—and Beth believed they were, also told her that the girl who sat in that room with her was indeed a hurting, broken child—not a monster. But she was going to need to get far more from Erin soon, because saying, "Yes, my father hurt me," was not going to be enough when the court date arrived—not nearly enough.

Beth tried to pry her mind from wondering what the rest of Erin's story was as she sat in her office with Donald Whitman later that afternoon. He was sitting across from her, slouched in a chair. For the first ten minutes, she couldn't get a word out of him. Then he spent the next ten ranting in, what seemed to Beth, a foreign language. She couldn't understand most of what he said, but she did understand that he was very angry. If she was getting it right, he was angry with his parents.

"Donald … Donald … please. If you want me to understand anything you're saying, you're going to have to start speaking English." Beth put up a hand. "Before you start to argue with me, let me say, I've been speaking English a long time. And the stuff that was just coming out of your mouth … wasn't it."

Donald relented. "I'll speak English if you'll at least stop calling me Donald. Only my parents call me that."

"Okay. What would you like me to call you?" Beth inched forward in her chair.

"Donnie."

Beth nodded, the hint of a smile on her face. "Alright, Donnie, would you like to tell me why your behavior changed so suddenly a few months ago?"

"Nothing changed," he said shrugging. "This is who I am. My parents just don't want to accept it."

Beth let out a breath and got up from the chair. "Well, your parents aren't the only ones who think you've changed. I talked to your teachers and they all said that until a few months ago you were an ideal student. They said that you suddenly became moody and uncooperative. You let your grades slip from straight A's to C's and D's. You quit the chess club and started hanging around with a whole new group of kids. Your teachers are worried about you. They said you had a real chance to go to any college you wanted, but now that might not happen," Beth stopped and studied Donnie's face for a moment. He looked sullen and moody, but beyond that, she was sure she had seen him react to what she had said about his grades and his friends.

Still, he just shrugged it away as he got up and started to pace around the room. "So what?" he said.

"Do you really want to ruin your future?"

"So what if I do?" Donnie said with a hint of anger in his voice. "Why should anyone care?"

"Why shouldn't they? Is there a reason why you think your parents wouldn't care about you?" Beth asked furrowing her brow.

"Because they don't care ... not really. They just care that I'm not becoming the son they want me to be," Donnie said as he continued to pace the floor.

"And what kind of son do they want you to be?"

"The kind who wears a suit to work every day and comes to their stuffy parties with a polite smile for everyone. The kind who makes a lot of money and has the right house and the right car. Hell, they probably want to pick a wife for me too. It doesn't matter what *I* want or who I really am. They only love the image of what I should be."

Beth let out a breath and scratched her head as she sat back down on the arm of the chair. "Sit down for a minute, Donnie," she said.

He scowled, but sat back down on the couch across from her. She looked him in the eye as she spoke to him. "You don't want to be what your parents want you to be, I get that. But is *this* really who you want to be?" she asked gesturing to his attire with her hand. "Because I don't think it is and I'm wondering ... why the big show? What do you think you're gaining from this new behavior?"

Donnie shrugged and looked down but didn't answer so Beth continued to talk. "You're putting a lot on the line with this. I mean, you gave up your old friends, your good GPA. You may not be able to get any of that back ... not the way it was. Not to mention that you're hanging out with a bit of a rough group now. Is that really the way you want it?"

"I do miss my old friends," Donnie said. Then looking up at her, "And I liked getting good grades, but I had to let them go to get in with this gang."

Beth got up from her chair and moved over to sit next to Donnie on the sofa. "And you really wanted to hang out with them."

"Naw. Not really. But I didn't know how else to get through to them."

"Your parents, you mean?"

"Yes. I had to make them give up on the idea that I would be the son they wanted. Then maybe who I really am would be okay."

Beth gave Donnie a searching look. "And who exactly is that?" she asked.

Donnie took a deep breath and looked down to his lap where he was fidgeting with his fingers. "I want to be a mechanic," he said in a voice so soft Beth could barely hear him. "I like working with my hands and I like cars."

The corner of Beth's mouth twitched up with the hint of a smile. Now she was seeing the real Donnie and she felt sure she was going to like him. "Donnie," she began, "I think it's time you told your parents the truth. Maybe they won't be as upset about it as you think."

Donnie cocked his head to the side a little and looked at Beth with a smile starting on his face. "Well, I'm thinking they'll at least like it better than this," he said gesturing to his clothing. "But they're going to be pissed that I pulled this on them."

"Did you ever try to tell them the truth before you began this new persona?"

Donnie shook his head. "They wouldn't have listened. Anytime I say I'm interested in something that they don't like, they just act like they didn't even hear me.

"To them having a kid is just a status symbol. They've never tried to know me. They only see me the way they want me to be."

"I'm sorry to hear that, Donnie. Now that I'm getting to know the real you a little, I think you're a real nice kid," Beth paused and looked Donnie in the eye again. "You have to tell them and do your best to make them see the real you. They might not like it, but you need to be honest with them anyway. Be a mechanic if that's what you want. Don't let them, or anyone, tell you that that's not good enough."

Donnie nodded with a broad smile. "You're alright. I'm glad I talked to you."

"I'm glad you did too."

Beth drove home with the radio loud, singing along to the music. She was feeling good; happy about the progress she'd made with Donnie and hopeful about the step forward with Erin. She pulled into the driveway next to Nolan's sensible tan Chevy. She had always thought it odd for an artist to choose such a plain looking car.

She was looking forward to seeing Nolan. It had been late when she got home the previous night and he was already asleep. She checked her makeup in the visor mirror, making sure she looked her best. Then she hurried to the front door.

As soon as she stepped inside, Lulu pushed up against her legs and begged for attention. Beth rubbed the dog's head. "There's my girl," she said. "Did you miss me?" Lulu nuzzled against her in response. "Yes, I love you too, sweet girl. Now, where's Daddy?"

Lulu, smart dog that she was, took Beth's hand in her mouth and pulled her down the hall and straight into the bedroom. There, Nolan lay on the bed wearing nothing but a pair of silk boxers. Beth smiled in approval and patted Lulu on the head one more time before shutting the door and closing the dog out of the room.

"Looks like Lulu brought me to the right place."

"She's a smart dog."

"I hope you didn't get too cold waiting for me like that." Beth sat down on the edge of the bed next to him.

"No," he said trailing a finger down her throat to the buttons on her blouse where he went to work undoing them. "I had thoughts of you to keep me warm."

Beth smiled. "You called Juanita and asked her to let you know when I left, didn't you?"

"I might have." He took one of her hands in his and pressed it to his lips. "But thoughts of you would have kept me warm either way."

Beth kicked off her shoes and snuggled up close to him on the bed. "That's sweet …," Beth began, but was cut off when Nolan covered her mouth with his.

Later, Nolan snuggled up close to her, kissing her neck. "Welcome home," he said. "I was hoping to do that last night, but you got back so late."

"I know. Katie's going through a hard time. I wanted to stay with her as long as I could. Sorry about that."

"After the time we just had, the last thing you need to do is apologize."

She turned on her side smiling at him. "So … you want dinner?"

"Sounds good. Let's go see what we can rustle up in the kitchen."

Five minutes later they were both in their bathrobes and slippers and Beth was watching as Nolan looked through the fridge.

"Maybe we should go to the store soon. There's not much in here." Nolan glanced at her. "We do have a frozen pizza."

"That sounds good. I'll get the oven heating." Beth walked toward the oven. Nolan took the pizza out of the freezer and placed it on a pizza pan.

When Beth walked over to him, he was arranging the pepperoni in star formations.

"You know … it's going to taste the same even if it doesn't look perfect."

"I'm an artist. Did you expect me to leave it looking all haphazard?" He said without looking away from his current work-in-progress.

Beth smiled, wrapping her arms around his waist. "I guess that could never happen. I don't know what I was thinking."

Nolan finished with the pizza, dusted off his hands and faced her. "Are you making fun of me and my art?"

"No." She grinned. "I'm making fun of you and your frozen pizza."

"There's a penalty for making fun of me."

She raised her eyebrows in challenge. "Oh yeah? What might that be?"

"Well if I had a jar of sauce you'd be in trouble." He walked to the sink. "But since I don't—" Turning on the water, he spun around to splash her face with it.

Her jaw dropped with the shock of the cold water. "I can't believe you just did that!"

"Well believe it, honey." He smirked.

"You're going to pay for that."

"What are you going to do about it?"

She walked to the sink and pushed past him. Then she picked up the sprayer and hosed him with the already running water.

It only took him seconds to overcome the shock and lunge toward her. He grabbed her around the waist and wrestled the sprayer from her hand. Then he turned it on her and she gasped as the water ran down into her robe. But before she could react, and with the water still hitting her, Nolan kissed her. She felt a jolt of sudden arousal and pleasure. Her mind jumped back to another place and time when she'd first kissed Nolan, so many years before.

Rebecca L. Marsh

# Chapter 22

On a warm Saturday in mid-February, I asked Ellen Sue if I could go for a walk. She said, as usual, that it was fine as long as I didn't go too far and I was home in time for dinner.

Normally when I went out for walks I stayed in the neighborhood, but that day I decided to walk behind the house and see what I found beyond the trees. The forest brought back a lot of bad memories, so I had avoided it ever since leaving my mother's house. But that day I craved the peace and solitude offered there.

I smiled, touching the bare branch of a tree. I wasn't thinking about the beatings or even worrying about Jack. It felt good to be so happy.

Jack was going to be adopted soon, and the McMillan's were looking into adopting me. I was in no rush because I was happy just to be with them. I wasn't even having the nightmares anymore ... not often anyway.

I started to hum a little tune as I wound through the trees and bushes, careful not to get caught by the briars. Up ahead I could see a gap in the tree line and hear a rushing stream. As I got closer, the beauty of the place overcame me. Grass grew at the edge of the tree line and then the land dropped off slightly to the stream. Someone had built a wooden bridge across it.

I stepped onto the bridge and, holding the railing, looked out over the stream. The water gently flowed over rocks and sand, while bare tree limbs arched overhead. Despite the time of year, birds were singing. In my mind, I saw what it would look like when spring came and green leaves formed a canopy. It was so peaceful. I sat down on the bridge and took my shoes off, then scooted to the edge and dangled my feet into the water. It was cold that I gasped, but it felt good. Feeling alive and free, I sat there for a long time, letting my feet nearly freeze before putting on my shoes.

I was just tying the laces of the second shoe when I heard someone clear their throat. I looked up, and standing over me was a teenage boy. He had short brown hair and intense brown eyes. "You're in my spot," he said in a matter-of-fact tone, staring down at me.

"Your spot?" I asked. "I didn't see your name on it."

"You don't know my name," he said with a smirk.

I rolled my eyes. "Funny. I don't see anyone's name on it … so what makes it *your* spot?"

"Well, it is on my uncle's property, but that's not why I call it my spot."

I blushed a little at hearing I was trespassing. "Sorry. I guess if your uncle owns it, then I should just go." I hopped up and started to walk past him.

He stopped me with his arm. "I didn't say you had to leave. I just said it was my spot … my special spot. I come here to draw." He held up a pad with the other hand. "I'm an artist. Or I want to be anyway. My name's Nolan Christopher. What's yours?"

I wasn't sure what to think of him, but I decided it wouldn't hurt to tell him my name. "I'm Beth."

"Well, Beth, I guess I could share my spot with you as long as you don't interrupt my drawing."

"Thanks, but I need to go home now anyway. It's almost dinner time."

I pushed past him and started to walk away when he called out. "You can come back sometime if you want to. I might like the company."

"We'll see," was all I said as I went on my way. He didn't see the smile that spread across my face.

I was still smiling when I got home.

"That must have been some walk," Ellen Sue said when she saw me. "Your smile's so bright it could blind someone."

I went to the kitchen cabinet, took out plates and began setting the table. "It was a nice walk. I went down behind the house and found the most beautiful place in the woods. There's a stream there and a bridge. It's so pretty."

Ellen Sue nodded. "I know that place. If you're going to spend time back there, you better watch out for poison ivy."

"I will." I sat down at the table I had just set. Ellen Sue put the finishing touches on dinner and for a few minutes, we were both quiet.

Then she set a bowl of mashed potatoes on the table. "So ..." She glanced at me. "Was it just the woods that made you so happy?"

I blushed looking down at the table. I was embarrassed by the question and wasn't sure I wanted to talk about it with her. I was dying to call Katie.

"Does the boy have a name?"

My cheeks grew hot and I didn't look up. "How did you know?"

"I know it's hard to imagine now, honey, but once upon a time, I was a teenage girl too. I know that smile. Now, are you going to tell me who he is, so I can put a face to my worries?"

I lifted my head a little but didn't meet her eyes. "You don't need to worry. I mean, it's no big deal. I only talked to him for a second." I looked at her. She gave me a patient but expectant expression that said, *tell me his name already!*

"His name is Nolan."

"Well, now we're getting somewhere. Does he have a last name?"

"Christopher."

"Then he must be related to Lewis, the man who owns that property." She held up one finger, yelling out, "John! Dinner's on the table."

"He is," I said. "His uncle owns it."

Ellen Sue nodded as she sat down at the table. "I think I know the boy you're talking about. He lives down the street. Sort of tall and gangly with brown hair?"

"I wouldn't say "gangly," but yeah, that's him."

"Almost all teenage boys are gangly. It's not a bad thing. He'll fill out."

"What are you ladies talking about in here?" John asked sitting beside his wife.

"We're just talking about the boy Beth met today," Ellen Sue responded.

I looked down again, trying to hide my embarrassment from John.

"Meeting boys, are you?" John gave a teasing smile. "Do I get to meet him?"

"Now, John," Ellen Sue began. "Give it time. *She* just met him."

Somehow the two of them managed to keep the conversation on Nolan all through dinner, and I was glad to escape to my room after the dishes were washed. There I could dream about Nolan Christopher in peace.

When my homework was completed, I called Katie and talked to her for more than an hour about the short time I had spent in the woods with a boy.

I didn't see Nolan again for a couple of weeks. As much as I wanted to return to the woods and find him on the bridge, I didn't have time because I was a backstage helper with the school play.

At last, the day before my birthday, I found time to walk in the woods, which was okay with Ellen Sue since she was tired and wanted to lie down.

When I came to the bridge, Nolan wasn't there. My heart sank as I looked at the empty bridge. I frowned realizing how much I'd wanted him to be there. It was silly, I told myself. I had only met the boy once. It shouldn't be a big deal whether I saw him again or not—but it was.

I tried to push the disappointment away as I stepped onto the bridge. I would just enjoy the beauty of a nice, sunny day. After all, the birds were singing, and a few wildflowers were starting to bloom. Once again, I removed my shoes and dangled my feet in the flowing stream while I rested my head on my arms on the lower railing. The water glistened in the sunlight and I could see a few tiny minnows swimming.

"There you are!" I jumped when I heard a voice from behind. I spun around and saw Nolan.

I placed a hand over my racing heart. "Don't sneak up on me like that. You scared me half to death. How did you manage to walk up so quietly?"

He smiled down at me and kicked off his shoes. "I have my ways." He sat down next to me and placed his drawing pad in his lap. "I was starting to think you weren't going to come back here."

I looked down nervously, not sure if he was glad to see me. "I'll go if you want me to. I just like this spot ..."

"Don't be silly," he interrupted. "I told you last time you could come back if you wanted to. I just thought I'd see you sooner."

I kept my head down just enough to hide the smile creeping across my face. "I just got too busy."

"Understand," he said nodding. "I've been a little busy myself working on a paper for English class. I haven't had much time to draw, but I still come down here with my homework sometimes. It's a nice place to work if you don't mind not having a chair or a desk."

"I guess you don't." I glanced at him. He turned to me, grinning. He was even cuter than I remembered. His skin was tan even though spring was just beginning and tiny dimples sprung up on his cheeks when he smiled. His hair was cut short, but still long enough to look a little messy and his eyes were full of life and dreams.

"It does get a little uncomfortable sometimes, but at least my little brother doesn't pester me when I'm here."

I nodded and tucked my hair behind my ear. Part of me wanted to tell him that he should be glad to spend time with his little brother, but I wasn't ready to tell him about my life and past yet. "I understand."

"Yeah, little brothers can be a real pain in the ass." He tapped his pad. "Anyway, I'm glad to be done with that paper. Now I can get a little time for my drawing. So what were you so busy with?"

"Me? Oh, I was helping with the school play."

He furrowed his brow in thought. "I don't remember seeing you in the play."

"That's because I wasn't in the play." I pulled my feet out of the cold water and set them in the sun to dry. "I was helping behind the scenes."

"I see. I usually help behind the scenes myself." He placed his feet in the sun next to mine. "You know, painting the set and stuff like that. But I didn't have time this year. My class load has been murder."

I nodded and, for a few minutes, we sat silently in the sun with the early spring breeze drying our feet. As I put on my shoes, he looked at me closer. "You know, it's funny. I don't think I've ever seen you around school."

I looked down. "We probably don't go to the same school."

"Why? What grade are you in?"

I glanced at him shyly. "I'm in the eighth grade."

"You're still in middle school?" he asked. "That means you're only thirteen, right?"

"Actually, tomorrow's my birthday and I'll be fourteen."

"I thought you were older, but I guess we can still be friends." He put his shoes on and scooted farther away from me. "And ... happy birthday."

"Yeah, thanks." My heart sank. Being friends wasn't what I had hoped for, but he was sixteen, and I was too young.

Spring turned into summer and my school vacation began. Katie was home for a couple weeks, and we had a great time doing sister stuff together. However, she had to spend the rest of the summer doing an internship at the aquarium in Pine Knoll Shores out on the coast. So, it was just John, Ellen Sue, and I until Katie came back for a one-week visit at the end of the summer.

The weather was nice; hot, but not too hot, and that spot in the woods was even more inviting now that the tree canopy was lush and green with the wildflowers blooming—and Nolan was next to me. We waded in the stream or walked through the trees, and talked about our friends and how great it was to be free of school for a while. Then we'd sit on the bridge and dangle our feet in the water while Nolan drew, and I pretended to read. I hardly remembered a word.

Focusing was difficult around him because my head was always filled with daydreams. When I looked at him though, I could see that he wasn't thinking about me the same way. All he thought about was his art.

One day, about halfway through the summer, I knocked on Ellen Sue's bedroom door to let her know that I was going to the woods.

"Come in," she called. She sounded tired and I thought maybe she was coming down with something.

I found her sitting on the side of the bed near the nightstand where the phone sat. "Did you hear the phone ring?"

"No, it must have been when I was using the hairdryer. Why? Who was it?"

"Martha." She looked up at me. Then she motioned me over to sit with her. "Martha was calling to let you know that the Zimmerman's have a court date next week to finalize the adoption."

I nodded. I had known this was coming, the words still hit me like a punch to the gut. Even though Karen had assured me that I could see Jack just as much, I still felt like I was losing my baby brother.

Ellen Sue put her arm around me and squeezed. "He's still your brother, Beth. That can never change."

"I know. And I'm glad he'll have parents taking good care of him, but ..." I took a deep breath. "We won't have the same parents or the same house ever again. That shouldn't bother me. I mean at least we're both safe, but ..."

Ellen Sue turned me toward her and looked me in the eye. "It makes perfect sense that this bothers you. He's your brother. But I promise you'll always get to see him and he won't stop being your brother. And soon you'll both have new legal parents." She smiled.

"Really?"

"It won't happen until at least the end of summer, but yes."

I smiled, letting her know that I was happy to be with her and John. Still, the empty feeling remained. She hugged me and then asked, "What did you want me for anyway?"

I looked at her, confused.

"When you knocked on the door, what did you want me for?"

"Oh. I was just going to let you know that I'm going to the woods for a little while. I mean, if it's okay with you."

"That's fine, dear. You tell Nolan I said hello."

I blushed and left without answering.

Ten minutes later I was on the bridge with Nolan, dangling my feet in the water while he leaned against the railing with his sketchbook. His hand flew over the paper as he drew.

We were quiet for a few minutes, but then he asked. "So, did you have a good morning?"

I shrugged. "Yeah, I guess."

"That's good. I wish I could say the same."

"Why? What happened to you this morning?" I turned to look at him.

"My stupid little brother happened. That little pain-in-the-ass took one of my sketchbooks and threw it into the toilet. Ruined every sketch." He shook his head. "And the worst part is my mother only grounded him for one day! Can you believe that? He is so spoiled. Sometimes I just hate him."

Anger flashed through me. "Don't talk about your brother like that."

He furrowed his brow at me. "You sound like my mom. Are you on her side or something?"

"I'm not on anyone's side. You just shouldn't say you hate your brother. You're lucky to have him."

"Oh, really? I'll happily give him to you if you want a little brother so badly."

I jumped up, and standing over him, yelled, "I do have a little brother, and I wish he was around to pester me. You should feel lucky to have yours!"

We glared at each other for a moment. *If only I could put the words back in my mouth.*

"Why isn't he around to pester you?"

I looked down at the boards under my feet, releasing a breath. I knew I would have to explain what I'd said but I wasn't sure how he would react to the truth.

"We were taken away from our mother almost two years ago. We're both in foster care now."

"But you're not in the same home?" He looked at me with interest.

"We were for a while," I told him. "Then I freaked out a little one day and scared our foster mom. She didn't think she could handle my issues, but they wanted to keep Jack. So, I came here to a new foster home, and he stayed with them. I get to see him once a week. I really miss having him around all the time." I slumped down on the bridge. Looking out over the stream, I tried to let go of the hurt I felt. I glanced over when I felt Nolan move in beside me.

"I'm sorry for what I said. You're right. I should be nicer to Peter. I don't really hate him."

I nodded but didn't look at him. "I'm sorry too."

"For what?"

"For yelling at you. I know that it's normal to fight with your siblings. It's really not you that's got me upset today."

He gently rubbed my back. I knew it was just a friendly gesture, but I couldn't help wishing it were more. I wanted to move closer to him, but I stayed where I was.

"What happened today?" he asked.

"My caseworker called to let me know that Jack's adoption will be official next week." My voice broke.

"Oh. I guess you don't want him to be adopted."

"No." I shook my head. "It's not that. The Zimmerman's are nice and I know he's happy with them. It's just that I feel like I'm losing him. Like if he's their kid, then he's not my brother anymore. And I know he still will be, but I guess there's a part of me that hoped somehow we could live together again. Then I could see him more than once a week."

As Nolan's hand moved across my back again in a soothing manner, I felt a tear trickle down my cheek.

"I'm really sorry, Beth," Nolan said. "I wish there was something I could do."

"You're a friend ... that's something."

As the summer days passed, Nolan became, not just a friend, but a confidant. Little by little I opened up and talked about my past; about the Zimmerman's, Jack and John and Ellen Sue. I gave him a very watered-down version of what had happened in my mother's house. That was a subject I avoided.

We also talked about other things; music, our favorite movies, our friends at school. We had fun together, and that summer was shaping up to be the best I'd ever had. Even the summers I had spent with Aunt Amy didn't measure up.

I usually went to the bridge late in the morning, and Nolan was already there with his pad and pencil. I'd read while he drew, but eventually, I'd stop reading and talk to him or splash around in the water. He'd try to keep drawing at first, but it didn't take long before he got distracted and put down the pad. Then we'd walk in the woods or wade in the stream, talking until we both had to go in for lunch. And most days we were right back out there after lunch.

By the middle of July, I had a golden brown tan despite all the shade, and I had gotten to know Nolan Christopher pretty well.

Around that time, John and I noticed how much Ellen Sue was sleeping and urged her to see the doctor.

I went with her to the first appointment, but they didn't tell us anything that day. They were going to run tests and see if they could determine the cause.

That afternoon when we got home, Ellen Sue went to her room to lie down and I went out to the woods to see Nolan. He was there, as always, with his drawing pad, his hand moving across the paper. He looked up for a moment and we greeted each other. I sat down on the wooden planks and pushed back against the railing. I didn't read, but just sat and looked at nature's beauty.

After a short while, I looked over at Nolan, who was sitting up against the opposite railing. "What are you drawing today, anyway?"

He shrugged without looking up. "Just what I see."

"There are a lot of things you can see right now." I rolled my eyes at him. "Are you drawing the trees? Or a bird? Or the stream?"

"No."

"Then what is it?"

He looked up for a moment. "Nothing. It's just a picture."

"Show me," I demanded.

"No."

"Why not?" I was getting more curious the more he was evasive. And now I had to know.

"I just don't want to, okay?"

"You've shown me other pictures."

"So?" He gave me an annoyed look. "I don't want to show you this time. And it's my drawing, so I don't have to."

Before he had a chance to think, I lunged across the bridge, grabbed the pad from his hand, and took off running deeper into the woods. He leaped up and ran after me. I laughed as he chased me, but it was soon clear that he was faster.

He soon caught up, and tried to grab me, knocking me down. He scrambled for the pad when it fell from my hand, but I snatched it up again before he could get his hand all the way around it. As he reached for it, his foot hit a tree root and he fell forward, landing right on top of me.

The air was knocked out of my lungs as his weight came down on me, but I held onto the pad. When he reached for it again, I held it up away from him and glanced at the drawing.

I was stunned at what I saw. The drawing wasn't finished, but I could tell it was me. When I looked away from the drawing, Nolan was looking at me intently. A flash of heat surged through me, and butterflies swarmed in my stomach.

As our eyes locked, my heart beat wildly against my ribs. My breath caught in my throat and time seemed to stand still. My fingers loosened and the pad dropped from them, plopping onto the ground. I placed my hand on his shoulder. Then Nolan lowered his head and, ever so gently, brushed his lips against mine, sending a shiver up my spine. Our kiss lasted no longer than a second before he pulled away, but it felt like forever.

When I opened my eyes, Nolan was looking at me uneasily. He got up and moved to a tree a few feet away from me, and leaned against the trunk. I could still taste him on my lips, and I felt warm inside.

A few seconds later, he looked at me with a sober face. "I'm sorry. I shouldn't have done that."

I shrugged. "Why not?"

He took a deep breath, and I could tell he was trying to let me down easy. "I really like you, Beth. I mean, I like hanging out with you and talking and stuff. But you're just a kid."

"I'm only two years younger than you." I protested.

"Two and a half."

"Okay, two and a half, but that's not so much. I'll be in the same school as you next year."

I couldn't say why I held onto him so hard after only one brief kiss, but the idea of pretending it had never happened felt like a stab to my heart.

"Yeah, the same school, but you'll be a freshman and I'll be a senior."

I shook my head. "So what? It's not cool for a senior guy to date a freshman girl, is that it?"

"No … some do. But I wouldn't feel right about it. You're only fourteen." He stopped and moved closer to me, taking my hand in his. "I really do like you, Beth. And in ten years our age difference may seem like nothing at all, but right now it's too big a difference … At least for me."

I wanted to keep protesting, tell him how he made my heart beat faster, but the words got stuck in my throat. I was almost certain that he felt something for me too, but he wasn't backing down about my age. I nodded my head and pushed back my tears.

That night I called Katie and told her about the kiss and what Nolan said after.

"Don't give up hope, little sister," she said. "He kissed you, so you know he likes you. And he drew a picture of you."

"Yeah, but he's an artist. He draws pictures of everything. And for all I know he kisses lots of girls."

"But, Beth, he didn't want you to see the drawing. I think that's because he didn't want you to know how he feels about you. Give it time. He may come around on the age thing."

I hoped that Katie was right and that Nolan would change his mind, but I stopped worrying about him when something bigger dropped into my life.

# Chapter 23

Two days after Nolan kissed me, we learned the results of Ellen Sue's medical tests. She had inoperable pancreatic cancer. She planned to fight, but her prognosis was very bleak.

As summer turned into fall, the process of John and Ellen Sue adopting me halted so they could focus on her chemo treatments. I tried not to worry because they assured me that when Ellen Sue was better, the adoption would go forward as planned. But what if she didn't recover?

Time crawled as I watched Ellen Sue wither from the chemo. She became weak and frail, a total contrast from the exuberant woman she has once been. Some days I barely recognized her. I assumed most of the household chores, and Katie came home every weekend. Between the two of us, the outcome was a sad reminder of all that Ellen Sue had always done for us. John thanked us anyway, for putting our best foot forward.

Watching John was equally difficult. His face seemed to age with every passing day. His hair grew whiter and his eyes lost their sparkle, leaving him a mere shell of the man I had met two years before.

After six months of treatment, the doctors told Ellen Sue there was nothing more they could do. Her life was ending.

For a few days, all any of us could do was cry. Then, one Saturday while Katie was home, Ellen Sue called us to the kitchen table for a family meeting. She looked a little better since she was no longer on the chemo and at times I could almost make myself believe she was getting better. Of course, that wasn't true. The doctors said she would feel better for a little while because her body didn't have to deal with the chemo. Her hair would grow back and her color would improve, but the cancer was still spreading.

To our surprise, Ellen Sue even cooked dinner for us that night. "No offense, girls, but we have to eat a real meal once in a while. And since I'm feeling a little better, I wanted to cook."

"Well, I don't think anyone here is going to argue about you being the better cook, Mom," Katie said. "But what is this meeting all about?"

Ellen Sue smiled at us. "I have a request for all of you." She stopped, and we looked at her with complete attention. "I know it's the middle of winter, but the doctors don't think I have much more time before I get really sick. So, I want to take a trip, a family vacation."

We all looked at each other and nodded. Then, shrugging his shoulders, John said, "If that's what you want, darling, just name the place, and we'll all go there."

"Now wait a minute, John. I know you would do it in a minute, but it'll be harder for the girls missing school. Especially you, Katie."

Katie and I smiled at each other. "We can handle it, Mom," Katie said. "We just want to spend time with you right now."

John placed his hands on Ellen Sue's shoulders and squeezed, letting her know he felt the same way. Ellen Sue reached out and took one of my hands and one of Katie's. "Then how do you all feel about a tropical vacation in Hawaii?" She looked over her shoulder at John. "I know it will be a lot of money for that kind of trip, and our savings are down from all the medical bills, but I really want to get away from here and go someplace warm with my family just one more time."

"Don't you worry about the cost, darling." John kissed the top of her head. "I'd take you to the moon if you wanted me to."

Our trip to Hawaii was wonderful. The four of us had such a great time in the warm tropical breezes, soft white sand, and the clearest water I've ever seen.

We spent every day together. We went scuba diving and para-sailing. Katie and I even tried a few surfing lessons, but we spent more time in the water than on the board.

Ellen Sue was feeling pretty good the whole week, and it was a joy to be with her.

When we got back from Hawaii, however, Ellen Sue started to get very tired again and her condition deteriorated fast. In less than two months she was hospitalized. A few weeks later, John, Katie, and I stood around her bed, and watched her slip away from us.

The last time I saw Ellen Sue, she took my hand and said, "Beth, I love you, and you are my daughter."

The funeral was held on a Wednesday in early March, just days before my fifteenth birthday. The weather had been warm for a few days, but turned cool and crisp that day, and some of the flowers that had started to bloom sat wilting in the flowerbeds. They seemed to know that the person who had cared for them was gone.

At the gravesite, John held Katie and I close, and from behind me, Jack reached his hand out to hold onto me from where he stood with Matthew and Karen. People I loved were there to support me, including Martha, but this day was even harder than that last day with Mama.

About a month later, I came home from school to find John sitting in the living room waiting for me. He sat in his favorite chair, but the TV was off, and he wasn't reading a book or the paper. He looked sad and distraught.

Thinking that he was having a bad day with grief, I sat down on the couch. "You're home early," I said. "Is there something wrong?"

He raised his head and looked up at me. His eyes were filled with pain and, after all, he had been through, he looked much older than his years. For a moment he didn't speak, but just watched me. Then he shook his head saying, "I'm a selfish old man, Beth, but it's time I stopped."

My brow furrowed in confusion. "What are you talking about?"

"This isn't fair to you. You're fifteen years old. You should be out having fun. Not at home taking care of an old man who can't even smile anymore."

"I want to take care of you. I love you, John." I looked into his sad, dull eyes as they filled with tears.

I went to him, and he hugged me. "I love you, too. That's why I have to give you up."

I froze as the shock of his words washed over me, feeling as if my whole world was falling away. "No, please." I shook my head against his shoulder.

I pulled away and looked into his eyes again. I could see he was hurting just as much as me. "But I don't understand. You and Katie are my family now. You're going to adopt me … Aren't you?"

His face filled with shame as he dropped his head. "I can't do it by myself. Not when I'm like this. I'm not much good to anyone now. Katie's grown and on with her life, but you still need parents. And right now, here with me, you don't really have any." He looked back up at me. "It's not right that you should be taking care of me. I'm ashamed of that. You deserve more."

"But I don't want anything else, John." My eyes searched his for some hope that he would change his mind. He turned his face away, unable to endure my gaze. "I want to be here with you."

He placed his hands on my shoulders and looked at me again. "I will always think of you as my daughter. It's because I love you so much that I want you to have better than this." For a moment he just looked at me. "I've already talked to Martha. You'll stay with me until she has a place for you, but she doesn't think it will be too long."

I stayed by John for a few moments, frozen in shock. I just couldn't believe this was happening. This was supposed to be my home, and these people my family, forever. Now John was telling me that I had to start over again with another home and a new family.

Intense pain replaced my shock. I jumped up and ran away from John and out of the house. I didn't think about where I was going. I just ran. Moments later I realized that I had run into the woods toward the bridge.

I sprinted paying no attention to the path. Small branches lashed against me, and briars tore at my skin. I didn't care. I barely noticed, because my heart ached so much that no other pain compared.

When I came to the bridge, I was crying so hard I could no longer see where I was going and I stumbled when my foot hit the first wooden plank. To my surprise and relief, Nolan caught me as I fell. I allowed myself to collapse into his arms. They were strong and warm around me and, I wished I could stay there forever, hidden from the rest of the world.

"Beth, it's going to be okay. I know it's hard right now. But things will get better."

I shook my head against him. "No, they won't."

"Well, I know it seems that way now, but it will get easier."

"It's not about Ellen Sue. That's not why I'm upset."

"Something else happened?" He eased us both down to sit on the bridge. "What could be worse?"

Another wave of emotion swept over me, and I couldn't answer right away.

"Beth, you're trembling. What's going on? Is it about your brother?"

"No. It's not about him. I'm upset because I have to move." I glanced at him.

His brow furrowed in confusion. "John wants to move now?"

"No, not John. Just me."

"But … I don't understand." He shook his head a little, and I thought I heard pain in his voice. "Move where?"

I sniffled, trying to hold back another flood of tears. "John doesn't think he can be a good parent to me all by himself, so I have to go to a new foster home."

"Where?"

"I don't know yet." My body quaked with more sobs. I leaned into Nolan's shoulder and just cried for a while. He tried to soothe me, his hand caressing my back.

"I know how much you love John and Katie. I'm sure you're going to really miss them."

I looked up at him, my tear-filled eyes meeting his. "I will miss them. But as much as that hurts, It's even worse when I think about not seeing you anymore. I don't understand it, but when I think about it …" I placed my hand over my heart. "I can't breathe."

Part of me couldn't even believe I'd told him that, but I didn't feel any shame in telling him or worry that he would reject me. Maybe that didn't even matter anymore. I just couldn't keep the feelings I had for him bottled up inside.

He kept his eyes locked on mine for a few seconds. Then, without saying a word, he leaned down and brushed his lips against mine.

His kiss was not deep, but tender and when I opened my eyes, his face was still close to mine and he touched his hand to my cheek in a gentle caress. "You never know, Beth," he said. "Maybe we'll see each other again someday."

# Chapter 24

"And you did see him again," Erin said with a hint of a smile.

Beth raised her eyebrows in response. "Did I?"

"You said his name was Nolan Christopher, right? And your last name is Christopher. So, you married him."

"I guess you were paying attention."

"How did you meet him again? Did you keep in touch?"

"No, we didn't keep in touch. I had no idea where I was going until the day before I left, and he was leaving the next year for college."

"Then how did you find him again?"

Beth studied Erin, encouraged by what she saw. Erin leaned in closer over the table, resting her head on her hands with her elbows on the table. Her body was no longer rigid with stress. She almost looked like a normal teenager waiting to hear a big secret.

*This is progress*

"Lisa found him for me," Beth responded to Erin's question.

Erin looked at her quizzically as she reached into a snack size bag of Oreos that Beth had brought for her. "Lisa?"

"Yes, Lisa ... or Ms. Larson ... your lawyer. She and I were friends in college and throughout graduate school. And while she was in law school and I was getting my masters in psychology, she met a guy and they started going out all the time." Beth looked up and saw that Erin was engrossed in the story. "When I complained about never seeing her, she decided to set me up on a blind date with one of her boyfriend's friends. I wasn't really thrilled about it, but she made it impossible to say no. Funny thing is, when we got there, it wasn't really a blind date because I already knew the guy. I just hadn't seen him in a long time."

"Wow! That's so cool. It's like fate."

"It's amazing, when you think about it, how things can work out even when you feel sure they can't. When I had to leave John and go to a new foster home, I didn't think I would ever be as happy again as I'd been when Ellen Sue was alive."

"Then you were happy again." Erin looked at Beth. Then she shook her head. "It's not the same for me. I killed my father. Nothing's going to change that."

Beth took a deep breath. "That's true, Erin. Your life will never be the same again. However, telling me what made you do it, might help your chances of having a good life again."

Erin glanced down at her lap.

"Erin, you already told me that your father hurt you," Beth said. The five words Erin had given her during their last meeting had been, "Yes, my father hurt me."

Now Beth needed more. "What I'm wondering is, did you ever try telling someone when it was happening?"

Erin shook her head, but stayed silent.

"I believe that he hurt you, but I need to know why you felt you had to kill him to make it stop. Why didn't you go to someone? A teacher or counselor?"

Erin raised her head, making eye contact. She didn't look like a happy teenager anymore. Her lips were curved into a frown and her eyebrows were drawn together. "When your parents are important, no one's willing to listen to you. No one wants to hear bad things about them."

"I think Mrs. Abernathy would have listened. She was very concerned about you when I talked to her. She noticed that your parents were more interested in their social status than in you and Kayla."

"She was a good teacher. I'm sure she would have tried to help. But someone would have stopped her, or convinced her I was making things up."

"How can you be so sure of that? You didn't try."

"*I* didn't, but I know someone who did. And it didn't turn out well for him."

"Tell me about him."

Erin looked unsure. "I don't want to use his name."

Beth nodded her understanding. "Then we'll call him Mr. X."

Erin took a deep breath and gathered her courage. "Mr. X was a good friend of mine. And before my father ever did anything to me, his father hurt him.

"His father was … well, let's just say he was a pillar of the community." Erin sounded more like an adult than a teenager. "And no one would ever have imagined he could do anything wrong. He knew all the important people and went to all the most important events. He was smart and funny and everyone loved him. Just like my father." Erin looked down again, and Beth could see she was fighting tears.

"Do you need a minute, Erin?"

She shook her head and looked at Beth again. "I'm okay. The thing is, Mr. X really loved his dad too, but then things changed."

"How did they change? Do you know?"

"I guess the pressure of the public eye got to his dad. He started to drink a lot and he was mean when he got drunk."

*How familiar that sounds*

"His wife left him. Of course, everyone in town figured it had to be her fault. I mean what kind of a woman ran off and left her husband and son behind. He got drunk and then he got mad at every little thing. He beat Mr. X sometimes, but he never put marks on his face. And most of the time it wasn't even physical."

Beth furrowed her brow. "If it wasn't physical, then what was going on?"

Erin thought for a moment. "I guess they call it mental abuse. Mr. X's dad just said horrible things to him. It made him feel like everything that went wrong was his fault." Erin stopped for a moment, taking a breath. "The worst part was how his dad made him think he was the reason his mom left."

Beth nodded. "What did Mr. X do about his father?"

"Nothing for a while. But then he started having trouble in school, anger problems. The school counselor talked to him and Mr. X told him everything. He asked for *help*."

"The counselor didn't help him?" Beth leaned back in the rickety metal chair without breaking eye contact.

"He meant to. Then he talked to Mr. X's dad. After that, he didn't believe Mr. X anymore."

Beth gave Erin a questioning look. "I don't understand what the father could have said that would make a counselor think a troubled kid made everything up."

"I don't know what was said, but his father must have convinced the counselor that Mr. X was crazy, because two weeks after that talk, Mr. X was sent to a mental hospital."

Beth wasn't sure what to say in response, but she was definitely going to look into this further. She didn't feel like Erin was lying, but she wanted to see for herself if any students from Erin's school had been sent to a mental hospital. And if so, she wanted to try and find out what the grounds were for sending him there.

Erin looked at Beth, trying to gauge her response. "You know, I probably would still have gone to the counselor, or to Mrs. Abernathy if it was just me I was worried about. I mean I don't think even the mental hospital could have been worse. But it *wasn't* just me. I had to think about Kayla."

Beth took a deep breath, trying to wrap her mind around all Erin had told her. She could understand how wanting to protect a younger sibling could make a person go to drastic measures. She could even understand making a self-sacrifice. There was still one thing she didn't understand.

"But why won't you talk to me and tell me what he did to you?"

Erin shook her head and her face darkened. "I want to tell you ... but I still have to think of Kayla."

Beth was not only confused by Erin's words, but frustrated as well. She thought she was getting through, but again she'd hit a wall. "Erin, your father's dead. What's going to hurt Kayla now?"

The young girl's face looked miserable as she stared across the table. Beth's frustration melted away and she only felt sympathy. *What was done to this poor girl?*

"My father wasn't the only danger in that house."

Beth's mind raced in circles as she drove back to her office. The guard had interrupted again, and Beth had never gotten Erin to tell her what other dangers there were for Kayla. What else could there be? What was going on in that house?

As soon as she got into her office, Beth researched any and all newspaper stories or other information she could find online about Erin's school. It was a great school that educated many bright, young minds, so there were a lot of stories about their students. Most of them were about Stonewood Academy students winning various awards, but then Beth found the one she was looking for. The headline read, "Stonewood student sent to upstate mental facility."

Beth skimmed through the article. She learned that Mr. X's real name was Justin Thomas, son of a local judge, Arthur Thomas. According to the article, Justin was sent to the facility after suffering a mental breakdown, supposedly the result of his mother running off the year before. There were several quotes from Justin's "very concerned father" that made him sound like a model parent, but that's not the way Erin had described him. So Beth had to wonder, was Erin wrong about all this or was Judge Thomas an amazing smooth-talker who was able to convince everyone his son was mentally ill?

Beth might never know. The article did, however, confirm most of Erin's story. And Beth was beginning to understand the difficulties in being the child of an influential figure.

But she was reaching out to Erin, believing in her, and still, the girl held back. What was she afraid of?

Beth would have to wait to find out. Tomorrow was Friday and she didn't have any more time to spend with Erin until Monday. She did, however, have a meeting scheduled with Donald Whitman's parents tomorrow morning. And his mother didn't sound happy when she made the appointment.

"Dr. Christopher, we brought Donald to you and trusted you to help him," Mrs. Whitman said with an exasperated look. "And instead of helping him, you've turned him into a … a mechanic!"

Beth took a breath before she began and tried not to let them see how stuck-up she thought they were. "Mrs. Whitman, I didn't turn your son into anything. I just helped him work things out so he could tell you the truth about why he acted out." Beth stole a glance at Donnie, who was seated behind his parents, next to the door. He smiled at her and nodded his approval.

"How can you sit there and defend what you've done?" Mr. Whitman chimed in. "Donald is strong and smart and has the opportunity to be anything. Fiddling with cars is beneath him."

"I'm sorry you feel that way. But Donnie *is* smart and I think he knows what he wants." Beth held up a hand when Mr. Whitman started to interrupt her. "I am a child psychologist, Mr. Whitman. It's not my job to convince your son to be what you want him to be. It is my job to help him understand his own feelings and actions. I'm very sorry if you aren't happy with the results."

Mr. Whitman sat stunned, his face getting redder each second as it contorted with anger. He looked at his wife. "Regina, can you believe the nerve of this woman? Talking to us that way!" He stood up and straightened his suit jacket. "We're leaving now. We'll just have to find someone else to help Donald."

"Dad," Donnie spoke up from behind. "You can't fix this. It's who I am. And it isn't her fault."

Mr. Whitman gave his son a hard look. "We'll see about that."

Donald looked back at Beth as his father began to herd him out the door. He smiled at her and mouthed the words, "Thank you." Beth nodded at him in return and hoped she had done enough for him.

When she was sure the Whitman's had had time to leave the reception area, Beth walked out of her office and met Juanita's glance.

"Don't pay no attention to them, Dr. Christopher. They nothing but snobs," Juanita said in her Spanish accent. "You make that boy smile again."

"For now. But they're not going to stop trying to change him."

"They might try, but he strong boy. I can tell this."

Beth let out a breath. "With parents like that, he'll need to be if he's going to stay true to himself."

Juanita nodded. "He can do that now. You show him how to be honest with them ... and himself. He won't let them take that away from him."

Beth patted Juanita on the back with a smile. "Thank you, Juanita. Sometimes I think you're *my* therapist. You probably ought to be charging me for it."

"Some things free with friendship. We all need a little encouragement now and then."

"It's time for lunch, friend. Would you like to join Lisa and me?"

"No, thank you. I have date with sandwich and nice looking man on TV," Juanita said clicking on the TV in the empty reception area.

"Okay." Beth headed for the outer door. "I'll be back in an hour."

Beth arrived at the diner before Lisa, so she found a shady table outside and put in their order. Chicken fingers and fries for her and a house salad with Italian dressing for Lisa.

A few minutes later Lisa stepped up to the table and tossed her briefcase down on the empty bench next to her seat, then sat. She blew out a breath. "Crazy week."

Beth nodded. "It has been that."

"Yeah, I guess you've had to deal with even more than I have. How's John doing anyway?"

"He's getting worse. Katie and I did have a few lucid minutes with him." Beth pushed her hair back from her face.

"I'm sorry to hear he isn't doing too well. I'm sure Katie is beside herself."

"She's having a hard time with it. I think my visit helped a little."

"I bet she's glad to have you right now," Lisa said just as the waitress came out with their food.

"Anything else I can get for you?" the waitress asked.

"No, thank you. It all looks good." Beth picked up a fry and popped it into her mouth. Then she looked back at Lisa, who was removing the onions from her salad and pouring on the dressing. "I'm just glad I could be there for Katie ... and John. They did so much for me." Beth paused then decided to change the subject. "So, what's been going on with you this week?"

"Well besides losing the Collins case, I took on two new cases that honestly don't look very promising. On top of that, I had to go see the school principal because Josh started a food fight on Tuesday." Lisa stopped and took a bite of her salad before continuing. "Last but not least, Anna's teething again. And this time she's getting molars so we're not getting much sleep." Lisa shook her head. "If she starts up tonight, I may have to get out the whiskey."

"To rub on her gums?"

"Actually I was going to get the whiskey out for me." Lisa looked up at Beth with weary eyes. "Then maybe I'll be able to sleep through the crying."

Beth let out a giggle and Lisa gave her a dry look.

"I'm sorry." Beth tried to hold back another giggle. "I guess it has been a long week for you. I have some good news though."

"Fabulous! Lay it on me."

"I got Erin to talk to me a little." Noticing a bright look come over Lisa's face she held up a hand. "Don't get too excited. She didn't give me any details. She did say her father hurt her."

"That's all? Because we can't go very far with just that."

"I know. I asked her why she hadn't told anyone when it was happening. Why she didn't ask for help."

"And what was her answer?"

"She said she was afraid to because a boy she knew had gone to the school counselor for help with his father and he ended up in a mental facility. She was afraid of what would happen to Kayla if she was sent away like that."

Lisa raised her eyebrows. "That's quite a story."

Beth told Lisa the rest of what Erin had said about her friend and about what she had found out from her own research.

Lisa nodded. "I know who you're talking about now. Judge Thomas, right?" When Beth nodded back, Lisa went on. "He's a really nice guy, Beth. I've met him."

"That doesn't mean he was nice at home. A lot of abusers have the people outside their home totally fooled."

Lisa relented. "I guess that's true sometimes. But how does this help us?"

"It might not, but talking about this friend is one step closer to Erin talking about her own problems." Beth paused to take a bite of her chicken. "There is one other thing she said, though. And I can't make sense of it."

"What's that?"

"I asked her why she wouldn't tell me what her father had done to her now that he was gone," Beth looked up and met Lisa's eyes. "She said she's holding back because of Kayla."

Lisa furrowed her brow. "Why is she worried about Kayla now?"

"That's the interesting part. And the part I can't understand. She said her father wasn't the only danger in that house."

Lisa thought for a minute as she chewed a bite of salad. "Do you think Victoria is abusive too?"

"Maybe. But Erin only aimed the gun at James. Besides that, why would Victoria punish Kayla for what Erin said about James?"

"Hard to say. I'm starting to think this family might be able to put new meaning to the word dysfunctional." Lisa looked up at Beth again. "I hope we can figure this all out soon. In two weeks it goes before the judge."

# Chapter 25

Sunday morning, Beth and Nolan went to Beth's father's house for brunch with the family. After they finished eating, and the mess was cleaned up, the men went into the living room to watch a NASCAR race. Beth, Grace, and Ashley stayed in the kitchen with the baby, who was now settled in his infant seat taking a nap. The conversation between the three of them was light. Grace talked about Sarah and told them how disappointed she was that things didn't work out between Sarah and her neighbor's nephew. "She gave it another chance after that first date and then he told her she wasn't really his type. Can you believe that?"

Then the conversation turned to the topic of gardening, which Beth was not at all interested in. Grace told Ashley about the tomatoes and cucumbers she was growing. "Let me show you," Grace said.

When Ashley reached to pick up the infant carrier, Grace stopped her. "Beth's not interested in seeing my garden. She can stay with the baby."

Ashley gave Beth an uncertain look.

"It's okay," Beth said. "Ronnie is right in the next room."

Ashley smiled, happy with the moment of freedom. She and Grace walked out the back door leaving Beth alone with Hunter.

Beth looked into the carrier at the tiny person inside. She reached out a cautious hand and touched his little foot, breathing a sigh of relief. "Well, at least I can touch you without losing it."

She sat there a minute watching him sleep; his chest rising and falling with each breath, eyes shut tight and little hands rolled into fists. He looked so peaceful and angelic.

Beth felt so ashamed that she couldn't get closer to him. "I'm a terrible Aunt," she whispered to him. "I hope you'll forgive me someday. I really do love you, little man."

"He'll know that." A voice came from the direction of the door and Beth looked up to see Grace standing there. "And who knows, maybe soon you'll feel able to hold him. When you've worked some things out."

"I hope so." Beth sucked in a long breath. She glanced around the room. A few things had been replaced in recent years, but a lot was still the same as it had been when Beth was a teenager. The same wallpaper was still up on the walls, the same baskets still hung on the wall, and the same old oak table still sat in the breakfast nook, covered with a floral print tablecloth. In the middle of that table sat a somewhat misshapen clay pot filled with artificial lilies.

She looked at that pot and she could remember the year Sarah had given it to Grace for mother's day. The same day, Ronnie knocked it off the counter and broke it. Grace wouldn't hear of throwing it away so she found as many pieces as she could and glued them together. She said the small holes that were left by pieces that had shattered too small to glue added character.

Looking around, Beth thought of all the good times she'd had while living there. She remembered laughs and hugs and a lot of great meals; along with love and plenty of good advice. It wasn't the first great home she'd had, but it was one she was glad to still be hanging on to.

That might be just why Erin was getting to her so much. The look in her eyes—broken and hopeless, and her words about why she stayed silent, "My father wasn't the only danger in that house." So what else was there? What was she afraid was going to happen to Kayla if she talked? And then there was the thing that bothered Beth the most—even if she could get Erin talking, would it help her in the long run? Would Erin ever know what it was like to live in a good home?

Beth brought herself back to the present and found her stepmother looking at her curiously. "You okay, honey?"

Beth smiled nodding her head. "Yeah, I'm fine. I was just thinking about all the great times we've had together in this house, and how glad I am that I ended up here."

"I'm glad of that too. I only wish it had happened sooner." Grace wiped her hands on her pink striped apron before giving Beth a hug.

"You know what they say." Beth pulled back from the hug to look Grace in the eye. "Everything happens in its own time."

Grace's brow went up. "How did you get so wise?"

"A couple of great ladies taught me." Beth gave Grace a kiss on the cheek. "I'm lucky. I ended up with a great family," she said, her voice thick with emotion. "So many kids never get that."

Grace met Beth's eye and held them for a long moment. Then she raised a hand and patted Beth's cheek. "And some do. Even when it seems impossible."

Sunday night, after an early dinner with Nolan, Beth decided to have a glass of wine to help her relax. She took her glass out the back door, letting Lulu out along with her, and sat on the patio to finish the wine while her dog ran around the yard.

When her glass was empty, she called Lulu and went back inside. It was only nine o'clock, but Beth was ready to relax. She brushed her teeth and got into bed with Nolan to watch a movie. Nolan flipped the channels for a few minutes until he found The *Wedding Singer*. It was a cute, funny movie and she had enjoyed it in the past, but tonight Beth found herself drifting off before the movie was even half over.

Suddenly she was alone in a dark, silent room, lying in bed. She got up and struggled to see in the dark. The room

191

seemed familiar. Yes, she knew where she was. It was the room that had been hers in her mother's house. She blinked her eyes, trying to get them to adjust, but it was too dark.

Then she heard someone shouting, and after that a scream. It must be her mother. Jeff was hurting her.

Beth felt a chill go through her when she realized she didn't know where Jack was. She had to find him. She put her hands out in front of her to keep from running into anything, and walked forward until she felt the wall. Feeling her way to the door, she turned the knob with care, so as not to make any noise, and opened it.

The yelling was louder now, but she was pretty sure the fighting was going on in the living room. Still she had to be certain, so she peeked around the corner to make sure the coast was clear. Seeing no one, she ran across the hall to Jack's door and opened it, but what she saw inside was not Jack's room at all.

It was another girl's room, filled with white painted furniture and pink frills. Beth had never seen it before. She stood there confused for a few seconds trying to decide what to do next and how to find Jack. Then she realized the fighting had stopped. She started to turn back toward the door, but stopped when she heard a loud pop.

Her heart pounded and she felt a lump form in her throat. *What had just happened?*

She eased around and was surprised to see a girl standing in the doorway. Her head was down and sandy-colored hair fell around her shoulders. She wore a nightgown with lavender rose buds and ruffles on it and a smattering of red across the front. In her right hand she held a gun at her side.

Beth stood still, not sure what to do. The girl lifted her face. It was splattered with blood, but Beth could see who it was… Erin. She looked right into Beth's eyes, her body trembling with fear and said, "It's still not safe here. Help me. Please!"

Beth sprang upright in bed, her heart pounding, as she awoke from the dream. Her body was damp with sweat and she was trembling. She glanced at Nolan. He was still sound asleep, so she just sat still until she felt her heartbeat slowing down. If anyone knew she was having nightmares about her past that segued into Erin's case—. Proper procedure would be to step down, let another psychologist take Erin's case. But Beth couldn't do that. Deep down she knew this was the only way to help Erin. It was starting to work. She could see that. And she absolutely couldn't fail this child.

Falling back on her pillow, Beth willed herself back to sleep. Soon this would all be over. She would find the answer. She had to.

Rebecca L. Marsh

# Chapter 26

Martha came for me the Saturday following John's call. Katie came home from school to say goodbye. We stayed up most of Friday night talking and crying together. She promised to always be my sister, no matter what happened and she made sure I had a number to call her whenever I needed her.

She was angry with John for sending me away, but I begged her not to be. He was a broken shell of a man after everything that had happened and he didn't need any more heartache or loss. As much as I hurt, I knew John was only doing what he thought was best for me. Perhaps his hurt was even deeper.

When Martha arrived at the house Sunday morning, John carried my bags out to the car and we said our good-byes. John hugged me tight whispering, "I'm sorry. I'm so sorry."

Then I hugged Katie, who didn't want to let go. We both had red, swollen eyes from crying. "I love you, little sister," she said. "And don't forget to call me."

Glancing back at them, I got into the car with Martha and headed to a new home. I didn't even try to imagine what it would be like. I didn't care, because no matter what it was like, it could never be home. I was losing that and I couldn't imagine any place ever feeling like home again.

Instead, I closed my eyes and took myself back to the bridge in the woods and the feel of Nolan's lips against mine, the sweetness of his touch. I wanted to remember every second of that kiss and never forget.

My daydream came to a stop when the car bumped down a rocky dirt road and stopped. I opened my eyes and looked around. In front of me was a simple gray, ranch-style house. Around the house was nothing but trees. There were no neighboring houses, which was very unsettling to me.

I looked at what was around me feeling dismayed. My heartbeat and breathing sped up. I pushed my body back into the seat of the car as much as I could and closed my eyes. *I want to go home! Please just let this be a bad dream and take me home!*

When I opened my eyes, Martha was turned around in her seat looking at me. "I'm sorry you have to move again, Beth. I really thought you would be with the McMillian's for good."

I nodded with a sniffle. "It's not your fault, Martha. It's not anyone's fault this time."

Martha nodded back still looking sad. "Your new foster parents are Mark and Leslie Kessler. I talked to Leslie on the phone yesterday, but only briefly. They've been foster parents for several years now, but I've never worked with them before."

"I guess they should be okay, though," I said, "If they've been doing this a while." That's what I hoped anyway, though I felt very uneasy.

"They should be." Martha's tone did not instill confidence. "And they have another foster child with them now. A sixteen year old boy named Jamie."

"So I'll have a foster brother." I thought that might be something to look forward to. I had never had an older brother before.

"Yes … The thing is, Beth, they've never had a girl before."

My brow furrowed as I tried to understand why Martha was pointing that out to me. Seeing my worry, she attempted to make light of it.

"I'm sure it won't be a problem. I mean we haven't had any problems with them in the past."

I nodded my head again, unable to shake the feeling of worry that I sensed from her.

She turned back to the front and jotted something down on a scrap of paper, then turned back to me again. "This isn't normal procedure, but I want to give you my number at home just in case you ever need me."

I looked into her eyes. She didn't want me to see how deep her concern was, but it was clear she was worried. And with all she had done for me, I knew she'd brought me to this home only because she had no choice.

I forced a smile. "I'm sure I'll be okay. But thank you, Martha. You've done so much for me."

She took my hand and closed it around the paper. "Let's go meet them."

Breaking my gaze away from her eyes, I got out of the car. I walked around to the trunk with Martha and helped her get my bags out and carry them to the front door of the house. Martha rang the bell and while we waited for an answer, I looked down at the pretty blue suitcases that held my things. I remembered the day that Ellen Sue had taken me shopping and bought me a "proper set of luggage." Before that, all my things had been taken from place to place in two very old, worn suitcases.

Thinking about her, a stab of pain went through my chest. I thought of Ellen Sue as my mother and I missed her terribly. I wished when the door opened, she would be standing in it with her arms open to me. Of course, that wasn't going to happen.

A moment later the door to the house did open and a plump woman of about forty smiled at me. She was a little bit homely, but wore no makeup. Her light brown hair was neatly combed and she wore a cheery rose-colored dress.

The woman came forward and wrapped her arms around me, squeezing me tight. My body stiffened but she didn't seem to notice. She pulled away from me, still smiling and glanced back at a man who stood behind her.

He was tall and thin and looked scruffy, with brown hair that was a little long and about two days of stubble on his face.

"I'm Leslie," the woman said, "and that's Mark." She made a gesture to the scruffy man. His lips twitched into something that wasn't quite a smile and he raised his hand in greeting to me then let it fall back to his side. His mannerisms seemed to indicate general disinterest, but there was something about him that was very unsettling.

Leslie's enthusiasm seemed unstoppable and I wondered, as she motioned Martha and me into the house, if her face hurt from smiling so much. We moved into the house, leaving the luggage at the door.

The living room was simple. A brown tweed couch and a matching love seat sat at a right angle from each other with an end table in between. Across from the couch was a low table with a TV on top.

There was a thin, lanky boy sitting on the couch watching a cartoon on TV. He had short blond hair and caramel-colored eyes that looked zoned out. Leslie motioned to him. "This is Jamie."

"Hi." I tried to look at him, but his eyes didn't leave the TV screen.

Mark slapped his hand down on the couch cushion. "Snap out of it, boy, and say hello."

"Hi," Jamie said. He looked at me but his eyes still seemed glazed and expressionless. I wondered if that was the way he'd always been, or if being here made him that way. I hoped it was the former.

Jamie turned back to the TV and I followed all of the adults into a small kitchen. It had dull gray linoleum on the floor, dark stained wooden cabinets that were old and scarred, and butcher-block countertops. In the corner sat a small table with mismatched chairs.

It was a little depressing to look at, but I told myself that it didn't matter how it looked or how old it was. *I shouldn't judge them by it.* On the way there I had thought I didn't care what this place was like, but now I was desperate to believe it was a good place. However, the feeling in my gut told me different.

We left the kitchen and walked down a dark hallway. Leslie pointed to a closed door without opening it. "That's our room if you need us at night."

The next door she opened and revealed a boy's room with little decoration. "This is Jamie's room. He's next to yours. But don't worry he's a real quiet boy and sleeps good at night."

I thought about the nightmares I used to have and wondered if I should warn her in case they came back. I decided not to.

Leslie opened the next door and I couldn't believe what I saw. It was as if we had gone into a different house. It was very clean and beautifully decorated, although it seemed like it should belong to a much younger girl. The walls were a pale shade of blue at the bottom and light pink at the top with a white chair rail in between. There was an oak dresser against one wall, a matching vanity table on another and on the far wall sat a canopy bed with a floral spread on top.

Martha and I both looked at Leslie with surprise. She blushed. "I guess you can see that I always wanted a little girl."

I could see that, but it didn't make me feel warm or welcome. It made me feel weird and uncomfortable; like standing in a crowd with a spotlight on me.

I grabbed Martha's hand and wished she wasn't going to leave me here. There was nothing I wanted more than to walk out the door with her.

But an hour later Martha drove away and I was left behind with the Kessler's. The first night wasn't too bad. Leslie cooked a pork roast and we all had dinner together. She wasn't quite the cook that Ellen Sue had been, but she wasn't bad.

While we ate, Leslie talked non-stop, asking me questions and telling me all about them. Mark and Jamie were quiet, but Mark kept looking at me with a strange smile that sent a shiver up my spine.

After dinner, Jamie went back to his spot on the couch and Mark joined him. Leslie went about the house cleaning and I went to my room to unpack.

Things stayed pretty quiet for the first few weeks as I settled into a new school. The teachers were nice and helpful, but I had trouble making friends.

I wanted to get to know Jamie better, but that proved hard as he rarely talked to anyone. He spent most of his time outside carving wood into shapes with a pocket knife. On a couple of occasions, I sat outside with him and attempted to start a conversation. He gave simple, closed answers to my questions and I decided he really didn't want to be my friend. Maybe he didn't want to be friends with anyone.

That only left Mark and Leslie to talk to, but I stayed away from Mark as much as I could and Leslie's bubbly attitude was something I could only take in small doses. I had never imagined that anyone could be too cheerful.

I was grateful each Saturday when Martha came and picked me up for my visit with Jack. Seeing my little brother, happy and well cared for, was the highlight of every week. I dreaded leaving him and going back to the Kessler's house, but knowing he was in a good place was the most important thing. For that, I could face most anything.

About a month after moving into the Kessler's house, I was out walking around one day when Jamie called me over. I was surprised. It was the first time he had ever talked to me other than answering my questions.

I walked over to him, curious to say the least, about why he had called me. "What's up, Jamie?"

He looked up at me and handed me a piece of wood he had carved. "I made this for you," he said.

I took the piece of wood in my hand, surprised by how heavy it was. It looked like a small baseball bat, about half the size of a regular bat, with flowers carved into the bottom end.

I looked it over, then looked back at Jamie. "Thank you, Jamie. It's really nice of you to make me something."

He nodded but said nothing.

"It's really heavy for its size."

"It's a very hard wood."

"I guess it must be more difficult to carve hardwood."

He glanced at me, seeming to survey me. "Yeah." Then he walked away and left me standing there holding the bat.

That night I lay in bed looking at the intricately carved flowers on the bat. Jamie was surprisingly talented. I ran my finger over it, feeling how smooth his work was and wondered how long he'd worked on it and why he'd done it at all. Did this mean he liked me and wanted to be friends after all? Or did he just want to give it to someone and I happened to be walking by?

Taking one last look at it, I slipped the bat under my bed and turned over to go to sleep.

Two nights later, I was just getting ready to go to bed when Mark came into my room without knocking. I was glad I was dressed, but the nightgown I wore felt thin and inadequate with his eyes on me. Not knowing what to do, I stayed where I was, sitting on the bed and asked, "What is it? Do you need me for something?"

He nodded, his eyes flickering with a smile that never touched his lips, as he inched closer to the end of my bed. "Yes, I do need you for something…" He crept closer, his eyes roaming over my body, and I pushed back into the pillow that was propped against the headboard in an effort to stay away from him. I couldn't back up anymore and if I tried to get up and go around him, he could stop me. I thought about yelling out for help, but my voice seemed trapped in my throat as he eased himself onto the end of the bed.

"This is going to be our little secret." He crawled toward me on all fours. I felt panic rip through me. What was I going to do? I had to stop him somehow.

Then, as he lunged forward to grab me, I remembered the little bat under my bed. I dodged his grab, knocking him back a little, and threw my hand under the bed. I felt the bat under my fingers and I was glad I had not pushed it under there any farther.

I pulled it up just as Mark began to come at me again, anger lighting his eyes now. I lifted the bat over my head and brought it down hard, hitting Mark squarely in the head. He tumbled backward and landed, unconscious, on the floor at the foot of the bed.

For a moment I sat there in my bed, stunned by what had happened. I wasn't sure what to do. Then I remembered the phone number Martha gave me. I grabbed the handle of the drawer in my nightstand and yanked it open just as Leslie came running in to see what the loud crash had been.

I pulled a little slip of paper out of the drawer before looking up at Leslie. Staring down at Mark in horror, she crouched down and touched his head where it was bleeding. Then she looked up at me. "What happened? Did you do this?" Her eyes began to fill with tears and she shook her head. "Why would you do this? Why would you hurt him? He was only coming to tell you goodnight."

"No... That's not why he was here." I pushed past her and ran into the kitchen to get the phone.

"Mark? Mark, can you hear me? I'll get you help. You'll be okay," Leslie said and I knew I had to be fast with the phone. I punched the numbers in and waited impatiently as it rang on the other end.

On the third ring, Martha picked up. "Hello?"

"Martha? I need your help. Please! Come get me ... and hurry—"

Leslie grabbed the phone out of my hand. She glared at me and I backed away. She dialed 911 and told the operator her foster kid had gone crazy and hit her husband over the head with something.

For a moment I stood listening to her talk. Then I wanted to get away from her, but I didn't know where to go. I couldn't go to my room since that's where Mark was. And I couldn't run away or Martha wouldn't be able to find me. I believed she would help me. She might be the only one who would. So I grabbed my jacket that hung by the door. I slipped it on over my nightgown and walked outside, sitting down on the porch to wait for Martha.

Despite the fact that the house was out in the woods by itself, it was only minutes later when I heard sirens approaching.

The ambulance arrived first and the EMT's pushed past me as they hurried into the house with their gear. I watched them and wondered for the first time if Mark would be okay. I didn't like him and I hated what he had wanted to do with me, but I didn't like the way I felt when I thought he might be dead. If he was dead, then I was his killer.

*Was it even possible I had hit him that hard?* That little bat was very heavy and I imagined it could do plenty of damage with the right amount of force. I tried to think back on the moment and decide how hard I'd hit him, but it had all happened so fast. I couldn't be sure.

If he was dead what would happen to me? It was possible no one would believe he tried to hurt me. There was no evidence because I'd hit him before he grabbed me. If they didn't believe me, what would they do with me?

That thought terrified me and I had to know if Mark was alive. I rushed into the house and hurried through the living room. The hall was empty as I entered it and the only sounds came from my room. Then I saw Jamie peeking out of his room from behind the door. He looked over at me, and with little expression, he met my eyes and nodded slightly, as if in approval, before closing his door.

I crept down the hall. I didn't want anyone to see me. I just wanted to hear what was going on. I got close to my room and heard voices. One of them was Mark's.

"How bad is it, doc?" Mark asked.

"It looks like you're going to need a couple stitches and you probably have a concussion, but you'll be fine. Let's get you on this stretcher and take you to the ER."

I backed up and away from the room feeling relief wash over me. At least I knew I hadn't killed him. However, that didn't mean I wouldn't still be in trouble.

I found my way back into the dark living room and curled into the corner of the couch hoping not to be noticed. That's when I heard another voice coming into the house. "Beth!" Martha called as she came into the open door.

The EMT's came into the living room with the stretcher at the same time and pushed past Martha. Leslie hurried behind them and Martha stopped her.

"What happened?" she asked.

"That little brat you gave us hit my Mark with a bat," Leslie said in a fiery tone. "And for no reason at all … she just went crazy!"

"That doesn't sound like Beth. Where is she? I'll take her with me tonight. And I'll get someone out here to stay with Jamie until you get back from the hospital."

"I'm right here," I said coming out of the dark corner.

Martha stretched one arm out toward me and, with no thought, I ran over to her. She put her arm around me while Leslie glared at me. Her eyes bore into me and I wondered if she wished she had hit me when she took the phone from me.

Five minutes later Leslie left for the hospital and I was alone in the living room with Martha. "We have to wait here until another social worker comes to stay with Jamie," she said. "So, why don't you use this time and tell me exactly what happened here tonight."

I nodded and told her everything. With tears in my eyes, I said, "I didn't want to hurt anyone, Martha, but I had to get away."

Martha wiped my tears away. "It's okay, Beth. You did what you had to do. But now I have to ask you something and it might be hard for you to answer."

I nodded, looking right into her eyes.

"What exactly do you believe he was going to do to you?"

My brow furrowed as I tried to get the words out. It was hard to answer. "I know what he was going to do to me. He wanted to ... to rape me." I broke into tears again. Martha wrapped her arms around me and held me tight.

"It's going to be alright, sweetie. You stopped him. Thank God you stopped him!"

Yes, I'd stopped him, but now what?

Rebecca L. Marsh

# Chapter 27

It was late when Martha dropped me off at child services. I was tired and didn't really care where I slept. At least I felt safe there.

I stayed at child services for almost a week before Martha came back to see me with news. I figured she would be taking me to another foster home and I hoped it would be better than the last one, but my expectations were low.

When I saw the somber expression on her face, my heart fell.

She met me in a small TV room on the second floor of the building and as soon as she came in, she embraced me. "Hi, Beth. How are you doing?"

I shrugged. "I'm alright. But you don't look very happy. What's going on?"

"I've been arguing your case with my superiors all week. But I'm afraid I don't have very good news for you."

"What is it, then?" I wanted to get the bad news over with. If not another foster home, what else could they do with me? Would I be punished for hurting Mark? Could they send me to jail? The possibilities ran through my head and I began to panic.

"I'll start with the bit of good news I have," she said. "The Kesslers aren't going to press charges. We convinced them the implications of your side of the story would make them look bad no matter how it turned out … The bad news is, without any physical evidence we can't prove Mark was trying to hurt you." Martha looked me in the eye. "Sweetie, I believe you, one hundred percent. I've pleaded your case with everyone in social services, but they don't all know you like I do, and Mark has been very convincing."

"What does that mean, Martha?"

"Your case and your history have been looked over. And some feel this incident coupled with the incident at the Zimmerman's house is evidence of violent tendencies."

I shook my head, not believing my ears. "But he attacked me! And the thing at the Zimmerman's was over two years ago. I didn't hurt anyone then. It was just a teddy bear!" I gave her a helpless look. "Did you tell them why I did that?"

"Yes. I told them all about it. I tried, Beth. I really did." Her expression was as helpless as mine.

I looked at the floor. I didn't want to be angry with Martha. I knew she cared about me. "So what did they decide to do with me?"

Once I stopped crying, Martha helped me gather my things, then drove me to my new home; a group home. They had decided that I was too high risk for foster care. The house was a large Victorian painted a pale shade of blue with white trim. There was a big maple tree in the front yard and flowers were planted along the walk. It didn't look like a bad place … but looks can be deceiving.

The home was run by four women. Two that stayed during the day and two that were with us at night.

There were seven other girls living there. All were between the ages of twelve and eighteen. And we were all paired with a roommate. I got lucky. I was paired with a thirteen-year-old named Brenda who was placed in the home because she suffered from psychological trauma that caused her to have extremely violent nightmares. During the day her condition manifested itself in the form of severe stuttering.

Brenda was quiet and non-threatening. I could not say the same about the rest of the girls. One had been taken out of foster care because she was caught setting fires in trash cans. Two girls were there because they had injured other children in their previous foster homes. One had scars all over her arms from cutting herself. I wasn't really sure about any of the others, but they were not people I wanted to mess with.

They picked on Brenda sometimes and I wanted to stand up for her, but I feared that doing so would only result in me, and maybe Brenda, getting into a fight. So I did my best to follow Martha's advice and kept quiet and out of the way.

Sometimes that was difficult. I had to push my way through the kitchen at meal times in order to get any food. Most of the time I got food for Brenda as well. She was younger and more vulnerable than I, so I acted like a big sister, trying to help her.

Martha managed to convince her supervisors to let me continue my visits with Jack. They had to be supervised by a social worker, but at least I got to see him.

About six weeks after I moved into the group home, I woke up one morning to find Brenda crouched in the corner of her bed. She stared straight ahead, but didn't seem to see anything; at least not what was really there. She looked terrified and stuttered uncontrollably in what seemed like gibberish.

I got out of bed and went over to her. "Brenda? Snap out of it. Whatever the dream was about, it's over now."

She continued stuttering and staring straight ahead. She didn't seem to notice me at all.

I waved my hand in front of her face, trying to get her attention. "Brenda, come on, wake up." I hoped this was some variation of sleepwalking. Her eyes were open, but maybe she was still asleep, still dreaming. Nothing I did woke her.

I ran down the hall to get Lila, one of the social workers who stayed with us at night. Halfway down the stairs, I yelled out to her. "Lila, please come quick! There's something wrong with Brenda." I heard movement coming from the living room and then Lila appeared at the bottom of the stairs.

"What is it, Beth?" she asked, concern in her eyes.

"It's Brenda. She looks like she's awake; I mean her eyes are open. But she's just sitting there stuttering. She doesn't seem to see me and I can't understand anything she's saying."

Lila rushed into my room right behind me and hurried over to Brenda. She tried to talk to her, just as I had. Then she tried snapping her fingers in front of Brenda's face and shaking her gently. "Brenda, come on, sweetie."

After a few minutes of trying, Lila shook her head and sunk down on the side of Brenda's bed. She turned to me. "Beth, go get Marge and tell her to call for an ambulance," she said referring to the other night shift worker.

I ran downstairs where I knew Marge would be making breakfast. "Marge!" I yelled almost breathless by the time I reached the kitchen. "Lila wants you to call for an ambulance."

Marge furrowed her brow at me. "Is someone hurt? Was there a fight?"

I shook my head. "No. It's Brenda."

"What's the problem with her? I'll need to know when I call. Is she sick, or did one of the other girls hurt her?"

"I don't know what's wrong with her. She looks like she's awake, but she doesn't respond to anyone … she just keeps stuttering. Something's really wrong."

"Okay." She put her hands on my shoulders. "Don't worry. I'll make the call. I'm sure she'll be okay."

I nodded, but I wasn't convinced.

The ambulance got there within minutes and paramedics wheeled Brenda out on a stretcher. I watched it drive away.

After the ambulance left with Brenda inside and Lila riding along with her, I went inside and begged Marge to let me stay home from school and wait for news.

"No, ma'am!" she said. "You're going to school and hopefully when you get home, we'll know something about Brenda."

I sat silently through all my classes, preoccupied with Brenda. When the bell rang at three o' clock I was the first to jump up and run for the door. I waited for what seemed like an eternity on the bus before it reached my stop.

When I got off, I didn't linger on the street talking to friends like the other girls. I hurried home and rushed inside to find Caroline, one of the daytime workers, sitting on the couch with a magazine. She looked up at me and smiled.

"Hi, Beth," she said. "You sure got home in a hurry."

"Yeah, I'm worried about Brenda. Have you heard anything?"

"They're still running tests. Lucy's with her," Caroline said referring to her daytime counterpart. "She went straight there and took Lila's place."

I moved closer to Caroline. "Do they know anything?"

She shrugged her shoulders. "They've ruled some things out. But the rest is just speculation right now."

"What do they think is wrong?" I sat down next to her on the couch. But as she opened her mouth to answer, the other girls came bursting through the door in a flurry of movement and noise.

"Hi, girls," Caroline said. "Snacks are on the kitchen counter. One package of chips each and that's all." Then she turned back to me. "Sorry, sweetie. What I was going to say is that right now, they think Brenda had a mental break."

I furrowed my brow at her. "What does that mean?"

"It means she just couldn't handle the stress anymore. Her mind sort of shut down to escape from it."

I looked into my lap. A lot of bad things had happened to me, but I didn't feel like I was anywhere near losing it that bad. Was I just kidding myself, or was I stronger than Brenda? Was it possible that Brenda's past was worse than mine?

"Caroline?" I looked back up at her. "What happened to Brenda that messed her up so bad?"

Caroline let out a sigh and looked at me with sympathy. "I'm afraid I can't tell you that. Just like I can't share that kind of information about you with anyone else except other social workers." I nodded. I could understand that, and I was glad the other girls would never know the details of my life history either.

"If she did have a mental break, what will they do to fix her?"

Caroline shook her head. "If it is a mental break, there isn't a lot they can do."

"Then what happens to her?" I asked with a hint of panic in my voice.

"She'll have to go to a mental hospital for long-term care."

"How long term?"

"There's no way to know. She would have to stay there until she becomes responsive again, which may or may not happen."

Now I was scared. "You mean she could be like that forever?" The words sputtered from my mouth.

"It's possible. It's also possible she could be talking again tomorrow. These kinds of things are unpredictable. The mind is just so complex. And everyone responds to things in their own way."

I didn't sleep much that night. I couldn't stop thinking about Brenda. I hoped she would snap out of it and be okay. She was a sweet girl; one of few I had met in this home. I wished I knew what had hurt her so much. I'd never even asked her about her past and why she ended up here. Now I wished I had and I wondered if that could have helped her. Maybe she would be sleeping in her bed now instead of in the hospital. Maybe we could have helped each other.

As these thoughts ran through my mind, I also wondered what might have become of me if Mark Kessler had managed to rape me. What if I hadn't had that bat? Could I have ended up in that hospital staring at the wall? I shuddered at the thought and silently thanked Jamie again for his gift. I'd brought it with me when I moved and kept it under my bed. I felt safer knowing it was there.

Two days later, Brenda was sent to the mental hospital with no change in her condition. Two weeks after that a new girl was assigned to my room. Her name was Hailey and while she wasn't as mean as some of the other girls, she wasn't pleasant either. She constantly glared at me and sometimes she took my food. I missed Brenda.

Rebecca L. Marsh

# Chapter 28

After a long, but productive day with patients, Beth sat at home watching TV and feeling generally good about the outcome she'd had with Lindsay Arnold. Lindsay had come to an understanding with her mother and was learning to accept her father's absence in her life. She no longer needed Beth's help.

For Beth, seeing a patient get to the other side of their troubles was like a natural high, making her feel happy and warm inside. It was the reason she loved her job.

Her good mood had led her to stop on the way home for pizza, her favorite celebration food. Then it had led to something even more wonderful with Nolan, who was still grinning like an idiot as he worked on a new sketch.

Needing some comedy, Beth turned on the TV. The news flashed up first. They were talking about James Clifton again and Erin's upcoming trial. His picture flashed on the screen and Beth shivered. There was something about his face that tickled at the edge of her memory, but she couldn't figure out why. In any case, the news was not what she was in the mood for. She flipped the channel and found a rerun of *Home Improvement*. Somehow the episode she had seen on a few occasions before seemed twice as funny in her current state of mind. She laughed out loud as Tim Allen glued his forehead to a table.

When the phone rang, she reached over and picked it up, looking at the caller ID. It was Katie and Beth couldn't help herself as she answered, "Hello, Nolan's sex shop." This got a stifled laugh from her husband.

"Well you're in quite a mood," Katie said. "Have a good day?"

"Yes, I did. One of my patients no longer needs me … And … well, I already told you the rest."

"Yeah, that's great, little sis." Katie didn't sound very happy.

"You sound awful glum. What's up, Katie?"

Katie sighed. "Aaron came by … and things got a little out of hand."

"Really?" Beth raised her eyebrows. "What happened?"

"He came by to pick up his final paycheck. It was late, and I was the only one still there."

"Always the last one out."

"Yeah, and he knows that so I'm sure he picked that time on purpose. Anyway, I gave him his check, but he kept following me around, begging me to forgive him and take him back."

"Take him back romantically or give him his job back?"

"Both. He swore he wouldn't take advantage of me." Katie paused for a moment. "Beth, he got down on his knees and begged, really begged. What do you say to that?"

"I don't know. What did you say to that?"

"I told him to get off his knees and stop whining like a baby."

Beth let out a snicker. "Yeah, that sounds like you."

"But then he got real close to me … and he smelled so good … and he looked so good. We were standing in front of the big tank, and the sharks were swimming right by us. There's just something sexy about that, you know?"

Beth furrowed her brow trying to think of sharks with massive teeth as sexy. "Not really."

"Well there we were, the two-story tank glowing in front of us and he kissed me. And I don't know what came over me. I mean I went weak in the knees. That hasn't happened to me in years. Then I lost all control. I dropped my clipboard and the next thing I knew we were on the floor … ripping each other's clothes off."

"Right there in the aquarium, huh?" Beth pulled her legs up into the chair. "How was it?"

"It was great, but so unprofessional. And I still don't know what to do about him."

"I guess that means you haven't given him his job back yet."

"No. I haven't done anything else yet. When it was over, I pushed him out the door, cleaned up and went home. But I'm freaking out here. I don't know what to do."

"Do you want to get back together with him?"

"Oh, little sister, I want to do so many things with him. I just don't know if I should. And I don't know if it's really me or just some kind of hormonal thing. You know, the ticking clock and all."

"Okay. Well, I'd rather not hear about all the things you want to do with him. So what can I do to help you?"

"I think I need to see that baby. Do you think it would be okay if I came for a visit this weekend?"

"Sure. You're always welcome."

"You don't think Grace would mind me stopping by?"

"Of course not! She'd love to see you."

Thursday Beth was in her office pulling out all the case files for the patients she was going to see that day. When she got to Erin's she stopped and held it in her hands for a moment. She was going to spend the better part of the afternoon at the detention center. She would tell Erin the last part of her story ... and then, she hoped, Erin would start to tell hers.

Rebecca L. Marsh

# Chapter 29

I was out of school on spring break. I preferred to be in school, away from the group home and the other girls who lived there.

My sixteenth birthday had passed a week earlier and all I had to show for it was the yellow and purple fading remnants of a black eye. One of the girls gave it to me when I refused to give her my biscuit at dinner one night.

I looked out the window in the living room watching sprinkles begin to fall from the gray clouds when Martha's car pulled up outside. Martha was not assigned to any of the other girls here so I knew she was here to see me. I watched her get out of the car, and stand in the drizzle for several seconds as she stared at the house.

When the doorbell rang, Lucy answered and let Martha in. They spoke in hushed voices for a few minutes before coming into the living room.

"Alright, girls," Lucy said as they walked in, "I need all of you to go up to your rooms now." She placed a hand on my shoulder and in a softer tone said, "You stay, Beth."

The other girls protested as they left.

I tried to search Martha's face for answers, but she resisted making eye contact with me until all the others were gone and out of earshot. When she did look at me, she seemed to struggle for composure. I had never seen her so upset. I felt a cold stab of fear in my heart.

"What is it, Martha?" I pleaded. "What's going on?"

"Beth, sit down please."

"I don't want to sit down. Just tell me what's going on."

She looked right into my eyes and her expression was full of pain. "Sit down," she insisted. I walked back to the couch and sat. She sat next to me and began to fidget with her fingers, looking down and avoiding my eyes. She seemed to be having trouble choosing her words.

She sniffled a little, and reaching up, she wiped a tear from her eye. "I hate that I have to tell you this. In the ten years I've been a social worker, nothing I've had to do has ever been this hard."

Unsure of how to respond, I shrugged my shoulders. "Why? Are they sending me to jail now?"

I was trying to lighten the mood, but when Martha looked up at me she was sobbing. I shook my head, unable to imagine what could be so bad. "Please, Martha, tell me what's going on."

"It's Jack," she spat out.

"What do you mean?" The words spilled out of me. "What's wrong with him?"

Martha's face seemed to break. She fumbled in her purse and pulled out a tissue to wipe her eyes. "Oh, Beth, There's been an accident"

Fear gripped my heart. "An accident? Is Jack okay?"

"No, he's not okay ... he's ... he's dead."

The words hit me like a fist to my stomach. All the air rushed out of me and I struggled to get my breath, as the world spun around me. I shook my head furiously. "No!" I jumped up from the couch and backed away from her. "No! He can't be dead! He's just a little boy! This is a mistake. It has to be a mistake." I searched her face for the answer I wanted. She only shook her head, meeting my eyes with her own.

Martha got up and moved toward me, but I kept backing away. "No! It isn't true. You're lying!" Tears began to flow. "Why are you lying to me?"

She moved forward and grabbed me by my shoulders in one fast motion. "I'm not lying. I wouldn't do that to you." She shook me a little and got right in my face forcing me to look her in the eye. "It's a terrible truth, but it *is* the truth. And hard as it is, you have to face it."

"No … no, no!" I yelled again, fighting to pull away from her, but she held on tight.

"It can't be true!" I cried. "He can't be gone. He's just a little boy!" I continued fighting to pull away from Martha, but she held on, pulling me closer until I finally stopped fighting and collapsed in her arms. My body quaked with sobs and I couldn't got my breath. Martha wrapped me up in her arms.

We cried together for a long time, and when it seemed I had no tears left she continued to hold me close until I pulled away. I looked at her with my face red and swollen. "How did it happen?"

"Are you sure you're ready to hear that right now?"

I nodded.

She took a deep breath and collected herself, wiping her eyes with a tissue. "He was at Lake Keowee with his parents," she said.

I nodded. I had known about the trip.

"He went out swimming with a friend without asking permission and he tried to dive into the water where it was too shallow. His head hit a rock. The other boy tried to get help, but he wasn't fast enough. Jack—drowned, Beth"

In the back of my mind, I could see Jack's nine-year-old body lying face down at the edge of a lake. Pain seared through me. "I didn't protect him."

Martha shook her head. "No, sweetie, don't think like that. There's nothing you could have done to stop what happened. This isn't your fault."

Tears started to roll down my cheeks and my voice broke when I spoke again. "I'm his big sister. I was supposed to protect him."

"Sweetheart." Martha took my hands in hers. "He was miles away from here. This was an accident. It's not anyone's fault." She paused for a moment, pulled out another tissue, and wiped tears from my face. "I know this hurts … more than anything else could, but don't make it worse by placing blame."

I nodded but I didn't think Martha or anyone else could really understand how deeply this news cut through me. When Ellen Sue died I didn't think any hurt could be deeper. I could never have imagined this.

That night I couldn't sleep. Every time I closed my eyes, the image of Jack in the lake came back and I found myself overcome with emotion. I cried into my pillow several times. I begged God to change it; to bring Jack back to me. Then I got angry with God for letting Jack die and silently raged at him.

By the time the sun came up, I had run out of tears and rage and was sitting on my bed staring at the wall.

Hailey woke up and sat up in her bed, glaring at me as usual and pushing strands of messy brown hair from her face. "You look like shit," she said before getting out of her bed and leaving the room.

The minutes of that day dragged by as I sat in my room. I had no desire to eat or even to leave my bed. I cried off and on. At some moments I thought the tears might never stop and at others, it seemed my eyes were a dry well. Lucy and Caroline came in once in a while to check on me. They both tried to console me, but each time I pushed them away. I knew their intentions were good, but there were no right words to soothe this pain and I didn't want to hear anyone try.

Late that afternoon, from sheer exhaustion, I fell asleep on my bed. I slept straight through till the next morning. When I woke up I saw that someone had covered me up. I stayed in bed for at least an hour after I woke up, not wanting to face the day. I tried to go back to sleep, looking for a blissful escape. Sleep refused to take me.

I sat up when a knock came at my door. Caroline poked her head in without waiting for a reply. "Beth, I see you're awake."

I nodded, and she went on, "I need you to get dressed now. Martha's here and she's brought someone with her who wants to see you."

"Who?" I hoped it was someone I could refuse to see.

"I don't know who he is, but Martha says it's important and wants you ready in ten minutes."

I let out a long breath. An argument was pointless. "Fine. I'll be ready in just a few minutes."

"Okay. She's going to wait for you in the meeting room."

"Alright." I wondered why she wanted to meet me there. She usually talked to me in the living room or in my bedroom. Why the formality today?

I dragged myself out of bed and threw on some clothes. Then I went into the bathroom and brushed my hair and teeth before walking down the hall.

Martha waited for me in the hall. The meeting room door was shut and there was no one with her.

"What's going on, Martha? Caroline said someone was with you." I gestured to the empty space around us.

"He's waiting for you in there." She pointed to the meeting room door. "I wanted to talk to you first."

I shrugged my shoulders in a disinterested gesture. "What about?"

"First of all, I talked with the Zimmerman's and the funeral arrangements have been made. The viewing is tomorrow night. I'll pick you up at five o' clock and take you to the funeral home." Martha took a breath. "The funeral will be Saturday morning."

"Will you be picking me up then too?"

"I'm not sure about that yet. Do you have appropriate clothes? If you need something I can come by tomorrow morning and take you to the store."

I looked down at my feet, a wave of grief washing over me. "I have something." I thought of the dress I had worn to Ellen Sue's funeral. I hadn't worn it since and I had hoped to never wear it again. I wondered if many kids my age had been to two funerals in a single year.

Martha angled her head to look at my face and bring my attention back to her. I looked up and wiped the tear that had escaped.

"Now let's talk about the person who's waiting to see you," she said in an odd tone that seemed to indicate that I should know who this mystery person was.

I gave her a confused look. "Okay. Who is it?"

"Well, he says he's your father." She raised her eyebrows at me. "The funny thing is … there's no father listed on your birth certificate and when I asked your mother about it four years ago, she said she didn't know who your father was." She paused for a moment and let that soak in. "So … is there something you want to tell me?"

I took a deep breath and tried to figure out the best way to explain. "I didn't know him until I was ten. We met by chance and after talking to me a few times, learning who my mother was and some other stuff, he figured it out."

"Did you have any relationship with him?"

I nodded. "He was furious with Mama when he found out she'd kept me from him. He insisted on visits. I spent one day with him every weekend."

"Was there a problem with him? Was he abusive too?" There was concern in her eyes.

"No. Never."

"Then why in the world didn't you tell me about him before?" she asked with exasperation in her voice and hands thrown up in the air. "You could have avoided the foster homes." She gestured around her. "You could have avoided living here."

"I needed to stay with Jack. I didn't know we would be separated."

"It's possible he would have been willing to take Jack too. We could have asked."

"And he might have said no. I wasn't willing to take that chance."

"And when the two of you were separated ... why not tell me about your father then?"

I shrugged and turned away from her, crossing my arms over my chest. "Why should I want him if he doesn't want me?" I turned, looking at Martha and trying to keep my emotion under control. "He didn't come looking for me. I figured if he really wanted me, like he said he did, he would have tried to find me."

Martha put her hands over her face and paced the hall for a few seconds. Then letting her hands fall she looked me in the eye. "Well, he wants to see you now." She motioned to the door. "We've probably kept him waiting long enough."

I took one step toward the door and stopped.

"What's wrong?" Martha asked.

"I'm not sure I want to go in there." There was a feeling rising up in me that I didn't think I could describe. "I haven't seen him in so long. I didn't think I would ever see him again."

She hugged me and stroked my hair. "I know this is a lot. You're going through so much right now ... but, Beth, if he was good to you before, then I think you should give him a chance. Talk to him. Ask him why he didn't come for you. Who knows, this might be a really good chance for you. Maybe you could get out of here and have a real home again."

I looked at her, searching her face. I couldn't even begin to think straight. All I had were raw feelings; pain and despair over losing Jack, and conflicting feelings about seeing my father again. Martha's face was filled with encouragement as she urged me to the door and I felt I had to trust her. She had never steered me wrong. I reached for the knob and turned it. Then with a deep breath, I pushed it open and stepped inside.

Dad stood by the window, looking out. He turned to look at me when the door creaked. He hadn't changed much. He wore the same short haircut and goatee, but the goatee was now flecked with more gray. His blue-green eyes were filled with concern and also, I thought, pain.

I saw his eyes register shock at the sight of my bruised eye. He came forward and reached out to me as if to inspect the damage, but I pulled back from him. He dropped his hand and looking somewhat defeated said, "Hi, Beth."

"Hi."

He motioned to the small wooden table and I moved to take a seat. He joined me, sitting on the other side. He looked down for a moment, then met my eyes. "I'm really sorry about your brother." He paused putting his face in his hands. When he looked at me again his eyes glistened with moisture and his voice was thick with emotion. "I've been trying to figure out what I want to say to you, but all the words I come up with seem to fall short. I don't know how I can ever tell you how sorry I am that I didn't come for you four years ago. I wasn't there for you and I'm so ashamed of that."

His voice was earnest, but I needed more. I needed reasons why he hadn't come to my rescue. "Why didn't you?"

He wiped tears from his eyes. It took him a moment to answer and I got the impression he was choosing his words with care. "It sounds like a stupid, hollow answer now. I feel foolish saying it, but it was because of that last time I saw you … Do you remember? It was the day I saw bruises on your arm. The day I tried to take you away from your mother."

I nodded.

"You convinced me to leave without you. I was so worried about you, but you were only worried about your brother." He shook his head and stroked his goatee again in an absent gesture. "You tried to tell me Jeff had hurt you by accident. I didn't believe that. I was scared for you and I wanted to keep you safe. But you said if I took you away from your brother you would run away to get back to him. I could tell you meant it. So I left you there … against my better judgment."

He stopped for a moment and a tear rolled down his face. I was taken in by his pain, but still, I was mad at him. He had no idea what I had been through.

"That's the reason I didn't come after you when I heard you'd been taken away from your mother. I wanted to, Beth. I really did. But I didn't think it was what you wanted."

I furrowed my brow, trying not to cry. "I still don't understand. Why didn't you think I would want you to come?"

He started to reach for my hand, but stopped when I pulled back. "Because I thought you wanted to stay with your brother. I never thought about the two of you getting split up." He looked at me with such deep regret that I almost moved to take his hand. "I wish I had known. I wish I had come for you. I never would have let you end up in a place like this if I had known. And I missed you. I missed you so much. When I saw in the paper yesterday the story about what happened to Jack, I decided it was time to find you … past time."

His eyes dropped to the table. "I won't blame you if you never forgive me. I've been no kind of father to you. But I thought you were with your brother. I thought you were somewhere safe."

A part of me wanted to reach out to him, cry with him and hold onto him. But I couldn't. I kept my emotions under tight control as he fought to control his.

We sat for a moment, neither knowing what to say next; how to repair the rift. Then he spoke. "Grace and I are going to the funeral on Saturday. We would like it if you'd allow us to pick you up and take you with us."

I looked him over. I still felt anger toward him, but I remembered Martha's words. Maybe this was a good chance for me.

"Okay." I nodded. He tried a smile, his face brightening a little with hope. Instead of smiling back I got up from the table and left him alone.

# Chapter 30

I didn't realize until I was dressing the next day for Jack's viewing that I was treating my father the same way I had treated my mother after I went into foster care. I had given him nothing but cold distance. I'd done that to Mama out of resentment because she didn't take better care of Jack and me. Because she had stood by while Jeff beat us and didn't try to stop him.

Now I had to think, did my father deserve the same treatment? I was upset because he didn't save me, but when he had once tried, I wouldn't let him. And the reason he didn't come for me was the same reason I hadn't told Martha about him myself.

It had taken me close to two years to give Mama anything other than anger after I left her house. Could I afford to keep being angry with my father?

I was almost sure he was the one who called the police that night. I couldn't know for certain. Martha had only told me the call was anonymous. I couldn't imagine one of the neighbors had decided to make a call like that. They never had before. And really, with as far apart as the houses had been, I wasn't even sure any of the neighbors could hear anything.

I struggled to pull up the zipper in the back of my dress. Then looking in the full-length mirror, I smoothed the silky black fabric with my hands. Lucy had pressed it for me and it looked perfect, maybe too perfect for such a terrible occasion.

I had slipped on some sheer pantyhose and black shoes with a low heal. I was fully dressed and had brushed my dark hair that now hung, bangless, just past my shoulders. My feet held to the spot I stood in like lead. I couldn't bring myself to move from that spot. The thought ran through my head that maybe if I didn't move, if I didn't go to the viewing or the funeral it wouldn't be real. So I just stood there staring into my own sad eyes.

I'm not sure how long I'd stood there when a knock came at the door and Lucy poked her head in. I looked at her but didn't speak, so in the absence of an invitation, she moved into the room and stood behind me looking into the mirror with me.

Lucy was a round Hispanic woman who managed to fix herself up in such a way that she often attracted more approving glances then most of the women who were half her size. She ran her fingers down my hair, then touching a finger to my face near the bruised eye she said, "How about I take you into the bathroom and fix this eye up?"

Still staring at my reflection I said, "I don't think I can do it ... I don't think I can leave this spot."

Lucy frowned at me in the mirror. "I'm so sorry, honey," she said with her hands on my shoulders. "But you need to do this."

"It's too hard." My voice broke on a sob. "I can't go there and look at him."

"I know ... it's hard. But you have to do it. You won't be able to move past this until you do." She paused for a moment running her hands up and down my arms. "Now come on, sweetie, dry those tears and let me fix that eye for you before Martha comes."

Lucy did a more than impressive job fixing my eye. When I looked in the mirror that bruise seemed only a memory. But even with the beautiful job she'd done on the makeup, my cheeks still seemed far too pale and my eyes looked like blue-green clouds ready to spill over at any moment.

*Did anyone else know what it was like to be in this much pain? Had anyone else ever been this sad?* At that moment I didn't think it possible.

By the time Martha got there, I felt almost as if I was in a trance. Martha took me by my shoulders and led me to the waiting car.

As she drove us toward the funeral home, I sat in the back seat, not speaking a word. And as we moved closer to our destination I felt, with each turn of the wheels, a pressure in my chest that pushed down and made it harder and harder to breathe. By the time we arrived, my breath was coming in shallow bursts and the weight of my grief seemed to hang around me, almost as if it were tangible.

The car pulled to a stop and Martha got out, but I just sat there in my seat staring out in front of me. *This isn't real! It can't be real!*

Hot tears stung my eyes when Martha opened my door. "It's time to go in now."

I shook my head. "No. Please don't make me go in there."

"You don't need to do it for me, honey. You need to do it for you." When I didn't budge she spoke again. "And if not for you, for Jack."

She knew me well, knew just the right button to push. I would do anything for Jack.

I closed my eyes for a moment, gathering courage. Then, taking a deep breath, scooted across the seat and out the door. Martha put her arm around me and led me to the wide porch at the front of a big white house.

As she led me in the front door, I could smell flowers and an odd musty smell, like the way clothes smell after they've been packed away. Despite the odd smell, the place was beyond clean. Everything seemed to sparkle. The floor was a dark wood, polished to a shine and the walls were pale blue, which matched my mood.

The first room beyond the foyer was lined with chairs and floral-print sofas. There was a table in the middle with a large vase of flowers on it. I walked in and sat on one of the sofas. Martha sat down next to me and held my hand.

Since I was a family member, we had arrived early. Not many people were there yet. Of course, Matthew and Karen were there, and after I'd been sitting there for a few minutes, they came into that room and approached me. Matthew knelt down in front of me. "Hi, Beth. How're you doing, sweetie?"

I looked at him, his face full of concern and hurt. Then I looked up at Karen, who stood to the side of him, and saw in her eyes the same deep despair that I felt.

"Not too good," I said in a whisper. "But I guess you know that."

He nodded, and as we both began to cry, I leaned forward and hugged him.

When I let go of Matthew he got up and Karen, who was wiping tears from her eyes, knelt down and hugged me too. "Do you want to go see him?" she asked as she stood back up.

I shook my head feeling my chest close up again.

"We'll go with you," Matthew assured me but I only shook my head again.

He nodded, "Okay. I know it's hard. Maybe you'll feel up to it in a little while."

"We'll come back and check on you," Karen said.

Martha and I sat there a while longer as people began to arrive. Many of them were people I didn't recognize and I figured they were friends and family of the Zimmerman's. Then I saw someone come through the door that I did know, my father.

He glanced around until he saw me and then walked over. Just like Matthew had done, he knelt down in front of me and without worrying how I might react, he took my hands in his. "Hi, sweetheart," he said as if we'd never been apart. And even though I had pulled back from him just the day before, even though I had been mad at him, at that moment his presence felt comforting and safe. I leaned into him, laying my head on his shoulder, and let tears fall.

"I'm so sorry you're hurting." He kissed the top of my head.

"She's been sitting here since we arrived an hour ago. She hasn't been to see him," Martha said to my father.

*Had it really been only an hour?* It seemed like an eternity.

I heard my father sigh as his arms went around me in a gentle hug. Then he pulled back, raised my chin, and forced me to look him in the eye. "Come with me, Beth. We need to go see your brother."

Trembling, I shook my head. "No. I can't."

"You need to say goodbye to him." When I didn't budge from my seat he continued. "I'll be right with you. You can lean on me all you want. But you need to see him, even if it's just for a few seconds."

I took a couple steadying breaths, then with legs that felt like Jell-O, I got up and let my father lead me into the room where the casket sat. I held his arm tight, making sure he was close, as we walked up to the white box that was held up by a long wooden pedestal.

As I looked into the box, I could feel my breath quicken and a small gasp escaped my mouth. Jack's body lay there on a bed of white silk. He was dressed in a blue suit with a blue and white striped tie. His hair was combed to perfection and his eyes were closed as if he were sleeping. He looked so small and fragile.

I closed my eyes and prayed for strength. I wanted to turn and run away, pretend this wasn't happening. But that would only be a fantasy and the truth would find me. The clock couldn't be turned back.

Opening my eyes, I looked at Jack. Touching a hand to his cheek, I felt coolness where once there had been warmth. "I love you, Jack," I whispered. "I always will love you. We have to say goodbye now. But I'll never stop thinking about you." Tears streamed down my face and fell into the casket leaving wet stains on the white silk. Then, with my voice weak and trembling I said, "Wait for me in heaven, buddy."

I turned back to my father, who had stayed at my side, and found his arms waiting for me. He hugged me tight and the love I felt from him gave me strength. Then, as we turned away from the casket, someone came through the doorway who I had hoped to never see again. I stopped frozen next to my father as Jeff walked in with my mother on his arm.

I sucked air in sharply and held it as years of horrifying memories washed over me. It hadn't even occurred to me they would be here. But regardless of what the state had decided, they were Jack's natural parents. They were there before me whether I was ready or not.

Mama gave Dad a disgusted look before turning her tear soaked eyes to me. It had been two years since I had last seen her and those years had not been kind. She'd aged a great deal. Her face showed the stress of, I had to assume, many beatings. But she would never admit they were happening.

"Oh, Beth." She moved toward me with her arms outstretched. I backed away, but her arms still found me and pulled me into a limp hug. Jeff looked on with his face molded into the expected expression of grief, but his eyes showed indifference, even at the wake of his son.

I breathed in the scent of Mama's perfume with my eyes closed. She had always worn that same scent. It's funny the things you grow to miss.

Mama turned away from me and walked up to the casket. Then she looked at the table next to it where there was a picture of Jack and under it an engraved nameplate that read "Jackson Matthew Zimmerman." I watched my mother's face change from grief to shock and at last to red-hot fury.

Matthew and Karen stood near the casket and I could tell they saw the change as well.

Mama picked up the nameplate and spun toward the Zimmerman's. "This is *not* his name! How dare you change his name?" She jabbed her forefinger toward Jack and with her voice rising said, "This is *my* baby and this is not his name!" Mama reared back and launched the gold nameplate straight at Karen, just missing her. "You take my baby away and then you think you have the right to change his name? Who gave you the right?!"

I'm not sure what came over me, but I found myself charging at my mother, my voice just as loud and powerful as hers. "The state gave them the right, Mama! And whose fault is that?"

She looked at me in disbelief. After all that had happened it still never failed to surprise her when I didn't take her side. "How can you say that?" she asked me, her voice lowering to a near whisper.

I didn't drop my voice. I glared at her, rage in my eyes as I raised my hand and pointed to Matthew and Karen who stood horrified by this display. "They took care of Jack. You could have gotten us back." I gestured to Jeff. "But you choose him instead of us!"

Mama shook off my comment about Jeff as if it had never been said. "They took care of him?" Her voice rose again with each syllable as she threw her hands toward the casket. "This is how well they took care of him!"

"This was an accident, Mama! They loved him and *they* never hurt him on purpose!" I screamed it at her, my voice filled with venom. Then for a few seconds, I glared at her while she looked back at me, shock, hurt and even a little confusion filling her eyes.

The entire funeral home had gone silent and everyone seemed to be holding their breath while they waited to see what happened next. I looked at Matthew and Karen. Matthew nodded in my direction gratefully. He held Karen close as she sobbed into his shoulder. I looked back at Mama who still hadn't recovered from what I'd said. Then shaking my head at her, I turned and walked back to my father's side.

As I moved into his waiting arms, I looked up at his face. I didn't see anger in his eyes, but only pity as he looked at my mother who had fallen to her knees on the floor, weeping.

I wondered what he thought when he looked at her; the woman he had fallen in love with one summer. Could he see even a remnant of the girl she had once been? Or just the pitiful ghost of a person she'd become.

She was, I realized as I watched her on the floor, the one thing I hoped to never become.

Dad put his arm around me and turned me away from Mama, guiding me to the door and back to Martha who was still waiting for me in the front room. She looked at me with both surprise and pride on her face. "Wow!"

I winced a little realizing that everyone there was very aware of what had gone on. They had all heard me *and* Mama.

Martha moved forward and wrapped her arms around me. "I'm sorry you had to deal with that, sweetie. But you did a great job of it. You've got guts, kid."

When Dad came the next morning to take me to the funeral, I was waiting for him, ready to get it over with. I wore the same black dress, the same shoes. Lila had ironed the dress again so it looked fresh.

When we got to the car, Grace, Ronnie, and Sarah waited there for us. They had all changed since I'd seen them last. Grace wore her hair a little shorter. Ronnie had sprouted up so tall and Sarah was no longer a baby.

Ronnie jumped out of the car as I walked up and greeted me with excitement. "Beth! I missed you." He grabbed my hand and pulled me into the backseat with him.

He beamed at me, not seeming aware of the hurt I was feeling. His smile was warm and genuine and too much like Jack's for me to look away from it. I gave a weak smile back to him.

"I missed you too, Ronnie." I looked around him to the little girl in the next seat who was almost eight now. "And I missed you, Sarah."

She looked at me, then sunk back into her seat without responding. Clearly, she didn't remember me. She'd been so young the last time I saw her.

Ronnie chatted the whole way to the church. I heard all about his school, his teacher, and his friends. I listened but I wasn't able to contribute much to the conversation. Ronnie didn't seem to mind, and I didn't mind listening to him. He was so much like Jack.

When we arrived at the church Dad instructed Ronnie and Sarah to be quiet and still once we went in. The speech must have been meant for Ronnie since Sarah hadn't said a word. Both of them nodded and obeyed as we went in and found a seat right behind Matthew and Karen in the second row. Martha showed up a few minutes later and sat down with us.

The service was short but beautiful. The preacher spoke about the difficulty in losing a child, going on to assure everyone that Jack was with God in heaven now, smiling down on us. When he was done several people came forward to say what a wonderful child Jack had been and how lucky Matthew and Karen were to have gotten him.

When the service was over everyone drove to the cemetery for the conclusion. Mama and Jeff were there but they stayed in the back and they stayed quiet.

At the end of the graveside service, the casket was lowered into the ground. Then white roses were passed out and everyone went by the casket and dropped the roses. When my turn came I stepped forward and looked down on the glossy wooden casket that now sat in a vault in the ground. Emptiness filled my soul, and I realized how much of my life I'd been living for Jack.

"I love you, Jack," I said on a sob as I dropped the rose.

I walked back to Dad feeling emotionally drained. I wanted to go home, fall into my bed, and sleep the rest of the day away.

When I reached him, Grace stood next to him but the kids had already gone to the car. Dad pulled me close and hugged me and I didn't resist.

"Beth," he said when we separated. "I talked to Martha and arranged for you to go to lunch with me today so we can talk."

I looked at him and then at Grace. "Is Grace coming too?"

"No," Grace said. "You and your father need to talk alone right now. So he's going to drop the kids and me off at home and then take you out for lunch."

I nodded. "Okay."

Dad took me out to a quiet restaurant. It was on the late side for lunch, so the restaurant wasn't too busy and we were seated right away at a booth near the back. At first, we just sat looking at the menus, but after our order was taken, Dad started to talk.

"I can't tell you enough how sorry I am that I haven't been there for you these last few years." He shook his head and looked down at the table. "And to find you living in that place … I'm just so sorry." He tried to keep control, but a tear slipped down his cheek.

My heart went out to him. I reached out a hand and laid it on his arm. "I've only been there for a few months. Most of the time I was in a really good place with people who really cared for me."

He looked up. "Tell me about them. I want to know all about where you've been and who you've been with."

"John and Ellen Sue ... those were their names. They had a daughter named Katie. I still call her every month." I didn't mention that I'd been lying to her ever since I left her parents' house. I told him how they had wanted to adopt me and how good they'd been to me. Then I told him about Ellen Sue getting sick and how heart-broken John had been when she died. "He loved me, but he wanted me to have a happy home and he didn't think he could give that to me anymore."

"He sounds like a good man. I hope I'll meet him someday."

"Me too." I didn't tell him about the Kesslers. The look of guilt on his face was something I couldn't bear to multiply.

"I've been talking to Martha quite a bit in the last couple days."

I nodded, not really sure where this was going.

"I told her that I want you to come and live with Grace and me," he said.

I looked at him for a moment before responding. *Did he really want me? Or was it just the guilt?*

"There's no proof that I'm your father, so blood tests will have to be done. After that, if you want to, you can come live with us ... Do you want to live with us, Beth?"

"I ... I guess so."

"I can't force you. And I wouldn't, even if I could. This is your choice." He paused for a moment stroking his goatee. "It is what *I* want. You need to know that, Beth. I want you with me. I want to know you."

His eyes were filled with emotion and sincerity. He really meant it.

I started to speak but he held up a hand. "I know I can never make up for the time I've missed with you. That's not what I'm trying to do. But I want to get to know you ... starting right now."

Despite the sadness of the day, I felt a smile playing at the corners of my mouth. His sincerity reminded me of how much I had loved being with him before. I found myself nodding my head. "I do want to come live with you, Dad. I missed you."

Moisture welled up in his eyes as he took my hand in his. "I'm glad. I'm so glad, sweetheart. We'll make things right now."

# Chapter 31

As Beth finished her story, Erin watched her intently. Her expression seemed thoughtful, but Beth couldn't tell at all what was going on in the girl's mind. She waited a few moments, staring across the table and hoping for Erin to say something.

"I've told you my story, Erin. Now it's your turn." Beth tried to sit without rocking in a chair that had one short leg.

"Did you ever see your mother or Jeff again?"

"Not while she was alive. She died a few years ago and I went to the funeral. Jeff was there, but I didn't talk to him." She had tried very hard at the funeral to not even look at him.

Erin nodded. She seemed to still be sizing Beth up. "Did you ever tell anyone in your family about Mark Kessler?"

"Not at first. But I started having nightmares again and it came out in therapy."

Erin bit her lower lip. "What did they think of you when they knew?" She was looking hard at Beth and the more answers Beth gave the closer Erin looked to tears.

"My family didn't think any differently about me than they had before I told them. They just felt sad that I'd gone through that and been punished for defending myself. Everyone wanted to help me." Beth reached for Erin's hand as tears began to spill from her eyes. "Just like I want to help you."

"You really do know what it's like, don't you? But you're so lucky to have people that love you. I only have Kayla. My mom hates me because of it." Erin was still trying to hold her hurt inside, but her control crumbled and tears began to flow freely.

"Your mom hates you because of what?"

"Because ..." She cast her eyes downward. "Because of the way my dad loved me."

A sick feeling built up in the pit of Beth's stomach as she began to get a picture of what Erin was trying to tell her. She closed her eyes for a few seconds and prayed for God to give her the right words, the right questions. She needed Erin to keep talking, letting her in. If Erin closed off again, Beth wasn't sure what she could say to get her talking the next time.

Beth gave Erin's hand a squeeze. "I know this is hard, but I need you to tell me what exactly you mean. In what way did your father love you?"

Erin's face scrunched up as she fought for control. She closed her eyes for a moment, then she looked at Beth with an expression that seemed sad and shameful at the same time. "He loved me the way he loved my mom." Her voice broke and sobs took over as soon as the words were out.

It was all Beth could do to keep from crying herself. She had been trying to get Erin to talk for weeks now. For a while, she had suspected that Erin's father had raped her, but to know for sure, to hear Erin say so, was even more heart wrenching than she'd imagined. She looked at Erin with sympathy and wondered if she could really help. Was it even possible for her to be whole again when her innocence had been stolen from her by the person who was supposed to protect her? This was worse, Beth knew, than what she herself had been through ... worse than the beatings.

Beth took a deep breath and prayed for strength. She was going to have to ask Erin some very hard questions.

"Erin, I'm so sorry for what you've been through. I know what you're telling me, but for the record, I need you to be specific. What exactly did your father do to you?"

Erin lifted her head and searched Beth's eyes with her own. She opened her mouth to speak, but the words didn't come. Her brow knit together as tears spilled over her rosy cheeks again. *How does anyone hurt a child this way?*

Beth waited patiently, holding her hand, for Erin to regain control. "It's okay, Erin. He can't hurt you anymore. Just try to tell me what he did to you."

Erin looked back up and swiped tears away with the back of her hand. "He ..." She fought hard to remain in control. "He raped me."

As soon as the words were out her composure broke and tears poured out. Beth got up from her chair and stooped down next to Erin's. She wrapped her arms around the child and held her while she cried. There were more questions to ask, but they could wait. For now, Erin needed to let herself cry and know that someone in this world cared about her pain.

Beth called Lisa as soon as she got back to her office. Lisa didn't have a lot of time left before Erin's court date. She needed the new information as soon as possible. She would probably want to be there the next time Beth talked to Erin so she could ask her own questions and hear everything for herself.

Helping Erin was still a long shot, Beth knew. There wouldn't be any physical evidence to back up Erin's claim. The judge might believe her, and then again he might think she was lying to try to save her own skin. But at least they had something to go on now.

Lisa picked up the phone on the second ring.

"Lisa, its Beth. I just came from the detention center and I have big news for you."

"Talk to me, honey!" Lisa's voice came through almost bubbling with animation.

"She talked."

"She talked? You mean something we can use?"

"Well, she hasn't told me everything yet, and I don't know if you'll be able to convince a judge to listen when there's no evidence, but she told me why she shot him."

"Was it abuse, like we thought?"

"Definitely. He raped her."

"Shit, that's terrible!"

"You should have seen her, Lisa. I wished I could drag that son-of-a-bitch out of his grave and shoot him myself." Beth paced her office with the phone in hand.

"This might sound callous, but that's actually a very good thing. With no physical evidence, we both know it's going to be very hard to convince the judge. If we hope to even see a lighter sentence, he's going to have to feel her pain."

"That's one more problem," Beth said. "It took weeks to get her to talk to me about this. How will we get her to testify?"

"Well, that's a problem for me to deal with. You did your part." Lisa paused, then said, "Did she say anything else?"

"No. I didn't want to push her too hard." Beth sat down in her desk chair and swiveled to look out the window where the sun was now setting.

"When will you be able to go back out to the detention center with me and talk to her again?" Lisa asked. "I don't want to wait too long. There are a lot of questions I'm hoping she'll be willing to answer now. But I'm thinking she'll feel more comfortable talking to me if you're there."

"I can't do it tomorrow, my schedule is full. I have a three-hour slot already blocked out for Erin on Monday."

"That'll work. What time should I meet you out there?"

Beth looked at her calendar. "I'll be heading out there right after lunch. How about meeting me at the diner and then we can drive out there together?"

"Sounds good."

"You got some time this weekend?"

"Not much. Josh has a soccer game on Saturday. And Sunday is always busy, but for you, I can make some time. Especially now that you've worked your magic with my client."

"Just doing my job. I was hoping you would be available Saturday night. Katie's coming to town." Beth turned in her chair and opened her file drawer to look for the files she needed to take home.

"Girl's night out, huh? I think I can fit that into my schedule. But I'm going to have to sweet talk Keith into staying home with the kids ... by himself."

"I'll have Nolan go over and hang out with him."

"The guys watch the kids while we go out? I am liking the sound of that, my friend. Do you think we could go to Dominic's and watch the drunks try to sing?"

"That sounds like something Katie would enjoy and since I'm aiming to help her unwind ... I think Dominic's would be perfect

"Is Katie stressed about John?"

"That's part of it, I'm sure, but it's not the main issue for her at this moment. She's having man problems and she's not sure what to do about it."

"I'm sure we can help her figure it all out. Listen, I gotta go now. See you Saturday, okay?"

"See you then."

Rebecca L. Marsh

# Chapter 32

Katie arrived in town Saturday morning. She and Beth spent some time catching up, then went out for lunch and shopping, leaving Nolan to his sketches. He didn't mind having some alone time to work on his art. When he was finished he would probably take Lulu to the park for a walk and do a little people watching before heading over to stay with Keith.

Beth and Katie enjoyed a light lunch, saving room for an indulgent dinner later, and bought new outfits to wear when they went out. Then they came home, took showers and in their tradition as sisters, did each other's make up before heading out to Dominic's to wait for Lisa.

They got there early enough to secure a table in the bar area that offered a good view of the stage, which would be nice later when the karaoke started. They ordered drinks, a beer for Katie and a margarita for Beth, and talked.

It was about forty minutes later when Lisa arrived, looking out of breath and tired. "Sorry I'm late, girls." She sat down at the table.

Beth squinted at her. "You look terrible, Lisa. And there's something in your hair."

Lisa wiped at her hair. "I think it's a few of Anna's cheerios. Could you help me get them out?"

Reaching across the table, Beth pulled the small pieces of cereal out of Lisa's hair. "What happened to you today?"

"It really started last night and just kept going," Lisa began. "Josh was having monster dreams and kept Keith and I both up almost all night. I think I finally got to sleep around four o' clock and then my little sweet Anna, who got a full night's sleep, woke me up again at five thirty."

"So, on an hour and a half of sleep, I had to take Josh to his soccer game. We went home after that and we all took a nap along with Anna today. Then Keith had to take Josh to a birthday party while I took Anna to a play date."

"Sounds like a long day," Beth said.

"You have no idea. And it gets better. At the play date, Anna got into a fight with her little friend Anthony and they started throwing cheerios at each other. I guess I got hit in the crossfire and didn't realize it.

"Then Keith was late getting back from the birthday party and that's why I didn't have time to fix my hair and makeup before I left. Of course, it would have been nice if my dear husband had bothered to tell me about the cheerios in my hair."

"Wow," Katie said. "That's some day. And all we did was shop."

Lisa gave Katie an unamused and somewhat threatening look. "Just rub it in why don't you."

Katie sat back holding up both hands. "Sorry."

"Maybe you'd like to order a drink," Beth said to Lisa.

"Good idea." Lisa signaled a waiter. "Cup of coffee, Please," she said to him.

"I was thinking you might want something a little stronger after a day like that." Beth smiled.

Lisa angled a look at her. "Are you kidding? As tired as I am, if I drink anything alcoholic I'll be asleep on this table in the next half hour. And I came to hear the drunks sing. So I need caffeine." Lisa leaned in closer to Beth whispering, "And you two better not drink many of those things, because I can tell you now not to count on me as your designated driver. I already feel lucky to have made it here alive."

"Okay." Beth leaned back in her seat. "Well, I'm sure your day will give Katie something to think about. She's considering the possibility of having a family."

"Really?" Lisa raised her eyebrows in Katie's direction. "And I thought you were having man trouble."

"Yeah, that too," Katie said.

"She's not serious with anyone right now. She's just trying to decide if she wants to have a family or not ... With or without a man," Beth said.

"I see," Lisa said as her coffee arrived and was placed in front of her. She put in some creamer and two packets of sugar. "Well, I won't lie and tell you it's easy. But don't let my day scare you. This was an extreme situation. And no matter how crazy it gets, or how sleep deprived you are, when your baby smiles at you, it's all worth it."

A few minutes later the conversation turned to Katie's boyfriend problems. Then the waiter returned and they ordered dinner. They talked and laughed and stayed until almost eleven o' clock watching the karaoke, which was pushing the envelope for Lisa who was barely holding on at that point.

And since Lisa was in no condition to drive, Beth drove her home while Katie followed in Beth's car. Then, after dropping off the half-asleep Lisa, Beth and Katie went home for the night.

Sunday morning Beth, Katie, and Nolan drove to Grace and Ron's house for brunch. Ronnie and Ashley would be there so Katie would get the chance to meet Hunter.

When they arrived, Grace was overjoyed to see Katie. It had been over a year since Katie had come to visit.

"Katie! It's so good to see you, sweetie!" Grace hurried forward to hug Katie, seeming very small next to Katie's tall and sturdy frame.

"It's good to see you too, Grace." Katie returned the hug. Grace released Katie and hugged Beth and Nolan before ushering all of them into the house where the wonderful smells of bacon and waffles already filled the air.

They walked into the living room where Ashley and Ronnie snuggled on the couch while Ron held little Hunter on his lap.

Katie said hello to the lovebirds on the couch and then went straight to the baby like a moth to a flame. "Oh, he's just beautiful!" Katie gushed earning proud smiles from the parents. "Can I hold him?"

"Certainly," Ron said lifting the small bundle so Katie could take him. He made a fussing sound, unhappy with being awakened by the movement. But Katie cradled him and rocked him back to sleep. She looked at the baby, peaceful in her arms and a smile spread across her face.

With Katie settled with Hunter, and Nolan enjoying a conversation with her father, Beth decided to go to the kitchen and help Grace finish getting the meal ready. "Can I help out?" she asked walking into the sunny kitchen.

"Oh, honey, I can put you to work. You can make the waffles. The batter's already made. You just pour it onto the iron, close it up, set the timer and when you hear the ding, you take it out," Grace said.

"I think I can handle that." Beth poured batter onto the iron.

"Is Katie enjoying her visit?"

"Yeah, it's been good. We went shopping yesterday and then had a girls night with Lisa."

Grace smiled. "That does sound like fun. Did you do each other's make up?"

"Of course." Beth grinned in return, not a bit surprised that Grace knew all her little habits.

"She really seems to be enjoying Hunter too," Beth said. "Maybe she'll decide she wants one of her own."

"Well if she ever does have one, you tell her I'll be happy to stand in as a surrogate grandmother ... If she wants."

"I'm sure she would love that." The timer dinged and Beth dumped the waffle out on top of a stack of them. "To be honest though, I never really imagined Katie having a baby. But she looks pretty good out there … Better than I've been."

"Maybe she'll decide she doesn't really want a baby, who knows. But sometimes seeing the end coming for your parents can make you think about your own life."

Beth nodded. "She feels like if she doesn't have kids, her family will end with her. I guess I don't feel that way because of Ronnie and Sarah. But on my mother's side, I'm all that's left and I don't remember going through any of that when Mama died."

Beth's comment was met with a curious silence from her step-mother. Beth waited a few seconds and then said, "You mean you don't have any wisdom to share on that topic?"

Grace turned and just looked at Beth for a moment. Then leaving the stove, she walked over, placed her hands on Beth's shoulders and looked into her eyes. "There are some questions you can only answer for yourself." Then without another word, she went back to the stove, turned it off, gathered up her bacon and a bowl of fruit, and motioning for Beth to bring the waffles, headed into the dining room. Mere seconds later everyone was at the table; talking, eating, laughing and passing the baby around to everyone but her, and Grace's wise words left her mind for a time.

That afternoon Beth stood in her driveway and hugged Katie goodbye as she left to head back to Wilmington. Beth was glad she and Katie had always stayed in touch. They'd had a lot of good times together and had helped each other through some hard times as well.

Beth spent the rest of the afternoon doing household chores while Nolan prepared his lesson plans for the upcoming week. After that, they cooked a light dinner together and ate before settling down to watch a movie on TV.

It wasn't until she was in bed that night that Beth began to think about her conversation with Grace again. Lying there in the dark, Grace's words came back to her. *There are some questions you can only answer for yourself.*

That thought spun around in Beth's mind like a mouse in a wheel. Why didn't it bother her that her mother's family might end with her? Her grandparents were both dead now, along with her mother, and all that was left was Aunt Amy and herself. Amy never had any children, or even married for that matter. So Beth was the only hope of the family going on. Yet it didn't bother her that it might not. Why was that?

Truth be told, she didn't even think much about her mother's family anymore, at least not until recently. When she went to her mother's funeral, Amy had been there. They'd made eye contact a few times, but Beth hadn't even made the effort to speak to her. She had just attended the funeral and left. She had been uncomfortable seeing Jeff and wanted to leave as soon as possible. Was that really the reason she had avoided talking to Amy, though?

When she really thought about it, she realized she had been relieved when she and Jack had gone into foster care rather than going to live with Amy or her grandparents. She also realized that Martha had never told her why she hadn't gone to live with family ... and she'd never asked, never felt a need to ... until now.

# Chapter 33

Monday morning came with a gloomy start, making Beth want to stay in bed, but she pushed through the morning with patients and by the time she met Lisa for lunch the sun was shining and the clouds were nothing more than a memory.

The two ate their lunch on the restaurant's patio, enjoying the sun, and then hurried off to the detention center to see Erin, each driving their own cars.

Beth wasn't sure what to expect. She hoped Erin would be open to talking with Lisa. She also hoped they weren't putting Erin through the painful process of reliving a horrific experience only to get the same result in court. It frustrated Beth to feel so certain Erin was telling the truth but have no way to prove it.

They went through the usual procedures entering the detention center. After which, a guard, one Beth had seen several times before, led them into an interview room where Erin sat waiting. She sat with her elbows on the table and her head in her hands. She looked like nothing more than a sad little girl.

Erin glanced up at them, and Beth forced a smile. "Hi, Erin. How are you doing today?" Without waiting for a reply, she walked to the table and sat a bag of M&M's down in front of Erin.

Erin didn't return the smile. In fact, she looked terrified, like a wounded animal waiting for the slaughter. Still, she picked up the bag of candy and held it in her nervous hands. She glanced up at Lisa and then down at the candy again, toying with the bag. "I guess you want me to tell you what I told her," she said to Lisa.

"Yes." Lisa walked to the table and took a chair. She put her briefcase on the table and opened it, taking out a small stack of papers. "I'm also going to set up a recorder." She removed the recorder from her briefcase and placed it on the table. "And I'm going to have to ask you some questions. This won't be easy, Erin. I'm going to be asking you to tell me what happened with more detail than you did when you talked to Dr. Christopher."

Erin didn't look up, but she nodded and Lisa continued as Beth took a seat.

"Erin, did your father hurt you?" Lisa asked.

"Yes," Erin mumbled.

"I'm sorry, Erin, but I need you to speak clearly for the record."

Erin looked up with sad eyes and said, "Yes, my father hurt me."

"How exactly did he hurt you?"

"He raped me," Erin said after a brief pause. It came out a little easier this time.

"When did this occur?" Lisa asked without pause. This wasn't the first time she'd had to do this kind of questioning with a teenager.

Erin tore open the bag of M&M's and put a morsel into her mouth before answering. "It started on my thirteenth birthday."

"Then you're saying your father was raping you for two and a half years?"

"Yes."

"Did he hurt your sister, Kayla?"

At this question, Beth noticed a flicker of rage and defiance in Erin's eyes but her voice stayed even. "No. But he would have."

Lisa looked up at Erin and saw the hard expression on her face. "We'll come back to that later. Did your father ever hurt your mother?"

"Not as far as I know."

Lisa nodded flipping to the next paper in her stack. "Did your mother ever hurt you or Kayla?"

Erin paused a moment and thought about her answer. "Not physically."

Lisa met Erin's eyes trying to gauge truth from lie. She moved on to the next step in her questioning, the part that was certain to break Erin's calm.

"Erin, I want you to tell me about your thirteenth birthday."

Erin's brow furrowed and it seemed to Beth she could actually feel the girl's pulse quicken. "Tell you about it?" Erin asked.

"Yes. I need to hear an account of exactly what you say your father did to you." Lisa looked up and saw the hurt and fear in Erin's eyes. She reached a hand out and covered Erin's. "It's okay. Just take your time and tell me what you remember."

"I remember all of it." Erin's voice broke a little. "I can't forget it."

Erin closed her eyes and took a deep breath. Beth could imagine a little of what Erin felt. Telling the horrors of your life was a bit like deciding to jump off a cliff, hoping you land in deep enough water.

"It was a Tuesday. I was excited when I got home from school. I was thirteen and we were going out to celebrate. My parents said they would take me anywhere I wanted, so I picked pizza. That might not seem like a big deal, but it was something Kayla and I never got. Mom and Dad only took us to fancy restaurants.

"We went to Mario's, and it was great. We got pizza, just the way I like it, and Dad gave us quarters for the video games. He even played some himself. After that, we went home and ate birthday cake and watched a movie before bed. Dad kept looking at me funny, but I didn't worry about it. I was having so much fun."

"When did the fun end?" Lisa asked.

"After I went to bed that night."

"What happened then?"

"My father woke me up late at night. He was on my bed straddling me and when I saw him it startled me. I started to scream, but he slapped his hand over my mouth to stop me." Erin began to sob, but she continued. "He said, 'Don't yell, honey. You're a big girl now and I'm going to show you what big girls do.'"

Beth felt a chill go up her spine hearing Erin's words.

"He sounded drunk. He was close to my face and his breath stank," Erin continued. "I was scared of him for the first time ever. I never liked my parents that much, but I'd never been afraid of them either."

"What happened next?"

"He told me he would let go of my mouth if I promised to be real quiet, so I nodded and he let go. Then he started touching me. He ran his finger down my neck and opened the buttons on my pajamas. It was all I could do to keep quiet, but I was afraid that yelling would make him do something worse." Erin's lip trembled. "Nothing could have been worse."

"What did he do next, Erin?"

Erin fought back emotion. Beth could see her breath coming in short gasps.

"Next, he … he—" Erin's face broke and tears spilled out as she tried to relay her most painful memory.

Lisa looked at Beth and nodded in the girl's direction.

Beth got up and took her chair to the other side of the table. She sat down and rubbed a hand down Erin's back as she sobbed. "It's ok, Erin. He can't hurt you anymore."

Erin turned her tear-streaked face to Beth and said, "He touched my nipples and I begged him to stop. 'No, Daddy, please.' But he didn't stop. He smiled at me, a scary smile. His hands ran down my body and into my pajama bottoms and I begged him again to stop. But it only seemed to make him like it more.

"He got rougher and nearly ripped my pants when he pulled them off. I cried, but tried not to make any sound. I felt so scared, but I didn't want Kayla to see what was happening." Erin shook her head and said with a whimper, "I didn't want anyone to know what was happening."

Beth took Erin's hand. "It's not your fault. You have nothing to be ashamed of."

"It doesn't feel that way," Erin said weeping. "I feel so much shame every day. I think I must have been really bad to deserve what he did."

"No, Erin, you weren't. He was sick and you were a victim. No one deserves that." *Except maybe those who commit that crime against their own children.*

Lisa, trying to keep a professional distance from the emotions of her young client, made eye contact with Beth and nodded. So Beth took the lead in getting Erin talking again.

"I know how hard this has to be for you. But you've made it this far. We need you to tell us the rest. What happened next?"

Erin looked at Beth with the sadness of a wounded puppy and Beth's heart broke for her. Then Erin squeezed her eyes shut and fought the swelling emotion back under control.

"He opened his pants and pulled them down a little. I could … I could see … things a daughter shouldn't see, and I just wanted to escape, so I closed my eyes and turned my head away. Then—" Erin shook her head. Her face was scrunched up and tears ran down her cheeks. "Oh, God, it was so horrible." She sobbed and wiped her face with a tissue that Beth handed her. "My eyes flew open when he shoved inside of me. It hurt. It hurt so much. I cried and cried, begged him to stop hurting me. But he didn't stop." Erin held her face in her hands, letting some of the emotion out. Then she picked up her head and glanced at each of the women sitting with her.

"When it was over, he got up and said to me, 'Happy birthday, princess.' Then he left me there, just like that. I spent the rest of the night crying into my pillow."

Beth put her arms around Erin and let her cry. When her tears were all used up, Erin looked up at Beth and whispered, "If you see Mrs. Abernathy again, will you tell her something for me?"

"Sure," Beth said, "what is it?"

"Tell her I'm sorry I was so mean to her. She was nice to me. She didn't deserve to be treated that way."

"I think she knows your anger wasn't really meant for her. She cares about you, Erin. It would break her heart to hear what you've told us today."

Erin nodded then looked at Lisa. "Do you have any more questions for me?"

"If you're up to it today, yes,"

"I'm okay now. Let's get as much of this done as we can today."

"Okay." Lisa looked over her papers. "Did you tell anyone about what your father was doing to you when it was happening?"

"No. I was too ashamed. And I didn't think it would help."

"Did your mother or sister ever know? Did they see or hear anything that you know of?"

"Kayla didn't know ... Well, she knew I was upset and I'm sure she noticed the changes in me and in my parents—"

"What changes in your parents? Did your mother know what was going on?"

"My mother never saw anything. I mean it's not like she was there watching. And I don't know if she heard anything. I tried always to be quiet so Kayla would never know. But somehow my mother knew ... or she knew something anyway."

"What do you mean?"

"She was different after it started ... cold, but only with me. At first, that was all, but as time went on and my father's visits continued, she got nastier."

"Nastier how?"

"Well, she continued to be cold and distant. She treated me like an obligation. I mean, she had always been that way a little with me, but after the … visits began, she started to make it very clear she didn't want me around, that I was a burden. And she said things too… mean things."

"What kind of things did she say? Give me an example."

"Well anytime my father was nice to me, she would say something like, 'you might think he's yours, but he'll always be mine!' And then a few months before … before I killed him, she started calling me a tramp and a whore. She would say it when only I could hear her, whisper it under her breath."

*Wow!* Beth knew what it was like to have a parent say terrible things to you. But this went beyond disturbing.

Lisa stopped for a moment, clearly just as shocked as Beth was, but keeping the shock hidden under a professional facade that never wavered. Beth understood the need for that, but was always a little amazed at her friend's level of control.

"Erin," Lisa said, "This went on for the last two years and you never told anyone?"

Erin shook her head. "No, I didn't tell anyone. I didn't think anyone could help me."

"Alright." Lisa straightened her papers and put them in her briefcase. "I think it's pretty obvious, but for the record, did you kill your father because he was raping you?"

Without a moment's hesitation, Erin looked Lisa in the face and said, "No."

This time Lisa was not as able to hide her surprise, and for a few seconds, she just stared into Erin's face. "No?"

"No," Erin repeated. "That's not the reason I killed him."

Lisa furrowed her brow. "Was your father hurting you in some other way?"

"No."

"Then I'm afraid I don't understand. If it wasn't the rapes and he wasn't doing anything else to hurt you, then why *did* you kill him?"

"I didn't do it for me at all. I did it for Kayla."

"Why? You said he wasn't hurting her?"

"No … But he would have."

"What do you mean? How do you know that?"

"He was going to start raping her too. I've known that, been sure of it, since the first time he did it to me."

"How could you be so sure of that?"

"Because … she was the pretty one. Daddy always said so. And I could tell by the way he had started looking at her. It was the same way he looked at me right before my thirteenth birthday … hungry and sinister, like a lion waiting to strike. I didn't know what it meant the first time," she said with a sob. "I was so stupid. But when he started looking that way at Kayla, well I knew what it meant and I couldn't let him have her too. So, one night when he was asleep, I snuck into his study and stole the key to his gun cabinet. Then I waited a couple days, as long as I could. But the night before Kayla's birthday was as long as I could wait. So that night when he was in the living room watching TV with mom and Kayla, I went into his office again and I opened the cabinet and took out a gun. Then I shot him."

"I didn't kill him for me. It was too late for me. I was already ruined and I had accepted that. But I *had* to save Kayla. I couldn't let her end up like me."

Beth sat listening. She knew that look, the one Erin spoke of. She'd seen it on the face of Mark Kessler from the first time she'd met him.

"But, Erin," Lisa said, "If you were so worried about Kayla, why did you shoot your father right in front of her? Didn't you think that would hurt her?"

Erin's head dropped, her hair cascading off her shoulders to surround her face. "I didn't want to do that." She looked back up at Lisa, a pleading look in her eyes. "I would have waited and done it after he was asleep—after Kayla was asleep in her own room, but Dad always looked at his guns and locked his study before going to bed. I couldn't get in there after that and he would have noticed if one of his guns was missing."

Lisa nodded, a sad look on her face, as she picked up her briefcase and recorder and stood up. "Okay, Erin, that's all for now. I'll be back to see you again soon ... And, Erin, you did well."

Beth turned to Lisa as they left the detention center and walked back out into the sunlight. Taking Lisa by the arm, Beth stopped them both on the sidewalk. "She's telling the truth, Lisa. I believe her absolutely."

"I do too and I wish I could tell her everything will be okay now that she's told us her story. But I can't." Lisa shook her head. "If it had just been about her it would be simpler. Bringing Kayla into it complicates the matter. I mean hearing what was done to her, a judge might believe her and take pity on her, reduce the charges and lighten the sentence. But to tell that judge she killed him because of something she believed he would do to her sister, while that sister is oblivious to it all, that's another matter. I just don't know what the judge will do. I can't even make a guess because I've never dealt with a case quite like it."

Beth's mind trailed off into thought.

"Got something on your mind that you want to share with the class?" Lisa said.

"No one's even talked to Kayla, right?"

"Right, but Erin says Kayla didn't know anything."

"Erin *thinks* Kayla doesn't know. But their mother knew even though Erin doesn't think she ever saw anything ..." Beth stopped for a moment. "I think we need to talk to Kayla. Maybe Erin wasn't as quiet as she thought."

"I'm sure I could get the judge to allow that in light of what Erin told us. But I'll have to talk to her. I can't take you in there and since she's a minor, her mother will have to be there as well."

"Yeah, I wish there was some way around that. There's no telling how that might affect what Kayla is willing to tell you."

"That's true. But I think you're right, it's worth a shot. I'll set it up and let you know what I find out," Lisa said with a shoulder shrug as the two parted ways. Then Lisa turned back and called, "I'll do my best for her, Beth."

Beth nodded. "I know you will. You wouldn't know how to do anything else."

# Chapter 34

Tuesday morning Lisa called to let Beth know she'd set up an interview with Kayla on Friday. Beth was so anxious waiting for the results that it made the rest of the week seem more like a month.

When Friday came, and Lisa finally called, she told Beth very little. She said that the meeting had been delayed waiting for a child advocate to arrive after the start of the interview. Apparently, Victoria had gone crazy when Kayla began to tell Lisa what she knew and had to be restrained and removed after trying to hit Kayla. Then she proceeded to bite one of the security guards who came to take her out of the room. She would be undergoing a psych evaluation very soon. And Kayla would be going into state custody pending the results.

Lisa went on to say that Beth had been right in thinking that Kayla knew more than Erin thought. When the advocate had arrived and the meeting continued, she had provided Lisa with the testimony she needed to argue Erin's case in court.

Beth thought she might go crazy herself waiting to find out what Kayla had said, but she was quickly distracted when, later that night, she and Nolan packed their suitcases for a weekend trip to Wilmington to see Katie and John.

They left first thing Saturday morning and pulled up in front of Katie's apartment just after eleven. In her usual way, Katie came running out to meet them before they could even get out of the car. "Hey, little sister!" She ran up to the car, a big smile on her face. "I'm so glad to see you!" She looked over and threw a smile at Nolan. "And you too, Nolan."

After hugs were exchanged they took the luggage inside and sat talking while they waited for the pizza that Katie had already ordered.

"So," Katie began, "you seem to be in pretty good spirits. Things going well?"

"Actually they are. I had a breakthrough with my most troubled patient and I've managed to go a few nights without nightmares."

"That's great!"

"Yeah, so how are things with you?"

"Okay." Katie looked a little sad. "Dad's getting worse though. It's been over a week since he last remembered who I was."

Beth nodded but didn't get a chance to say anything because the doorbell rang and Katie jumped up to answer it.

"It's pizza time," Katie said carrying the box into the kitchen. Beth and Nolan got up and went in to join her.

"That smells good," Beth said.

Moments later they sat down in the living room to eat pizza and decide on a movie to watch.

They all settled on *Evan Almighty* and before she knew it, Beth was laughing so hard tears were streaming down her face. Beside her on the couch, Nolan sat holding her hand and lightly stroking her arm.

The next day all three of them drove to the nursing home to see John. As soon as they got there, one of the nurses approached them and spoke to Katie. She was a short Hispanic woman with a quick smile. "Good morning Ms. McMillan."

"Good morning, Rosa. We're here to see my father."

"Of course, but you should know he's having a rough start today. He was very upset and confused. They had to give him a sedative to calm him down. He may already be sleeping again."

Katie put a hand on the nurse's shoulder and Beth could tell they had gotten to know each other. "That's okay, Rosa. We know what to expect."

"Alright then, go on in." Rosa walked away.

Beth, Nolan, and Katie went down the hall and an orderly let them into John's room. He was on his bed tossing and turning. The group walked to the bed and gathered around John. "I'm here, Dad. It's me, Katie. Beth's here with me, and Nolan."

John squinted up at them, shaking his head. "I don't know you," he said as he tried to focus on each of the faces looking down at him. "Who are you? Why am I here? I want to go home."

Katie cast a sad look at him. "This is home now, Dad."

Hurt, confusion, and a little anger flashed on his face but the sedative was starting to work and he was growing too sleepy to fight.

"Shhh," Katie said in a soft tone. "Just relax now, Dad."

He used the last bit of energy he could muster to shake his head again. "I want to go home ... I want t ... t ... to ..." Then he drifted off.

Beth looked up at Katie and saw tears in her eyes. She reached out and took Katie's hand as their eyes met. "We're losing him, Beth. I don't know if he'll ever know me again."

Beth nodded. "I know."

Nolan looked at the two women and patted his wife's arm. "I'll just go see if there's someplace to get coffee around here."

"Okay, thanks, honey."

As he walked out of the room, Beth and Katie looked at each other again. "It's gonna be okay, Katie. I'll be here for you. The whole family will."

"They're great people, your family."

"Katie ..." Beth looked at her sister earnestly. "Your family was there for me when I needed someone. They became my family. Even when I went to live with my father and Grace, I still thought of you and John as my family too. I hope you'll let my family be yours now also. Nothing would make them, or me, happier."

Katie nodded as her eyes filled with tears again. For a few moments, the two of them just stood looking down at John.

Beth was the first to speak again, "So, did you decide about the motherhood thing?"

"Not until yesterday." Katie met Beth's eyes.

Beth furrowed her brow. "Okay … what did you decide then?"

"I think I'd like to have a child, but I don't want to have a baby alone. I don't want to do it until the circumstances are right. I want to have what you have first." Katie stopped and looked at Beth. "I was watching the two of you yesterday and that's what I want. I know at my age it may be too late to have kids by the time I find that someone, but I don't want to have them with just anyone."

"What about Aaron? Are you still seeing him?"

"I was." Katie sighed. "I'm going to break it off though."

"I thought maybe he was the one for you. You seemed to really have something special with him."

Katie shook her head. "What I have with Aaron is a strong physical attraction and great sex. It's not love. It's not what you and Nolan have, not even close."

They were both quiet for a moment and Beth squeezed Katie's hand before letting go of it.

"You know, now that I think of it, the last time I remember really being in love was when I was in college. And that guy dumped me for a short, busty freshman," Katie said.

"His loss." Beth grinned at her sister and got a smile in return just as Nolan came back in holding a tray with three cups of coffee on it.

Nolan looked at the two women as he offered the coffee and a slight smile spread across his face. "Gotta love those sister moments. One of these days I'm going to find out what you girls talk about that turns tears into smiles and smiles into tears."

Beth and Katie smiled at each other and both said, "It's a girl thing. You wouldn't understand."

They stayed with John for a while, watching him sleep, and Beth knew he would be gone soon. She also knew she may never have another lucid moment with him, that he may never again look at her with recognition. It pained her to think that when his final moments came and she said goodbye to him, he wouldn't know her.

She tried to find comfort in the fact that she would still remember him; his smile, his kindness and the way his eyes used to twinkle. She would never forget what a great father he was or the love he'd given her.

Rebecca L. Marsh

# Chapter 35

Erin was brought before the honorable judge Walker on a Tuesday morning. Beth sat in the front row behind Lisa and waited for her turn to testify. Beth had been out to see Erin during the previous week. She seemed better now that she'd told her story—as if a weight had been lifted. She was relieved to know that Kayla was safe and away from their mother. That was more than Erin had hoped for. It was still going to be a long, hard road for her. She would never again be a normal teenager. Once innocence was lost, it wasn't possible to get it back.

Kayla was there with her caseworker in the same row. Victoria had been found psychologically incompetent and was spending some time in the hospital's psych ward. She would only be brought in to testify.

Beth watched as the police officers who had arrested Erin told the story of a terrible murder scene. Their voices were filled with passion when they told the judge that the murder of James Clifton was pre-meditated and cold-blooded. Beth could see in their eyes how much they wanted Erin to suffer for what she'd done. But they didn't know how much Erin had already suffered. If they did know, she wondered, would they feel differently?

After the police officers, the prosecution brought in their psychologist to talk about Erin's state of mind. Then they brought in Victoria who looked like the perfect victim when the prosecutor questioned her, but fell apart and became angry when it was Lisa's turn. It wasn't very hard to get her to show her true colors.

The trial was closed to the public and only certain people were allowed in the courtroom, but everyone in the room listened intently as Erin told her story in heart-shattering detail. Erin cried, but continued all the way through. Beth was proud of Erin's courage.

The hardest part to watch was the prosecutor questioning Erin. Harry Turner was a tall, trim man of about forty-five years. He had light brown hair that had begun to show flecks of gray and intense brown eyes. He wore a dark gray suit with a red striped tie. *That color was supposed to show power and confidence, wasn't it?*

He did seem very sure of himself, but Beth hadn't ever known a lawyer that wasn't, at least not in the courtroom.

He paced in front of Erin for a few seconds, gathering his thoughts, before starting. "Miss Clifton, How long had you been planning to murder your father?"

Erin flinched at the question, then answered with resolve, "For about two months. Ever since he started looking at my sister like she was an entrée."

"You say that he raped you. Was he raping you when you pulled the trigger, ending his life?"

"No."

"Why didn't you report this alleged rape?"

Erin paused a moment, choosing her words. "My parents were wealthy and well known in this town. I didn't think anyone would believe me." Erin's voice was calm and even.

"But you could have gone to the hospital and the evidence would've been there to support your story," Turner said. "Why didn't you?"

Turner expected Erin to get flustered by this question, Beth was sure, but Erin remained calm.

"I should have, but I was only thirteen the first time and the hospital is miles away from my house and my school. I didn't feel I could trust anyone. I didn't even know a doctor could tell what had happened to me." Erin paused looking down for a moment then she looked back up and directly at Turner's face. "I also didn't want to tell anyone because I was ashamed."

"I see." Turned continued to pace the floor. "So you were too afraid and ashamed to come forward then, but now you're not ... How convenient. And we're all supposed to believe you with no evidence. Then you can get away with murder, is that it?"

"Objection, your honor," Lisa said, "badgering the witness."

"Sustained," said Judge Walker.

Erin spoke up and answered anyway, "Think about it for a minute Mr. Turner, if your father had raped you when you were thirteen, how many people would you have wanted to tell?"

Beth watched as Mr. Turner stood there for a moment, stunned by Erin's response. "No further questions," he said before turning and walking back to his seat.

Beth herself was next on the stand. Her original reason for spending time with Erin was to get her side of the story. But once that story had been told, it had been her job to gauge Erin's mental state now and also at the time of the murder. That was what she would be testifying to here.

She was nervous because she knew that her testimony was not really a big help to Erin's defense. She was sure Erin had never lost control of her sanity. She'd killed her father knowing exactly what she was doing. That meant the officers were right. It was pre-meditated. And the judge might not care that Erin did it because she believed it was the only way to save her sister.

The last one on the stand was Kayla. Beth knew Lisa had saved Kayla for the end because she wanted that testimony to be the freshest in the judge's mind when he made his decision.

Kayla took the oath to tell the truth, then settled into the chair on the witness stand. She wore a light blue dress that made her big blue, angelic eyes stand out. Per Lisa's instructions, it was in a style girls Kayla's age rarely wore, making her appear younger and more innocent.

Lisa went through the basic questions. Then she started asking the important ones.

"Kayla," Lisa began, "did either of your parents ever hurt you?"

"Well my mother tried to hit me the first time I talked to you, but other than that, no."

"Were you ever aware of either of your parents hurting your sister?"

"Yes," Kayla said without hesitation.

"In what way did they hurt Erin?"

"Mom just said a lot of mean things to her, called her names. But Dad ... well ..." Kayla paused, seeming to have difficulty saying the words out loud with so many people watching.

"What did your father do to Erin?" Lisa prompted walking a little closer to Kayla.

Kayla looked down at her lap. She took a steadying breath, then looked up at Lisa. "He raped her." Her voice was little more than a whisper.

"How do you know this?"

Kayla's face looked almost ashen.

"When it first started more than two years ago, I really wasn't sure what was going on. But I heard Erin crying sometimes. I also heard banging sounds and a couple times I heard Erin begging our father to stop."

Lisa tilted her head trying to make eye contact with Kayla who looked into her lap and twisted her hands together. "Stop what? Do you know what he was doing that she wanted to stop, Kayla?"

"For a long time, I didn't know. But a couple weeks before ... before she shot him, I heard Erin crying again and I also heard that banging noise. I had never before gone to her room to see what was going on, and I don't know what made me go that night, but I did ... and I saw what he was doing to her."

"What exactly did you see?"

The room was silent except for the clicking of Lisa's heals on the hardwood floor.

Kayla looked up to answer the question. Her face was streaked with tears and her lips trembled as she spoke. "I saw my father on Erin's bed. He … he was on top of her … and …," Kayla's voice disappeared into a sob as more tears rolled down her face.

"It's okay, Kayla. Take your time," Lisa said handing Kayla a tissue.

Kayla dried her eyes and collected herself. "He was on top of her and his pants were off. Erin's nightgown was pushed all the way up around her neck. He was …," Kayla's voice trailed off and came back much quieter. "He was raping her. The headboard was banging the wall, making that noise. Erin was crying, begging for help … But I didn't help." Kayla's face seemed to crumple with grief. "I was so scared. I ran back to my room and got in my bed. I didn't help her … I didn't help her then and I didn't help her later either."

"You're helping her now." Lisa made eye contact with Kayla. Then she looked at the judge and said, "No further questions, your honor."

Lisa went back to her seat and Mr. Turner came forward.

"Miss Clifton, your sister says she was too ashamed to come forward and tell someone what happened to her. Why didn't you tell anyone when you saw what was happening? If your father really was raping her, then why *didn't* you help her?"

Kayla's face filled with sadness as she struggled for an answer. To Beth, she seemed almost as helpless as a five-year-old. Her mouth quivering, Kayla said, "I was just scared. I thought about telling someone, then I imagined what might happen to Erin, and to me if I told the wrong person."

"I find it hard to believe you didn't have one person to tell whom you knew you could trust. All those teachers at your school, they were all against you and Erin?"

Kayla was not as cool under pressure as her sister and by now she was so upset she couldn't even speak. Lisa jumped up. "Objection, your honor!" she said. "The witness has already answered the question. How many ways does Mr. Turner intend to ask it?"

The judge looked at the prosecutor. "Mr. Turner, do you have any *other* questions for this witness?"

Turner gave a slight huff at being shut down. "No, your honor," he said before walking back to his seat.

Beth glanced at Lisa and saw a hint of a smile. Maybe things were looking up. The judge told Kayla she could step down, and closing arguments were made. Then court adjourned for the day. The judge would come back with his decision the following day.

Beth struggled for sleep that night. All she could think about was Erin. She wondered if the judge believed Erin and Kayla. Or did he think the girls were making it up to cover a murder?

Beth rolled over in bed, trying not to disturb Nolan. She had testified in several juvenile cases, but she'd never felt this connected; never worried so much about the outcome. Erin had suffered terrible abuse at the hands of her father, as Beth had with her step-father. But Erin was not the first similar case she had dealt with. Somehow she was different and Beth couldn't figure out why.

Around three-thirty Beth fell into a fitful sleep. Her dream began in the living room of her mother's house, except there was nothing there. No furniture and no other people. She looked around the empty space. It looked like it had the day she'd first seen it when she was four years old, but there was something different. Beth walked to the wall in the front of the room where the window was and ran her hand across it. It had dents in it here and there, and scars in the paint. These were the marks made by years of violence.

So where did everything go? Beth had never been back to this house after the police came that night when she was twelve. She'd never seen it empty again after they first moved in. The walls had been smooth then, the paint unblemished.

Beth glanced into the kitchen as she approached the hallway. She could see the crack in one of the cabinet doors that came from a plate hitting it when Jeff had hurled it in an angry rage. An image of her mother crouched in a corner, hands over her face, came to mind.

She shook that off and continued down the hall. She peered into the room her mother had shared with Jeff. Then she walked into Jack's room. It sat empty like the rest of the house, but for some reason, she could hear the faint sound of music. She realized it was the music from the mobile that hung over Jack's crib when he was a baby. The sound brought back memories and also pain. Beth raised a hand to her cheek and wiped a tear away.

She walked out of that room and went into the one that had been hers. The walls were scarred in here also. Beth walked to one of them and ran her hand along it. Then, reaching the closet, she opened the door and looked in, remembering all the times she had tried to hide in there. She could see herself, just a girl, huddled in the back corner with Jack. The two of them trembling and trying not to make any noise.

As the image faded away, Beth turned and was surprised by what she saw behind her. It was Jack; looking as he had just before he died. He smiled at her and held a hand out toward her. She stepped forward, without even seeming to make the decision to do so, and reached her hand out to his. He grabbed it and they stood there looking at each other.

"I've missed you," Beth said.

"Don't miss me. I'm always with you."

Beth glanced around the room again. "The house is empty, but not like it was when Mom and Jeff and I first moved into it. The walls are scarred from all the times Jeff threw things at them. But I never saw the house empty after we left. I never came back after that night when the police came. So why is it like this?"

"You left the house, but what happened here never left you. You don't live in it anymore, but the scars are still there." Jack pointed to the wall where the window was, the one they had used to escape when they could. "Look closer. The scars are starting to fade … some of them."

Beth looked at the wall. Some of the marks were fading away. But others remained dark. "Not all of them."

"No. Not all of them." He looked into her eyes.

"Is it because of Erin? I'm still worried about her."

"It's not about her. These are your scars"

Beth shook her head. "I don't understand."

"Look inside yourself."

Beth stood there holding Jack's hands and she tried to understand what he'd told her. She shook her head. "I don't understand. Can you help me?"

"There are questions you have, questions that were never answered, questions you never asked."

Beth thought about the questions that had come to mind when she'd talked to Grace about Katie. The questions of why she and Jack hadn't gone to live with Amy or their grandparents. Was that what he was telling her now? Was that the reason the scars weren't all healing? She hadn't thought she needed to know, but maybe the questions ran deeper than she believed.

Beth never spoke these thoughts, but Jack seemed to know anyway. "Yes," he said. "Those are the questions. If you want the scars to heal, you need to ask them."

Beth started to speak again, ask more questions about what to do, but Jack faded from sight and she was alone.

She awoke and looked at the clock beside the bed. It was only five oh clock, but she didn't feel like she could go back to sleep. She got out of bed and headed for the shower. After she was showered and dressed, she went into the kitchen and got out some eggs to cook along with a couple of frozen biscuits.

Fifteen minutes later Nolan walked out of the bedroom in his bathrobe, squinting his eyes against the kitchen's bright light and scratching his head.

"You're actually cooking breakfast? Did Grace's spirit come during the night and take possession of your body?"

Beth rolled her eyes at him. "Very funny. And, yes, I am actually cooking breakfast."

Nolan looked Beth over. "You've already had a shower and gotten dressed. How long have you been up?"

Beth glanced at the clock on the microwave. "A little over an hour."

Nolan furrowed his brow at her. "Why so early?"

She shrugged. "I just woke up and didn't think I could go back to sleep. So I figured I would make use of the time."

"You just woke up?"

Beth let out a breath. "I had a weird dream."

"A nightmare?" Nolan asked with concern.

Beth shook her head. "Not a nightmare, just a weird and very vivid dream."

"Okay." He shrugged his shoulders. "I guess if it gets me biscuits and scrambled eggs on a Wednesday, I should just shut up and be happy."

"I guess you should," she agreed, set a plate down on the counter in front of him, and scooped a portion of eggs onto it. "The biscuits are in the toaster oven. Help yourself."

They sat down at the table and ate breakfast together, which almost never happened. Then Nolan headed for the shower and Beth decided to get a jump on the day and headed to her office to look over some paperwork before she went to the courthouse to hear the judge's decision.

Beth arrived at the courthouse with time to spare and was in the front row again when Judge Walker came out and sat down on the bench. After everyone was seated, the judge addressed the court. He'd arrived at a decision. He asked Erin to stand up, then addressed only her.

"This hasn't been an easy case for me to decide," he began. "This is a very serious crime, young lady, and there isn't any doubt you committed it."

Erin nodded, acknowledging the truth. She didn't look down or avert her eyes from him.

"There are, however, circumstances to this case that I feel must be taken into account. It was a terrible thing that was done to you. However, that does not excuse murder. Your life was not in danger and you were not under an attack of any kind when the murder was committed. There were other avenues you did not even attempt. And I can tell you, there are many people out there who would have been more than willing to help you regardless of whom your parents were."

The judge looked at Erin over the top of his glasses and continued. "You should have looked for help rather than resorting to murder. However, I can understand how a young girl might not know how to get help or where to look for it. I can also understand the fear and helplessness you must have felt. Most importantly, I don't believe you are a threat to society."

Judge Walker paused and took a sip from his water glass. He glanced around the courtroom, then turned his attention back to Erin. "I'm sentencing you to six months in a juvenile detention center. You will continue your school there for that time and you will have both individual and group counseling. When your sentence is up, you will either be returned to your mother or go into state custody. That decision has not been made yet."

The judge banged his gavel and said, "Court adjourned."

Erin continued to stand for a few minutes and Beth wondered how she felt about the judge's decision. This outcome was very good, all things considered, but no one wanted to hear that they were going to be locked up, even for six months.

Lisa put an arm around Erin. "It's going to be okay, Erin. I'll be checking on you. And I'll do everything I can to make sure Kayla's in a good place."

Beth reached forward and put her hand on Erin's back. Erin turned and looked at her, a hint of a smile crossing her lips. "It's okay," she said to Beth and Lisa. "This isn't so bad. I can handle it. And besides, the judge is right." She looked down at her feet. "I'm sorry for what I did. I believed that killing my father was the only way to save Kayla. I didn't think I could trust anyone to help me. Now I know I was wrong. I know that because I've gotten to know the two of you. And you've made me see that there are good people all around me, people who would've helped me." She looked at Beth. "And people who understand what I've been through.

"But I committed a terrible crime and I have to pay a price for it. I knew I would." Erin stopped for a minute looking at Lisa and Beth. Her eyes began to well with emotion. "What I didn't know was that I would meet two really wonderful people that would do so much to help me. I'm grateful for what you've done. And I feel good because I know you'll be looking out for Kayla. I never expected things to turn out this good."

Lisa and Beth both hugged Erin. Then Kayla walked up with her social worker. She hugged Erin and they both cried a little before Erin was escorted out of the courtroom.

Once Beth and Lisa were outside the courtroom, Lisa said, "It wasn't a win, but it was more than I hoped for when I took the case. And that's because of your help. I know it was a hard case for you. You really had to put yourself out there and open some old wounds. Thanks for doing it."

Beth shrugged. "I think maybe some wounds need to be reopened."

Lisa's eyebrows went up. "Really?"

"Yeah." Beth nodded. "Erin's given me a lot to think about. I realized there are some things I never gave much thought to before. Now I think I should."

"Is that the psychologist taking advice from a patient?"

"Maybe so. Erin's not like any patient I've had before. She's pretty amazing, really."

Lisa nodded in agreement. "That she is. I'll never forget the look on Turner's face when she turned his question around on him. She never let him get the better of her."

"She's tough, she's had to be."

"Yeah, she is. I think she's going to be okay, even in Juvenile detention. Most girls who've been through what she has wouldn't ever make it to okay. But I think she will."

"If anyone can do it, she can."

"Yeah," Lisa said. "Hey, why don't we go out on Friday night? We'll celebrate Erin. Are you free?"

"Sure. You want the husbands along or is this just a girl's night?" Beth asked with a smile.

"We can make it a foursome. I figured I would be going out this weekend either to celebrate or drown out my sorrows depending on how this case turned out so I already lined up a babysitter."

"Great. We'll meet you at Angelina's at seven then."

"Okay. See you then."

# Chapter 36

Beth enjoyed dinner Friday night with her husband and their friends. They celebrated the end of a difficult case, they talked and they laughed. However, in the back of her mind, Beth kept seeing Jack's young face and hearing his voice, the words he had spoken in her dream. She couldn't seem to get those words out of her mind. She needed to talk to Martha.

She'd kept in contact with Martha over the years and occasionally worked with some of Martha's "kids." So first thing Monday morning, Beth called social services.

"This is Martha Edmonton," Martha's familiar voice came on the line.

"Martha, its Beth Christopher."

"Beth! It's good to hear from you. How are you doing?"

"I'm doing fine, Martha, but I was hoping I could come in and talk to you sometime."

"Sure. I could meet with you here tomorrow afternoon, or I could meet you somewhere today on my lunch break if you're in a hurry."

"Lunch sounds good. Where should I meet you?"

"I usually go to Carrolton's Deli and my break is at noon."

"Great. I'll meet you there."

Beth was at the deli five minutes early so she found a table and waited for Martha to arrive. When Martha got there, both of them ordered sandwiches, then Martha looked at Beth and asked, "So, what's this about?"

Martha still had the warm, dark eyes that made Beth feel at ease, but these days she was about twenty pounds heavier than when Beth had first met her and her dark hair showed little flecks of gray.

"I guess we're going to get right to it," Beth said.

Martha shrugged. "We can make small talk if you like, but I only have an hour and I do plan to eat while I'm here."

Beth nodded. "Okay. I wanted to ask you some questions about my case."

Martha furrowed her brow. "Your case?"

"Yeah, just some things I never asked back then."

"Okay, fire away." Martha took a bite of her turkey club.

"The first question I have is: why didn't you send Jack and me to live with family? You told me that night in the hospital you would look into the possibility of us staying with our grandparents or Amy."

Martha looked thoughtful as she finished chewing her bite of sandwich. Then she looked Beth in the eye. "Before we send a child to live with a family member after they are taken out of their home, we have to do a full background check on that family member. I couldn't send you and Jack to your grandparents because we discovered things that made them unsuitable."

"Can I ask what you found?"

"There were several instances in their history of the police being called to their house by neighbors who reported domestic violence." Martha brought her gaze back to meet Beth's. "There were also a few reports made by doctors in the emergency room of suspicious injuries."

"What kind of injuries? Who was injured?"

Martha took another bite and chewed it while Beth waited to hear an answer. "These reports came from when your mother and Amy were teenagers. They included broken ribs and a broken arm, along with bruises and abrasions that the doctors didn't feel matched up with the stories they were given."

"My mother and Amy were the ones that were hurt?"

Martha nodded. "Mostly your mother, but Amy too. And one time it was your grandmother."

Beth had never seen any of that in her grandparents. They had always been good to her.

She shook her head in disbelief and took a bite of her ham and cheese sandwich without really tasting it. "What about Amy? Why didn't we go to live with her?"

Martha stopped short of taking a bite and just looked at Beth for a moment. "Why are you asking all this now?"

"I'm not sure—I just feel like I need to know."

On a sigh, Martha said, "Alright … but there's no easy way to say this. Amy was asked to take you and Jack. She declined."

"She declined? You mean she didn't want us," Beth said flatly. She felt as if she had been slapped in the face.

"Now wait a minute, Beth." Martha touched Beth's arm. "You don't know what her reasons were."

Beth looked at Martha feeling anger rise up inside her. "Do you?" she asked in a tone that sounded more like a demand.

"Not precisely. But I know fear when I see it, and I believe she was afraid."

"Afraid of what? We were only kids."

"She said you and Jack were better off taking your chances with foster care." Martha paused, then said in a quiet tone, "Beth, It's very likely she was trying to get you both away from a family that had been abusive for more than just one generation … and …"

"And what, Martha?"

"Well, I don't know for sure, but it's possible she was the one who called the police the night you and Jack were taken from your mother and Jeff."

"No," Beth started in confusion. Even though she had no real way of knowing who had called the police that night, she had always believed it was her father. She'd never discussed it with him, but it had happened so soon after he'd found the bruises on her arm that she figured he may have been keeping an eye on her mother's house. She'd never even considered Amy. After all, Amy had known about the abuse for years without doing a thing.

"No," Beth said again. "I always thought it was my father who called."

Martha looked Beth in the eye. "No, honey. It was a woman who made the call. That much is in the police report, but she didn't give a name."

Beth's mind spun with all the information she was hearing. Trying to make sense of it, she let her mind jump back to that night. She thought about the moment she heard the sirens. Jeff had been standing over her, kicking her. Jack was just a couple feet away, and Mama was crouched by the wall crying. The police had stormed in, knocking down the door, and dragged Jeff off of her. There was a lot of yelling and shouting. Then, before Jeff was even out of the house, the paramedics had rushed in and started taking care of her, Jack and Mama.

Beth remembered being taken out of the house on a stretcher. She remembered the broken angel figurine on the floor ... and then as the memory flashed before her eyes, she remembered something else. The phone! It had been off the hook, lying on the floor and making that horrible beeping sound. And it hadn't just been knocked off the hook in the fighting, Beth realized. Mama was talking on the phone that night when Jeff got home. She was talking to Amy. She had dropped the receiver when Jeff came into the house. That must have been the thump she'd heard after Jeff came in that night.

*Could it really have been Amy that made the call?*

"Martha, Amy knew about the abuse for years. I realized that the day Jack was born. All those years she never did a thing. Why would she call the police that night?"

"I don't know. Maybe you should ask her."

Beth had never imagined she would see Amy again. She had certainly never thought of seeking her out, but maybe she did need to talk to her aunt again.

She nodded looking back down at the food she'd only picked at. She picked up a pickle and took a small bite. "Maybe I'll do that."

"Good. I think it might be good for you." Then, changing the subject she said, "I hear things finished up in court with the Clifton case."

"Yeah. She's going to be doing a little time in juvenile detention, but it could have been a lot worse. And she's got a good attitude about it." Beth paused and took a bite of her sandwich. "How's her sister doing? Do you know?"

"Yes, I'm supervising the case. Kayla's doing pretty well. She's in a good foster home."

"That's good. I'm glad to hear Erin will have a good place to go when she gets out of detention."

Martha looked down, taking another bite of her food and avoiding Beth's gaze.

"What's wrong, Martha?"

Martha took a deep breath and met Beth's eyes. "The family that has Kayla isn't willing to take Erin."

"Okay. That's not unusual with teenagers. But surely you can find a family that will take them both."

Martha's face was clouded with sadness. She shook her head. "Beth, I doubt we'll find a family for Erin at all."

"What do you mean?"

"Erin was tried as a juvenile, so her record will be sealed. But that doesn't erase people's memory. Her parents were well known and the whole thing was in the news." Martha furrowed her brow as she saw Beth's hurt look. "We'll look for a family to take her, of course. But I wouldn't pin a lot of hope on it. She'll probably go to a group home."

She shouldn't be shocked, Beth knew. In fact, she should have known all this without asking. But somehow she'd believed Erin and Kayla would be in a home together again when the sentence was over.

"Martha, Erin's a tough girl and I believe she could be okay with a lot of therapy ... but spending the rest of her youth in a group home away from her sister ... that could ruin her."

"I agree, but people are scared of her. And I can't make someone take her." Martha stopped talking for a moment and regarded Beth. "You know, we can always use more volunteers in the foster care system."

Beth's brow drew together. "Martha, are you suggesting I take the girls?"

She shrugged. "Well, you *and* Nolan. Things are still good with you two, right?"

"Yes ... but we can't take two teenagers," Beth said with exasperation.

"Why not?" Martha's expression was serious, almost hard as she looked Beth in the eye.

Beth fumbled for an answer. "Well, for one thing, I'm Erin's psychologist."

"Not anymore. The trial's over." Martha raised an eyebrow.

"She's going to need one again when she gets out of detention and I'm the one she's comfortable with."

"Beth, there are plenty of psychologists that would be willing to take her case. She needs a home. You know her and want her to have a chance. You can give it to her ..." Martha made a sound that resembled a faint laugh. "It's kind of funny actually how things come full circle sometimes."

Beth looked up, confused. "What are you talking about?"

"I mean how you've come back into contact with this family after all these years."

Beth shook her head, the confusion only deepening. "I still don't understand. When did I have contact with Erin's family before?"

Martha's eyebrows went up again. "I'm talking about your time with the Kesslers."

Beth stared at Martha, still not understanding.

"I don't suppose Jamie ever told you his last name."

"No. He didn't talk much." Then a look of shock struck Beth's face as she realized the connection Martha was talking about. That was why his face always gave her a shiver when she saw it on TV, why it seemed so familiar. Still, she couldn't believe it was true. "You're not saying that Jamie and James Clifton were the same person, are you?"

Martha nodded and Beth fumbled for words. "But that can't be true ... Jamie helped me ... He gave me the little bat I used to stop Mark when he attacked me. Jamie made that for me ... and I think he knew I would need it." She paused for a moment. "Are you telling me that boy grew up to be a man who would rape his own daughter?"

"I'm telling you that Jamie and James Clifton were one in the same. And he apparently did rape his daughter."

Beth shook her head again, trying to make sense of what she was hearing. "I don't understand. How could a boy who cared about a girl he barely knew grow up to be such a monster?"

"I don't have an answer for you on that one. But keep in mind the influence of his youth. After you left the Kessler's home, he stayed. In fact, he was there until he aged out of the system. And I heard he stayed with them for a while after that." Martha stopped for a moment and looked Beth in the eye. "Two other girls were sent to live with the Kesslers after you left."

"What! Why would they do that?" Beth felt her last bite of sandwich turn bitter on her tongue.

Martha only raised a brow again.

"Because no one believed me; no one but you," Beth said.

"Yes. They put another girl with them a couple months after you left ... a thirteen-year-old. She stayed there for about six months and then she was sent back to her mother. After that, they just had Jamie for close to a year before the other girl went there."

Martha paused and Beth urged her on. "Okay, so what happened with her?"

"She was there for about two months before she told one of her teachers that her foster father had raped her."

Beth shook her head. "That poor girl. And it didn't have to happen."

"I know, honey. But the only thing they had evidence of was that you hit Mark and knocked him out. There was no proof of the attack."

Beth nodded. "I know." She picked up her napkin and put it on her plate, though her sandwich was only half eaten. Then she gave Martha a quizzical look. "Do you think Mark raped the first girl too?"

"Probably, but she never said a word to anyone."

"What about Jamie? Do you think he was involved in the rapes then?"

"The girl that reported Mark didn't say anything about Jamie, but you never know. Maybe he was involved. Maybe he just watched. Maybe Mark made him watch. There's no way to know."

Beth shook her head trying to make all of the pieces of information she was getting fit in with everything she had previously believed. She couldn't do it.

Then she had a thought. "Martha, James Clifton was rich and pretty well known. How did he achieve that? Did the Kesslers send him to school?"

"No. Victoria Bentwood's parents did. It was through them that he came to be so well known too. He inherited Michael Bentwood's company."

"How did that happen?"

"The official story is that James and Victoria were madly in love and so her parents sort of adopted James into the family and put him through school because they wanted him to have a bright future. Then during the time he was in school, the happy couple got married and had a couple kids. Then Michael got sick and passed the torch on to his son-in-law since he didn't have any sons."

Beth gave a skeptical look. "Uh huh, so what's the real story?"

"Rumor has it, Michael and Amanda Bentwood were not so fond of James. They didn't like him at all, but then Victoria wound up pregnant so they did what they thought a dignified family had to do. They had a shotgun wedding, then sent James to school and carefully covered his past history up as best they could, so he wouldn't bring down the family reputation. Then, of course, Michael got sick and he had to pass on the business to someone. Victoria didn't have any business skills to speak of, being raised as a debutant and all, so it was either hand it to James or let it leave the family."

"It's leaving the family now."

Martha nodded. "That it is … Well, I better get back to work. I hope you got the answers you need."

"And then some," Beth said with a frown. "Thank you, Martha. It was good to see you."

"It was good to see you too, honey. You are, after all, one of my best success stories … and, Beth?"

"Yes?"

"Think about Erin. You could give her a great home. I can't think of a better person for the job."

"I don't know about that, but I'll think about it. Thanks again," Beth said as the two of them walked out of the restaurant and parted ways.

Beth got into her car. She turned off the radio and drove back to her office in silence. Her head was pounding with all the new information she was trying to process and the radio would only make it worse. She'd wanted answers, but had never expected it to be so hard to make sense of those answers.

All afternoon her mind kept racing back to the answers that had brought more questions. When she got home it was no different. She was quiet through dinner and continued to stay with her thoughts after that, trying to decide what to do with the new information. She didn't even notice the way her husband was looking at her until he spoke.

"Wanna tell me what's on your mind?"

She glanced up at him seeming almost surprised to realize she wasn't alone in the room. "Huh?"

He smiled at her. "I was wondering if you'd like to tell me what's on your mind."

"Oh ... well I saw Martha today."

Nolan nodded. He knew that Martha had been Beth's social worker as a child, but in recent years Beth had spoken of her only because they sometimes worked together with the same kids. "About your court case?" he asked.

"No. About my case," she answered. Then in response to her husband's perplexed expression, she continued, "You know all the dreams I've been having lately?"

He nodded.

"They made me realize there were questions about my past that I didn't have the answers to. So, I went to see Martha today."

"Did you get the answers you were looking for?"

"Yes ... but I still can't even wrap my head around the things she told me."

Nolan's eyebrows went up in interest. "Do you want to talk about?"

Beth smiled at him. He was always so considerate. She told him about her grandparents and Amy, but didn't tell him that Martha had requested that the two of them become foster parents for Erin and Kayla. She wasn't sure how she felt about that yet and didn't want to bring it up until she was. She also held back the part about Jamie and James Clifton being the same person. That was information pertaining to Erin's case and Beth felt it should remain confidential despite the fact that it was very much about her as well.

Nolan listened, as he always did, and let her talk through everything on her mind. Then they settled in together and started to watch a movie. Halfway through it she looked at him and said, "I think I have to see Amy."

Nolan, with his arms wrapped around her, nodded again. "I figured you'd want to."

Rebecca L. Marsh

# Chapter 37

Two days later Beth got in touch with Amy and asked to meet with her. They arranged to meet at Amy's apartment the next afternoon when Amy got home from work.

That night Beth tossed and turned all night. She wondered what kind of answers she would get from her aunt and hoped there wouldn't be anything shocking she didn't already know or suspect. She was still trying to make sense of the things she'd learned from Martha and wasn't sure she could handle any more surprises.

Beth got up early since she was already awake and once again her husband found her in the kitchen cooking breakfast when he got up. He walked into the kitchen groggily, scratching his head. Then he stopped and sniffed the air. "Pancakes and bacon this time?" He sat down on a stool at the counter. "And it hasn't even been a week since the last time I found you making breakfast on a weekday. Should I be worried?"

"No." Beth took a deep breath and turned around to face the stove again. "I just wasn't sleeping well."

"Dream?"

Beth shook her head but didn't turn around. "I'm going to see Amy this afternoon."

"Really?"

Beth figured he was wondering why she hadn't told him the night before. She turned to him saying, "I needed time to think. I feel really overwhelmed right now. I haven't had a real conversation with Amy since I was twelve."

Nolan's face softened. "You'll be fine. And I hope you get the answers you need."

Beth usually had appointments until five or six in the evening, but she'd rescheduled two of her patients so she could leave at three and meet Amy. She drove to the address Amy gave her and arrived at an apartment complex that was a bit nicer than the one her aunt lived in when she was a child. She parked her car and walked to the front door. Standing on the stoop, she closed her eyes for a few seconds. Then gathering her courage, she rang the bell and waited for Amy to answer.

When the door opened, Beth was surprised to see how much older Amy looked since she'd last seen her at Mama's funeral. In fact, she looked far older than her fifty-five years and Beth could only see a shadow of the person she used to be. Amy smiled, but Beth could tell somehow that smiles were rare for her. Beth supposed Amy didn't have much left in her life to smile about. She had never married or had any children of her own. Her parents were gone now, her sister was dead, her nephew was dead and her niece, the only living family member she had, stood in front of her for the first time in twenty-three years.

Amy stepped to the side and motioned for Beth to come inside. She ushered Beth into the small living room and they sat down. Beth glanced around the room, noticing how sparsely it was decorated. The walls were white and almost bare. There was a brown sofa that they now sat on and a matching armchair, along with a simple wooden coffee table and one similar end table. On the wall opposite the couch hung a small TV. There was nothing colorful to liven the place up. It spoke volumes to Beth about the woman who lived there.

"Can I get you anything to drink?" Amy asked. Beth's throat felt a little dry so she accepted a glass of tea.

Then they both sat again and for a minute or two they stared at each other, in uncomfortable silence. Amy spoke first. "You wanted to talk to me about something?"

Beth cleared her throat. "Yes. I went to see Martha the other day." Beth paused then said, "You remember Martha?"

Amy nodded and Beth continued. "I talked to her about what happened when I was twelve and now I have some questions for you."

Amy gave another slight nod, but didn't react otherwise, so Beth went on. "Martha said that you were asked to take Jack and me and you declined … Why?" Beth shrugged asking, "Didn't you want us?"

Amy sat silent for a moment, then put down her glass before looking Beth in the eye. "I wondered if you would ever come asking me that." She held Beth's gaze. Her expression was pained and she seemed almost near tears. "Of course I wanted you. But it was better for you both—safer— to go somewhere else."

Beth didn't look away. She had expected this answer. "Because of Grandpa?"

Amy's eyes widened in shock, but she was quick to recover. "Yes."

"Martha told me there were domestic disputes reported by Grandma and Grandpa's neighbors and that there had been suspicious visits to the emergency room back when you and Mama were young."

Amy's head bobbed in agreement with everything Beth said. "Yes, your grandfather had …" She paused, holding back emotion. "A violent temper."

"I don't remember him ever being that way when Mama and I lived with them … before Jeff."

"You were still so little then. You were cute, so most of the time he let the little things you did go. On the occasion he did get angry, your mother stepped in for you. She took his anger and his punishment for you."

Beth didn't remember any of this, but as she thought back to the first time Jeff had beat her, she remembered that her mother had tried to take Jeff's attention away from her.

She had tried to take the punishment for her, but Jeff wouldn't allow that.

"I guess that's what she was trying to do the first time Jeff beat me. She never tried it again though. She never did anything again except tell us to pretend to be asleep. Sometimes that worked." Beth shook her head as emotion started to get the best of her. "I always thought she was just weak. I wanted us to leave … to run away from Jeff and start a new life. I didn't understand why she kept taking it and acting like there was nothing wrong."

Amy wrung her hands in her lap. "She wasn't always like that," she said. "Believe it or not, when we were growing up, she was the strong one."

Noticing Beth's surprise, Amy said, "That's why she got most of the beatings back then. I always stayed quiet and tried to pretend it wasn't happening. Bella stood up for herself; she stood up for me too. She had a lot of spirit and grit." Amy gave a sad shrug. "But he beat it out her eventually."

Amy looked down and Beth could see the look of shame and hurt in her eyes that she had seen many times in her own eyes. "I wish I had known that side of her."

Amy nodded and a hint of a smile crossed her lips. "You would have liked her then." She picked up her glass of tea and took a shaky sip then set the glass down again, and as she did she noticed Beth's wedding ring. "You're married?"

"Yes. Seven years now."

"Are you happy? Is he good to you?" Amy asked and Beth knew she was really asking if Nolan hurt her.

Beth smiled. "I am happy. And he is good to me."

Beth saw relief on Amy's face. "I'm so glad. You've broken the cycle then. I decided when I was very young I was never going to get married."

"You thought it would turn out like your parents; like mom and Jeff?"

"It's not that I thought there weren't any good men out there or good marriages. I knew there were. I just didn't trust myself to find that. I was too afraid it would end up bad. And if it did, I would have been stuck with it."

Beth shook her head. "Why? Why wouldn't you have been able to leave if it was bad? Why didn't Mama think she could leave?"

"Because our father would not have allowed it and by then we were both far too afraid of him. Whatever desire we'd once had to fight was gone. We had learned to keep our heads down, do as we were told, and not take any chances." There was a hint of the old hurt and anger creeping back into her voice.

"But you did take a chance, didn't you? The night the police came and took Jack and me away?"

Amy looked her in the eye, startled that Beth could know this, but didn't respond.

"Martha thinks you're the one who called the police that night. I always thought it was my father who made that call, but Martha says it was a woman. She believes it was you and when I thought about it I remembered you were talking to Mama on the phone that night when Jeff got home … It *was* you, wasn't it?"

Amy's eyes were still glued to Beth's as her head began to nod in agreement. "Yes, it was me."

"But why?" Beth shrugged her shoulders. "Why then? You knew the truth about Jeff all along and you didn't do anything. Why did you call the police *that* night?"

Amy looked a little stricken by Beth's very straightforward question that came out more like a demand. She opened her mouth once, then shut it. She reached for her glass and took a small sip, then said in a whisper, "I always thought I was doing all I could to help. I took you kids away from there as much as Jeff would let me." She took a deep breath and thought for a moment. "Like Bella, I didn't think there was any more I could do. If I had done something about it, my father would have gotten involved. My fear of him was paralyzing."

"But then you did do something. Why was that night different?"

"Because I was there ..." She stopped for a minute, flustered. "Well, I wasn't *there*, but ... in a way I was. See, Bella never hung up the phone. I heard everything ... the shouting, the crying, glass breaking. It was like being a kid again, hiding in a corner and waiting for my father to find me.

"It was excruciating listening to him beating Bella and feeling so helpless, and yet I couldn't put the phone down. When I heard him go after you and Jack, when I heard the two of you screaming," she shook her head as tears streaked down her cheeks. "I couldn't stand it. I couldn't do *nothing* anymore." Amy's voice was firm now. "I hung up and called the police. I didn't give them my name, and I didn't stay on the line for them to ask questions."

Amy was quiet for a few seconds, but Beth sensed that Amy had more to say so she listened and didn't interject.

"I was so scared after I made that call. I was sure Bella would know it was me, and she would tell our father. I waited for him to come and punish me, but he never came." She looked up at her niece. "Bella thought your father was the one that called too. I never told her otherwise. I wasn't brave enough."

Beth nodded and reached out her hand to take Amy's. She felt sorry for this woman who had lived all her life in fear.

"That's why I didn't take you kids." Amy's eyes searched Beth's face for understanding. "If you had stayed with our family you would've ended up like me ... or like your mother. And Jack might have ended up like my father. I wanted you two to get away, have a better chance." She looked down again fighting emotion. "If I had known what was going to happen to Jack..."

"No," Beth said, "that's not your fault. No one could have known." She waited for Amy to look up at her again.

"He was happy. He was loved, and he was happy. His death was an accident."

Tears still running down her face, Amy met Beth's eyes. "Were you ... happy?"

Beth found herself feeling more compassion for her aunt than she'd ever expected, and a part of her wanted to tell Amy that she had indeed been happy. But that wasn't fair. Amy deserved to know the whole truth. "At times I was."

Amy searched her face, looking for some assurance that she'd made the right choice all those years ago.

"It turned out good for me." Beth took her hand again.

"I heard you ended up back with your father."

Beth nodded. "Yes, he found me after Jack died, and I was safe and happy there." Beth squeezed Amy's hand. "Thank you for seeing me and most of all for being honest with me."

Beth had noticed that while the walls in Amy's living room were mostly bare, there were two pictures hanging up. One was of Amy and Mama. The other was a picture of Beth and Jack from the summer before they were taken away. Seeing this, Beth realized she truly was all Amy had left and she felt deep sorrow for the life her aunt had been too afraid to live.

Then she thought about her mother and realized something odd. She felt almost the same mix of love and hate for her mother that she felt for Jamie. She wasn't yet sure how to sort that out.

Beth reached forward and gave Amy a tentative hug. "I'd like you to come visit me sometime and meet my husband. Maybe we could have dinner."

Beth saw surprise on Amy's face and also something else ... reservation maybe.

"Do you really mean that?"

It was fear, Beth realized. Amy was afraid to have anything because she didn't want to lose again. Beth nodded and gave her aunt a sincere look. "Yes, I mean it. I think we need to get to know each other again."

The fear left Amy's face and a wide smile spread across her lips. Her whole face brightened with delight and tears flowed again, but this time they were tears of joy.

# Chapter 38

The following week Beth took an afternoon away from the office and went to see Erin. Crazy as it was, she hadn't been able to get Martha's words out of her head, "She needs a home, and you can give it to her."

Beth had a hard time, however, even imagining becoming a parent for two teenagers and she had no idea how she would even begin to talk to Nolan about the idea. He wanted to be a father, but Beth knew this wasn't what he had in mind. She wasn't sure how *she* could even be thinking about it.

When Erin entered the visitation room and saw Beth sitting there, her face lit up. The guard escorted her to the empty chair, then left the room. Beth handed Erin a small bag of M&M's, bringing a wide smile to her face. Beth smiled back, but she felt sadness deep inside her knowing that moments of joy in this poor girl's life have been far outnumbered by moments of fear and pain.

She shook off the sadness and set herself in determination. One way or another, she had to make sure things got better for Erin.

So many kids that come out of abusive homes grow up and perpetuate the cycle. They become abusive themselves, or they chain themselves to someone who abuses them. Beth believed this happened because people tend to stick to what they know. If they grow up only knowing fear and pain, then perhaps they don't believe their lives can ever be different.

Beth was sure she had the life she did today because she'd spent at least part of her childhood in good homes. She knew a better life was possible and so she'd set out to have it. She had to make sure Erin got that chance too.

"So," Beth started, "how are you doing?"

Erin looked at her earnestly. "I'm okay." She shrugged. "I mean, I can think of places I'd rather be, but it's better now than it was before the trial."

"Are the guards treating you better?"

"A little, yeah. Do you think they know what my father did to me? Is that why they're being easier on me now?"

Beth gave a thoughtful look. "They're not supposed to. It was a closed trial. But who knows?"

Erin ripped open her bag of M&M's and poured a few in her hand. "Well, I'll take it, whatever the reason." She looked up from her candy and met Beth's eyes. "The therapist I'm seeing here is pretty good."

"I'm glad to hear that." Beth took an M&M that Erin offered her.

"Yeah. I really like the group sessions."

Beth nodded. "It helps to know you're not alone, doesn't it?"

Erin looked down now, very sullen.

"What is it, Erin?"

She shrugged, then began to wring her hands. "Before the trial, I was only thinking about what was going to happen next. I know I said I didn't care, and that was partly true. But I still wondered what would happen, and I thought about it a lot."

"That's understandable."

Erin glanced up and then back down at her hands. "But it's different now. That part's done and ... well, I've had to start really thinking and talking to the counselors about my father and everything that happened."

Erin looked up now and her face broke into tears. "I'm so ashamed of what I did. And I can't stop thinking about it. Every night when I go to sleep I see my father's face looking at me with dead eyes."

Erin was overtaken by emotion, and Beth reached out to her and held her hand, letting her empty herself of all the hurt and guilt that had built up inside.

A moment later, when she had regained control, Erin continued. "Now that I'm looking back on it, I can't believe I'm the one that took his life. Now I have to face what that means; who that makes me." She shook her head again. "I don't like what I see in myself now, and I'm trying to figure out how to deal with it."

"Erin," Beth said in a gentle voice. "You're not a bad person. He hurt you in the most terrible way. And you wanted to keep your sister safe."

"I should have looked for help."

"Yes, you should have. But you're just a kid, and you didn't know who to trust." Beth reached forward and lifted Erin's chin so they were looking each other in the eye. "When the very people who are supposed to protect you are the ones hurting you, you start to see the world as if it's a den of monsters. That makes it hard to trust anyone. You were in the worst kind of situation a kid can be in and when it was only you, you took the abuse and did nothing. But you felt a responsibility to help your sister. You wanted her to have a different fate. You did what you thought you had to do in order to keep her safe. And she is safe now.

"You know now that there are people in this world who care about you and would be willing to help you. It's good you see that now. It's also good that you understand the seriousness of what you did. I know you don't want to feel these things—guilt and shame, but it's good that you do … You feel those things *because* you're a good person."

The following Saturday Beth and Nolan went to Ron and Grace's house. When they got there, Nolan went straight into the living room to find Beth's father and Ronnie. Beth headed into the kitchen to see what Grace and Ashley were doing.

She found Grace holding Hunter while she sat at the table talking to Ashley. They both turned as Beth walked in.

Beth glanced around the kitchen, noticing the stove was empty and so was the oven. She raised her eyebrows at Grace. "You're not cooking today?"

Grace smiled at her. "Disappointed?"

"Maybe. Mostly hungry. Are we still having lunch?"

"Sure we are. But even I need a break sometimes. We're ordering pizza today."

"Oh," Beth said sitting down at the table with the other two women. "That sounds good."

"I'm about to get online and place the order. What do you and Nolan want on yours?"

"I'm fine with just pepperoni, but Nolan will probably want the works."

"Okay," Grace said as she opened up the laptop computer that sat on the table in front of her. She moved the mouse, clicking on the various choices to make their order. "I love watching it make the little pizzas on the screen." She made a few more clicks and then looked up. "It'll be ready in about twenty minutes."

"Are you having it delivered?" Beth asked.

"No. I need to stop into the drug store anyway, so I'll pick it up," Grace responded.

"I'd love to go with you," Ashley said. "I'll leave Hunter with Ronnie. I could really use a few minutes of me time."

Grace nodded and looked at Beth. "What about you? Want to come along?"

"No, I'll stay here."

The other two women got up and Grace tucked Hunter into his carrier seat then started to pick it up to take into the living room.

"You can just leave him here with me if you want," Beth said.

Ashley gave her the concerned look mothers were so famous for. "Are you sure?"

Beth smiled at her. "Don't worry. Ronnie's just in the next room."

Ashley nodded, then she picked up her purse and walked out of the room with Grace just ahead of her.

Beth looked down at her tiny nephew, sitting in his seat. He wore a light green outfit that said, "I'm so cute it's scary," and his arms and legs seemed to be in constant motion while he made soft sounds.

"I guess it's just you and me, buddy." Beth reached out a tentative hand and gave the baby's bald head a gentle stroke.

She let out the breath that she hadn't even realized she was holding. She felt some relief that the touch didn't provoke any panic, and so she reached for his small hand and allowed him to grab one of her fingers. His grip was tight, but she was still ok.

Maybe the problem was fixed now that she'd gotten all her answers. Maybe the fear was gone now.

She watched Hunter as he held her finger tightly, regarding him with reservation. Then she closed her eyes for a second, gathering her courage.

"Okay," she said to herself, "there's only one way to find out, right?"

She reached into the baby seat and moved her hands under the baby, making sure to support his head, and lifted him up. She brought the baby close and cradled him in her arms. Standing there for a moment she considered how she felt.

She was Okay, she realized. There was no fear—no panic.

Hunter was snuggled in close to her and looking content as he cooed at her. She smiled at him and her eyes grew moist. "I think I'm Okay, little man. We can start to get to know each other now."

Beth was enjoying the quiet moment with her nephew when her father walked into the kitchen. He started to head for the refrigerator, but stopped short when he saw Beth holding the baby. For a few seconds, he just stared, then said, "Well look at you!"

Beth glanced up at him and smiled. "Looks like I beat the fear, Dad."

Ron smiled back. "Looks like you did."

Ron leaned down and kissed the top of Beth's head, and then he kissed the top of Hunter's head. When he straightened back up, he started to the fridge again and pulled out a can of soda. As he headed back to the living room, Beth said, "I talked to Amy last week."

Ron stopped where he was, and Beth could see some surprise register on his face. "Oh?"

"I had a few questions I needed to ask her … I've learned a lot lately." She looked at her father's face. He met her eyes, but didn't say anything. "I found out she was the one who called the police the night Jack and I were taken away from Mama's house." She paused for a moment and searched his eyes. "It happened right after you saw those bruises on my arm; when you tried to take me to live with you. I always thought you were the one who called the police."

Ron walked over to where Beth sat and knelt down so they were face to face. He took one of her hands in his and looked her in the eye. "Sweetheart, if I had known what was going on in your mother's house that night, I wouldn't have called the police. I would have killed that bastard with my own two hands."

Beth sat still for a moment, seeing the sincerity on her father's face. "Then I'm glad it happened the way it did. Jeff did enough harm in this world. I'm glad he didn't also turn my dad into a killer."

After their lunch with the family, Nolan took Lulu to the park for the afternoon, and Beth toiled around the house cleaning. In reality, she was pretending to clean while she tried to figure out how to ask her husband for one more thing; one very big thing.

She had seen his face light up when he saw her holding Hunter. And he had every right, after all his patience, to expect her to say, "Honey, it's time. Let's have a baby." He certainly would not expect what she was going to propose instead. It was unfair to him. She knew that. But everything in her was screaming for her to do this.

It was almost six by the time Nolan got home. Beth was in the kitchen making dinner and was alerted to his return by Lulu, who came running in first and began begging for scraps.

Beth smiled down at the dog. "Sorry, Lulu, I don't have anything for you right now."

"Got anything for me?" Nolan asked walking into the kitchen behind the dog. He was smiling and his shirt was sweaty. They had been running, Beth decided.

"Of course." She leaned forward to meet his lips.

"You're making dinner." He gave an approving look. "What are we having?"

"Pot roast ... but don't expect it to be as good as Grace's."

He raised an eyebrow at her and she knew that was his way of saying, "Why would I ever expect that?"

She rolled her eyes at him. "Anyway," she said in an exasperated voice, "it'll be ready in about twenty minutes. How was the park?"

"Good." He grabbed a bottle of water from the refrigerator and sat down on one of the bar stools at the counter. "I spent some time drawing. Then Lulu and I played Frisbee. Lulu met a friendly bulldog when she was chasing a wild throw, and they played together for a while. I decided it was time for a run when the bulldog started humping her. Then we came home."

Beth looked at the dog that was still sitting nearby, tail wagging, hoping for food to drop. "Lulu, you're not supposed to let the boys do that on the first date!"

"Face it, honey, she's easy. She didn't even try to play hard-to-get."

When the food was done, Beth and Nolan went to the table and began eating while the dog continued to beg. Beth had reverted back into her thoughts and was very quiet throughout dinner.

"The pot roast was really good, Beth. Grace would be proud," Nolan said.

She looked up at him, startled out of her thoughts. "Huh?"

He raised an eyebrow at her. "And they say men don't listen."

She smiled. "I'm sorry. I'm just thinking through some things. What were you saying?"

"I was complimenting you on the pot roast."

"Oh." Her smile broadened. "Thanks."

"It's true," he said. "If you keep up all this deep thought, you might teach yourself to be a really good cook." He reached out and touched her hand. "The food's been great lately ... but I kind of miss my wife. Any idea when she'll be back?"

Beth's smile faded, and she moved back into her thoughts. "I'm working on bringing her back." She looked down at the table, tracing a finger along the wood grain. "I'm almost there ... but there's one more thing I need."

He shrugged. "Okay, what is it?" His expression told her he wanted to do anything possible to help her and that warmed her heart. Nevertheless, she wasn't so sure he'd feel the same once he heard her request.

She gave him a hesitant look. "I've been thinking about something for the last few days ... ever since I went to see Martha." She stopped a moment, trying to find the right words, wishing there was an easy way to say this.

"Okay ... and?" Nolan urged her to keep talking.

"I was asking her if the sister of the girl I've been working with for Lisa was doing ok."

Nolan nodded. "Just use her name, Beth. It's not like I don't know who she is. Her case was all over the news for a while there."

"Yeah, I guess it was. Well, I was asking Martha about Erin's sister, Kayla. I wanted to know how she was doing and if they had found a good family for her. Martha said they had, but that the family she's with isn't willing to take Erin when she gets out of detention."

"I guess that's no big surprise. She's going to be a hard kid to place, I imagine."

"Yes, she is." Beth looked her husband in the face. "Martha had a suggestion about that."

"She did?"

"Yes, but I don't think you're going to like it."

He shrugged and his brow drew together. "Why should it matter to me?"

Beth took a deep breath. "Because she suggested we take the girls."

For a moment there was silence, and Beth thought she saw a number of different emotions cross her husband's face. Once the shock cleared, anger won the battle.

"What! Are you kidding? We're not foster parents."

"I know that. She was asking us to become foster parents. We could do the training while Erin is in detention."

"You're seriously suggesting we do this?"

"Yes." She looked into his eyes, searching for understanding. "I think I need to help these girls."

He shook his head in disbelief. "I can't believe you really want to do that. Become parents to two teenagers?"

"I know it's asking a lot. But no one else will do it. They need a home."

Nolan was pacing now while Beth sat very still at the table. "There's a reason why no one else will do it. That girl is in detention for killing her father. Remember that?"

"Yes, I remember. He was raping her, Nolan. For two years he was raping her."

Nolan stopped pacing and looked at her. He was quiet for a moment, stricken by the idea of a father raping his own daughter. Then he shook his head. "We'd be bringing a convicted killer into our home. How can you be sure she's not dangerous?"

"The judge doesn't think she is. That's why he only gave her six months."

"I don't care what the fucking judge thinks!" Nolan's anger flared in a way Beth almost never saw. "I don't want to be a father to two teenagers I've never even met! I wanted us to have our own family! Is that too damn much to ask?"

Beth was taken aback, her eyes wide with shock. "It's … not too much to ask," she stammered, her voice little more than a whisper. "We used to talk about having a family, kids of our own. I know you've been waiting for that, waiting for me. I know I haven't been a very good wife to you." She looked up at him, meeting his eyes. "It's not fair what I'm asking of you. I know that. But it's what I need."

He shook his head again in disappointment and disbelief, but his voice came out softer when he spoke again. "I can't believe you're actually asking this."

Beth could see this was not going well, but she felt such a strong need to help Erin—like it was what she was meant to do.

"Can we just talk about it? Erin's really a good kid"

"I don't want to talk about. I don't even want to think about it."

There was silence again as they stared at each other. Beth felt dismayed and saddened by the look she saw on her husband's face—like he didn't know who she was. Then he grabbed his jacket from the hook by the door and put it on.

"Where are you going?" Beth asked, fear rising up. She needed Nolan too.

"I don't know. But I need to go somewhere else right now." He opened the door and walked out without looking back. A moment later, Beth heard his car start and pull away from the house.

She sat there at the table for a long while. Tears rolled down her cheeks as she took shallow breaths. She wasn't exactly crying. What she felt most were numbness and shock. She and Nolan had experienced a few little spats in the past, but he had never walked out and left her alone and she had no idea what this meant.

When the phone rang, Beth was still sitting at the table with dirty dishes and a cold platter of pot roast in front of her. She rushed to answer it, thinking it might be Nolan, and almost knocked her chair over. When she picked up the phone, it was not her husband's voice she heard. It was Lisa's.

Beth glanced at the clock on the stove and saw it was almost nine thirty. She had been sitting at the table for more than two hours.

"What is it, Lisa?" she said in a sad, weary voice.

"Just thought you might want to know your husband is over here. What happened? He's been ranting for the past hour and a half about you wanting to adopt a killer."

"Is he staying there tonight?"

"He'll have to now. You know Keith's way of counseling someone through a tough time is to give them a drink and make sure the glass is never empty. Nolan isn't really making sense anymore, and I imagine he'll be passed out very soon ... So what's up? Spill!"

"He was talking about Erin."

There was a pause, and then Lisa's voice came back. "Explain."

"I went to see Martha this week, and I asked her about Kayla. And, well, long story short, she suggested that Nolan and I become foster parents and take Erin and Kayla when Erin gets out of detention."

There was a brief silence from the other end of the line, then Lisa said, "Well, that's interesting. I take it you want to do it?"

"I didn't at first. But it kept nagging at me, popping into my head all the time. I told you after the trial that some old wounds need to be reopened."

"Yeah, I remember."

"Well mine were opened and I want to heal them this time, not just put on a Band-Aid. The process of healing them led me to discover things about my past that I hadn't even given much thought to before. I got the answers to my questions and I even reconnected with Amy. Still, something was missing and I think this is it. I need to give back. My childhood was hard, but there were a few great people along the way that helped me through it. If it were not for them, I may have ended up a very different person. I want Erin and Kayla to have that too. And Martha doesn't think anyone else will take them."

"Wow! I feel like I've missed a lot. When did you see Amy?"

"Thursday. I had some questions to ask her."

"But you said you reconnected. Does that mean you'll be seeing her again?"

Lisa's lawyer's mind didn't miss a thing.

"I hope so. I told her I wanted her to meet my husband." Beth let out a breath. "I just hope when she comes over I'll still have one. He was really upset when he left. I don't think he's ever been that mad at me before."

Beth waited for a response from her friend, hoping, of course, for reassurance. The phone remained silent, not a word from the other end.

Beth relented, let out a sigh and said, "It's a lot I'm asking of him. I know that. And it's not fair; it's not what we planned. I don't know. Maybe it's too much to ask."

"What if it is?" Lisa asked her candidly.

Beth wrinkled her brow. "What do you mean?"

"If you had to choose between helping Erin and keeping your marriage together, what would you choose?"

Beth sucked in a breath. Just hearing someone say those words felt like being punched in the gut. She couldn't imagine life without Nolan. However, this need to help Erin was not something that even felt like a choice anymore.

"I don't even think I can consider that choice right now, Lisa. I was hoping you would tell me that Nolan just needs time and he'll come around."

There was a brief pause and Beth didn't like that. Then Lisa spoke up in a less than reassuring voice. "Maybe he will ... maybe not."

Beth let out another long sigh and, needing support, sat down at the table again and rested her head on one hand. "Sometimes I think you should be the therapist. You really get straight to the point and make a person think about their choices."

"Yeah, well, lawyers know how to ask the tough questions too."

"That's the truth. I was hoping you would help me lick my wounds and tell me everything will look better in the morning."

"I'm not Mary Poppins. I think you know me better than that. Besides, tomorrow you would wake up and the problem wouldn't just be gone." Lisa paused, and for a few seconds, there was silence. "Listen, the kids are at my mom's house tonight and Nolan's going to be out soon. I think Keith can handle things here. Why don't I come over and stay with you tonight?"

Beth glanced around the empty house and felt the loneliness of it, despite the presence of the dog that was lying on the floor snoring. She didn't want to be alone with her worries, she realized.

"That would be nice, Lisa. Thanks."

Less than fifteen minutes later Lisa was at the door. Beth let her in and hugged her. They talked for a few minutes, but there was little more to say about the situation, so they both got pajamas on and got in Beth's bed to watch a movie. Lisa chose a Jim Carey movie, trying to cheer Beth up. It distracted her enough that she was able to fall asleep.

When Beth woke up the next morning she found Lisa in the kitchen, sitting at the table with a bowl of cereal and a cup of coffee. She padded to the coffee maker and poured herself a cup, then joined Lisa at the table.

Lisa looked up. "Hey there, sleeping beauty. Feel any better today?"

Beth shrugged.

Lisa nodded. "Yeah, I'm sorry. Listen, I hate to bail on you at a time like this, but I've got to leave soon to pick up the kids."

Beth sipped her coffee, wincing as it burned her tongue. "That's okay. Thanks for coming last night. It was good to have the company. Don't worry about me. I'll be alright."

"Call me later if you need to talk." Lisa carried her coffee cup and bowl to the sink. She grabbed the small bag she'd brought from home the night before, slung it over one shoulder and headed to the front door. Then she stopped and looked back at Beth. "Listen, I know it's causing you a lot of marital trouble right now, and I don't know how it's all going to work out, but I think it's really nice that you want to do this for Erin and Kayla. And who knows, maybe Nolan will come around."

Beth watched as Lisa turned and headed out the door. Then she got up, and grabbing a granola bar from the pantry, headed back into her bedroom with her coffee cup. She finished her small breakfast, took a shower and dressed for church. She needed guidance and she couldn't think of a better place to find it. However, as she headed out the door, she realized that, while she wanted to be in the presence of God, at the moment she wasn't really up for casual conversations with other people. So, instead of heading to the church she and Nolan often attended, she headed for one she hadn't been to in quite a while.

She pulled up a few minutes later in front of the church she had attended when she lived with John and Ellen Sue. It had been many years since she'd been here and she doubted anyone would know her now. She could be alone with her thoughts and the preacher's words.

Walking toward the building, she couldn't help but remember that first Christmas Eve with John and Ellen Sue. This church had felt like magic to her that night. Now she hoped it would provide comfort and direction.

She walked in and sat in the back row. She was a little late and the service had already started with announcements. A few minutes later the choir began singing, *How Great Thou Art,* and she closed her eyes as she listened. The music was beautiful and Beth felt warmth fill her heart as she listened.

Then the minister gave his sermon. It was about compassion and when she left at the end, she found herself even more certain about helping Erin and Kayla. But what about her marriage? What about Nolan? She couldn't stand the thought of losing him. So where did that leave her?

She wandered back to her car, and a few minutes later found herself driving toward the park. When she got there she was hungry, so she found a vendor selling hot dogs and bought one, then settled down on a bench to eat.

She watched the people around her, some out walking their dogs, others spreading blankets on the grass to have picnic lunches. Turning her head to the right, she could see the children playing on the playground. She watched them running and laughing and she thought about the day Nolan had proposed to her.

They'd sat on a bench near this one and he'd gotten down on one knee in front of her and asked her to marry him. She hadn't been surprised. They'd already talked about marriage and they both knew they were headed in that direction. That took nothing away from the magic or sweetness of the moment. After the proposal, they'd watched the children on the playground and talked about the family they planned to have in a few years.

Seven years later, they still hadn't started that family. Neither of them was getting any younger. Nolan had been so patient with her. Now, as she watched the children, she was sorry for how unfair she'd been to him.

By the time Beth got home, Lulu was beside herself with the need to go outside. Beth let her out in the fenced backyard, then sat down on the couch and flipped through the channels on the TV. Nothing appealed to her, so she turned it off and lay down, closing her eyes.

She woke up to the sound of the door opening and glanced at the clock. It was almost four thirty.

Nolan walked in with his head down and Beth knew right away their argument had not yet ended. He closed the door behind him and hesitantly made his way toward her.

She looked up at him. "I'm glad you're home."

He nodded but said nothing. They stared at each other for a moment, then he headed down the hall to his study. He didn't come out until dinner and, even then, he said very little. When the meal was finished he said, "I'll just sleep on the couch tonight," then headed back to his study.

*So that's how it is.* Their fight wasn't over. Beth was desperate to make things better, but she knew Nolan well enough to know he wasn't ready to talk. Really there was little left she could say, so she gave him his space and didn't argue when he took his pillow out to the living room later that night.

Beth got into bed alone, hating how empty the bed felt. She wished she knew what he was thinking; if there was any chance he would come around to what she needed. What would she do if he didn't? That thought was too painful, so she pushed it aside, closed her eyes and waited for sleep to take her.

Rebecca L. Marsh

# Chapter 39

The following weekend, Beth went to her father's house alone. She and Nolan were talking to each other again, but only about bills and things that needed to be done. They were sleeping in the same bed, but they didn't touch one another. It was better than silence, Beth supposed, but still nerve racking and uncomfortable. Even so, she could not back down.

When her father and Grace asked where Nolan was, Beth made an excuse about him needing to prepare a lesson, but her words sounded hollow even to her own ears.

Brunch was ready almost as soon as she got there. She had planned it that way, hoping to avoid alone time with Grace. The woman was way too insightful and Beth didn't feel ready to talk about what was happening between her and Nolan.

Even without the time alone, Beth could feel her step-mother's gaze bearing into her throughout the meal. It reminded her of the time she'd almost gotten away with going to Tennessee on an overnight trip with Alex Marshall back in the eleventh grade. She had covered her bases by telling her father and Grace she was spending the night with Terri, one of her high school girlfriends. She was sure her parents hadn't found out the truth, but somehow Grace had known she was hiding something and had beaten her down with that gaze. After four days of it, Beth had reached her breaking point and blurted out the truth in the middle of dinner.

Beth wasn't sure if she somehow gave herself away, but, in any case, Grace always knew when she was keeping something secret. Sooner or later Beth always talked.

She looked at Grace again and saw the gaze had not yet stopped. She let out a breath. *I guess I'm not very good at keeping secrets.*

When they finished eating, Grace took some plates and headed into the kitchen to do the dishes. Beth cleared the rest of the table and brought the dishes to the sink. Then Grace turned and looked at her, concern in her eyes. "What's going on with you?"

Beth let out a long breath and prepared for the talk. "Nolan and I are fighting." She looked down at her hands, twisting her fingers.

"What about? Is he pressuring you about kids again?"

"Actually, I'm the one pressuring him. It's just not the kids he wants."

Grace furrowed her brow in confusion.

Beth walked to the small kitchen table and sat down. Grace followed her.

"I want Nolan and me to become foster parents."

"I see." Grace nodded. "Well, I think that's wonderful, dear, but maybe it's something you should wait on until you have a child of your own first. That is what Nolan wants, right?"

"Yes, but it's not that simple. I don't want us to become foster parents for just any kids. I have specific ones in mind; two girls I feel a need to help. And they're going to need a home in about six months."

Grace watched her carefully now. "Really?"

Beth nodded, but Grace's look told Beth that her step-mother was thinking of the news. As Martha had pointed out—everyone knew about Erin.

"Two teenagers. It's a lot to take on. And they have a troubled past." Beth looked down at her hands. "I feel like I need to help them. It's something I can't let go. If there was someone else who would take them, someone I know would be good to them, I'd be overjoyed. But it's unlikely anyone will." Beth looked up at Grace and met her gaze. "They need a good home and the love they've never been given before ...

They need what I got with John and Ellen Sue ... and with you and Dad."

Grace nodded and her eyes looked moist. Beth went on. "Nolan is really against it. He's barely talking to me." She shook her head and looked away. "I haven't been fair to him. We had plans. He has a right to be upset with me."

Grace was silent until Beth looked at her again. "Sweetie, I do understand how he feels. He does have a right to those feelings, but thinking we can plan our lives out is just an illusion. If you feel that helping those girls is what you're meant to do, then you have to listen to *those* feelings." She squeezed Beth's hand. "Maybe that will mean being a foster parent to them or maybe there *is* another solution that you haven't found yet. But, honey, trust what you're feeling."

Emotions welled up inside Beth. Despite the strong feeling she had about helping the girls, a part of her had been hoping her step-mother would tell her to do what her husband wanted. That was the safer path.

Beth's eyes filled with tears and Grace reached out and took hold or her hands. "What's wrong?"

"What if I lose Nolan?"

"Oh, honey!" Grace leaned forward and gave Beth a hug.

Then Grace said, "Sweetie, let's think about this. Does wanting to give these girls a home mean you don't want to have children of your own?"

Beth shook her head. "No. I still want to have my own kids. I think I'm much more ready to handle it now. I don't feel so scared about it anymore. I just feel that I need to help the girls first."

"Have you told Nolan that?"

Beth looked down feeling a little ashamed of the simplicity of the mistake Grace suggested. "No," she admitted. "I thought we needed to sort this thing out first."

"Well, dear, perhaps telling him what you just told me would help him to be more receptive to your request. Tell him, and then give him some time to sort it all out. Maybe he'll come around."

"You think so?"

She shrugged. "You never know."

Then another thought occurred to Beth. "Grace," she said, "what do you do when you feel both love and hate for the same person?"

Grace looked thoughtful. "Focus on the love."

Beth nodded, thinking about that and realized it was the answer she needed. She would focus on the love, and she'd be able to forgive her mother.

When Beth got home, Nolan was doing some yard work. So she went inside and looked over some of her case files and notes for a while. An hour later Nolan came inside and took a shower. Beth was waiting for him in the bedroom when he got done.

She sat silently on the bed while he got dressed in clean clothes. Then he looked at her. "You seem to be waiting for me."

She nodded. "I was hoping to talk to you." She could see a look in his eye telling her he didn't want to talk yet. "You don't have to say anything. I just want you to listen for now."

He signaled his agreement to listen by sitting down in the chair that faced the bed. "I don't know if it will make any difference or not, but it has occurred to me that there are some things I haven't told you; things you should at least know.

"I told you a couple weeks ago about my visit with Martha." Nolan nodded and Beth continued, "There was one part I didn't tell you. I chose not to tell you this because, at the time, I didn't think you knew that Erin Clifton was the girl I was working with for Lisa and I was respecting that confidentiality. However, this bit of information is not just about her, it's about me too. Now that you know I was working with her and also because I'm asking you to consider giving her a home with us, I think it's something you should know." Beth looked down, letting out a sigh. "The funny thing is, Erin doesn't know what I'm about to tell you, but it's part of the reason I feel such a need to help her."

Beth looked back up at Nolan and saw he was listening in earnest. "When Martha asked me about becoming foster parents for Erin and Kayla, she made a comment about everything coming full circle. I had no idea what she was talking about. When I asked her about it, she was surprised I didn't understand. She said she was referring to my time with the Kessler's when I was fifteen. I still didn't understand." Beth watched her husband's face. She wanted so much, at this moment, to reach for his hands; to have a physical connection with him. She wasn't sure he was ready for that though, and she didn't want to lose the momentum she had going with the conversation.

"Nolan, do you remember me telling you about the boy that lived there with me? Jamie?"

Nolan nodded. "The wood carver." He gave her a quizzical look and shifted in his chair. He wasn't just listening to appease her now, he was becoming curious.

"Yes, that's the one. I never knew much about him, not even his last name." She paused for a moment looking into her husband's curious eyes, wondering if he was figuring it out. "But he helped me. He carved a bat for me out of a very hard wood. I didn't know why he'd made that for me; I mean, of all things, a bat. That bat saved me the night Mark Kessler came to my room with the intention of raping me. I think Jamie knew I would need it. I think he knew what kind of a man Mark was and he wanted to help me.

"That's why I couldn't believe it when Martha told me that Jamie's last name was Clifton." She paused letting that piece of information sink in. "When I left that terrible place, he stayed. I guess somewhere along the way that kind, quiet boy turned into the same kind of monster he was raised by. He saved me, but he destroyed his own daughter."

Beth shook her head. It was still a lot for her to think about. "Maybe it's crazy, but I feel like I need to make up for the part of Erin's father that I got to know and she didn't; the part Mark Kessler took away. I need to give her the love he couldn't."

She paused for another minute and let her words soak in. "Nolan, I know you want to have a baby." Now she did reach forward and took her husband's hand. "Our baby. And you've been waiting a long time for me to be ready." She furrowed her brow trying to hold back the emotion that brimmed inside of her. "You've been so patient, and to be honest, for a while there, I didn't think I would ever be ready. I wasn't sure I could be a mother.

"I've worked through a lot of things lately. Fear isn't ruling me anymore." She looked into Nolan's face smiling as tears ran down her cheeks. "I was able to hold Hunter. I was finally able to hold my nephew. I think I'm ready now, Nolan, to have those kids we've always talked about."

There was silence for a moment and they stared at each other. Then Nolan broke the silence. "Are you saying you want to have a baby now?" he asked, hope springing into his eyes.

"Yes … well soon anyway. I also want to take the classes to become foster parents. And if no one else is willing, I want to open our home to those girls." She shook her head. "No, I *need* to open our home to the girls. I *need* to help them."

She squeezed his hand. "Just think about it, please," she said before getting up and leaving him alone.

# Chapter 40

All week Nolan was quiet and thoughtful. They didn't talk about what was an elephant in the room, but Nolan was sweeter and more willing to hug and cuddle, which Beth took as a positive sign.

When the weekend came, Beth packed a bag and left for Wilmington to see Katie and John. John's health was getting worse with every passing day and, as hard as losing him was for her, she knew it was hitting Katie harder. She wanted to spend some time with her sister and lend her support. She also thought giving Nolan a weekend alone might help him think some things through.

Beth arrived at Katie's apartment late Friday night. Saturday morning they spent some time together talking and after lunch the two of them went to see John. He was in and out of sleep the entire time. When he was awake he suffered deep confusion that led to hysteria. More than once he had looked at her and Katie and begged them to tell him where Ellen Sue was, without having any idea who they were.

His confusion and almost total loss of memory were heart-breaking for Beth and Katie alike. Spending time with him was a highly emotional experience and by the time the two women left, they were both overcome.

When they got to the car, Katie leaned against it and searched her purse for a tissue. Beth looked up. The sun was setting and the sky was filled with pinks and reds along the horizon. Beth admired the view, appreciating it in a new way thinking about how fast life could go by.

"This gets harder every day." Katie wiped her eyes. Then with a sigh, she said, "I need to go somewhere I can relax. Let's drive out to the aquarium. We can get dinner on the way."

Beth smiled. "You're probably the only person I know who finds her job relaxing."

"The job isn't always relaxing," Katie said as they both got into the car, "but the place is. Plus I'm off duty right now and they're closing soon. After hours is the best time to be there. It'll be quiet; just us and the fish."

"Yeah … and the sharks."

This brought a mischievous smile to Katie's face. "Well as long as Aaron doesn't stop by, the sharks won't be a problem."

Beth let out a small laugh as Katie started the car and headed toward the Fort Fisher Aquarium.

When they arrived, only a few cars remained in the parking lot. "Perfect," Katie said, "only a few staff members are still here."

They walked inside and Beth followed Katie through the exhibits, glancing at the different fish and other sea life as they went along. Katie moved with purpose. Beth guessed her sister knew exactly where she wanted to go.

A few minutes later, they walked out a door and entered an area that was like an enclosed forest. There were lots of plants growing and some areas were like ponds. There were quail walking around and in one area, box turtles hid under leaves. They walked around a circular path and stepped onto a wooden deck that overlooked the exhibit holding an albino alligator.

Katie seemed to relax as soon as they got there. She leaned on the railing and admired the alligator. "I love this place. It's so natural, so simple."

"It's nice, but I'm not sure I would call an alligator relaxing." Beth looked at the creature as it seemed to slither along in its pond and made a sour face at it. "Couldn't we go back inside with the fish?"

Katie looked at Beth shaking her head and smiling. "You're such a wus, little sister. It's not like she can get out." Katie gestured around the enclosure. "Stop worrying for a few minutes and try to get into the spirit of this very natural environment. Out here there are no worries, no problems that weigh you down, and no difficult decisions. These creatures just live."

Beth nodded and the two of them stood silent for a few minutes, Beth trying hard not to look at the alligator. It was dark outside now and the enclosure was lit only by moonlight. As she soaked in the sounds of the animals and breathed in the fresh air provided by the plant life all around, she could understand why Katie found the place relaxing. It was like being in a forest ... without the bugs.

"I'm glad I have you," Katie said. "You have no idea how much your visits are helping me right now."

Beth rubbed Katie's back and said, "It's the least I can do. I want to be here. He was a father to me too."

"Yeah, I know."

Katie let out a sigh. "Beth, I've been living alone for two decades now and I've always loved it. Then Dad gets sick and now every time I go home the emptiness feels like it's swallowing me alive."

"To tell you the truth, I've been feeling pretty alone myself lately." Beth leaned on the railing alongside Katie. Somehow the alligator seemed a little less intimidating now; almost like a friend that only knew how to listen.

Katie turned and studied Beth, trying to read her expression. "What's going on, sis? Are you and Nolan having problems?"

"You might say that." Beth shrugged. "I hope we'll have it all worked out soon, but I'm not really sure."

"Wanna talk about it?"

Beth looked at Katie's open face. No matter what she was dealing with in her own life, Katie was always willing to listen to anyone else's troubles. Beth wondered how it was possible that someone this wonderful was still single. She told Katie as much as she could about what was going on between her and Nolan.

Katie nodded, and without speaking the two of them stayed for almost another hour and enjoyed the peacefulness

327

of the deserted aquarium. Katie understood why Beth needed to help Erin and Kayla. Beth didn't need her sister to say anything to know that. Katie had always been able to understand Beth's feelings even though she'd never been through the things Beth had. That was part of what had always made their bond so strong and so special.

Katie spoke again saying, "Maybe we can solve both of our problems with one solution."

Beth gave her a quizzical look. "What do you mean?"

"Do those kids you told me about have to stay in the same county?"

"No, in fact, it would be better for them if they didn't. They do have to stay in the state. But Martha doesn't think they'll be able to find anyone to take them regardless of where in the state they look."

Katie looked Beth in the eye and said, "What about me?"

Beth's forehead crinkled. "Are you saying what I think you are?"

Katie nodded. "I've thought about becoming a foster parent before. I mean that's how I got you for a sister. I always found excuses not to do it. I was too busy and didn't have the time a child would need. But these are teenagers. They wouldn't need as much time as a younger child would." She nodded, but the gesture seemed to be more for herself than for Beth. "This could be a great thing, for both me and those girls, and I think now is the right time."

Beth was taken aback. She had not expected this from her sister, but once she recovered from the surprise and thought about it for a minute, it all made sense. It was a perfect solution. Katie was lonely and needed someone just as much as the girls did. Also, Beth would know, beyond the shadow of a doubt, that Erin and Kayla were safe and well cared for.

Added to that, moving to Wilmington would take them away from the place where their parents were well known, away from the place where James' murder had been on the news for weeks. They would have a chance to start over.

It was a good idea—a wonderful one, but Beth felt a sense of loss run through her. Despite the issues it had caused with Nolan, Beth realized now that she had become attached to the idea of taking the girls herself. It would be better for the girls, though, to come here and it would be good for Katie too. Beth could still be an aunt to them and watch over them. However, she wondered if Katie really knew what she was getting into.

Beth looked at her sister. "I think it's great that you want to do this and I know you would be a good mother to these kids, but you should know they have an abusive past and will need a lot of help."

"I pretty much figured that from what you told me already." She smiled. "I know there will be challenges. I think I can handle it. And if I need help, I know a great psychologist that'll let me call her day or night."

Beth grinned at Katie. "That's true," she said, embracing her sister.

When Beth got home Sunday night, Nolan came out of the house and greeted her with a hug. "I love you," he whispered in her ear, then let go of her and went to the trunk to get her bag. Nolan acted like he was relieved to have her home; almost as if he hadn't been sure she would come back.

Beth stood in place for a moment, mystified by her husband's welcome. She wasn't sure what this meant.

She walked into the house behind him and followed as he carried her bag into the bedroom.

"Sit down," he said, sitting on the bed and patting the place next to him, "I want to talk to you."

Beth did as he asked.

"I'm glad you're home," he said with an almost sheepish look.

"Yeah, so am I." Beth watched her husband intently, curious about his behavior.

Nolan fiddled with the ring on his finger. "I've been thinking a lot this weekend."

Beth nodded and Nolan went on. "I thought about what you told me, and I want to say I'm sorry for how I've been acting. It's a good thing that you want to do, and I can understand why you feel such a need to do it." He gave her a sorrowful glance that held with it so much love. "It was just so unexpected. After seeing you hold Hunter, all I could think about was us having our own baby. I didn't want to hear anything that didn't fit with that plan.

"But the truth is," he said turning and placing his hands on her arms. "I love you so much. I can't imagine my life without you. And I know part of the reason you're here with me, able to love and be loved, is because of the kindness and love you got from John and Ellen Sue."

Nolan's hands dropped and he looked close to tears. "Of course you want the Clifton girls to get that same kind of love. I feel terrible for not being more supportive of the idea. They deserve to have a good home and we can give that to them."

Beth scooted close to her husband and put an arm around his waist, leaning her head against his shoulder. "I love you, too, Nolan. I can't imagine life without you either. I can't tell you how much it means to me that you're willing to help the girls."

She turned him to face her and looked him in the eye. "They *are* going to have a good home. But not with us."

Nolan's face crinkled in confusion.

"Katie has been very lonely since John's mind started to go and it's made her start thinking seriously about having a family of her own."

"Yeah, I know," Nolan responded still confused about why the conversation had turned to Katie. "Didn't she decide she didn't want to have a kid until she found Mr. Right?"

"She decided she didn't want to have a baby until she found Mr. Right, but I told her about the girls this weekend and, to my surprise, she said she'd like to become a foster parent for them. She wants to do it. It's perfect, really, because Katie won't be alone anymore, and Erin will get away from the place where everyone knows who she is and what she did. She might get a real chance to start over ..." Now Beth trailed a finger down Nolan's chest and kissed his lips passionately. Then smiling at him, she said, "And we could start working on our family."

Nolan beamed at her and took both her hands in his. "Are you sure you're okay with that? I know you wanted to be the one to help the girls."

Beth smiled back at him and nodded. "It felt like a loss when Katie first volunteered, but the truth is, going to Wilmington will be better for them. I'll still be helping them. It's through me that Katie knows about them and wants to help. I know they'll be safe and loved with her. And I'll still be able to watch over them."

Nolan hugged her. "I'm glad to have my wife back, and I can't wait to get started on that family of our own."

Rebecca L. Marsh

# Chapter 41

About six months later

Beth arrived at Katie's apartment in Wilmington right behind Martha, who drove Erin and Kayla there. She bounced in the passenger seat like an excited child while Nolan smiled and shook his head at her from the driver's seat. Behind her in the car were her father and Grace who'd come in support of Katie. They were almost as excited as Beth.

It was a beautiful fall day with a deep blue, cloudless sky. The sun was warm on Beth's face as she got out of the car and rushed toward Katie, who stood on her front stoop. Three months earlier they'd stood together at John's funeral, crying as they remembered what a wonderful father he'd been. That had been a very difficult day, but the hope of this day coming had helped them both through it.

"I can't believe this day is finally here," Katie said, her voice filled with a cautious anticipation.

Beth beamed. "It's here, sis. You're going to be a great mother."

"You think?" Katie's face showed a little nervousness now as they watched the two young girls pull their suitcases from the trunk of Martha's car.

Beth turned to her and looked her in the eye. "I'm sure of it, Katie … And your parents would be so proud of you."

Katie's eyes welled with tears. "I wish Mom and Dad were here today."

"They are," Beth said, glancing up at the beautiful sky. "I know they are."

Katie looked past Beth to where Nolan, Ron, and Grace stood. "And so are they," she said with warmth in her voice.

Beth nodded. "They wouldn't miss this day either."

Moments later the group dispersed as they took Erin and Kayla's things inside. Beth stayed behind and watched the group walk into the apartment. It warmed Beth's heart to see Erin so happy. Someday she would tell the girls who their father had once been, that he was the one who'd saved her. First, they needed time to heal and get used to their new life.

Beth turned and looked around at her surroundings. Everything seemed peaceful. This would be a good place for the girls to start a new life.

Beth was so wrapped up in thought, she didn't notice when someone walked up behind her, and she was startled when a hand touched her on the shoulder. She turned and found herself looking at Erin.

"Dr. Christopher?"

Beth smiled at her, pushing some of her sandy hair back from her shoulder. "Erin, I'm not your psychologist anymore. You can call me Beth now."

"Okay, Beth," she said looking at her feet and blushing at the familiarity she didn't yet feel. "I just wanted to thank you for all you've done for me ... and Kayla." She looked up now. "I didn't think you could help when I first met you. But you did ... and you changed me. You were a light in the darkness—my rainbow. The world doesn't look as scary now." She glanced around at her new surroundings. "And this day ... it's the *very* best day."

The next thing Beth knew, Erin had her wrapped in a hug. She felt joy flow through her, and she knew she was healed. The scars of her past would no longer trouble her or wake her in the night.

Erin pulled back, tears on her cheeks and a smile lighting her face. "I never thought things could turn out this good." Then she glanced down at Beth's belly that was a little rounded. "She's very lucky, you know, to have a mom like you."

Then Erin turned, and with an eagerness to begin her new life, she walked into the apartment. Beth watched her go, feeling as if happiness might burst from within her, and touching her rounded stomach she thought, *no, I'm the lucky one.*

# About The Author

Rebecca L. Marsh is an author of women's fiction and member of the Paulding County Writer's Guild. She grew up in the mountains of Western North Carolina, and now lives in Dallas, Georgia, with her husband and daughter.

When she isn't writing or taking care of her family (cats and dog included), she occasionally likes to make home-made candy and work on her scrapbooks (she is woefully behind).

Visit her website at rebeccalmarsh.com

Or follow her on Facebook at

Author: Rebecca L. Marsh

# ACKNOWLEDGMENTS

A special thanks to those who took the time to help me in any way—all my early readers. Thank you to Steve Schofield and Ken Vinson for the information you provided on the workings of the law (I know it's been a while now and you might not even remember). Thank you to the Paulding County Writer's Guild for all the help you have given me. I could not do this without you. Thank you to Heather Trim especially for creating a beautiful cover for this book, and all the other help you have given me. And, most of all, my family for standing by me, especially Joe and Maegan.

# NOTE FROM THE AUTHOR

Thank you for reading *When the Storm Ends*. I value all my readers, and hope you have enjoyed it. If you'd like to leave a review on Amazon or Goodreads, I would greatly appreciate it.

Thanks for your support!

Made in the USA
Columbia, SC
11 November 2018